A Bright Power Rising

Noel Coughlan

A BRIGHT POWER RISING

Cover Illustration © Marek Purzychi
(http://igreeny.deviantart.com/)
Maps © Rob Antonishen (http://www.cartocopia.com/)
Morpheus Font was used with the permission of Eric Oehler

Edited by Finish The Story
(http://www.finish-the-story.com/Editing.htm)
Additional proofreading by Proofed to Perfection
(http://www.proofedtoperfection.com/)
Formatted by Polgarus Studio
(http://www.polgarusstudio.com)

Published by Photocosmological Press (http://photocosm.org/)

Paperback Edition 2014: ISBN:978-1-910206-02-7

For my wife, Colette,

who made this book possible.

Acknowledgments

I thank my friends and relations who suffered through my various drafts, who were hounded out of weddings and other family occasions to discuss cover designs and other issues at short notice, and whose input made this book a much better work—Evan Coughlan, Padraig Coughlan, Deirdre O'Gorman, Brendan Murphy, John Logan, Mags Murphy, Joe McInerney, Kirsty O'Neill, and Orla McGrath. I also want to thank Colm Murphy for his advice on setting up Photocosmological Press.

Rob Anstonishen turned my crude maps into something far more professional. He was able to transform my rather dense vision into something beautiful. Thanks again, Rob!

Thanks also must go to Marek Purzychi who designed the beautiful cover of this book. He was absolutely great to work with.

Thanks to Marina and Jason Anderson at Polgarus Studios for formatting the paperback.

I want to thank the good people at the Finish The Story for all their editing work: Alicia Dean (proofreading); Bryan Thomas Schmidt (copy editing), and Claire Ashgrove (developmental and line editing). I'm particularly in Claire's debt for all the work that she put into the book. I also want to thank Pamela Guerrieri-Cangioli, Amy Raubenolt, and Kevin Cook from Proofed To Perfection for all their help. Hopefully, these acknowledgments don't read too badly because I edited them by myself!

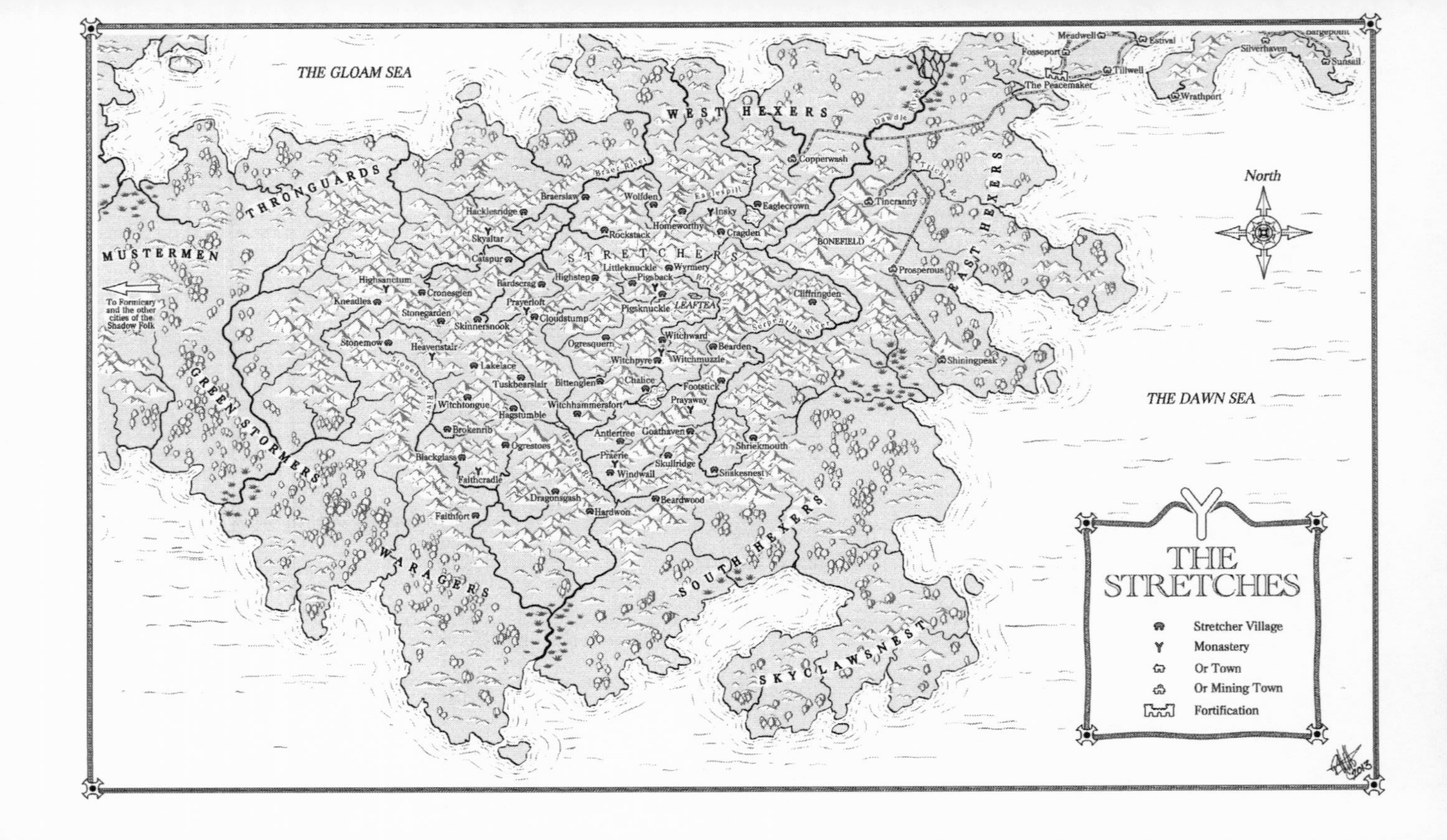
THE STRETCHES
Stretcher Village
Monastery
Or Town
Or Mining Town
Fortification
THE GLOAM SEA
THE DAWN SEA
North
WEST HEXERS
EAST HEXERS
SOUTH HEXERS
STRETCHERS
THRONGUARDS
MUSTERMEN
GREEN STORMERS
WARAGERS
SKYCLAWSNEST
To Formicary and the other cities of the Shadow Folk
Meadwell
Estival
Silverhaven
Sunsail
Fosseport
Tillwell
The Peacemaker
Wrathport
Dawdle River
Copperwash
Trickle R.
Tincranny
BONEFIELD
Prosperous
Cliffringden
Shiningpeak
Braer River
Eaglespill River
Braerslaw
Wolfden
Insky
Eaglecrown
Hacklesridge
Homeworthy
Rockstack
Cragden
Skyaltar
Catspur
Littleknuckle
Wyrmery
Pigsback
Highstep
Highsanctum
Cronesglen
Bardscrag
Kneadlea
Stonegarden
Prayerloft
Pigsknuckle
LEAFTEA
Skinnersnook
Cloudstump
Serpentine River
Witchward
Bearden
Stonemow
Heavenstair
Ogresquern
Witchpyre
Witchmuzzle
Lakelace
Tuskbearslair
Bittenglen
Chalice
Footstick
Stonebeck River
Witchtongue
Witchhammersfort
Prayaway
Hagstumble
Brokenrib
Antlertree
Goathaven
Shriekmouth
Ogrestoes
Prairie
Skullridge
Blackglass
Windwail
Snakesnest
Faithcradle
Heathen River
Dragonsgash
Beardwood
Hardwon
Faithfort
2013

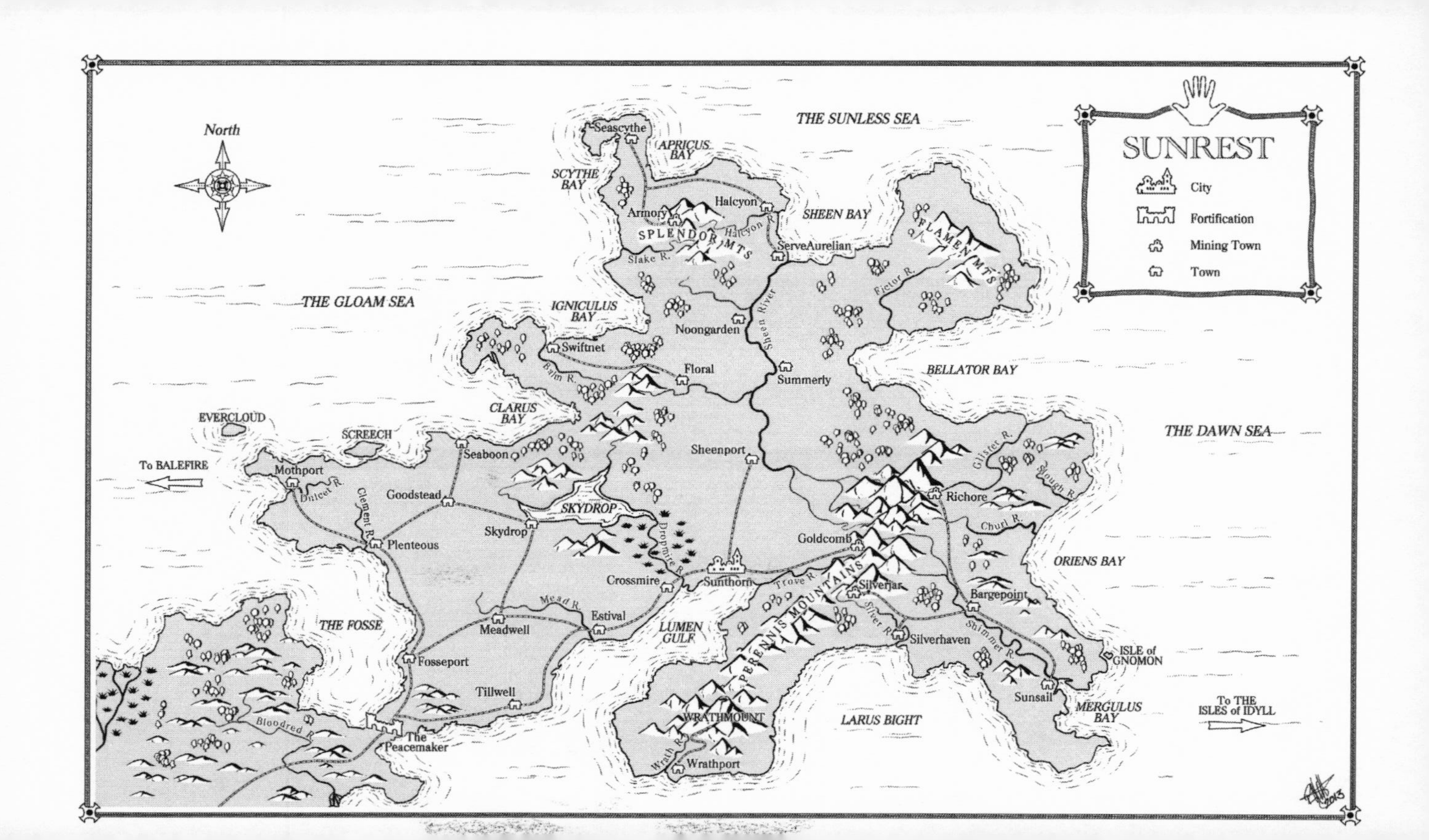
SUNREST
City
Fortification
Mining Town
Town
North
THE SUNLESS SEA
THE GLOAM SEA
THE DAWN SEA
Seascythe
APRICUS BAY
SCYTHE BAY
Armory
Halcyon
Halcyon R.
SPLENDOR MTS
Slake R.
SHEEN BAY
ServeAurelian
FLAMEN MTS
Fictor R.
IGNICULUS BAY
Noongarden
Sheen River
Swiftnet
Floral
Balm R.
Summerly
BELLATOR BAY
CLARUS BAY
EVERCLOUD
SCREECH
Seaboon
Sheenport
To BALEFIRE
Mothport
Dulcet R.
Clement R.
Goodstead
SKYDROP
Skydrop
Plenteous
Dropmire R.
Crossmire
Sunthorn
Goldcomb
Richore
Glister R.
Slough R.
Churl R.
ORIENS BAY
Trove R.
PERENNIS MOUNTAINS
Silverjar
Bargepoint
Silver R.
Silverhaven
Shimmer R.
Mead R.
Estival
Meadwell
LUMEN GULF
THE FOSSE
Fosseport
Tillwell
Bloodred R.
The Peacemaker
WRATHMOUNT
Wrath R.
Wrathport
LARUS BIGHT
Sunsail
MERGULUS BAY
ISLE of GNOMON
To THE ISLES of IDYLL

Or Legion Ranks & Structure

Officers	Unit	Sub-Units	Legionaries*
Legate Tribune Prefect	Legion	Six Cohorts	5193
Centurion Superior	Cohort	Six Centuries	865
Centurion Secondary Centurion	Century	Twelve squads	144
(Legionary) Senior	Squad	Twelve legionaries	12

*Includes Officers

PROLOGUE

Never enter the forest.

The Gilt Spider, the Elfin hunter of men, waited there with webs of silken gold to catch naughty little boys. Granyr had warned her son many times. Why had he not listened?

Because he was too young, still clumsy at speaking, grasping only half of what was said to him. The fault was hers. She should have kept a better eye on him. A moment of distraction had robbed Granyr of her reason for living.

Stifling her sobs, trying to rub away the tremble in her hands on her skirt, she stared helplessly at the wood encircling her farm. There was no time to search the house and shed again, not if he had blundered into the forest.

The sensible course, however demeaning, was to summon help from Pigsknuckle. If she raised the alarm, the villagers would form search parties and cover a lot more ground than she could alone. But her heart screamed otherwise. If they had let her settle in the village instead of this wild, lonely place, her child would be safe. If her husband was still alive, things would be different. She fought unwanted images of a great, y-shaped cross drenched in his blood. This was his family's reward for his sacrifice: his wife made a pariah; the son he had never seen lost and perhaps dead.

May the Forelight damn the Pigsknucklers for their conceit. She had to find her boy.

Instinct, primal and desperate, swept her forward, her son's pet name bursting from her chest. "Lilak, where are you?"

As she punched her way into the monster that had swallowed her child, briars mauled her face and hands, tugged and tore at her dress. Her gaze sifted the sun-dappled gloom. Any glimmer of movement might be her son. She tried to steady her rasping breath to hear his plaintive whimper.

Soon, she was adrift in the monotony of the forest, as lost as the child she sought. She shivered at the prospect of the approaching night, an inevitable pall declaring all hope dead.

A howl filled the forest and reverberated through her. Other wails rose up in answer. Her fingers sought her knife, but the scabbard was empty. She groaned at her stupidity. The blade lay in the hut, forgotten in her panic to find her child. She could only guess at the proximity of the wolf pack, but if they found her unarmed and alone, they would kill her.

Granyr searched the forest floor for a fallen branch to use as a club. Most were too rotten, too flimsy, or too unwieldy, but she eventually found a suitable one. The rough bark of her makeshift weapon chafed against her calloused palms. Its heft was reassuring, though it would be no match for a wolf pack.

A high-pitched squeal tore through the wolves' madrigal. Her terror forgotten, she rushed toward the cry, her cudgel cradled in her arms. It had to be her son.

The howling ceased. Barking and snarling tore apart the silence. A lupine yelp was cut short by the sound of a heavy blow.

She veered toward the noise. Hunters must have happened upon the wolves' trail. Help was nearby.

She heard the whisper of the stream before she stumbled upon it. Blood tinged its trickling waters. Shivering at the prospect of what she might find, she headed upstream. A lupine corpse bled into the brook—its body twisted awkwardly, the skull crushed in and its lower jaw unhinged and hanging in an incongruous grin.

Another yelp alerted her that the wolf's slayer had struck again.

Granyr rushed toward the cry. Beneath a broken tree stump lay another dead wolf. Rivulets of blood flowed down its muzzle from a single puncture wound between its eyes.

A soft whine drew her attention to the bushes to her right. She cautiously probed the foliage with the club. The stick brushed through the leaves unharmed. Raising her weapon above her shoulder, she stepped into the thicket.

A snarling frenzy of fur, legs, and jaws writhed in mid-air in front of her. She brought her cudgel down on the beast, delivering a glancing blow that sent it into a convulsion of rabid barks. Unnerved by the futility of her strike, Granyr stared uselessly at the creature as it swayed from side to side. It took time to gather her thoughts. The wolf posed no threat. Hanging upside down by one paw, it could not reach her.

She glanced up at the rope from which it dangled. It was a light yellow-green cord, surprisingly slender given its obvious strength. No mortal hand could make a rope so fine. The maker of the trap was not a Stretcher, like her, or even human. It had to be the Gilt Spider. The trap holding the wolf had been intended for unwitting trespassers in the Elf's domain.

The memory of a thousand childish nightmares made her back away from the wolf. She turned and ran in no particular direction. The forest whirled dizzily about her. A gantlet of branches lacerated her face and hands.

She burst from the oppressive gloom into the clearing around her home where she collapsed, weeping, and pounded the ground beneath her fists. Lilak was still lost somewhere in the maze of shadow behind her, perhaps already the Gilt Spider's prey.

"Forelight, I beg you. Protect my son," she pleaded, but her heart cried otherwise. The saints claimed that the Forelight was love itself, but what love had he shown to her? He had stolen her husband and now her boy.

She picked herself up. Her grubby fingers tried to brush away the blood, sweat, and dust caked to her face. The sun was already slipping behind the holy mountain called the

Pig. Night was spreading over the valley. She couldn't abandon her son to it. She needed a torch and her knife.

Utterly spent, she trudged toward her home, dreading its chill emptiness.

A healthy pillar of smoke rose from her home. Surely, by now, the fire should be ash. A small figure stood at the entrance. She quickened her pace. Aching muscles strained as she ran to her son and clasped him to her bosom. Here was Lilak, alive and safe! Praise the Forelight! Someone must have found him—the same person who had tended the fire—but that mystery could wait. For this exquisite moment, it was enough to embrace her son, to feel his arms hugging her neck; to have his sweet, childish babble tickle her ear. The horrors of the forest no longer mattered now. She had Lilak again.

Granyr gently held him at arm's length. "Never wander off again," she chided, attempting to conceal her relief with a frown. "Do you promise?"

Lilak nodded with innocent solemnity. She pressed him to her once more. Something in his hair attracted her attention, an alien thread of gold among the black. Its significance squeezed her chest so tight she could hardly breathe. The real Lilak, her Lilak, was gone forever. The Gilt Spider had taken him and what stood before her was a cruel fraud.

She shoved the sham boy away and screamed.

PART 1
GRAEL

Chapter 1

A beauty as proud as the sun,
Are the tears of the Golden Light.
Beware the eyes of the Fair One
Lest those bright fires consume your sight.

~From *Alackalas and the Fair Princess.*

Every step pulled the Pig a little more from the sky. Already, distance had reduced its snowy peak to just another crooked tooth in the jaw of the Stretches Mountains. Whenever the sight of his mountain folded into the winding terrain, Grael feared it lost forever.

Before him, a rope stretched. One end was knotted around his wrists, the other tethered to a cart bloated with wares amassed by the Jinglemen on their trading expedition. No doubt some of these goods were ill-gotten, like Grael.

From beneath the canopy stretching over the Jinglemen's precarious pile, Harath Melkath glared, as cold and distant as the mountain that bred her. A purple bruise marred her left cheek. Her red hair was disheveled. Their captors had ripped her halo from her head and tied the circlet of twisted white and blue cloth across her mouth. The profane sight was so sickening that Grael struggled to look upon it. To her credit, the daughter of the most powerful man in Pigsknuckle maintained her customary haughtiness, even when bound and gagged. Grael wanted to offer her words of consolation, but the accusation in her stare kept him silent. She blamed him for their plight, and it was difficult to disagree. If he hadn't attracted this scum to Pigsknuckle, she would still be safe there.

His own halo clung to his head by a single braid. It danced a precarious jig against his temple with each step, threatening to forsake him at any moment. The prospect filled him with dread. It was all he was, all he believed in. A tangible statement that he was a Stretcher, a true worshiper of the Forelight. The colors even proclaimed him as a Pigsknuckler. What was he without it?

He picked up his pace. If he could slacken the rope, he might be able to grab the halo before it fell off completely.

A whip lacerated his shoulder with the force of lightning. His legs wilted, and he fell. The wagon dragged him along the grating earth, straining his shoulders and arms to the point of breaking.

The air filled with the tinkle of dancing metal that gave the merchants their name. Their leader, Tarum Sire, halted his horse by the cart. He yelled to the driver, "Don't pull him apart, Hackit. He's no good damaged." He looked down at Grael. His bearskin coat created the impression of great bulk. From a necklace of black feathers and shell beads hung a wooden fish. "Are you all right, boy?"

"I am fine," Grael said, ignoring his scrapes and pains as he quickly picked himself off the ground to prove his point. To say anything else put his value in question. Tarum's concern was limited to his coin pouch, and he had no use for a cripple.

Grael's eyes sought Harath. Her wide-eyed concern salved his pain. For the first time that he could remember, she looked on him with sympathy.

"He was trying to escape," the grinning bundle of rags driving the cart slurred, directing a malign stare at Grael. "He was trying to reach the girl so he could free her."

Tarum Sire's belly laugh brimmed with smug menace. He stroked the ends of the black mustache curving to his chin, his frosty blue eyes narrowing. "For your sake, I hope that was not your intention. Remember, boy, you are a long way from your village. This is the Gilt Spider's land, and no place for solitary travel."

Grael glowered at the Jingleman. Threatening him with children's tales! Despite what mothers told their innocent broods, the chances of being taken by the Gilt Spider were remote.

Tarum Sire stared at him for a moment, then threw back his head and shook with laughter. "Besides, you wanted to go to the city of Formicary," he sneered. "You are just entering through Shackle Gate."

"Aye, for you, it's the wrong gate," Hackit mocked. "But it's the gate that pays us best." He peered down at Harath. "Don't worry, deary. I'm sure the Sire has finer things planned for you than working in the mines."

"No less back-breaking, though," Tarum Sire quipped.

Harath kicked against the side of the cart.

Tarum Sire's fat laugh lingered as he galloped away. Hackit's wheezing cackle choked on a fit of coughing. He cracked his whip. Grael was thankful that it was directed at the hides of the draught animals and not his. The cart shuddered forward.

Still smarting from his fall, Grael trudged behind. The gentle clapping of his halo was gone. He moaned. The final concession to his slavery had been made. Better to be the Gilt Spider's victim than to suffer such humiliation.

As the sun slipped behind the darkening mountains, the caravan halted by a small stream. Exhausted and aching, Grael plunked down on a tuft of grass and watched the Jinglemen set up camp. Soon they were all sprawled around the smoking campfire, waiting for their dinner. The smell of cooking meat made Grael's mouth water.

Hackit looked at him and smiled. The old Jingleman leapt up. He chuckled softly as he limped over to his cart. "Pardon, deary," he said as he rummaged inside. His search terminated in a wheezy laugh. What was Hackit up to?

Hackit carried a bag under his arm as he returned to the campfire. "Let's see what treats the young lad has brought us."

Tethered like an animal, Grael listened to the Jinglemen as they divvied out the contents of his backpack.

"Hey, Pigsknuckle boy," Hackit quipped as he licked pastry off his fingers. "Your mother's a good cook."

Another Jingleman sighed. "Pigsknuckle, where the streets, if there were any, would be paved with goat droppings."

Tarum stood up and puffed out his chest. In a baritone voice reminiscent of Widan Melkath, Pigsknuckle's politician, he swung one arm wide and said, "Welcome to Pigsknuckle, at the foot of the Pig, the last place for pilgrims to have a dump without committing sacrilege on the holy mountain till they reach Pigsback."

The taunts lingered with Grael in the dark, cold night. It was hard to accept his squalid fate. There had to be some way to escape the horrors of Formicary's mines, and free Harath from a certainly despicable fate, but Grael couldn't find it. The cord lashed around his wrists was too stout to break or chew through. Appeals to the Jinglemen's compassion were futile, and he had nothing with which to buy his freedom—his captors had already taken everything he possessed. Concocting some kind of hidden treasure to whet the Jinglemen's avarice and bargain for his release was a tempting gambit. Alone, he might have risked it, but he could not put Harath in even greater jeopardy. Nor could he abandon her if a chance for flight arose. They must escape together or not at all. But such an opportunity was unlikely. Her presence was a stronger fetter than any rope.

"Are you all right?" Harath whispered.

It was the first time she had ever spoken to him. Shyness had always made him avoid her. She had been like an Elfin maiden, a prize too great for a mere mortal like him.

"I'm fine." His answer was reflexive. "They didn't hurt you, did they?"

"My honor is intact."

Grael's cheeks burned. The possibility had never entered his head. "How did they catch you?"

"We had better be quiet in case they hear us. I've had enough of being gagged."

"I meant no offense."

She made no reply.

"Harath, are you there? Say something."

The silence reproached his crassness. He had set out to Formicary partly to win her admiration. Long before he left Pigsknuckle, his imagination had mapped out his adventure as a series of simple steps. After a profitable stint as a mercenary, he could return home as a rich man like Garscap Torp and ask for Harath's hand in marriage. Now, with his plans ruined by the Jinglemen's treachery, his one guilty consolation was that circumstances had conspired to throw him together with Harath. And almost the first word out of his mouth had caused her to spurn him.

***

The Pigshead was an ideal hiding place, secluded and forbidding. From an early age, Pigsknucklers learned to avoid the eerie geologic feature, a ridge protruding from the precipitous mountainside. The promontory's gentle slope terminated at another precipice and inclined inward, creating the impression of a giant snout. This, legend maintained, was the face of the mountain.

The villagers fervently believed those who trespassed in its shadow risked waking the monster. Saints knew this was nonsense. A saint had petrified the creature, and miraculous works by a priest of the Forelight could not be undone so easily. But the tenets of childhood still haunted Saint Charlin, so he tread softly.

The object of his visit was another nightmare of his youth—the Gilt Spider. The very name conjured terror. Every time a hunter failed to return home or a child disappeared, it was whispered.

He raised the hem of his cassock and splashed across the little stream beneath the snout. The shade concealed a cave entrance.

"Forelight, protect your servant, the humblest of saints," he whispered so softly that only his god might hear him.

He squeezed into the narrow opening. The crevice constricted around him, forcing his body into ever more elaborate contortions in order to progress. Plunging through the earth like this was unnatural, but he had no choice other than to push forward. It was tempting to seek reassurance from whatever sliver of sunlight that had followed him into this rocky vice, but in the cramped space, to even glance back risked injury, entrapment, or worse.

Relief at stumbling into the wide inner chamber was tempered by the knowledge that he had to suffer that dreadful passage again to exit. A sweet scent dispelled a little of the cavern's earthy smell. Neat rows of slender candles on the floor wove a shifting web of light and shadow across the ceiling. At the far end stood two y-shaped crosses. One was the Forelight's holy symbol, a furka, in gold. The other was the Gilt Spider, dressed in the black robes of a saint, arms raised high and head pressed against one shoulder, in the prayerful pose of a devout Stretcher. Though Charlin had witnessed this before, the incongruity of the scene remained jarring.

The Elf ceased his prayers, dropped his arms to his side, and turned to face Charlin. Candlelight sparkled in his amber eyes and polished his flaxen skin into living gold. On a mess of aureate curls rested the black halo of a saint. The creature's beauty was alien and had a distasteful taint of femininity. Charlin directed his gaze at the floor to avoid the Elf's hypnotic stare.

The Elf's dulcet tones filled the cave. "Has something happened to Saint Sebryn?"

"The abbot of Saint Odran's remains in good health," Charlin replied.

"You never call it Pigsback," the Elf observed.

"I am not here to discuss names. Saint Sebryn sent me here on an urgent matter. Harath Melkath, the daughter of the Politician of Pigsknuckle, has disappeared."

"Sebryn knows better than to blame me for her vanishing."

The lack of indignation in the creature's voice made Charlin shiver. It was a pity that Saint Sebryn was not hale enough to do his own unsavory errands. The abbot might be convinced of this creature's good faith, but the unearthliness of the Elf made Charlin's instincts scream otherwise.

"Of course not." Charlin almost choked on his words. A cough exacerbated his discomfort.

The Elf filled a cup from a pitcher and passed it to Charlin. He sipped, then sipped some more. The beverage was like a wine, but Charlin didn't recognize the fruit. An aftertaste of something sweet and delicate lingered—honey perhaps. It was rather good, and it softened his cough.

"It's one of my few luxuries from home," the Elf said. "You were saying?"

"Saint Sebryn wants your help to find the politician's daughter. On the same day she vanished, some wandering traders—we call them Jinglemen—visited the village. They may have abducted her." Charlin's cheeks reddened. "If that's the case, then they hold another hostage—my brother. He secured passage with them to Formicary."

"Why do the Pigsknucklers not pursue these Jinglemen?"

Charlin took a deep breath. "They don't suspect the Jinglemen. The Pigsknucklers believe the Gilt Spider took her."

"You didn't disabuse them of this fallacy?"

"The decision was Saint Sebryn's. The Pigsknucklers must not suspect this arrangement." Charlin waved one hand vaguely around the cavern.

There was a hint of impertinence in the Elf's wan smile. "But surely they would accept such an insight as a saintly miracle. The Pigsknucklers could pursue the Jinglemen, and I could be left in peace."

This interrogation was irksome. Nobody else would dare question a saint's decision. "To claim a miracle where there is none is a terrible sin. Besides, by now the Jinglemen are well beyond the reach of Pigsknuckle. Any pursuit by the Pigsknucklers would have to be negotiated with the other villages along the Jinglemen's route, and of course, with the monasteries to which those villages owe allegiance. Progress would be slow at best. It may also lead to unanswerable questions from other saints."

The Elf raised an eyebrow. "Unanswerable questions?"

"We cannot lie under any circumstances, *as you know*. The best we can do is to avoid the truth."

"Indeed. If I find the Jinglemen, and they have your missing girl, what am I to do? I took a vow of pacifism. My reputation alone may not be enough to free her."

"Saint Sebryn has instructed me to release you from your oath, if you are willing." It was sickening to loose the Gilt Spider again upon an unsuspecting world, but this creature might be Grael's only hope.

The Elf was silent for the longest time before he spoke. "I will do as Saint Sebryn wishes."

Charlin slipped Saint Sebryn's scroll from inside his cassock. He unrolled it and read the beginning. "Place your hands on the furka." His voice trembled as he began the convoluted rite to absolve the creature of its sacred pledge.

Chapter 2

The unlucky, the foolish, the bold,
The Gilt Spider's latest prey await,
Enshrouded in webs of silken gold,
Their snarer's keen blade to carve their fate.

~From *Alackalas and the Fair Princess.*

Days turned with the wagon's wheels, slow, grinding, and unmerciful. Whenever the vehicle stuck in mud or hit an obstacle, Grael became another beast of burden. The rest of the time, the wagon dragged him along, wringing out his last vestiges of hope.

Hackit took a particular dislike to him, seizing every opportunity to goad him with his whip. Once, early on, Harath made the mistake of trying to stay Hackit's hand.

"Leave him alone," she had blurted as the leather seared Grael's shoulder, forcing him to his knees.

"Leave him alone," Hackit repeated, raising a finger with each word. As each finger curled back into his palm, the whip flicked at Grael. The first blow left him face down in the dirt. He squirmed as the second and third lashes struck his back.

"Anything else to say, deary?" Hackit asked. "Mm? Mm? I thought not. As for you, boy, if you don't get to your feet now, you never will."

After that she never intervened again, but whenever Hackit lashed Grael, the concern in her gray-green eyes salved the sting. The foul old lecher ignored Harath most of the time, probably out of fear for what Tarum Sire might do, should he damage her. Scars would lower her worth to Formicary's whoremongers.

Every evening, Grael watched the Jinglemen gather around the fire to eat and swap the same old bawdy tales and grubby dreams of wealth and sexual adventure.

Tarum Sire was deaf to his men's pleas for grog. "In a foreign land it is best to stay sober," he growled when pushed on the subject.

Their dry revelry soon lapsed into listlessness, and one by one, they drifted away to their bunks to sleep off the night.

This enforced temperance was a great comfort to Grael. He shuddered at the possible drunken antics of such coarse imaginations. Particularly with a beautiful woman in tow.

But Hackit was the most persistent petitioner, the most plaintive, the most fawning. "It's bitter cold," he lisped one evening as he stroked his dirty beard. "It makes my old bones shiver. I could use a little something to warm me up."

Grael held his breath. Would Hackit succeed this time?

"Drink your tea then," Tarum Sire grunted.

"Ah, Sire, tea might burn fingers and sting the mouth, but it goes cold in the belly. I need a proper warmth there. Something to last through the night."

Tarum Sire pointed to the fire. "Eat it, if you must."

"What?"

"Eat the flame. Like one of those fire swallowers in Formicary. Then you will have plenty of heat in your belly."

Grael exhaled as the Jinglemen snickered at Hackit's expense. On other occasions, such gentle teasing had been sufficient to silence the old Jingleman.

But not this night.

"True, Sire," Hackit said. "The flame looks right warming, no mistake. But there's one problem. I might singe my beard."

Grael tensed at the Jinglemen's chuckles.

"Hackit's beard's so greasy, if it caught fire, it'd burn like a candle," Scaral, the heavy Jingleman with drooping eyelids, said, patting Hackit on the shoulder.

Hackit grinned, exposing his sparse, rotten teeth. "Ah, please, Sire. One sip of firewater, enough to moisten the tongue and fortify the stomach, and I'll be happy for the rest of the trip. You won't hear another word from me. I promise by the Seven Lights."

"Go on, Sire," Gristle said. His fingers played with the copper beads in his long, silver beard. "Nobody has ever seen Hackit happy before."

"I don't know if I can take Hackit being happy," Tarum Sire said with a devilish grin. "Or recognize him, for that matter."

"Never mind about making him happy," Scaral said. "Making him shut up all the way back to Formicary—that's worth a few sips of liquor."

"Sips?" Tarum Sire repeated.

"It's bad for a man to drink alone," Gristle said, his face radiating mock innocence as his hand polished his bald pate. "Unhealthy. Would you not agree, lads?"

Exaggerated nods and playful smiles expressed hearty approval for the sentiment. A few licked parched lips at the prospect.

As Tarum Sire played with his mustache, Grael silently begged the Forelight. *For the love of your servants, keep this unbeliever from succumbing to this temptation. This once. Please.*

Tarum slowly rose to his feet, sauntered to one of the wagons, and retrieved a small ceramic jar. The other Jinglemen, giggling like naughty children, scattered and sacked their belongings, mustering a variety of cups and bowls to receive the precious libation.

"Where's your cup, Sire?" Hackit asked as his leader uncapped the jar.

"Someone needs to stay sober enough to stand guard," Tarum Sire said.

"Aye. Someone does, but not you, Sire. Let Kaven do it."

Kaven, who was hardly older than Grael, expressed his disapproval with a violent howl. But the others pacified him with effusive praise for his sacrifice and solemn promises of recompense.

Grudgingly, Tarum Sire collected his drinking vessel—an ornate bronze goblet. He poured some of the jar's contents into it. Nodding in the direction of his prisoners, he raised his goblet. He gulped down a mouthful of the spirit with wolfish pleasure.

Grael's heart shriveled. So this was how the Forelight answered his prayer. He had been stupid to hope for more. Miracles were for saints, not for common folk like him.

The other Jinglemen roared with pleasure, passed the jar around, and toasted the munificence of their leader. The jar emptied quickly and was discarded, and the sullen Kaven was dispatched to fetch another.

Harath thrashed about in the back of the wagon in a frenzied effort to loosen her binds. Spurred by her efforts, Grael strained against the rope around his wrists, biting and gnawing at it with rabid fervor, though it was too stout to break.

The Jinglemen jeered at his exertion till the sting of Hackit's whip ended it.

"Enough!" Hackit snapped. "Can't even have a drink in peace. This is what I get for being so nice." He grabbed Grael by the hair, dragged him over to one of the wagon wheels, and seizing another rope, wrapped it around his neck.

As the noose closed, Grael kicked and screamed. Hackit punched his face and pulled the rope so tight that every breath hurt his throat. Grael tried to pull it with his bound hands, but the futile attempt only tightened the noose.

The Jinglemen laughed and joked, thoroughly entertained.

"Lashed to the wheel, you won't be going anywhere tonight. That's for certain," Hackit said. "As for your girlfriend…" He unwrapped a stained, ragged cloth from around his wrist. Its original colors of white and blue were barely distinguishable.

Grael's neck burned as he twisted his head to get a glimpse of what was happening in the wagon. His inability to see either Harath or Hackit emphasized his helplessness.

"Remember this," Hackit said.

The wagon creaked and groaned as Harath struggled with the Jingleman. Hackit squealed with delight as her screams choked off. His colleagues clapped and cheered and toasted Hackit's prowess.

"Thanks to you, deary, we've been dry a long time," Hackit murmured. "The sire was afraid if we got too boisterous we might knock down your value. Of course, the sire is the worst drunkard among us. Once he gets a taste of the liquid fire, he cannot stop himself from having another and another. That's why I made sure he joined our little celebration. Sober, he was likely to cut it short. Don't worry. When he is nicely tipsy, I'll remind him you're here waiting for him. After he's had his sport, there'll be no reason the rest of us can't." Hackit's chuckle decomposed into coughing and spluttering.

Grael chewed again on the knot holding his wrists, more out of frustration than any hope of freeing his hands. He was nothing more than an audience to Harath's danger.

"I bet you're sorry now you begged us to take you from your village," Hackit croaked as he plodded back to the campfire.

Shock halted Grael's biting a moment. The tilt of Hackit's head indicated the comment had been directed at Harath, not Grael. The notion of her begging vagabonds such as these to whisk her away to some foreign land was beyond scandalous. It was preposterous. The woman in the wagon could not be the daughter of the Politician of Pigsknuckle. She had to be an Elfin impostor, a changeling of some sort. And yet, Grael's heart vouched that his fellow prisoner was the genuine Harath Melkath. Why would she choose to leave her village in such a sordid fashion?

He continued to gnaw on the bindings despite the scrape of the noose against his throat with his jaw's every movement.

The mountains snuffed out the sun. Clouds crept across the sky and blotted out stars just glimmering to life. Soon, only the campfire pierced a little corner of the implacable, starless night. The Jinglemen's merrymaking became more rambunctious with every clink of an empty jar striking its discarded predecessors. Even the luckless Kaven sneaked a few swigs of forbidden spirit.

Conversations became incoherent, random, and sodden. Scaral's rambling, pointless story about a one-legged whore in Formicary was cut short by the brothers Chalas and Asurach, who were inspired to fart a tune from the grassy plains of their birth. Gristle and a wiry, bow-legged man called Anorsop had to be held apart after Anorsop took offense at Gristle's urinating on his wagon. The next instant, when one of their comrades fell on the fire, their feud dissolved in manic laughter.

Grael spat out the few broken fibers in his mouth and studied his bindings. The rope exhibited little evidence of his effort.

Tarum Sire hushed the others as though trying to bring some decorum to the proceedings, but then started a rendition of an old fireside favorite: the difference between riding a woman and riding a horse.

"You know, you could show us," Hackit slurred. "You've a horse, and you've a woman yonder."

"I doubt you could tell them apart, you old codger," Tarum said, guffawing and pounding Hackit's back.

The gathering convulsed in laughter.

Grael exhaled a trembling breath as the moment of danger passed and the high jinks swept onward. A few revelers played a knife game till they tired of nicking their fingers, while others danced sloppy jigs to the contorting tune of Gristle's flute. Chalas and Asurach wrestled. Scaral crawled into the bushes and vomited. Kaven forgot all pretense of being sober.

Tarum Sire rose to his feet and turned his back on the merriment. Hackit's rotten grin was ugly with triumph as Tarum wobbled toward the prisoners' wagon.

"She won't be worth much after you finish with her," Grael said. It was a heinous argument, but he had no other. "Would you rob yourself of a fortune for a few moments of pleasure?"

Tarum paused. With his back to the fire, he was an impenetrable black mass. "You may be speaking good sense. Unfortunately, my balls are deaf to your advice." He chuckled and walked by Grael and out of sight behind the wagon.

"Beloved Forelight, save your innocent servant from this heathen!" Grael pleaded. "If you are to ever answer one prayer, let it be this one. Please!"

As Harath gave a muffled scream, Grael punched the side of the wagon with his bound hands and kicked his legs in frustration. The rope around his neck pinched his throat as her scuffle with the Jingleman shuddered through the wagon. The defeated Tarum emitted a pained groan as he fell from the back of the vehicle and thudded against the ground.

As Tarum climbed to his feet, his stream of curses dissolved into booming laughter. "Damn, woman, you kick like a mule." His voice brimmed with reluctant admiration. "You've more spirit than the rock breaker fastened to the wheel. Maybe I won't throw you to the others when I'm finished. Maybe I'll make you my wife."

Harath let out a defiant growl. She flailed and kicked the sides of the wagon as Tarum staggered toward it.

"If you hurt her, I'll kill you!" Grael yelled.

Tarum took no notice. The other Jinglemen cackled and guffawed.

Grael glared at them in turn. "I'll kill you all!"

At that moment, a shapeless, shifting silhouette burst out of the night and leapt over the campfire. The shine from the flames revealed the cloaked figure's face, as passive as a golden idol. The eyes, glittering and cold, were at once beautiful and inhuman. Elaborate spiked axes flicked at the awed Jinglemen with serpentine grace. Anorsop gurgled a final scream as his punctured throat sprayed a bloody mist over his appalled comrades. Chalas, sitting victorious atop his brother, slumped over, dead. Asurach threw aside the corpse sprawled over him and chased his brother's killer into the night.

"Come back!" a sobered Tarum called as he ran to the fire. "Come back, you fool!"

Somewhere in the fright shivering through Grael was relief for Harath. She was safe, for now, thanks to the mercy of the Forelight.

"What was that?" Kaven asked, eyes shocked wide.

"The Gilt Spider," Hackit whispered.

Grael's relief wilted as Hackit stretched a finger toward him.

"That pup summoned him!" Hackit cried. "He threatened to kill us all, just before the Gilt Spider appeared!"

Tarum snorted and slapped down Hackit's hand. "Why would the Gilt Spider do the bidding of a Stretcher?"

"If it was the Gilt Spider, then we're fortunate," Gristle said. "By all accounts, he never leaves behind corpses, much less survivors. We won't see poor Asurach again."

"The Gilt Spider'll be back for the rest of us," Hackit said.

"And we'll be ready for him if he does," Tarum Sire said as he delivered a rousing kick to the snoring Scaral. "Get up! Gristle and Kaven, get rid of the corpses. I don't care where you put them. Just get them out of my sight. The rest of you can encircle the camp with fires. Nobody sleeps tonight. Don't fear the Gilt Spider. Elves bleed the same as any other race."

"You've killed one, have you?" Kaven asked hopefully.

Gristle filled Tarum's silence. "No."

***

Like the Jinglemen, Grael stared into the nocturnal abyss, striving to discern a creeping shadow against the blackness. First light brought some relief, despite Hackit's dire warnings that the day belonged to the Gilt Spider.

"What makes you say that?" Kaven demanded.

"Stands to reason," Hackit said. "The Gilt Spider is an Elf. Elves serve the Golden Light, the torch of day."

"All Hackit or the rest of us know about the Gilt Spider comes from the ravings of drunken Stretchers," Gristle muttered.

Hackit pointed to Grael. "The boy may know more. He's from these parts."

Grael's relief at the loosening of the constriction around his neck was brief. The Jinglemen hauled him to his feet.

Gristle seized Grael's hair and pressed the point of a knife to his throat. "You had better spill everything you know about the Gilt Spider, because if we have to ask your girlfriend, you'll never talk again."

Grael wracked his memory. "I've never seen one of the Fair Folk before. Few in my village have, and then only as a fleck of yellow in the distance. Golden they are, and ageless. Their beauty surpasses all other races."

"We all saw one last night," Tarum said. "Can't say much about its beauty."

Grael talked through Tarum's comment. "The splendor of their womenfolk is such that they have to be cosseted away and guarded by monstrous, misshapen beasts, for the briefest glimpse of their beauty drives the beholder mad with desire. A hero of my people, Alackalas, took one as his wife, but he could only behold her as a reflection in a mirror lest her unmitigated beauty drive him insane. In the end, the precaution was not enough to save him. Most Elves live in great cities where the sun rises. They have a few settlements in the mountains, like the one in the valley of Martyrsgrave, but rarely stray beyond them. The Fair Folk have taken little interest in Stretchers for generations.

"The Gilt Spider is the exception. He is a hunter of men. The unwary and the foolhardy that wander the forests are his usual quarry, but he has even been known to snatch an untended babe from its crib. Those whom he steals are never seen again. They say that nobody sees him and lives."

"Enough!" Tarum Sire bellowed. "The boy knows no more than what he overheard from his mother when he was bouncing on her knee. Last night, our attacker had nothing more magic than surprise. If our guard had been sober and alert, he wouldn't have had that."

Kaven's lips parted to speak, then pursed in silent frustration.

As the Jinglemen walked back to their campfire, apparently forgetting Grael, he sighed softly and bowed his head in gratitude for this little mercy.

Tarum Sire continued. "I hope the Gilt Spider, or whoever he is, visits us again. Discounting Asurach, we number nine. The Gilt Spider numbers one. I like those odds. And I know someone in Formicary who would pay a fortune for the head of an Elf. A fortune."

"Who?" Hackit asked, scratching his ear.

"Never you mind," Tarum Sire said. "I know him, and that is what is important. Scaral and Kaven, you bury our fallen friends deep. If the Gilt Spider wants their remains, he can dig for them. The rest of you, strike camp."

***

"Asurach!"

Jinglemen galloped past Grael. As their horses skidded to a halt, they leapt down and crashed through the undergrowth.

The wagon halted where Asurach's corpse hung by the neck from a tree. His eyes were bulging horrors. His tongue, swollen and black like a hideous slug, extended from his mouth. A dagger pinned a note to his chest. Sickened, Grael could hardly look upon it. He had never seen anything so horrible.

Before he could warn her, Harath strained over the goods piled in the wagon to glimpse the commotion. She shivered at the sight of the dead man and quickly turned away, her eyes squeezed shut as though she was trying to wring the image out of them.

The Jinglemen gathered beneath the dead man, untied the noose of yellow-green cord from the tree, and lowered the corpse to the ground.

"What do we do with him?" Gristle asked. "Dig another grave? It'll be dark soon enough, and I don't fancy camping in this forest."

Tarum Sire shrugged. "Asurach ran off. He left us. We owe him nothing. Leave his body for the crows."

It took Kaven a while to unravel the noose's knot, but Tarum insisted the cord must not be cut. The Elfin rope was worth more undamaged. While Kaven fumbled, the other Jinglemen puzzled over the parchment.

"I can read," Tarum declared as he seized it. He frowned. "It's gibberish. Some foreign script."

"Ask the boy. He might be able to make sense of it," Hackit squealed.

As the document was thrust in front of Grael, he heaped silent curses on the old Jingleman for again drawing unwelcome attention to him. Some of the characters were familiar from inscriptions in the monastery of Pigsback, but a hint of comprehension, however slight, would earn him a violent interrogation.

He shook his head and returned the Jinglemen's stares with unfeigned apprehension. "I am a humble shepherd's son. What would I know of writing?"

"We should squeeze him a bit to make sure," Hackit slurred.

"Let the boy be. We've no time to waste on such nonsense," Tarum Sire muttered. "The day will soon turn against us, and we must be clear of this forest before nightfall." He tossed the parchment into the bushes.

"Don't throw it away," Hackit squeaked, scrambling after it. "It might be worth something."

Tarum Sire's scornful laughter filled the forest. "Scoop up a few cowpats while you're at it, in case they're worth their weight in gold." His mirth collapsed into frustration. He yelled, "We cannot read your message, you stupid bastard!"

The echo of his cry melted into the silence of the mountains.

A loud, melodic voice resonated like thunder through the valley. "Give me the boy and girl, and keep your lives."

The hair lifted on the back of Grael's neck. The astounding horror of the Gilt Spider's demand tingled through him like a venom, leaving only a dead coldness in its wake. He trembled.

Harath looked at him with glassy eyes, her mouth agape, her face white with fear.

"Don't listen to him," Grael pleaded. "For the love of the Forelight, don't hand us over to the monster."

"I couldn't care less about you or your god," Tarum grumbled as his gaze searched the encircling labyrinth of forest for the speaker. "Tell me this, Gilt Spider. Why do you want them?" he boomed.

"They are my prey, and I am hungry."

"And why would the corpses you left at our camp not satisfy your hunger?"

"They are buried. They are stale."

"Why did he not eat Asurach? He wasn't buried." Tarum muttered. Opening his arms wide, he yelled, "Like them fresh, do you? Come down here and collect your dinner."

"I desire the thrill of the chase. Free the Stretchers, and I will find them. You have until the sun sets. Their lives for yours. Make your choice."

"How do we know you'll keep your part of the bargain?" Tarum asked.

He waited but no reply came.

Grael's sense of impending disaster was mirrored in the faces of most of his captors as the caravan traveled on through the forest. Tarum Sire was the sole exception. He appeared to be in a perpetual daze, as if fascinated by some puzzle. When Gristle and others hinted they should surrender the Pigsknucklers to the Gilt Spider, Tarum smiled and waved away their veiled entreaties.

"A wooden coin for your thoughts," Hackit asked him as he rode alongside the old man's cart.

"A wooden one?"

"If I offered anything but wood, you would hold me to it. What are you thinking?"

"If the Gilt Spider was as almighty as everyone believes, he wouldn't need to bargain with us."

Tarum kicked his horse into a canter, leaving Hackit mumbling nervously behind him.

Grael found some comfort in his utterance. Clearly, Tarum was all that stood between the Gilt Spider and his quarry. The other Jinglemen would hand over their prisoners in a heartbeat. This twist of fate was peculiar and disconcerting. Last night, Grael had begged the Forelight to smite Tarum Sire. Now, the captives' only hope depended on his survival. At least, until nightfall, when the Gilt Spider's deadline passed and the Jinglemen's decision was made for them.

The day stretched mercilessly. Every moment dragged. Would the sun ever drop from the sky?

Occasionally, some random Jingleman drew up beside Hackit's wagon and exchanged whispers with him. Grael was too far away to overhear, but they had to be discussing the Gilt Spider's ultimatum. They might be even plotting against their leader.

It was late afternoon when the Jinglemen found a satisfactory campsite in a wide glade rising gently above the endless forest. A jagged outcrop at the center provided a bulwark against the bitter cold wind. The black and gray corpses of campfires beneath the rock and the tree stumps that pockmarked the clearing indicated previous transient habitation. Two Jinglemen were dispatched to the rock's summit to stand guard while the others huddled around a newly kindled fire at its base.

Hackit and Kaven tied Grael and Harath together back to back and plunked them down near the fire. Hackit joined his comrades by the fire and fixed a malevolent stare at Grael. The other Jinglemen took little notice as they tracked the sun's slow, slow decline.

Grael mouthed a silent prayer to the Forelight to hurry the night. As the sun rested on the shoulders of distant mountains, a question from Gristle sent a shiver through him.

"Are we going to let the two kids go?"

"Gules rises yonder, fat and bright," Tarum said, pointing to the bloody moon smoldering in the ashes of the day. "There's no cloud in the sky or the threat of one. Our friend will not surprise us so easily on a night like this."

"So, you'll risk our lives to spite the Elf?" Gristle charged.

Tarum Sire's indulgent smile had a hint of deprecation. "For every risk I take, there must be a reward. In the end, we're all dead. We might as well be rich in-between."

"Is an Elf's head worth so much?"

"It is."

"I hope you're right."

The Jinglemen fell silent again as the sun slipped away like sand in an hourglass, till the last shining speck disappeared, and with it, any chance to reverse their course. They had defied the Gilt Spider's ultimatum and now must face the consequences.

Bloody moonlight seeped into the night, shaping the darkness into a discernible topography. The Jinglemen were restless and taciturn, their eyes fixed on the encircling moorland for any disturbance creeping through the vegetation.

Harath's head tapped Grael's shoulder as she leaned to one side. It was a comfort that she slept. He lowered their bound torsos to the ground and sought the same oblivion. The chafe of the rope, the awkwardness of his position, the prickle of the crushed foliage against his face, the sepulchral cold and the haunting specter of the Gilt Spider conspired to deny him. He turned to prayer to see him through the hellish night, knowing every whispered word brought its end closer.

A scream tore through the silence. A commotion of shadows flitted above Grael. Excited voices clashed in thunderous babble.

"Ruscondel's dead!"

"The Elf killed Ruscondel!"

The grim outcome of the battle whirling around him was as certain as the Gilt Spider's presence. Harath's fingers touched Grael's. He clasped her hand awkwardly as he listened to the Jinglemen's panicked cries.

"Get down!"

"Quick! Over there!"

"Get the bastard before he gets away!"

"Where is he?"

"There! There! There!"

"I can't see him."

"There!"

The crisp twangs of loosed bowstrings hushed the clamor.

"Got him."

Gleeful roars and congratulations gave way to confused dismay.

"He's up and running again." Hackit's foul slur was unmistakable.

"I hit him. He fell. You all saw him fall."

"Scaral, that may be, but he didn't stay down."

"We can't just lie here," Grael whispered to Harath. "We need to see what is happening."

With some difficulty, they lifted off the ground, and sat upright. Grael was facing the Jinglemen, a clump of jittery silhouettes against the firelight.

"Maybe the arrow missed him. Maybe he fell as the arrow was about to strike," Kaven suggested.

"Maybe he's made of gold, and the arrow bounced off him," Gristle muttered.

"The arrow struck his shoulder. I'm certain of it," another Jingleman insisted.

"You must have the eyesight of a bat to see that in the dark," Gristle said.

"Didn't slow him up much if it did," Hackit said in a hushed tone.

"Enough of this prattle!" Tarum Sire bellowed as he emerged from the huddle. "Either Scaral missed, or the Elf's armor saved him." His voice exuded confidence, but the light of the campfire revealed it as a lie.

"Did you see the stumpy arrow that killed Ruscondel?" Kaven asked. "Too small for a bow. The Gilt Spider must have thrown it at him. Imagine the strength to cast it that distance and pierce poor Ruscondel's armor."

"How did he see him in the dark?" Hackit asked.

Scaral began to explain. "We were climbing up the rock to take our turn on watch…"

"Shut up," Tarum said, turning toward the others, his face once again veiled by shadow. "Enough of this childish drivel. The Gilt Spider is as much flesh and blood as any of us. It isn't magic to run away."

"Flesh and blood he may be, but he's killed four of us so far," Gristle said. "And I think it's time to do my magic. Kaven, grab your stuff. We're leaving."

Gristle stomped over to his sleeping mat and started to gather his possessions. After a moment's hesitation, Kaven scurried after him and did the same.

"If you leave now, I'll make it my business to ensure no caravan will ever hire you again," Tarum said, shaking a fist.

Gristle continued to pack his belongings. "I'll have to take the chance."

"Damn coward," Tarum muttered as Gristle saddled his horse.

Gristle paused, then finished tightening the cinch. He swung stiffly into his saddle and waited in silence for Kaven to mount his animal.

Despite the risk of incurring Hackit's whip, Grael could not keep silent. "Don't go," he begged. "Please." Desperation inspired him. "The Gilt Spider is waiting for you out there. You stand a better chance as eight than two."

Gristle glanced coldly at Grael but made no reply. "Good luck," he said to his former comrades as he kicked his horse and galloped away, Kevan trailing behind him but glancing back several times. The thunder of hooves peppered with the tinkle of dancing metal faded into the night. Of the original twelve Jinglemen, six remained.

"Damn them, and damn the Elf," Tarum said. "I promise by the Golden Light that begot him, this ends tomorrow."

Harath's grip tightened, her nails dug into the backs of Grael's hands. The pain was a welcome distraction from his own fear. The Jinglemen were now as much their protectors as their captors.

***

Something squirming against Grael's back jolted him awake. The dampness of the night clung to his face like cold sweat. The first light of dawn had already formed a halo over the mountains.

Harath exhaled behind him. "I suppose we should thank the Forelight for surviving the night." Her voice was shaky.

"We'll be fine," Grael lied. He looked around the empty camp. Where were the Jinglemen? What if they had fled in the night? What if the Gilt Spider had killed them?

"Tarum Sire, are you there?" Grael called.

"Shut up, unless you want my fist for breakfast."

Grael's heart lifted at the sound of Hackit's slur. Even that devil was better company than the Gilt Spider.

As the morning strengthened, the Jinglemen emerged from melting shadows. They immediately set about striking camp. Ruscondel's corpse was placed in a shallow dent in the ground and covered with a thin, earthen veil. Grael and Harath were lashed to an uprooted tree trunk. Grael faced the outcrop. Harath, on the other side of the log, faced the forest's edge.

"Elf!" Tarum Sire roared from his horse. "You have won. Behold your prize, our humble offering to the Golden Light. Let us leave in peace and bother us no more."

As the caravan departed, Grael tested his bonds. He could hear Harath engaged in the same frantic struggle behind him. The Gilt Spider's precious cord held firm. Its use was a surprising oversight by the Jinglemen in their rush to flee. How far would they go before they realized their error? Tarum Sire would not be pleased.

The banal melody of the caravan slowly faded into the distance, till the only sounds were the whisper of the wind through the trees and the thumping of Grael's heart.

"What will we do?" Harath pleaded.

"We'll think of something," he reassured her, his voice thick with fear. What could they do but wait and pray for some miracle?

"Perhaps if we both leaned against the rope in the same direction at the same time?" Harath suggested.

"Let's try it," Grael said. Anything was better than sitting here placidly waiting for the Gilt Spider.

They shifted their combined weight left and then right, but the cord was too strong. If anything, it tightened its grip.

"He's coming!" Harath cried. "Oh, my sweet Forelight, he has a knife in his hand."

Grael turned his head to look, but Harath's flowing red hair obscured his view. He sought Harath's hands, but the trunk separated him from them.

"Remember, we live not for this life but the next," Grael said, suppressing the quiver in his voice. Creeping terror inside declared him a liar.

Harath burst into tears. "I have no next life, other than the endless torture of Hell. I am a sinner. I did not honor my father. I flouted the saints' law. And now, I am going to die and suffer eternal damnation. Oh, beloved Forelight, forgive me, please forgive me." She started screaming.

Grael strained to look back, but all he could see was a bloody knife and the flaxen hand that held it. The fantasy of a prayerful martyrdom died. Fear overwhelmed his senses. Convulsive terror shrieked though him.

And then, barely discernible through the din of his screeches, came miraculous words—the Forelight's Prayer. The voice was soft, tuneful.

Grael opened his eyes. The countenance before him possessed an unearthly beauty, but it was more like a mask than a living face with its unblemished, straw-colored skin and its smooth smile. Only the Elf's amber eyes sparkled with life. The wind played with the stranger's shock of golden curls, sometimes partially concealing the black symbols on his forehead: a disc above what looked like a bow and arrow pointing upward. The Elf wore no cloak. His breastplate was adorned with a simple depiction of the left half of a face. A convoluted weapon rested across his shoulders, its complex heads at both ends reminiscent of antlers. Small oval shields protected his forearms.

"You have no need to fear me," he said. "I am a Stretcher, like you."

"I thought your people worshiped the Golden Light," Grael said.

"I did, long ago," the Elf said. His gaze followed Grael's eyes to the bloody dagger in his hand. He sliced at the cord. "The blood belongs to one of your captors. I found him lurking in the forest, no doubt waiting to ambush me. This is a trap. Your captors left you here as bait. As soon as you are free, run to the forest in the direction from which I came. Let the mountains guide you home."

As the cord fell away, an arrow struck the Elf's calf. The agony twisting his bland features dispelled any illusion of invincibility. The Gilt Spider was flesh like any other creature.

The Jinglemen appeared from behind the promontory and the edge of the forest. The Elf's hands reached to the wooden rack across his shoulders. What had appeared to be a single weapon was a brace of identical wooden rods terminated at both ends with spiked, double-bitted axe heads. As the Jinglemen closed in, Grael grabbed Harath's hand and ran.

The Elf shouted after them, "Remember the true name of he who saved you. I am AscendantSun for this lifetime, Auctor always."

Grael glanced back before plunging into the forest. The Elf stood in the midst of the five surviving Jinglemen, his extravagant weapons poised for combat, like a wounded stag beset by wolves.

Chapter 3

To know beauty famed but unwitnessed
Is why I must scale this lofty spire,
To embrace a love both cursed and blessed,
Which poets dream of and kings desire.

~From *Alackalas and the Fair Princess.*

Through the forest they raced, plunging headlong through the foliage. It did not matter where they were going as long as it put more distance between them and the Jinglemen. Though Grael's instincts screamed otherwise, he gentled his pace to match Harath's. She was slower, and her long skirt kept snagging on bushes, hampering her. It was tempting to elevate the hem of the offending garment to disencumber her movement, but even in this crisis, such a liberty was inappropriate.

"I can go no farther," she gasped. "I need to catch my breath."

Grael glanced over his shoulder. The Jinglemen might be already in pursuit. "Very well."

She began to wander away, apparently oblivious of the possible dangers lurking in this unfamiliar forest.

"Where are you going?" he demanded.

"That is no man's business," she said, reddening.

Grael didn't know what to say. His ears and then his cheeks burned. "Very well. Be careful."

She regarded him disdainfully. "I won't go far…just far enough."

Grael pretended not to hear the rustle of foliage as she did what she had to do. He searched the undergrowth till he found a reasonably sturdy stick. It was better than nothing, but not much of a defense against a pack of wolves or a bear.

"Do you think we are safe?" Harath asked when she reappeared.

His nerves unwound a little at her presence. They were free, but they were lost, perhaps pursued, and armed with only a stick. Worse, they were provisionless, without even the protection of a halo…

"For the moment," he said. "But we need to keep moving."

She nodded. "Lead on."

***

By late afternoon, exhaustion slackened their pace to a trudge. Their progress homeward was even slower. The Pig was a useful direction marker, but it gave no indication as to what lay between them and their home. Impassable cliffs and a frothing river forced them to reverse their course twice. Grael watched for signs of people, friendly or otherwise. If Stretchers inhabited this foreign land, their hospitality wasn't guaranteed to two unkempt strangers drifting through their territory.

"Why did you ask the Jinglemen to take you to Formicary?" he asked Harath. The question had been thumping inside his head most of the day.

"Why did you want to go to Formicary?" she asked in return.

"To make my fortune," he said. *And come home and marry you and live happily ever after.* What a joke. "But I didn't run away. I got Widan Melkath's permission. He negotiated my passage with the Jinglemen."

"You got my father's permission, but not that of Lahan, your own father."

"Widan is the Politician of Pigsknuckle. His word is law. My father is just an ordinary man and happy to be one."

"And you weren't happy to be ordinary."

"You are the politician's daughter. You aren't ordinary."

Harath raised an eyebrow.

Grael continued, "I don't understand why you…you know…invited the Jinglemen to kidnap you."

"I needed to get away. My father planned for me to leave Pigsknuckle anyway. He wanted me to marry a politician from another village. If I must live among strangers, I might as well choose them."

"And how were you going to support yourself?"

"With honest work. I hoped I might be employed as a servant in Formicary."

Grael laughed. "The politician's daughter dreamed of being a servant."

She displayed the calluses on her hands. The welts on her wrists looked as sore as his own. "Do these look like proud hands to you? I was a servant to my father and my brother. Elsewhere, I might get proper recompense for my effort. Do you know I'm older than my brother Donmor? If I had been born a boy, he would be the one going to Formicary." Her face reddened. "What are you going to tell everyone when we get back to Pigsknuckle?"

"I don't know," Grael admitted. Was she asking him to lie?

"The truth is no more than I deserve, I suppose."

"We've both suffered enough for our foolishness."

"If you truly believe that, then swear to the Forelight you will keep my secret. Tell my father the Jinglemen abducted me."

"I'll not compound lies with sacrilege."

"So you intend to ruin me."

"As far as I am concerned, the Jinglemen kidnapped you. The details of your abduction are your own business." He sounded like his dad.

"Thank you." She kissed him, leaving the dew of her lips on his cheek.

Grael resisted the urge to return her favor. The girl was trouble. She had already persuaded him to lie, at least by omission, and now her over-familiarity stirred a mixture of unsavory emotions.

"I'm sorry if I embarrassed you," Harath murmured.

He coughed to clear his throat and struggled out a muddled apology. He had dreamt of her kiss so long, and now when she bestowed it on him, his first reaction was to condemn her. It made no sense. Why was he so horrified by such intimacy? The fault lay not with Harath but with him. He was afraid of what he might do, what sin he might be willing to commit for her.

Her indiscretion paled in comparison to the bawdy tales of the Jinglemen. He chuckled at his naivety in believing that he could cope with the licentiousness of Formicary.

"Why are you laughing?" she demanded.

"Nothing." He fumbled for a better excuse. "I was thinking of the Gilt Spider and our unexpected rescue. That the Gilt Spider should claim to worship the Forelight is such a queer notion."

"You believe the Jinglemen defeated him? But he's the Gilt Spider."

"Elves can die. Alackalas slew several of their greatest warriors to win his fair princess."

Harath scrunched her nose in disgust. "The Jinglemen are nothing like Alackalas. He was a hero."

"True. They don't fight fair, for a start. By now, they are on their way to Formicary with their precious trophy. I should have stayed and helped the Elf. I owed him that."

"How? You had no weapon other than your fingernails. The Elf told you to go. Besides, you couldn't abandon me to wander through this wilderness alone and become the prey of beast or man. I don't see what other choice you had. As you said, the Elf's rescue might have been a ploy.

I'm sure your mother told you to never trust the Gilt Spider."

"Did your mother also tell you that?"

"She died when I was young. My recollection of her is hazy."

"At least you still have your father and brother."

"True." Her voice was edged with a repressed bitterness.

"You don't like them," he said.

"I love my family. And I would love them all the more from the distance of Formicary," she said. "It must be nice to have a family like yours. No troubles to speak of. Saint Charlin is the eldest?"

"Charlin is the eldest, followed by me, my brother Maerbard, my sister Wanyr," Grael said. "Miona—she's obviously the youngest. When I told my parents of my plans to go to Formicary, I said they would hardly notice I was gone with the other three children to care for." He chuckled. "They didn't react too well. I've rarely seen my dad so angry. He was shaking with rage.

"We should find somewhere to camp for the night," he said. "It will be sunset soon enough."

They set up camp near a rocky brook. Grael found an edged rock, but it wasn't a great substitute for a knife. Even with both of them gathering materials, it took quite a while to lash a shelter together.

After some discussion, they agreed that they should light a fire. Wolves and bears were more of a concern than the Jinglemen, who had surely abandoned any pursuit and returned to their caravan by now. Without a bow drill, it proved quite a challenge, but eventually Grael managed to get some tinder to catch fire.

"Take off that rag on your back," Harath said. "I made a salve for your wounds."

His back burned with pain as he peeled off his shirt. Harath winced and breathed deeply through gritted teeth.

"Hackit greased my back with some stinky stuff they use on their horses for sores," Grael explained, reddening.

Harath brought him over to the stream and wiped away Hackit's vile unguent. The softness of her touch reached through his pain and comforted him.

She began applying her salve. Every gentle brush of her fingers was like a healing kiss.

"Hopefully, this will help your back heal. Let it dry a while before you put on your shirt," she said.

He glanced over his shoulder. She was smiling. For the first time since the Jinglemen seized them, she looked happy. Her eyes caught his, and he couldn't pull away. Neither of them moved, stilled by the spell of the moment. Only the thumping of his heart marked the passage of time. A resolve built of saintly edicts, custom, and propriety dissolved into a pool of longing. If her head tilted a little nearer, if he drew a fraction closer…

He wrenched his gaze away. The spell was broken. She bolted to her feet and strode over to the fire, arms folded.

"You can use the shelter tonight. I'd rather sleep in the open," he said. He had to keep his distance.

"You built it for both of us," she said, studying him.

"I'll only use it if it rains," he said, looking away. *Forelight, I beg you, test me no more. I haven't the strength.*

"If you are sure," she said.

He nodded and smiled. At least neither had acknowledged the moment with words. There was some comfort in that. Somewhere to hide.

They ate what meager fare was to be found in the forest and lay down to sleep, Harath in the shelter, Grael on the far side of the fire. A leaden exhaustion weighed on him, but he was too restless to sleep. The day's events spun in his mind. It was hard to believe so much had happened. The morning could have been a month ago. He kept reliving that moment with Harath, picking at it. Writhing emotions mocked his insistence that he had done the right thing. He longed for a second chance but was afraid he might let it pass again, or worse, seize it. Could anything good come of sin? He might be wrong, might have imagined the whole thing. Imagine reaching out to Harath only for her to pull away. Imagine her horror.

In desperation, he turned to the Forelight and prayed himself to sleep.

***

A narrow wooden bridge straddled the azure river. Grael greeted it with mixed emotions. It was proof of habitation, however transient, but offered no clue as to the identity of its builders. A furka would have established that the locals were Stretchers and provided a sanctuary with which to parlay with them.

"If there is a furka nearby, it is up there somewhere." He pointed to the ridge above them.

"And if we find one?" Harath asked as she rubbed the perspiration off her forehead with the back of her hand.

"We wait," Grael said. "Pigsknuckle's furkas are checked regularly. The local Stretchers must do the same. We should be able to convince them to bring a local saint to us, and he will ensure our safe passage home."

It was a shame that they had to be so guarded in making contact with others of their religion, but unfortunately, there was little amity between villages. But for the saints, there would be perpetual war.

"We haven't even halos. How am I going to face my father like this?" Harath said, pulling at her disheveled hair.

"We could be dead," Grael said. "Or worse. We could be slaves in Formicary. Widan will understand."

"Understand what? The shame I have brought on his family? His scorn already rings in my ears, heaping the curses of his father and his father's father on my head."

"He can hardly fault you for being the victim of abduction. If anyone deserves blame, it's me. I brought the Jinglemen to Pigsknuckle. I will tell your father that."

"Please, Grael, that is a noble gesture, but you mustn't."

"But what about you?"

She smiled. "I'll be fine. I'm tougher than I appear. My father will marry me off sooner and farther away than he originally intended."

Grael's heart sank. Of course, she was right. He was a fool to hope otherwise. Widan Melkath wouldn't want the likes of him as a son-in-law. At least, he hadn't done anything foolish last night.

"Are you okay?" Her concern only made it worse.

He pushed up the corners of his mouth into a smile. "I'm fine. Let's keep going."

They began the laborious climb up the incline. Every step was hard on the legs. Harath wobbled dangerously a few times, but the only sound from her was labored breathing. When they paused about half way up to catch their breath, they both sprawled out on the slope. Grael let out a sigh. It would be so easy to close his eyes and drift off to sleep.

Movement on the bridge made him sit up. Men were crossing. All six wore the same gray headdress. If it was a halo, it did not belong to Pigsknuckle. They were armed and in a hurry. One of them waved his spear toward the ridge.

"Run for your life," Grael hissed.

As he and Harath scrambled up the slope, he prayed to the Forelight they would find a furka on the ridge. Without that miracle, they were doomed.

Though he encouraged Harath not to look back at their pursuers, he couldn't resist glancing back to gauge their progress. The men were close enough for the gray of their halos to resolve into the entwined black and white of the village of Cronesglen, and they were gaining fast. Harath was too slow, too hesitant picking her way up the slope. Grael grabbed at her hand to pull her along

She snatched it away. "Leave me. Save yourself. I'll be safe. No Stretcher would harm a woman."

She might be right, but he couldn't just forsake her. "I'll not leave you, whatever happens."

"Go," she insisted.

"If you stay, so do I."

She rolled her eyes as she resumed her progress up the slope. She climbed faster than before, her previous circumspection forgotten. Her stumbles only added to the determination of her ascent. Grael, staying by her side, offered words of encouragement till she told him to shut up. The summit drew ever nearer, but the men from Cronesglen closed, too.

"Come back!" one of the Cronesmen cried. "There's no need to fear Cronesglen's welcome."

Clever language—not quite the guarantee of hospitality it promised. It reminded Grael of an old proverb: A good Stretcher never lies, but he may not always tell the whole truth. He cast a concerned glance at Harath, expecting her to waver, but she wasn't fooled. She didn't relent in her pursuit of the summit. There had to be a furka up there. Why else would the Cronesmen seek to stall them?

Near the top, the slope became so steep and rocky they had to climb with their hands. A large stone fork, painted black and white, stood farther along the ridge. Grael glanced back at their pursuers. So close.

"Run to the furka," Grael said. "I'll try to stall them." He only had a stick, but the men of Cronesglen would be hampered by the steep ground.

"If you stay, so do I."

They had no time for argument. They ran. A spear flew past Harath's shoulder and slid along the ground till it stopped at the base of the furka.

"You young fool!" one of their pursuers exclaimed. "You nearly struck the furka!"

"They were getting away," the spear-thrower pleaded.

"Better that they escape than the furka is injured," said a third man. "Better for you that you were never born than touch it with a spear."

Their distraction gave Grael and Harath time to reach the furka. They hugged its sculpted trunk and claimed its sanctuary.

***

Grael stared back defiantly at the five frowning Cronesmen, while the sixth sought their politician. The Politician of Cronesglen took forever to arrive at the furka. He was an old man, lean, with sunken cheeks and shoulder-length, snow-white hair. A white beard fringed his jaw. Crystalline shards as white as his hair fanned from his thorny crown.

Before Grael finished introducing himself, the politician silenced him with a wave of his hand. "What is the second commandment of our religion?"

Grael's brows knitted. What possible relevance did that question have? "To love the Forelight above all else."

"That is the first. What is the second?"

Grael blushed. "To love others."

"There's more to it. It is to love others as you love yourself. And the third?"

Grael rummaged his memory. "To reject the False Lights."

"Very good. Please pray to the Forelight. Both of you."

Grael and Harath recited the Forelight's Prayer.

"I am Radal Faral," the politician said. "Please forgive our wariness in extending our hospitality. Even if you wore halos, we would have been as cautious. In the past, rogues and vagabonds from the lowlands pretended to be Stretchers to enter our company and rob us."

"Did wariness make one of your men cast a spear at a fleeing woman?" Grael asked.

"What?" Radal Faral was aghast. He turned to the man beside him. "Joloth, is this true?"

The oldest of the pursuers, a plump man with a sandy beard and receding pate, stepped forward. His gaze fell to his feet, and he blushed.

"Here is the evidence," Grael said, pointing to the spear lying beneath the furka.

"I thought it belonged to you," Radal said.

"It's not mine," Grael said. "It lies where it landed. I wouldn't touch it, in case I might be infected with its dishonor. It belongs to one of your people, to the red-headed youth yonder."

"Then it almost struck the furka," Radal said. His glare shifted from Cronesman to Cronesman. "None of you chose to mention this. Not you, Fermad, who sought me, nor you, Joloth, my brother, who is old enough to have more sense."

"We thought the sinner best recount his sin," Joloth said.

"Falmor, what have you to say?"

The fiery-haired youth, his face burning crimson with anger and shame, directed scornful glances at his comrades. "I cast at the girl, not the furka, and I didn't know she was a girl when I threw it. In those filthy rags, from behind, at a distance, no man could tell. For all we knew, their intention was to smash the furka. I was defending it."

"Smash it with what? This stick? Her empty hands?" Grael muttered.

"Then, Falmor, your sin is at least not deliberate, but it's a sin nonetheless," Radal said.

Falmor tried to protest, but the Politician of Cronesglen shushed him. "Recklessness is a sin. Sacrilege, even through thoughtlessness, is a sin. To risk injuring a furka isn't merely an insult to the Forelight and a breach of the first commandment, it is to endanger our very home."

He picked up the spear, laid one end on a boulder, and stamped on the shaft. Falmor flinched as it split in two.

"Remember, the Witch People lived here before us, till the saints drove them away," Radal said. "The ghosts of their matriarchs still haunt Cronesglen. The furkas keep their evil at bay. If the furkas were destroyed, our valley would have to be abandoned till new ones could be erected."

Radal laid a hand on the young man's shoulder. "So, Falmor, this is what you'll do. You'll go to the monastery of Highsanctum and ask the saints to provide an escort back to Pigsknuckle for our unfortunate guests. Then you'll tell them your sin and take whatever penance they choose. It's hard for a layman to be just in such matters."

The features of the politician and the man whom he scolded shared a familial theme. Radal might have looked much like his son before the years whitened his hair and weathered his face. Father and son had the same blazing blue eyes, though in the case of the older man, their luster was tempered with wisdom.

"If it's your wish, Father, then I will obey it," Falmor said.

"Not my wish. My duty," Radal said. "Go now. I'll pray the saints are merciful, and that when you return, you'll be a little closer to being the man you could be."

Falmor nodded. "Then let that journey begin here. May I beg for the forgiveness of the lady for my sin against her?"

Harath nudged Grael in the ribs. "He is asking you. You're my protector. Apparently."

Grael's eyebrows rose at this astounding assault on his person, but his voice did not betray his surprise. "You may."

Falmor knelt and bowed his head.

"I forgive you," Harath said.

"Thank you." Falmor stood. His eyes glistened as he stretched his arms and pressed his head against his shoulder. The sign of the furka made, he headed down the ridge.

"We shouldn't let him go alone," Joloth said. "We're equally culpable. We should accompany him to Highsanctum and share his penance."

"One hand throws a spear," Radal said. "And it only takes two legs to walk up a mountain. Let him be."

Radal Faral was a better kind of politician than Widan Melkath, Grael decided. The former was more akin to the politicians of legend, dispensing wisdom with pious humility, while the latter, consumed by the perpetuation of his dynasty, wriggled like a fat grub through an interminable putrefaction of compromise and convenience. For a dangerous moment, if Radal had invited Grael to join his community, he might have accepted. Then again, many decent people lived in Pigsknuckle, including Grael's family. It was a shame they did not have a better leader.

"So, this is Widan Melkath's daughter," Radal said after Grael had introduced Harath. The politician's pitying smile suggested he shared Grael's opinion of her father. "How did you two end up here? It must be quite a tale."

For much of his story, Grael was as faithful to the actual events, only changing the details of Harath's initial seizure and avoiding mention of the liberties that Tarum had threatened to take. However, when it came to recounting the Gilt Spider's hand in their escape, the weight of legend proved too much. It was easier to portray the Elf's rescue simply as a failed bid to snatch them from the Jinglemen. Anything else might have offended Radal's sensibilities.

But at the last moment, stirring guilt made Grael blurt, "The Elf professed to be a Stretcher and claimed his goal was our rescue."

Radal smiled. "Never believe the promises of Fair Folk. Tomorrow, you and I will see if we can find the site of this battle and learn the fate of your captors. If any trace of them remains."

***

Grael shivered as whispers broke the brittle silence of his companions. In the daunting gloom of the forest, the Cronesmen huddled in a ring around Radal. He had brought more than twenty of his best warriors and a saint from Highsanctum to ward against Elfin magic. Even with numeric superiority and the Forelight on their side, every sweaty face was tense with apprehension.

"We will search the clearing after Saint Marden blesses it," Radal whispered. "I doubt we will find anything *unholy*. Not to belittle what our friend from Pigsknuckle saw, or thought he saw, but a lifetime's wisdom tells me a handful of mortals could not defeat the Gilt Spider. I expect to find no trace of either the Gilt Spider or those who fought him."

"Why did you bring so many of us then?" Joloth asked, his voice twitchy. "If you don't mind my asking, brother."

Radal shrugged. He leaned close to his brother, his eyes rounding and a smile stretching his lips. "Because I could be wrong."

If only Grael could have stayed in Cronesglen with Harath. The Gilt Spider was not the all-powerful fiend that the Cronesmen feared, but it would be better to never meet him again.

Saint Marden stood aloof from the gathering. His black garb blended into the shadows so well that he appeared like a disembodied head miraculously floating behind them. No beard hid the chinstrap holding his black halo on his balding pate. The old man's demeanor had an unearthly calmness as he mouthed silent prayers, the furka hanging from his halo dancing against his forehead to his unspoken words. He stepped into the glade. Raising his arms and pressing his head against one shoulder to make the sign of the furka, he prayed to the Forelight to cleanse the clearing of whatever evil haunted it. Finishing, he nodded to Radal.

Grael followed the Cronesmen out of forest. The Jinglemen's corpses lay strewn in a rough circle, already partly ravaged by beak, fang, and claw. Hackit's face leered at him. The old man's head was severed from his body. Not even scavengers dared to touch it.

"Should we bury or burn them?" Radal asked. "What would be appropriate for these foreigners?"

"They should have pouches around their necks," Grael said. "Tinder for fire. Earth for burial."

"What about a wooden fish? What could it mean?" Radal had retrieved it from Tarum Sire's corpse.

Grael shrugged. "I have no idea. Perhaps, he should be thrown into a river perhaps."

Radal sniffed. "We will bury him. Our rivers should not be polluted with scum such as this. Joloth, how do you read the signs?"

"The Gilt Spider was wounded. It left a trail of blood yonder. You are not going to suggest I follow it, are you?"

"Of course not. The Fair Folk are mischievous. Their signs cannot be trusted. Find this young man's caravan instead. It should be nearby."

"It's not my caravan," Grael said. He had assumed Radal Faral would claim it for Cronesglen.

"It's yours by right of your suffering."

"Then it should be equally Harath's."

"No woman other than a widow may own property, according to saintly law. The Jinglemen's possessions are yours."

Grael did not know what to say. It was too much. He had done nothing to deserve such a bounty. But it was pointless to protest saintly law. "And will you not take some of the contents in recompense for your hospitality?"

Radal shook his head. "If you wish to donate some of the goods to the monastery of Highsanctum, I will ensure they safely reach there, but Cronesglen will take nothing of the caravan. Consider it our penance for attacking you."

They found the three carts, the oxen that hauled them, and the Jinglemen's horses patiently awaiting their dead masters.

"You are fortunate," Radal said to Grael as he surveyed the vehicles and their piles of goods. "Most men who go to Formicary, if they live long enough to return home, never amass such wealth as you have in a couple of days. I hope you'll have the good sense to quit while you are ahead and put dreams of Formicary aside for good."

Grael massaged the bruise on the back of his wrist. "All I want to do is go home."

As he walked alone back to the clearing, the smell of burning flesh and wood assaulted his nostrils. Joloth and a half-dozen other Cronesmen stood around the Jinglemen's pyre, watching the fire peep through its thatch of branches.

Grael glanced downward. A dark slash of congealed blood clung to the foliage, no doubt part of the trail discovered by Joloth. Grael's eyes followed its direction to the edge of the forest. As his legs moved toward it, he faltered mid-step. What was drawing him there? Something more sinister than simple curiosity about the fate of his rescuer? He'd had his fill of adventure, and yet, something urged him to find the trail. Some part of him wouldn't let the riddle of the Gilt Spider rest.

Chapter 4

As the Consensus of Lineages could not cure him, it severed him from his lineage and his name, and condemned him to the island of Evercloud, so that no matter how loud he yelled, the seas would swallow his heresy.

-From *The Book of Judgments.*

He heard the hush. The only sound was the breathing of the sea, its soft churn against the shore. The seabirds sharing his island prison were silent. He threw on his sandals, left his little stone cell, and glanced about the decaying village. No birds swooped overhead. None were lighted upon the broken walls of the nursery, or the hall, or the storehouses, or the little vegetable garden. No birds rested on the little stone cells that had defied neglect and weather for a century or more. Even their favorite haunt was abandoned—the gaunt stone pillar that had been the village's gnomon, robbed long ago of its golden hand and precious gilding when the island was abandoned.

The Harbinger of the Dawn trod along the rough path that slashed back and forth down the hillside to where the cliffs could be surveyed. He peered over the low, ramshackle parapet guarding the unwary from the black precipices beyond. The air was empty. No winged sickles harvested the ocean. No ribbons of white festooned the cliffs. In the midst of their mating season, the colonies of guffawns, guillets, and waeries had disappeared. Not a single bird remained, as if some divine hand had wiped them from existence.

He slipped off his sandals, climbed over the wall, and down the cliff face. Abandoned nests lay along the ledge below. In some he found eggs. He wrapped his fingers around one. The shell was dead cold.

"Where are you?" he cried as he flung the egg into the sea.

The echo of his question taunted him. He was so utterly alone. Even the creatures of the air spurned him. Dedication to the Golden Light, Aurelian, had always prevented despair in the past. Suddenly, it was failing. Long ago, his people had banished him to this miserable rock. His race had denounced him as a heretic. The Consensus of Lineages, that self-aggrandizing parliament of bureaucrats and windbags, had insisted he was wrong, his beliefs fallacious and unnatural, his prophecies either fraudulent or the product of insanity. His own flesh had disowned him. Yet his faith in his calling had endured. So many years had passed waiting for the fulfillment of his prophecies, and the return of the Golden Light to his people. So many years longing for some crumb of divine favor to prove him right. This day, this very moment, that faith was dead. The lifeless wind had snuffed it out.

Only Aurelian could reignite it.

The Harbinger turned to the blinding sun, the embodiment of the Golden Light in the sky, and prayed. The light stung his eyes, but physical blindness was preferable to a spiritual one. He pressed his hands together, and keeping his four thumbs entwined, he revealed his palms to form the symbol of the open flower. The common prayers sanctioned by the Consensus were formulated by committee, not inspired by the divine, but they were as good as any in this crisis. He settled on the Five Name Orison.

"Aurelian, Bright Lord,
Let not the Darkness blind your servants.
Aurelian, Summer Plow,
Sustain your servants that they may thrive.
Aurelian, Night Breaker,
Free your servants from its tyranny.
Aurelian, Burning One,
Set your servants' hearts afire.
Aurelian, Unconquered Sun,
Give your servants their reward."

Five names and five prophecies. It was a marvelous coincidence. The five warring Lights, the five races of myrmidons that served them, the five names of Aurelian, the five prophecies revealed to his humble messenger—it fitted together perfectly. Why had he not noticed it before?

> *"A great darkness shall precede Aurelian's coming, as the night precedes the dawn.*
> *Aurelian shall divide from the sun, and the sky shall be his nursery.*
> *The faithful heart shall feel no shadow. Its only ambition shall be to serve.*
> *The City of Eternal Noon shall be reborn on the ruins of Gleam.*
> *The Lights who mocked Aurelian shall become his crown."*

This was his creed, pieced together from dreams. This was the cause of his suffering.

Damn the birds. Why should he miss them? They were the White Light's servants. The Lord of Storms had sent them to tease him. They offered him companionship and then forsook him to drive him mad with loneliness. The White Light's scheme would not succeed because its very existence proved that the Harbinger was right. Aurelian's rivals considered him a threat because he was destined to prepare the Ors for the return of their Bright Lord.

I must not fail, he thought. *I cannot. I am weak. I know it. Yet I have endured so much. The Golden Light sustains me.*

He ceased his prayers. They no longer mattered. His heart sang more eloquently than the weary lip service of the Consensus.

When the brand of the sun had cleared from his eyes, he scrambled back up the cliff. After he climbed over the little stone wall, the air shuddered. The wall crumbled, showering loose stones down the cliff. It was a miraculous escape. If he had lingered below a few moments longer, the falling debris would have killed him.

The collapse reminded him of the quake that struck the deathblow to the hallowed city of Gleam. Memories stirred of its walls cracking apart, folding and collapsing like torn fabric.

Something was happening around him, some kind of geologic seizure. The ground was steady, but rocks spilled from their perches and a peculiar shiver lingered in the air.

It ended as suddenly as it began. He hurried to the village to check his hut. He thanked the Golden Light that his little cell remained sound. Not a single stone had shifted. The other cells were untouched by the tumult. Elsewhere amid the ruins were signs of fresh devastation: toppled walls, loose stones rattled free of mossy shrouds. The gable end of the wretched nursery had dissolved into rubble.

The day's events filled the night and left no room for sleep. The White Light had taken away his winged companions. That was a certainty. The earthquake was a different matter. Was it also the White Light's doing, or was it the deed of another Light? Aurelian might even be responsible. Perhaps the five prophecies were about to be fulfilled at last. How frustrating. Great events might be happening elsewhere, and he was trapped on this forsaken island, severed by the sea from the rest of the world.

He was so blind, so feeble. The Golden Light's mind should be transparent to his oracle. He shouldn't have to hurl guesses at this mystery. He should know.

Then again, a mouth cannot see. Can it hear? No. It can only speak. A servant needed only knowledge specific to his function. He must have faith in his master.

***

A tickling on his cheek caused the Harbinger to wake. Dust sprinkled his face. A loud grinding sound like a thousand gnawing jaws closed in around him. Another quake, more sustained than the last.

He fled the hut, his blanket under his arm, and his sandals in one hand. He stood a safe distance from the cell till the tremor halted. When the ground calmed, he stared at the hut's entrance, afraid to re-enter. What had been a snug refuge from the weather was now a waiting tomb. He slept the rest of the night in the open with the blanket and a fire to ward off the damp air.

Over the subsequent days and nights, quakes of increasing intensity shook the island. Around noon on the fifth day, a loud bang crossed the sea. Another followed, and two more in quick succession, then others at random, as if the shell of the world was slowly cracking apart.

Scanning the sea in the direction of the booms, he saw clouds like prodigious black fingers reaching over the horizon. The inky plumes spilled across the sky with alarming speed, quenching the noon sun. The world was blind but for the lightning flashes that tore through the calamitous blackness.

Convulsive thunder shook the air. Hot, feathery ash began to fall. Balls of flame exploded against the earth. It was too dangerous to remain in the open, but the sturdiness of his cell could not be trusted, so he stood in its entrance watching the unfolding catastrophe, enduring each hot, choking breath, fear-stricken and awed.

At any moment, the vast conflagration might spill from the sky and destroy him. The sooner the better. At least this torture would be over. If only he could lie down and sleep till the flames took him. But it was impossible to look away from the cataclysmic spectacle. The world roared as though wounded. Stones rattled down on the domed roof of the cell. The earth trembled with pain. There could be no escape, no reprieve.

Then, in the midst of this destruction, a miracle occurred. A tapered light appeared atop the gnomon, its profile reminiscent of the edge of a hand. Was it blue or white? No, it was tinted a ghostly yellow. The Golden Light had sent him the sign he'd so desperately sought at the moment of his greatest despair!

Further calamities followed. A great boom deafened him as the incessant night blinded him. A thick mantle of ash smothered the island. The frothing sea surged up the island's precipices and ripped away chunks of land. But the greatest scourge of all, fear, was gone. Even when the golden hand disappeared, it burned on in his heart.

He murmured quietly, *"A great darkness shall precede Aurelian's coming, as the night precedes the dawn."*

***

Weeks of night passed before the sun pierced the terrible black pall over the world. It was weak at first, a sickly green disk smeared by murky shadows for a few hours around noon. The next day was brighter and stronger but brought heavy rains which lasted for a week. Black rivulets carried ash and filth off the island, into the sea. Then, one morning, the rain stopped and the sun burnished the skies, and the Harbinger could bathe once more in his master's light.

Evening was fast approaching. The retreating sun bled across the sky and the sea, inflaming everything with its violent color. High on the cliff, he watched a little black beetle-like boat struggle across the bloody channel that severed Evercloud from the mainland. Squinting, he sighted it between finger and thumb and imagined it wriggling vainly there. He pinched his fingers together, snapping the gap shut as if to crush the boat. The fate of his torturers would soon be in his hands.

The little boat drew close to the bottom of the cliff. Three figures, their garments tinted red by the sunset, scrambled up the rocks. They leapt from one black boulder to the next, till they reached the cliff-face. Then, they began a slow, painful ascent.

The Harbinger stood. Age and hunger made him stiff.

A guffawn alighted atop the only cell still standing after the cataclysm, the Harbinger's home. He picked up a pebble. "Welcome back, you faithless coward!" he cried as he flung the stone at the bird.

The stone missed, and the guffawn flapped away.

He awaited his visitors in the shadow of the gnomon. They were unmistakably flaxen-skinned Ors. Two had golden, shoulder-length hair, no doubt the current civilian fashion. The one in the center sported the cropped cut of a soldier. They wore the elegant finery of ministers on official business, but their dishevelment after their climb made their appearances comical. Their tunics were soiled, their hands blackened, and the names tattooed on their foreheads were partially obscured by dirt. The Harbinger recognized the lineages. The faces of a Soliferreum, a Consilium, and a Ferocitas were unmistakable. The ill-concealed horror on their perpetually young faces as they beheld him was strangely gratifying. To them, he must seem a living cadaver.

The Consilium in the middle apparently noticed the Harbinger squinting at his forehead. "FervidServant is my life name," he croaked. "I and my fellow ministers speak for the Consensus of Lineages."

"And what does the Consensus wish to say to this heretic?" the Harbinger teased. "It is early in the year for my new attire to be delivered. Or perhaps the Consensus feels that, given the unseasonably cold and wet summer, I need them now."

FervidServant blinked. "Pardon?"

"The Consensus, in its mercy, provides me a fresh set of clothes every year. I assume you are here to deliver it? The island provided all my other needs till recently."

FervidServant ordered one of his companions to give the Harbinger some food.

"Do not be afraid," the Harbinger said as he watched the Soliferreum's wary approach. "My aging is not contagious. As far as I know. Or fatal. Though it damned me more than any of the theological arguments the prosecution spun against me at my trial."

The Soliferreum gingerly handed the Harbinger a small loaf of bread and a water skin. The skin was too full for his frail arms to lift.

"Help him," FervidServant commanded.

But the other Ors didn't move.

Casting irritated glances at his reluctant companions, FervidServant picked up the water skin, opened the stopper, and began to dribble some of its contents into the Harbinger's mouth.

He drank what he could of the falling water as it washed his mouth and chin and neck. "Thank you," he said.

The bread inspired a strange revulsion. He took a bite and chewed the dry, tasteless dough. It was so hard to swallow. "Did you come from Mothport?"

"Mothport is destroyed. We rowed here from the city of ServeAurelian. The sea swept away all the coastal settlements as far east as Seascythe, and thousands of Ors with them. Even the Peacemaker's fortifications along the

Gulf of Fosse were damaged. It will take months to repair the wall," FervidServant said, his eyes glistening.

"May the sun open its arms to their spirits. If this island was a little more hunched, I might have shared their fate." And none would weep for him. "Do all the lineages survive?"

"They do."

"Well, that is some comfort, is it not? What a terrible loss a lineage would be." He bit off another chunk of bread. His appetite was returning. It was tempting to recount for his visitors the apparition of the golden hand, but they were unworthy of the revelation.

"And the Consensus sent you here to bring me this news?"

"The Consensus charged us with bringing you to the capital for questioning on the matter of these unnatural disasters blighting our land."

"Am I being accused of causing them?"

"No. The Consensus hopes you might be able to shed some light on their nature."

The Harbinger smirked. So, the Consensus was lost. The enlightened leaders of the Ors were stumped. The fine rhetoric echoing in their meeting chamber could not placate the cries of a people demanding an explanation for their sudden misfortune, so the Consensus turned to the Harbinger for the very reason it had exiled him.

"Tell the Consensus I will appear before it in due course, if it is the will of Aurelian."

FervidServant frowned. "You obviously do not understand. We are here to take you to the Consensus."

"I will make my own way to the city of Sunthorn if Aurelian wishes."

"How?" FervidServant blurted. His confusion was pleasing.

"Tell the Consensus this, also. None can compromise with the will of Golden Light. I prophesied the terrible darkness before the dawn, and it has happened. I prophesied the sun reborn in flesh, and it will come to pass."

"How will you come to Sunthorn?" FervidServant demanded, his voice quivering with frustration.

"The answer is here." The Harbinger opened his fist and pointed to its center, laughing. "Here in the palm of my hand."

"Enough ravings from this madman. Night fast approaches. We are leaving," the Consilium declared.

"What will you tell the Consensus?" one of his comrades asked as they walked away.

"I will tell it not to waste my time with such idiotic errands in future," he said. "Our land is in chaos, our people without shelter or food, and I am sent to trade jests with that ridiculous fool."

"Leave me the food!" the Harbinger yelled.

FervidServant grabbed a satchel from the Soliferreum and flung it in the direction of the Harbinger.

"You are not so certain Aurelian will fill your belly," FervidServant observed.

"You will change your tune the next time we meet," the Harbinger muttered to himself as he watched the Ors disappear down the cliff.

***

The Harbinger lingered in the decrepit stone village till he regained enough strength through nourishment and rest to climb down to the sea. His path was not the easier southern descent favored by his visitors. The western side of the island was a sheer rock wall bowing gently inward, but a large fleck of yellow shone on the black rocks at its base. Such a sign from Aurelian could not be ignored.

Slipping his sandals into the satchel on his back, he eased himself over the edge of the cliff. Progress downward was slow. Every movement wracked his body as he swung and jerked, striving for handholds. His grip slipped, and for a moment, only one hand held him to the cliff. With massive effort, he pulled himself upward, seized a ledge with his other hand, and planted his feet in niches in the rock. He continued down the precipice. Another might be afraid of plummeting to his death, but not he. What had he to fear, when the Golden Light guided him?

It took him most of the afternoon to reach the beach at the bottom. The object of his journey lay straddled across two boulders. It looked like a raft from a distance, but on closer inspection, it was a ragged sheet of pale yellow rock. Its spongy appearance belied a brittle hardness.

Scattered across the beach were smaller pieces of various sizes. Some fragments danced on the waves racing onto the shore. Farther out to sea, a rash of yellow specks bobbed on the water. The strange rock had to be a boat of some kind.

He pulled it down from its perch. Its lightness was surprising. He hauled it into the sea till the waves carried its weight. The evening sun was already painting the world in fire and shadow, as he flung himself onto the raft of pumice. He paddled out to sea till, overcome by exhaustion, he entrusted his fate to his god and let the flaming waves steer his course.

Chapter 5

From lands of endless summer came
This thornless rose, this sacred bloom,
Petaled with gold, shining as flame,
Its perfume all other loves' doom.

-From *Alackalas and the Fair Princess.*

Grael stole a glance at Harath. Her face was stiff with boredom as Saint Marden mumbled prayers by her side in the cart. He and Radal Faral conspired so successfully to keep Harath isolated from the rest of the caravan that she was more like their prisoner than their charge. Grael's hesitant intimacy with her in the forest was a happy memory and an impossible dream. He would give up his newfound fortune if he could have that closeness again.

He sighed.

"You'll be home soon enough," Joloth said. Joloth, always jolly, always nearby, always watching. It was hard to ignore the implication of this surveillance, but to challenge it might only serve to confirm the worst suspicions of Harath's guardians. Doubtless, it would be worse in

Pigsknuckle. Scandal, real or imagined, was never forgotten there.

Grael vented his frustration with a sigh. "If we were permitted to walk home by ourselves, we would be already there."

The saint ceased his droning and fixed his eyes on him. Grael stared back defiantly. Saint Marden looked away and started praying again.

"But you couldn't leave your fortune behind," Joloth said, clapping Grael's shoulder. "These carts aren't goats. They can't skip up the sides of mountains. That's the trouble with youth—not enough patience. All good things come to those who are patient."

Around noon, a loud bang, sharper than a thunderclap, shivered through the mountains. Here and there, the white mantles of mountains slipped, pouring feathery spumes of snow down their sides. After Grael and the Cronesmen had calmed the frightened horses and oxen, all eyes looked to the sky for the cause of the boom, but its faultless blue only deepened the mystery.

Joloth shrugged. "Maybe your Pig decided to turn over."

"If it did, I hope it did not roll over my village," Grael snapped, cutting short Joloth's half-hearted chuckle.

"I'm sure Pigsknuckle is safe," Joloth said. "As safe, at least, as my own village."

After giving thanks to the Forelight for his protection, the party continued their journey.

A dark gauze spread across the sky. The sun gradually dimmed throughout the afternoon till it was a cool, blue-green ball. The air had an unseasonable chill.

Grael overheard two Cronesmen whispering ahead of him.

"I've never seen anything like it. It's unnatural."

"See, I told you. Radal was right to give this treasure away. Ill omens follow it."

"Aye. I'm loathe to admit it, but for once you're right. Nothing good comes from the Gilt Spider. His spilled blood must have cursed it."

"Excuse me one moment, Grael," Joloth said as he quickened his pace. He squeezed between the two Cronesmen and clamped his arms across their shoulders. They exchanged whispers. One of the Cronesmen glanced sheepishly back at Grael. Joloth released them and drifted back to Grael's side.

"Don't mind those superstitious fools," Joloth said. "They have nothing in their heads except overeager tongues."

Grael nodded and tried to hide his disquiet behind a smile. The Cronesmen's exchange explained Radal's urgent generosity with the Jinglemen's possessions. What doom was Grael bringing home to his people, his family?

No. Radal was a righteous man. He could never be so devious. Besides, the Gilt Spider had never been near the carts. Though to be sure, Grael would ask his brother Charlin to bless it when he got home.

As the green sun slowly slipped behind the mountains, the sky raged with ocher, orange, and crimson, as if the world beyond the Stretches was afire.

***

The caravan was nearing Pigsknuckle when crimson snow began to fall.

"Hard frosts in the middle of summer and now this," Joloth muttered to Grael. "Blood dripping from the sky."

The snow turned to muddy water as it melted in Grael's palm. It had an acrid smell. "It's not blood," he said as he wiped his hands together. "Whatever it is." He brushed away a flake tickling his lip, afraid to taste it.

"Blood! The sun is weeping blood for the Gilt Spider!" a Cronesman cried.

"Shut up!" Joloth snapped. "I see no sun above us. Only dirty clouds."

"Utter no more blasphemies!" Saint Marden yelled from the cart. "Lest the Forelight strike you dead in his wrath. We are Stretchers. We recognize no god other than the Forelight. Only Elves and madmen put their faith in the divinity of Lights."

Radal joined Grael and Joloth.

"How much further is your village?" Radal asked Grael.

Grael looked for the Pig but it, too, was hidden behind the clouds. "Leaftea Lake cannot be far. There is a furka there."

The Politician of Cronesglen nodded. "Then we will camp there tonight, and Saint Marden can go to

Pigsknuckle in the morning." He wiped the blotches of snow from his pale face. "If there is one."

***

Grael crawled from under his sleeping skins and out of his makeshift shelter. The red snow was gone, like a dream. He slipped on his boots and strolled out of the copse, down to the lake. The horses and oxen were scattered across the surrounding brush. In the center of a loose circle of carts stood the furka, painted in Pigsknuckle's colors. Radal, Joloth, and several other Cronesmen were already up and about their chores. Saint Marden stood before the furka, his arms stretched in the air and his head pressed against one shoulder in the traditional devout pose as he droned through his prayers. To the east, against a bleeding dawn, the sun shone blue. A deeper shade of red stained the summit of the Pig, proof that the red snow was not a dream after all.

Saint Marden finished his prayers, dropped his arms to his sides, and walked over to Grael. "It's good you are up. I will go to Pigsknuckle to announce our arrival."

Grael pointed to the hill overlooking the furka. "If you head that way, you cannot miss it."

Marden bid farewell with a nod and began to pick his way up the hill. Grael headed on to the camp to see if he could do anything.

Radal sat by the fire, cooking breakfast. An unusually pensive Joloth sat beside him, apparently to keep him company. Grael glanced around, searching in vain for Harath.

"Good morning, Grael," Radal said.

"Hopefully, it will be a better day than yesterday," Joloth muttered as he prodded the fire with a stick.

"These are strange times indeed," Radal agreed. He glanced at the wagons. "Is Saint Marden finished with his prayers yet?"

"He has already gone to Pigsknuckle," Grael said.

Radal Faral stood. Joloth tossed his stick into the flames and joined him. "Everyone get over to the furka!" Radal roared.

"Do you think the carts are close enough?" Joloth asked.

"Too late to move them now," Radal said. "Besides, they're Grael's property, not ours."

Grael's confusion turned to indignation. "Pigsknuckle honors its guests."

Radal smiled. "But we're not Pigsknuckle's guests yet. Don't worry. I'm sure all will be fine. In strange times like these, it's best to be cautious."

Grael joined the Cronesmen by the furka. Only he was unarmed. The rest held spears.

"Where is Harath?" he asked Radal.

"She is sitting in that cart yonder," Radal replied. "I doubt she has anything to fear from her father."

Saint Marden returned with Saint Charlin, Grael's brother. On seeing Grael, Charlin's somber countenance lifted. He scampered over. His arms opened as though they were about to wrap around Grael, but evidently noticing Saint Marden's disapproving look, Charlin lifted them into the air. He leaned his head against one arm to form the sign of the furka and formally blessed Grael.

"I hear you've been busy," Charlin said, lowering his arms. "You must tell me all about your adventures. Where's Harath Melkath?"

Saint Marden said, "She's in one of the carts, awaiting her family to collect her."

"Widan will be here soon," Charlin said.

"When he arrives, I wish to speak to him privately, as one politician to another," Radal said, handing his spear to Joloth.

"Do what you must," Charlin said. "Matters of politics are not the concern of saints."

Joloth directed everyone's attention to the top of the hill, overlooking the lake. Widan Melkath was unmistakable. He was as broad as he was tall. The stiff frond of dyed red hair extending proudly from his jaw was reminiscent of a rooster's comb. From this distance, his thorny crown looked no different from any other villager's halo. The men of Pigsknuckle fanned out on either side of him. Everyone held a spear.

The concerned murmurs of some Cronesmen made Charlin chuckle. "Two saints and a furka protect you. Do you really think so little of the Stretchers of Pigsknuckle that they would attack you on this hallowed ground?"

At Radal's suggestion, he and Charlin walked up the hill. Widan strode down to meet them. The two politicians exchanged greetings.

Widan laughed.

Grael answered the politician's wave with another before realizing that it was intended for his daughter. Probably at Saint Marden's prompting, Harath had drifted to Grael's side. It was the nearest that they had been since their separation in Cronesglen. Her presence made him blush all the more. Hopefully, distance hid his embarrassment from the Pigsknucklers on the hill.

Radal said something to Widan that made him react with confusion and then anger. He and Radal locked in heated debate.

The Cronesmen around Grael glanced nervously at each other.

"Remember, here you are guests not only of Pigsknuckle but also of the Forelight," Saint Marden said. "Any man who commits violence this day will suffer an eternity in Hell."

Charlin intervened in the politician's wrangle.

Radal nodded.

Widan shrugged and fell silent. He fixed an icy stare on Grael. Did he suspect Grael had taken advantage of his daughter?

Widan began to plod down the hill. Radal and Charlin trailed after him.

As Widan neared the caravan, he smiled, but only with his mouth. His eyes looked like a dead man's. "I have you to thank for my daughter's rescue," the politician said, shaking Grael's hand. He yelled back up the hill, "Lahan Erol, come down here and greet your son."

Grael's father detached from the far left of the crowd of Pigsknucklers and slowly made his way down the hill. The gray frill of beard hiding his halo's chinstrap accentuated the raw redness of his face. His shoulders were hunched as though the world pressed down on them. This was the last thing he wanted—this celebrity.

"Welcome back," Dad said, his gray eyes nervously darting about the gathering.

Grael moved to hug him, but thought better of it, and offered his hand instead. His father had suffered enough embarrassment already without an over-ostentatious display of affection from his son before the entire village. Dad seized Grael's hand with both of his, and shook it with gusto, his lips splitting into a smile. Grael grinned. At last, he felt at home.

"Saint Charlin, would you mind blessing the carts before we take them back to Pigsknuckle?" he asked.

Saint Marden straightened. A frown clouded his face. "I already blessed these vehicles and their contents. The blessing of one saint should be enough to dispel any Elfin magic tainting them. A blessing from Highsanctum is as good as one from Pigsback."

Charlin's eyes narrowed. "I am sure my brother meant no offense. He doesn't appreciate that a saint is but an instrument of the Forelight's will. Your blessing was not made in the name of Highsanctum or *Saint Odran's*, but in the name of the Forelight himself."

Saint Marden nodded. "Indeed." His gaze drifted to the furka.

Widan clapped Grael's shoulder. "What makes you think your treasure is cursed? It's a wonderful boon for the village in these troubled times." He glanced at Radal. "Of course, these carts and their contents are yours, Grael."

"Dad, I've a present for you," Grael said. He retrieved the leather parcel he had discovered in one of the carts, and placed it in his father's hands.

"I'll look at it later," Dad said.

"Why bother to wait. Open it now," Widan said.

Dad fumbled with the knotted strings holding the wrapping together. He unfolded the leather sheet to reveal a long-handled hammer with a leather grip and an ornate metal head.

"It's too fine for work," Dad protested.

"Keep it," Grael insisted. "It's my gift to you."

"It is astounding," Widan said. "I knew you would make your fortune, but to do it so quickly… Astounding. And you saved my daughter. I am so delighted to have her back."

Harath's smile was as false as her father's, but the others did not seem to notice.

Widan leaned close to Grael's father and mumbled something. Grael's heart fluttered. Did he hear right? Did Widan mention something about a match?

"Well, no harm in discussing it," Dad said, almost choking on his words, his face bleeding embarrassment.

Widan threw an arm over his shoulders. "Come now. Your son and my daughter were together alone in a forest."

Memories stirred of that moment when Harath's eyes met his by the brook, when anything might have happened. Grael rubbed his cheeks with his trembling hand to conceal his blush. Hopefully, nobody else noticed.

"My son is an honorable man." The vehemence of his father's reply stirred a prideful tingle in Grael.

"And my daughter is chaste. I'm sure not even their shadows touched. But you know rumor can rob a reputation as easily as truth. Is that not so, Radal?"

"You know your village best," Radal said coldly.

Widan took no notice. "It's our duty to protect our children and their honor. I can think of no better husband for my daughter than your son, and I am sure you consider Harath an excellent choice for a wife. I would provide an ample dowry, though young Grael hardly needs it."

Grael silently urged his father to say "yes" and put the matter beyond doubt.

Dad smiled. "I'll discuss your offer with my wife." His positivity veiled the lack of commitment in his response. Grael wanted more, but it was the best that could be hoped for now given Dad's cautious nature.

"Very good," Widan said. For the first time, his smile reached his eyes. "Women give wise counsel on such matters. I've always found Harath to be a font of sagacity." He winked at his frowning daughter. "I'm certain Grael would find her opinions as useful as I do. Of course, she's by no measure a nag. She knows her place."

Harath directed an icy stare at Widan. "I promise to be as obedient to my husband as I have been to my father."

"I don't doubt it," Widan said, oblivious to her sarcasm. "What do you think, Grael?"

"I'll abide by my parents' decision." Hopefully, it would be the right one. His parents would see sense. He just had to have a little patience.

Widan waved to the other Pigsknucklers. "Come down. See this great trove that Grael Erol has brought home. Leave your weapons up there. These good men from Cronesglen are our guests."

The clatter of cast aside weapons filled the air as the men of Pigsknuckle spilled joyfully down the hillside.

One figure lingered on the hill in the midst of the discarded spears and knives. His complexion was like worn leather, and his black hair was splashed with white around the temples. But his clean-shaven jaw gave his face a certain youthfulness. He sat down on a rock and coolly regarded the boisterous celebration whirling around Grael.

"You look worried," Widan said. He followed Grael's stare. "Don't mind old Garscap. You know him. He's a fly always looking for an ointment to swim in. I bet he's just sore with jealousy."

He snorted. "So much for the big mercenary from Formicary. It took him half a lifetime to make his fortune, and he has boasted about it for what feels like another half a lifetime. It was nothing compared with what you've brought back to the village in a handful of days."

Widan looked about the assembled Pigsknucklers, his voice getting louder. "I hope those reckless youngsters who so admire the great Garscap Torp see him now for what he really is, which is nothing. He's not even a has-been. He's a never-was. He couldn't live as a saint so he moved to the village. He couldn't survive as a villager so he moved to Formicary. He couldn't make a living in Formicary so he came back to the village. I'd call him by the only true name he deserves, but I would not utter it this close to a furka. Even his own mother disowned him. A sad tale."

He patted Grael's shoulder. "His day is past, and it was not much of a day, either. Yours is just beginning."

Grael had been one of those same youths whom Widan mocked. Though Grael never followed Garscap around like Evram Erath, the mercenary's adventures had been the inspiration for his journey to Formicary. It seemed so childish now, so simple, and yet Grael's dreams were on the verge of becoming reality.

"Perhaps you intend to set out for Formicary again," Dad said.

Grael shook his head. "This adventure has cured me of such audacity. I want nothing more than a quiet life."

Dad nodded. "Then you'll be wanting a wife."

This was unreal. It could not be happening. It was like a fairytale, but in this case, the hero was not some ancient warrior-king but the son of a goatherd. Everything he had ever wanted was suddenly within his grasp.

Dad drew Widan aside. Their conversation was lost in the chatter of the crowd, but every gesture suggested deep negotiation. They moved apart a little and stared at each other with closed mouths. Something was wrong. A standoff. The match would not be agreed to today. It might never be.

Forelight, don't let it fall apart now, Grael begged.

Widan whispered something in Dad's ear. Dad smiled. They shook hands and walked back to Grael.

"The deal is done," Dad said, blushing.

"Your father drove a hard bargain," Widan said.

"The dowry is very generous," Dad said. "But no more than you deserve."

Grael's smile stretched till it hurt his cheeks. A giddy joy washed through him. He looked around for Harath. Surely, she, too, would be delighted by their match. Nobody understood her better than him. Nobody could love her more.

His glance met hers. No delight sparkled in her eyes, only the accusation of betrayal. She looked away, her face turning scarlet with anger. What was wrong? Did she not understand that the match was for her benefit as much as his?

So much for the fairytale. Perhaps, the Gilt Spider had hexed the treasure, and this match was part of the curse. All of the treasure in the world was worthless in the reflection of Harath's hate.

***

The triumphant celebrations below mocked Garscap as he watched his rival fawn over Grael Erol. Widan was far too happy, which meant that the fat fool thought he had turned this unexpected event to his advantage.

Old Thomol Mangal crept slowly up the hillside toward Garscap, bent over his walking stick like a three-legged goat. It must be a horror to rot away so, to know every day was just a wait for death.

A sandy-haired youth raced by the ancient. Evram Erath was almost unrecognizable. His mouth lacked the habitual, conceited slant that had given him his nickname—the Smirk. His face was crimson, his dark eyes were teary with rage.

"Widan Melkath is mocking you," Evram hissed. "You have every right to go down there and strike him dead."

Garscap raised an eyebrow. "Beside a furka, in front of two saints?"

"You must do something!"

"I am. I'm not making a fool of myself."

Garscap relished Evram's scowl, but testing his patience too much was pointless. Evram had so little to begin with.

"Anything I do or say today will play into Widan's hands," Garscap explained. "Let the Melkaths enjoy their victory. Let them have their sport at my expense. It'll do them no good in the long run. Now, no more talk of this. Thomol approaches, and his excellent hearing contradicts his general decrepitude."

The old man walked up to Garscap, tilted his head quizzically, and smiled. "Grael has amassed a tidy fortune.

When you came home from Formicary, you brought a horse-load of metal goods and amazed everyone. Now, Grael arrives with three wagons laden with riches."

Garscap's stare warned Evram against taking the bait.

The old man continued. "You boasted at the very furka below us that you tricked Widan into letting Grael go to Formicary by feigning your opposition to his departure. Now, Grael is the richest man in the village and will soon be Widan's son-in-law. I guess your jape did not work out quite as you intended." Even this miserable old cripple suddenly felt brave enough to mock Garscap to his face.

Garscap stiffened and growled, "Evram, please find my spear. It is somewhere up there."

Startled, the old man began to hobble back down the hill with surprising speed. "I meant no offense."

"The truth cannot offend a Stretcher," Garscap assured him.

"Are you going to attack him?" Evram whispered.

The sheer stupidity of the question was painful. The rock on which Garscap sat had more subtlety than the Smirk. The rock had enough sense to stay silent. "You don't cure an itchy nose by hitting it with an axe. The old man chose to needle me, and I needled him back. Nothing more than that. Evram, never forget the importance of patience."

Garscap's advice was aimed at himself as much as the Smirk. This business with Grael Erol had been a mistake, an unnecessary error. A few cheap guffaws in the immediate aftermath of Grael's departure weren't worth looking like a fool now. Frustration had gotten the better of his usual shrewdness. His campaign to topple Widan had stalled. Winning over the disgruntled fringes of the village had been easy, but the majority preferred the devil they knew.

Garscap needed a major issue to drive a wedge between Widan and his supporters, and he'd thought he had found it in Grael's quest to go to Formicary. Trick Widan into granting Grael permission to leave Pigsknuckle and watch the parent of every boy in the village turn against the politician for fear he might grant the same to their son. The scheme had such seductive elegance, but it had been fatally flawed from the start. It had relied too much on the imagination of these goatherds. Sometimes, Garscap was just too clever for his own good.

And Widan was damn lucky. The crops half-dead from frost, portents of catastrophe written across the skies, and suddenly a fortune arrived to secure his thorny crown.

"I found your spear," the Smirk said.

"That's nice," Garscap said, frowning at the interruption of his contemplation.

He had to be patient. Someday, a real opportunity to topple Widan would present itself, not a half-chance or quarter-chance like Grael's leaving. It was destined to come. Garscap's fate wasn't to become a worthless old man living in fear of being planted in his home by infirmity like Thomol Mangal. Garscap was marked for something better. Long after he was gone, the mountains would still echo with his name.

In the meantime, he could stir up a little trouble.

Chapter 6

Unlike other races, Ors are impervious to myth. For us, memory and history are indivisible.

-From *On Before History* By WorshipSun Fulgur.

Every morning since Grael's arrival, Charlin left his little stone house in the village and waded through the snow to Pigshead to check if the Gilt Spider had returned to his lair. Nobody thought to ask where he was going. Nobody dared. The villagers he encountered avoided his gaze even as they murmured hello. A few more timid souls jumped, when they realized that their paths might cross his, and guiltily changed direction. When he was first assigned to Pigsknuckle, such antics had been mildly comical but now they grated on his nerves. At least, they had some benefit in matters such as this. Thank the Forelight, his own family understood that beneath his saintly garb, he was still a man. Otherwise, he would be as cut off from life in the village as in the monastery.

Beneath a heavy pall of snow lay a murdered summer. Perhaps all those ominous portents, the quakes and bloodstained precipitation, the feverish, celestial colors, were testimony to the summer's violent death. There was no fire in the sky now—only an impenetrable blanket of ashen cloud.

Who or what had killed the summer? Everyone in the village looked to Charlin for answers. Was it the work of a devil or some punishment from the Forelight? Was it a spell of witches or Elves? He answered their pleading stares with encouragement to pray harder. The Forelight would protect them. All they needed was faith. It was the only real answer he had.

The little stream beneath Pigshead was frozen. He carefully crossed it, squeezed through the cave's narrow entrance, and plunged into pitch blackness. His journey was wasted. AscendantSun had not arrived yet. Perhaps he might never return. He might have died of his wounds on the way.

A cough disturbed the perfect silence.

"AscendantSun, are you there?"

"Saint Charlin, wait one minute."

Sounds of rummaging and scraping echoed through the cavern. A little shower of sparks briefly pricked the sepulchral darkness. Another shower of sparks followed, and then another. Golden fire dispelled the night. AscendantSun, sitting on his mat of straw, laid a lamp on the ground and lay down.

Charlin ran to his side and knelt down. "Thank the Forelight you are alive."

AscendantSun's face twinged with pain. A bloody smear showed through the bandage around his shoulder. "I nearly didn't make it. I was out of practice."

"Is there anything I can do?" Charlin asked. "I could take a look at your wounds."

"There's no need. They have already healed beyond the point of being life threatening."

Charlin smiled. "Thank you for saving my brother. And the girl. I have perhaps been charitable to you in the past..."

"A Stretcher should not deny forgiveness to one who asks it."

"Very true. Thank you. I was wrong to look upon you as a monster."

"I have been a monster. Not in the ways you imagine. Worse ways. Far worse. Before I began to wander the Stretches."

Charlin's smile wavered. "But that belongs to the distant past, and I am sure you have done penance for those crimes. The Forelight has forgiven you."

"I cannot forgive myself. I've tried, but I can't. It is too much."

"Remember the second commandment of our religion. You must love others as you love yourself. You must forgive yourself."

"I know. In time, perhaps. Will you hear my confession for my more recent sins? The Jinglemen's deaths weigh little on my conscience, but I still must atone for them."

"Of course. If you wish, you can retake your oath of pacifism."

AscendantSun shook his head. "Not yet. As soon as I am strong enough, I must go back to my own people for a while first."

"Why?" Charlin's question was louder than he intended.

"For two reasons. Here, these wounds will not fully heal. I'll be left a cripple. But if I return home, I can be cured fully. Also, I need to visit my friends in Tincranny—the other Elves who worship the Forelight, the Orstretcherists. The Forelight knows what madness these meteorological anomalies have unleashed among my people. These phenomena are unprecedented."

"I have never seen the like before," Charlin admitted.

"My memory stretches back to before this world began, and I have never seen the like either," AscendantSun said. "If I still clung to my old beliefs, I would be strapping on my armor in expectation of a second Light War."

Charlin's jaw quivered. His throat tightened. "I hope you are wrong."

"You don't mind if I close my eyes?" AscendantSun asked. "I'm so tired."

"Of course," Charlin said. He stood beside the Elf and, stretching his arms, silently prayed to the Forelight that AscendantSun's dreams would be peaceful.

***

A millennium dissolved in an instant, and AscendantSun returned to when he had neither name nor religion; to that first moment he awoke in a universe of amber light.

Curiosity reached out into the void above him. He crawled about the tubular envelope and slid his fingers across a surface so smooth it felt soft. He pressed against it, but it did not yield. Shaping one hand into a fist, he struck it. Pain. He clutched his pulsing hand and rocked till the ache subsided and curiosity returned.

He explored himself. He wriggled the digits on his hands and feet. He reached up to the fluttering portals through which he saw the world and discovered a whole range of strange shapes and textures with which to play.

Self-examination was forgotten when he spotted a shallow deformity protruding from the surface of the tube, about twice the expanse of his open hand. It had not been there earlier. He was certain. He crept over to it. What could it be? He extended one finger toward it. Touched it. Nothing happened. He moved a hand over its creases and crevices. The shapes and textures of the distortion were reminiscent of his face. Apart from that intuition, he had little comprehension of what it was. Its function was unimportant. It served to feed the naive curiosity of his senses.

It lit up. Its eyes popped open, and out of its mouth roared fear. He bounded clear of it to the far end of his universe. The face grew a head, a neck, and then a trunk. Two gracile arms extended from the torso, their terminal protuberances flowering into hands. On its pate danced golden flame.

He screamed his terror back at the luminescent figure, but it neither advanced nor withdrew, remaining rooted where it had sprouted. It continued to speak. The shock of its voice waned, and he began to recognize an attractive softness in its tone. The Other was smiling and waving to him as it repeated the same sound over and over: "Come."

He approached the Other with caution, his eyes fixed on it, his every muscle anticipating flight from indefinite menace.

"Good," the Other said as he neared. It stretched out one arm before it, an open palm facing the floor. A spherical depression formed on the surface beneath it. Yellow liquid poured from the Other's hand into the basin. When the bowl was full, the Other clenched its hand and pointed to the bowl of liquid. "Milk," it said, and it scooped some up in one hand, sipped, and smiled.

He warily mimicked the Other. The milk tasted good.

The Other pointed at itself. "Aurelian."

Then it pointed at him. "Auctor."

As Auctor stood before his god, he discovered happiness.

Aurelian was his constant companion, teaching him, playing games with him. Aurelian even haunted his slumber, his divine radiance permeating so deeply into the Or's dreams that Auctor sometimes did not know if he was asleep or awake.

Aurelian's patience was near infinite. There were occasions when some mischief angered him. He inflicted terrible pain then, and Auctor's world provided no hiding place from the Golden Light's wrath. However, this seldom happened. If Auctor was fatigued and uninterested in learning, Aurelian rarely coerced him. Auctor's absorption of each lesson was an inevitability. It filled his universe and persisted till he was forced to confront it. He had to eat whatever Aurelian served him because it was the only food available. He learned to walk upright because conditions made it impossible for him to continue otherwise. He learned to talk because the Golden Light increasingly ignored his grunts and gestures. Success was lavished with praise, and Aurelian's praise was what Auctor craved most.

This conspiracy of circumstance was the natural order of his cosmos. There was no room for faith or doubt. Only two beings existed: Auctor and Aurelian. Auctor had not summoned forth the cosmos. He had no mastery over it. The Golden Light was fused into its fabric and manipulated it at will. Aurelian must have created it.

As for Auctor, the Golden Light sustained him physically and spiritually. No food touched the Or's lips, no concept entered his mind, unless it came from Aurelian. The Golden Light's divinity was as axiomatic as Auctor's own existence.

The foundations of this blissful certitude were shaken when Aurelian told him that beyond his snug macrocosm existed a larger universe inhabited by other Ors. The divine pronouncement itself did not cause a shiver of doubt. To question the veracity of his god was unthinkable. It was the implication for his own imagined status that was perturbing. He was not as special as he had supposed.

Jealousy tortured him. He redoubled his efforts to please his deity. Auctor sought approval in Aurelian's slightest gesture but found only more reason for doubt. As his mastery of the nuances of the spoken word matured, he detected subtle reticence in his god's discourse. His competitors for the Golden Light's affection had to be responsible for this taciturnity. He wanted to ignore them, expel them from his thoughts, but in his weakest moments, he damned them with unarticulated curses.

Then came the wind.

Its unfamiliar chill woke him. He looked for Aurelian, but his god was gone. So, too, was one end of his universe. The chamber extended forever in one direction. Its relentless stretch was dizzying. His eyes pressed shut, he clung to the floor to stop himself from plummeting down the horizontal well of yellow light.

"Aurelian!" His cry echoed down the passageway.

He fought his paralyzing terror, because he had to travel down the tunnel. He had to find Aurelian. He forced his eyes open, though he dared not raise their gaze from the floor. He began to crawl, each hand reaching beyond the other, knees shuffling behind.

It took great effort to glance back at what had been his universe. The far wall of the chamber was its only recognizable vestige. As he crawled farther, it got smaller and smaller till it disappeared, and Auctor saw an endless corridor forward and back.

Loneliness weighed on him, but he forced himself on.

Ahead, a yellow-orange speck pricked the oppressive monotony of the tunnel. Could it be Aurelian? The possibility lifted him to his feet. Fear cast aside, he raced toward the saffron smudge.

As Auctor neared the figure, it became clear that he was not the Golden Light. The stranger's cropped, golden hair contrasted with Auctor's frizzy coiffure. His smiling face was similar to Auctor's, but there were differences. The eyes were larger, their irises a darker orange. The round, flat nose was slightly smaller. The faint chin was a little more pronounced. The oval, flaxen face was perhaps a little fleshier. This was one of the other Ors of whom Aurelian had spoken. His face was less symmetrical than Auctor's.

"May the Golden Light shine on you," the other Or said. "I am Lumen. Aurelian bade me meet you as you left your maturation tube, and bring you to him." He rested a saffron cloak around the shoulders of Auctor. "You will find it cooler in the city."

He helped Auctor slip on a pair of sandals. "Your path will be less smooth beyond the tube," he said as he took Auctor by the hand and led him through the mouth of the tunnel.

Before Auctor, a cavernous world gaped. Golden stars in the arched ceiling shone down on manicured gardens. Beyond towered a mountainous ziggurat, its burnished surfaces setting the horizon aglow.

Casual clapping attracted his attention to the scattered knots of Ors around him.

"They are welcoming you," Lumen explained. "It is a time of great joy for our race when a new Or joins us."

These Ors were not the phantom strangers he had hated. They were his brothers, at one with him, at one with the Golden Light.

Lumen pointed to the ziggurat. "Our destination—the Citadel of Eternal Noon. It is where the Golden Light and we, his servants, reside." He opened one fist and spread wide his fingers and thumbs. "The Citadel is shaped as a hand. What you see before you is but the tip of one thumb."

They crunched along the gravel paths meandering through the park. Everything was so new and fascinating: the hedges, shrubs and trees; the intoxicating bouquet of the gold and black flowers; the zestful bees; the burbling streams and diaphanous fountains. Only Lumen's gentle coaxing prevented Auctor from becoming lost in this new world.

"How long have you dwelt here?" Auctor asked.

"I came here long ago. Before these gardens were planted, when this land was waste. I was the first to emerge from the tubes. I was the Golden Light's sole servant till Consilium and others followed. As the Minister of Initiates, it is my honor to present newly emerged Ors like you to our Bright Lord and to supervise their orientation."

Auctor recognized only some of Lumen's words, but he comprehended their gist, and he did not like it. The servants of the Golden Light had a hierarchy, and Auctor was consigned to the bottom.

"Did you notice the square block of stone we passed?" Lumen asked.

"Yes," Auctor replied, his voice quivering with suppressed anger.

"You will find similar plinths elsewhere in the gardens and the citadel. Do you know what they are for?"

"No," Auctor said. They were too tall to be seats.

"The Golden Light had them installed when we built the gardens. They are for the future heroes of our people, the doers of great deeds as yet undreamed. They are to record our history as yet unwritten. The adventures of the Or whose likeness will adorn this plinth shall inspire songs and tales for eternity. It could be you on top of this pedestal, or me, or perhaps an Or still in the maturation tubes. Whoever it will be, his rank will not matter. Courage knows no station."

It was hard to fully grasp Lumen's speech, but the tone was exciting. It would be so wonderful to stand beside Aurelian atop the plinth, staring down on crowds of admiring Ors. Whatever great feats had to be performed to deserve such an honor, he must do them.

As the Citadel of Eternal Noon neared, it became apparent that the imposing edifice was bustling with activity. On every tier, Ors hurried purposefully, slipping in and out of winking doors.

Moving stairways straddled the levels. Lumen took Auctor's arm and helped him onto one. "Let the escalator do the work," he said with a smile as he patted Auctor's hand.

Auctor's little leap off the disappearing stairway at the summit brought another smile. Before them stretched large, palatial buildings, demarcated into blocks by broad, bustling thoroughfares.

"What are those places?" Auctor asked.

"Ministries, legion headquarters, sub-departmental offices," Lumen said.

He continued to hold Auctor's arm as he steered him through the crowds. The majority were armored. Over mail shirts, they wore a saffron tunic and pants and bronze cuirasses. Greaves protected their shins. Small oval shields covered their arms. A few helmets had crests. Lumen explained that these were officers, and the orientation of their crests denoted their seniority.

Some passersby recognized the Minister of Initiates and stepped aside. A few halted and honored Auctor with restrained applause. Most were too intent on their own business to notice. The throngs were thickest where Ors streamed into and out of ornate kiosks that punctuated the avenues at regular intervals.

"They provide access to the lower levels of the Citadel," Lumen explained. "Our destination, the Palm Yard, is located on this level, so we will not need to use them."

The Palm Yard was vast. It reverberated to beating drums and stamping feet. Across its expanse, saffron regiments of Ors paraded to and fro in practiced synchrony, shepherded by their barking officers. At the far end of the square stood a great burning hand, its fingers and thumbs splayed like the limbs of a tree.

"The Second Legion is on parade," Lumen said in hushed tones as though his words might disrupt the drill. "We had best skirt around the edges of the square. Our Bright Lord is at the flaming hand yonder. I must warn you that Aurelian will differ from his incarnation in your maturation tube. His face is more expressive. The flames on his scalp are livelier. His voice is more resonant. It is hard to explain. You have to see him to understand."

As they neared the Golden Light, Auctor gasped. The differences in Aurelian were less subtle than Lumen had suggested. Aurelian had legs! And he was standing on them!

Lumen nudged his charge and whispered, "Did I not mention about the legs? Oh, sorry. I forgot. He has legs. As you can see."

Aurelian's attention was fixed on the formations of warriors maneuvering across the Palm Yard. He turned to the Or standing to his left and said, "Very good, Consilium. As always, your legion is an example to the others."

"Thank you, Bright Lord. I am fortunate to oversee at your behest a legion of veteran troops. Instilling discipline in newer legions drawn from newcomers fresh from the maturation tubes is a far greater challenge."

"True, but the Second Legion is still the benchmark to which all others must aspire. Tell me this, Consilium. If I created an Eleventh Legion and made you its commander, could you raise it to the standard of the Second?"

Consilium's face tensed. "I would try, Bright Lord."

"Then I will place the Eleventh Legion in your care."

Consilium's spasm of displeasure warped into a smile.

"Know this, Consilium," Aurelian continued. "The challenge you face is far greater than you imagine. The time of the Ors' testing nears. This fetal age is about to pass, and a new, heroic age will rise in its stead. The legionaries of the Eleventh will need your wisdom and leadership if they are to survive the coming of days."

For a time, Aurelian and Consilium discussed the merits of the latter's lieutenants and settled on his successor as Legate of the Second. Aurelian's attention turned to Lumen and his charge. The Minister of Initiates bowed and encouraged Auctor to follow his example.

"Welcome, Auctor," Aurelian said. "Will you serve me now as I nurtured you in the maturation tubes?"

"Yes," Auctor murmured. Lumen's prompting made him add, "Bright Lord."

"Will you put your trust in me as I put my trust in you?"

"Yes, Bright Lord."

"Will you love me as I love you?"

"Yes, Bright Lord."

"Always remember, your soul is part of me. My light courses through your veins, sustains your body, fires your mind. I would no more cast one of you aside than cut off my hand. Remember that, and it will nourish your faith in difficult times, for your faith will be tested both here and beyond."

Auctor swore silently that he would never fail his god. How could any Or be so wicked as to doubt the Golden Light?

Aurelian continued. "This fair land is an oasis hewn from the desolation of Gules. In its parched deserts of rock and dust dwell my rivals and their vile spawn, who seek to usurp my authority over all things. With the first dawn, we shall march out to meet my foes and impel them to concede the fealty rightfully mine.

"We shall transform the deserts of Gules into gardens. The ravenous dunes shall still their creeping and bleed water. The gnawing winds of dust shall be beaten down by the gentle tears of a joyful sky. The rain shall make the very rocks crack open like seeds, and the earth will blossom with life. This we shall

do with the coming of days. And the Citadel of Eternal Noon shall be the capital of this greater paradise. It shall attest to the valor of the Ors. Its halls shall sing of their deeds."

The Golden Light's words rapped on Auctor's heart.

"That is our destiny, Auctor. Will you play your part?"

"Yes, Bright Lord."

"Lumen will show you to your quarters and assign your duties. Heed the words of Lumen, and the other ministers and legates, as if they spring from my lips. Farewell for now, Auctor."

And with those words, Aurelian's attention returned to the drilling troops.

"Bright Lord," Auctor summoned the courage to say. Lumen's grasp prevented him from nearing his deity.

Aurelian turned his gaze on him again. "Yes, Auctor?"

"May I stay here with you?" Auctor asked, his voice faltering.

Aurelian smiled. "When Gules is conquered, there will be time for such things. But for now, you must go with Lumen."

Lumen took Auctor's hand and gently led him away. Auctor did not resist but he gazed back at Aurelian for as long as his straining neck permitted. Losing Aurelian's radiance was like becoming blind.

In a blink, his dream transported him to another momentous day.

It was the day they went to war.

Regret teased Auctor as the cylindrical gnomon lifted its golden hand high above the Palm Yard. He was more than a match for the twelve Ors who formed a wide circle around the pockmarked column.

The participants' legions were identified by large, dark red numerals on the front of their saffron tunics. Each Or's meager panoply comprised two elliptic shields on his forearms and a brace of batonaxes racked on his back. They had nothing else. Even their feet were bare.

Aurelian rose from his seat, his pate of flames radiating a golden nimbus about his head. At his thunderous command, the Faith Melee commenced. Each legion roared on its entrant as the contestants bolted toward the pillar, the heads of their batonaxes flashing as they swung them from their racks. Whoever reached its apex first won a supreme tactical advantage. However, the quick start of the two foremost competitors proved their undoing. Batonaxes flung by slower rivals cut them down. When another contestant stumbled, his nearest opponent, Atriensis of the Ninth, seized the opportunity to drive a spike through his temple. While the victims' legions booed such underhand tactics, Auctor mourned the dead gallantry of the early Faith Melees.

Natator of the First and Cyathus of the Second joined in single combat. Their batonaxes whirled and lunged in a succession of classic attacks and counter-attacks. As the likelihood of a quick outcome waned and their rivals extended their lead, their tactics became more desperate. Cyathus hooked one of his batonaxes with the other and flicked them like a chain at his opponent's head. Natator dodged the strike, hooked the leading batonaxe with one of his own, and tried to wrest it from his foe. Cyathus lunged, liberating the batonaxe in his hand, and drove one of its spikes into Natator's chest. A rain of steel fell around Cyathus as batonaxes clanged against the pavement.

The Second cheered and taunted the First, but Cyathus wasted no time savoring his victory. Snatching up his dropped batonaxe, he raced after his rivals, who were already scrambling up the gnomon.

Two of the combatants on the far side of the gnomon were hidden from Auctor's view. Atriensis of the Ninth led the others, but Direptor of the Eleventh was so close behind that he might be able to seize the other Or's ankles at any moment.

"Direptor! Direptor!" Auctor chanted with the rest of the Eleventh, willing him on.

Atriensis paused to deliver a kick to his rival's head, but Direptor stabbed at the descending foot with a batonaxe. Atriensis screamed as the weapon punctured his leg. He flung a batonaxe at his assailant. Direptor deflected it with one of his weapons. It slid down the gnomon, struck one of the combatants farther down, and sent him crashing into the warrior below him. Both smashed into the ground.

As Direptor skirted around the wounded Atriensis and headed for the summit, Auctor and the Eleventh cheered and banged their arm-shields. If Direptor won, it would be the Eleventh's first triumph in the Faith Melees. Every Or in the legion would share a little of the glory.

Around Auctor, some were already talking confidently of victory, but he wasn't so sure. What was happening on the other side of that column?

As Direptor used his batonaxes to hook the top of the gnomon and heave himself up, another Or suddenly loomed above him.

Warning cries turned to groans as the Eleventh watched Gerulus of the Fifth behead their hero.

As Direptor's headless body fell, it struck Atriensis, and he, too, plunged to his death.

Auctor pressed his hands to his temples and shook his head. Direptor was dead, and all hope lost. If Auctor had been in his place, Gerulus would not have caught him so easily.

A corpse-like silence struck the Eleventh. The cheers of the other legions for the remaining contestants taunted it.

And then, the Eleventh recovered its voice. Auctor and his comrades roared again, not for victory but for vengeance, their cheers directed at Gerulus's opponents.

Gerulus circled the golden hand on the summit, waiting for his remaining foes. As though by unspoken agreement, Cyathus and Insignis of the Fourth paused beyond the reach of his batonaxes. Pugnus of the Sixth edged into view. He drew level with the others. Tackling Gerulus alone was certain death. His three challengers had to coordinate their attack to have any chance of defeating him.

At Cyathus's signal, the three Ors started to climb; unknown to his fellow conspirators, Pugnus paused before he reached the top. Gerulus dispatched Cyathus with a single strike, but Insignis managed to scramble onto the summit.

While they fought, Pugnus scurried atop the column and charged the duelists. As Insignis sank his weapons into Gerulus, Pugnus pushed both of them off the gnomon. They tumbled down the side of the column and hammered into the Palm Yard.

Gerulus was dead. Direptor had been avenged. A grim victory of sorts.

It was over.

No. Wait. From the carnage below, a bloody Or rose on unsteady feet. Gore obscured his face and his legionary emblem. He placed two batonaxes in the rack across his shoulders. He began climbing the column.

A lone handclap started. Another joined it. The claps multiplied into applause, and the applause coalesced into a steady beat, urging the anonymous hero onward.

His foe at the summit hurled down discarded batonaxes at him. Some sailed past the gnomon. Others glanced against the pillar and skipped harmlessly by him.

The legions cheered as each failed to strike. Their encouragement swelled with every new hold he reached. Some whispered that this was fate. This Or was destined to win. Nothing could stop him.

A collective groan followed him down the gnomon when he slipped and fell. Everyone divined from the sickening smack when he struck the ground that the contest was over.

The Or on the summit cried, "I am Pugnus of the Sixth Legion! I have won the Faith Melee. I have defeated all other challengers, and I beg our Bright Lord to receive me into his cadre of sentinels."

The pillar slowly sank into the Palm Yard till its summit was level with the floor. The Golden Light inducted Pugnus as a sentinel, while the broken remnants of his rivals were cleaned away.

"I could have beaten them all. I could have won," Auctor murmured under his breath. His instincts whispered otherwise.

Aurelian addressed the legions. "The final Faith Melee is over. My twelfth sentinel is chosen, and my bodyguard is complete." He gestured toward the sentinels standing behind him in their ponderous gold armor.

"Before me twelve legions stand," he continued as he raised his spread hands above his head. "Every Or in their ranks is my creation, my friend, my pride. I called you all out of myself, and I love you. You are extensions of my will, as much a part of me as my fingers and thumbs."

The legions cheered.

"We have long enjoyed this paradise wrought of gold and blossom. Yet, this is but a single grain of light glimmering in the famished soil of a sleeping universe. The time has come for that seed to germinate, for its golden rays to set that universe afire. The coming of days is upon us. The first dawn approaches. It shall open the gates of this citadel like the petals of a waking flower, and we shall march forth to confront our enemies. Here, you were the hands of my artistry." Aurelian closed his hands. "In the wailing deserts of Gules, you shall be the fists of my justice."

Everyone roared and clapped and stamped their feet and struck their arm-shields. Aurelian waved his hands to calm the tumult.

"In the wastes of Gules, you shall be tested. Mighty foes await you. False Lights shall attempt to steal your hope while their monstrous progeny try to take your lives. Even the desert shall persecute you. It shall choke you and blind you and burn you. But you shall triumph, because of your faith in me and your faith in each other. Victory is your destiny."

The ordered ranks of the legions melted into a crowd, and the crowd boiled over in adulation.

Auctor dissolved into this euphoria. Love for his god outshone all thoughts of self.

Aurelian made no effort this time to quell the riotous veneration. He stood there, his hands stretched open by his sides, as if soaking it in. Only after the legates and other officers had recovered their wits was a sense of decorum restored.

"Is the speech over?" someone asked as everyone hurried back to where they should be.

"What more need the Golden Light say?" Auctor replied.

The Golden Light parlayed with the legates. All eyes were on the legates as they returned to their legions. Everyone cheered and clapped as Aurelian's crown of flames spilled down his person, forming a veil of aureate radiance, behind which his corporeal form transmuted into a column of living fire.

"Forward!" Consilium roared, his order echoed by centurions down the line.

The Eleventh advanced. As it paraded by each legion, the Eleventh's centurions encouraged their troops to yell and beat their arm-shields. The other legions saluted in kind, but their response sounded hollow. The Eleventh had bested them.

"Quiet by the Second," passed down the line. The centuries behind Auctor were still taunting legions long passed by the vanguard.

Consilium strode before the Second Legion. He saluted its legate and then the troops he had once commanded.

"Consilium, Consilium, Consilium," the Second chanted. The Second's legate patted his predecessor's shoulder with heartfelt magnanimity. Not to be outdone, the Eleventh took up the cry. It had as much to be thankful to Consilium for as the Second. Consilium was being rewarded for his loyal service to the Golden Light with the honor of leading the army out of the citadel's gates, and the Eleventh was privileged to share it.

Consilium quivered before the adulation as though a blow had struck him. He rubbed his eyes with one hand, shook the hands of the Second's legate, bowed in the direction of the Golden Light, and returned to the vanguard of the Eleventh.

"Full voice for the First," roared the centurions.

The Eleventh held nothing back as it passed the hated First, the haughty legion of bureaucrats under Lumen's command. It was damned to guard the vacated Citadel, while the other legions surpassed it in glory. The Eleventh heaped on the First all the scorn a butterfly might have for the chrysalis that once had caged it.

Onward the Eleventh marched, toward the Citadel's gates. No Or had witnessed the great portal open. None had seen what lay beyond it. With a thunderous groan, the massive doors yawned wide, and the Citadel inhaled the desert's dusty breath. The writhing gust lashed the legionaries, but the allure of the scarlet light reaching through the portal enticed them forward. Auctor watched the silhouettes of Consilium and the vanguard appear to catch fire, and then melt into the confounding brilliance. Suppressing his apprehension, he followed them across the blazing threshold. History was about to begin.

The light resolved into desert and rusty sky as, once more, his dream shifted.

A saffron cloth, tattered and bloodied, danced on the wind across the sands. Auctor advanced with both batonaxes at the ready. There was a corpse close by, but it was not that of an Or. Swaddled in purple was a stinking mound of flesh. The color of its uniform marked it as a minion of the Purple Light. The stench of putrefaction emanated from the cadaver, but the rivulets of dark ichor seeping into the dust indicated the creature's demise was recent.

Auctor used a batonaxe to lift its lolling head from between its bulbous shoulders. The ashen face was so tortured, so ugly. The broken stump of a twisted horn pointed downward from the center of its protruding forehead. The huge eyes with cold white pupils and the gaping jaw, bristling with incisors, leered defiantly.

Ors had slain it, but it had been no easy adversary. Three arrows were embedded in its hide, and the fragments of a batonaxe lay nearby. From under the carcass, a lifeless hand protruded. A flaxen hand with two thumbs. A dead Or, probably the warrior who had finally felled the beast, lay beneath the Purpure.

Auctor found more slain Ors as he persevered toward the camp. The corpses were isolated at first, then appeared in growing clusters till they smothered the desert in all directions, and everywhere there were smashed faces, headless corpses, splayed ribcages, jumbles of limbs partially degloved of flesh.

As he wandered though this bewildering carnage, a landscape of torn tents and ruined baggage, an invisible hand squeezed his throat. Something more than the fetor of stale blood choked him. It was his first taste of humiliation. The sporadic carrion of Purpures did not obscure the completeness of the Twelfth's devastation. Here, at least, the unthinkable had happened. The undefeatable had been defeated. The immortal lay dead around him. The Twelfth had been the weakest of the legions, the runt of the litter. Its ranks were, for the most part, fresh from the tubes. They must have forgotten what little training they had and panicked when the Purpures struck. Surely, such one-sided slaughter would not be replicated if the Purpures attacked the Eleventh or the Second.

But the Golden Light had been with the Twelfth. Auctor had come here to report enemy troop movements to him. Where was Aurelian? Why had he not saved his children from this massacre?

A yellow gleam demanded AscendantSun's attention. A sentinel's gold cuirass winked at him amid the butchery. It lay at the feet of a naked Or slumped against a blood-spattered boulder. Around him lay the other accoutrements of a sentinel: a golden suit of mail almost consumed by the sands, a golden helmet shorn of its crest, a fragment of a winged arm-shield.

As Auctor lifted up the cuirass to examine it, the other Or raised his head. The dust rouging his cheeks was etched with parched tear tracks. He stared through Auctor with eyes so dead that the Or's motion seemed hallucinatory. It was the sentinel, Pugnus.

"Where is Aurelian?" Auctor demanded.

An eternity passed before Pugnus spoke: "Dead." The word was like a thunderclap and yet as insubstantial as a dream.

"It cannot be true."

"I saw him die. He was in his martial aspect—the pillar of golden flame. The Purpures tore through our ranks and flooded around him. They leapt on him, combusted, and dropped to the gound, screeching and wailing as the fire consumed them. But the number pouring on top of him was too great. He collapsed beneath its weight, and his flame sputtered and died. Through the Purpures' exultant howls, I heard him beg for mercy as they ripped him apart. There was nothing any of us could do then but die, and I failed even in that. Something hit me from behind, and I passed out. I awoke in the midst of this carnage. Aurelian's remains are gone, no doubt taken as a trophy by his killers."

"Why did you throw off your armor?" Auctor demanded.

"I could not breathe," Pugnus answered.

If the Golden Light was lost, then so were his children.

"I have no more tears to weep," Pugnus said. "I can cry no more."

"Are there other survivors?"

"I do not know. Of the sentinels, only I live."

"There must be other survivors. We must find them."

"Leave me here," Pugnus begged, as Auctor tried to pull him to his feet. "Let me waste the remainder of my useless existence praying for absolution for my failure."

"Come now. You still believe the Golden Light lives. Why else would you pray to him?"

"I saw him die."

"Are you certain? Do you really know what you saw? Who are we to know our Bright Lord's fate? We serve him, but we do not understand him. We know neither the breadth nor depth of his powers. Who are we to say this is his beginning and this is his end?"

The sullenness on Pugnus's face melted a little. Auctor's speech gathered momentum. The words coming out of his mouth surprised him. He was as much their audience as Pugnus.

"Remember what Aurelian said. He foretold the deserts of Gules would test us, and so it has come to pass. But he also promised us our faith would save us. Faith is not our right. It is our greatest duty. We must not despair. We must survive."

Auctor's words lifted Pugnus unsteadily to his feet.

"Yes, we must survive," Pugnus echoed hoarsely.

Auctor helped him strap his armor back on. Pugnus almost buckled beneath the breastplate's weight, but he refused to relinquish it, and Auctor was forced to support him. As they made their way out of the Twelfth's camp back into the endless desert, the wind picked up and gently drew a sandy shroud over the desolation.

AscendantSun's eyes opened. Gasping in the smothering darkness, he bolted upright. Where was he? A hand rested on his shoulder. He turned toward its owner. The face lit by the candlelight was a jumble of misshapen features. The creature drew back, evidently startled by AscendantSun's demeanor.

"Are you okay?" it asked with genuine concern. "You were weeping in your sleep."

That voice was familiar. AscendantSun took a breath and then another. The who, the when, and the where returned.

He wiped the wetness from his cheeks and mustered a half-hearted smile to reassure Saint Charlin. "I'm fine. It was just a bad dream."

The saint's face was full of curiosity, but he pried no further.

AscendantSun seldom dreamed of those times, and never before so vividly. An omen perhaps, but was it for good or ill? Hopefully, when he reached Tincranny he would learn more.

Chapter 7

In Martyrsgrave no man may thread,
Forbidden by saintly command,
A place of ruin and bloodshed,
Where heroes fell by Elfin hand.

~From *The Martyrdom of Coneyriddle.*

The wind howled in triumph around Grael as he crunched a path across the snow to the great hall. It was hard to believe that almost three months had passed since his return to Pigsknuckle. It had been the coldest, wettest, most miserable summer that anyone could remember. Now, instead of autumn, winter set in early, and some wondered if spring would come at all.

Once every week, he made this visit to his betrothed. Conversation was a pathetic, wilted thing under the dour gaze of her brother, Donmor. Its topics were limited to health and weather. Grael could not ask the one question most pressing on his thoughts: Why did she appear to regard him with such ill-concealed disdain?

He hammered on the door of the great hall. It creaked open a little, and Donmor Melkath beckoned him to enter.

Grael dropped his hood as he squeezed through the narrow gap, but the icy blast that followed him inside made him regret his haste.

"I'm not walking out in that blizzard," Donmor Melkath muttered as he slammed the door shut. "You two can take your stroll inside. The great hall is big enough. You can walk in a circle around it."

"And is our chaperon going to follow us around?" Harath asked as she ambled over to them.

"I'm going to sit by the fire. I can see you well enough from there." Donmor directed a threatening glance at Grael.

Grael's mouth dried. This was at last a chance to speak frankly, to learn Harath's true feelings, for good or ill.

Donmor joined the crowd huddled by the main hearth, leaving Grael and Harath in silence. Sly laughter greeted him as he sat down.

"I suppose we should walk," Harath said.

"Yes," Grael said.

They strolled for a time in silence. As he mustered the courage to speak, he evaded her gaze lest his nerve melt before it.

"The weather has been terrible," Harath observed.

"Forgive me," Grael blurted.

"For what?" Her voice was edged with irritation.

He summoned the nerve to look at her. "For this. For our engagement."

She paused mid-stride. She regarded him with rounded eyes and parted lips. She raised one hand to her chest, the fingers pressed against her breastbone as though trying to contain her heart. "You wish to end it?"

It was his turn to be shocked. "Only if you desire it. If you want, I'll set out for Formicary a second time, never to return."

Her brows knitted, and her lips pressed together into a wan smile. "So you would leave me here to suffer the scandal of your departure?"

"Whatever you want." Feverish with embarrassment, he could think of nothing else to say.

She crossed her arms and glanced at the crowd huddled around the fire. "At the moment, all I want is for us to continue our stroll before our stillness attracts Donmor's attention."

Her comment jolted him into action. They walked on.

She smiled. "Slow down. There's no need to go so fast."

He slackened his pace.

"Perfect," she said. "Now, what do you want?"

He wiped away the perspiration on his face with a trembling hand. "I'm sorry. You've seemed so disgruntled with the match, with me."

She snorted. "You weren't exactly enthusiastic about the match either. You only agreed to it to humor your parents."

"I did not!" he insisted.

She shushed him. "Too loud."

"I did not," he whispered.

"You said as much yourself. *I'll abide by my parents' decision.* Remember?"

"Did you not see how deliriously happy I was?"

She shrugged. "You had many reasons to be happy that day."

"Remember when we were by the brook in the forest? The evening of our escape? That moment when we looked into each other's eyes. Did you feel nothing?"

"I remember," she said stiffly. "I felt…I don't know what I felt." She sighed. "What does it matter? We are engaged to be married."

"It matters to me," Grael said. "I love you."

She blinked. "I think you have listened to *Alackalas and the Fair Princess* once too often." Her laugh was giddy.

A month of self-recrimination and hopelessness melted away in an instant. Emboldened, he declared, "You are my Fair Princess."

She flushed. "Oh my Forelight, you'll be reciting poetry to me next."

The temptation was irresistible. "You are the year's beauty distilled—fierce as winter, gentle as spring—"

"Another word, and I'm calling Donmor," she warned, but the sparkle in her eyes said differently.

"I have stared into the eyes of the Gilt Spider," he said, still intoxicated by his success. "I fear nobody."

"You can tell that to my brother. Here he comes."

Her tinkle of laughter deepened Donmor's scowl as he stalked over to them. "You two are too happy for my liking. What were you talking about?"

"The weather," Grael said.

Harath laughed.

Donmor's eyes narrowed. "I'm glad someone finds this weather funny. Grael, it's time you went home. My sister has chores to do."

Grael bid a joyful farewell to Harath and her chaperone and headed for home. As he made his way back to his parents' home, his high spirits insulated him so much from the cold, he forgot about his hood till the insistent burning of his ears reminded him to raise it.

As Grael entered the cabin, he was struck by its emptiness. Was it a portent of trouble?

"Where are the others?" he asked as he stamped his feet to knock the snow from his boots. He took off his overcoat and hung it by the door.

"We sent your brother and sisters to the Mangals," his mam explained. She looked more haggard than usual. Her face held a sickly pallor. Even her hair was grayer.

Grael nodded, and sat down across the fire from his parents. Its crackle and spit could not lift the oppressive silence as he waited for them to speak.

His dad's face was hidden beneath his age-tonsured crown. He kept eating stew, spoonful following spoonful with unwavering constancy, his eyes never straying from the contents of his bowl. He raised his head as he wiped a dribble from his ashen beard. His gray eyes looked at his son and then back at the bowl.

Grael had had enough. "What's wrong?"

Mam's lips pressed into a frown.

Dad cleared his throat and stared at Grael. "You must break off your engagement to Harath Melkath."

Mam nodded.

"Why are you both suddenly against me marrying her?" Grael asked. "You agreed to the match in the first place."

Mam directed a cutting glance at Dad. "Your father agreed."

"Well, I won't end the engagement," Grael declared. Not now. Not when Harath was finally warming to him.

"You're a man and can do what you want, but remember this," Mam snapped. "Widan is more interested in your wealth marrying him than you marrying his daughter."

Grael scowled. "That may be, but it doesn't mean he will get it. Do you think I'm a full fool? You trusted me to face the dangers of Formicary. You can trust me—"

"You cheeky…we did not!" Dad cried. "We tried to stop you."

Grael talked over his father's interruption. "You can trust me to deal with Widan."

"Nearly two thirds of your fortune is gone already in a few months," Mam said. "At this rate, it'll not survive the winter."

"One cartload was donated to Pigsback," Grael retorted. "Another went to feed this village. Are you suggesting I let our neighbors starve?"

"Of course not," Dad grumbled. "But your generosity is keeping the thorny crown on Widan's head. There'll not be many more Jinglemen through here before spring, if it ever comes. If food runs low, Widan and his cronies will get the blame. And like it or not, you are seen as one of his cronies."

"When you left Pigsknuckle for Formicary, you left us no choice but to accept it," Mam said. "My one consolation, though I did not realize it at the time, was I did not appreciate fully the hazards you faced. Now, danger comes looking for you again, and we can see it, and you seem blind to it. Tell me this: When did this love for Harath Melkath begin? You never showed any interest in her till her father proposed your marriage."

Grael blushed. "I never thought…" Embarrassment choked the words. *I never thought I was worthy of her.*

"Listen to me, son," Mam said. "Understand, we are not impugning the girl. We know she is a good girl, and she would make a fine wife. The problem is her father. He cannot be trusted. He arranged this marriage not for your benefit or hers, but for his own. Whatever he might hint, be under no illusion that he intends you to succeed him as our politician. The thorny crown is reserved for Donmor."

"I do not want to be the politician," Grael said.

"It doesn't matter," Dad said. "Widan's position is under threat. These are hard times, and many in the village are asking if he is still up to the task. Garscap Torp's support is growing."

"Not so long ago, some suggested I might make a good politician," Grael observed.

"But you do not want to be politician," Mam muttered.

"It shows their fickleness and the foolishness of relying on them," Dad said. "Sooner or later, the Changeling will challenge Widan, and things will get ugly."

It was a shock to hear Dad refer to Garscap by that cursed name. Though Garscap's enemies in the village habitually used it, Dad had always disapproved. He had maintained that it wasn't proper to cast such an accusation on even a man like Garscap Torp.

"Perhaps the old buck will defeat the pretender," Dad said. "Maybe, the young buck will win. Either way, it is best you stay clear of their butting horns."

"I'm not afraid of either of them," Grael said.

"You have no fear for yourself, but what about your family?" Mam asked. "Don't you care about your flesh and blood? What you do outside the village is your own business, but in Pigsknuckle, we all are bound to your actions. If you marry into the Melkaths, you tie our future to theirs."

"The last challenge to the Melkaths was when I was a youngster," Dad said. "The man was a Kuny."

"I've never heard of that family," Grael admitted.

"That is because the Kunys lost. Feuds over the thorny crown are brutal affairs."

"Please," Mam implored. The gray fear on her face made plain that she would not be swayed by appeals for Grael's future happiness. Grael needed more practical arguments.

"I won't be too popular with Widan for breaking the engagement," he observed. "Widan may decide that those who aren't with him are against him."

"We've considered that. You can tell him you must go to Pigsback to answer the call to sainthood."

"One saint in this family is enough!" Grael protested. "I have no interest in being another!"

"Hear me out," Dad said. "You stay there for a while. Perhaps a year. A year passes swiftly. Then you can come home as a layman if you wish. Widan's feud with the Changeling will be settled and forgotten, and you can live your life how you want."

"I will think on it," Grael said. His family's safety came first. But his parents' plan would cost him Harath. Unacceptable.

Which left only one option: elopement. Harath might be amenable to leaving Pigsknuckle. They could take enough of his treasure to live elsewhere comfortably. Obviously, he could not bring Harath to a den of thieves like Formicary. Radal Faral was a friend and an honorable man. He might let them settle in Cronesglen.

A stick tapped on the lintel of the door.

"Anyone home?" Widan's baritone voice was unmistakable.

Mam sighed.

Dad cursed under his breath as he stomped over to the door and opened it.

The entry filled with a massive black silhouette as the politician stepped inside. "I am afraid this is not a social visit," Widan said. "The village has been invaded."

"What? The village under attack?" Dad exclaimed. "Wolves of the four-legged or two-legged kind?"

"There are Fair Folk in the village."

"The children. I must find the children." Mam, as pale as death, leapt to her feet and rushed out the door, leaving it ajar in her haste. An icy breeze swirled through the cabin and tossed the fire.

"Fair Folk? What are they doing here?" Dad asked in utter disbelief.

"They are standing in the middle of the village, their arms raised over their heads with the piety of saints," Widan said. "I came here to seek your son's advice, since he knows more about the Fair Folk than any other villager."

"I met one, and then only briefly," Grael said, embarrassed.

"The little you know is more than the rest of us," Widan observed. "We know them only from old tales. You have seen one, spoken to him. I want you by my side when I parlay with them."

Grael directed a pleading glance at his dad.

"I had better help your mother," Dad said. "With your permission, Politician."

"Of course. Family must come first," Widan said, his voice soaring with extravagant indulgence.

"I will follow as soon as we are sure the children are safe," Dad said. He retrieved his overcoat from its peg by the door, and swinging it over his shoulders, slipped it on. He shook his head and murmured, "In her rush, Myryr's forgot her fur." He tucked her coat under his arm, snatched his spear, and dashed outside.

"I have always considered your father be one of the most decent men in the village," the politician commented. "Keeps to himself. Lives for his family. If more of us followed his example, Pigsknuckle would be a far happier place."

It was hard not to feel a little sympathy for Widan. He was so unaware that his admiration of Dad was far from reciprocated.

Widan continued: "We should go. Grab your coat and weapons, and follow me. Perhaps the one who rescued you is among our guests."

The village was a giant, muddy footprint in the interminable whiteness. At its heart stood the mightiest of Pigsknuckle's furkas, built by Saint Odran himself, according to legend. Beneath it, encircled by spears and taut faces, stood three poetic figures resplendent in shining bronze and yellow. They bore neither helmets nor weapons. Their arms were raised in the air, and their heads were tucked against their shoulders in a prayerful manner. But the pale yellow luster of their complexions and the crystalline sheen of their ocher eyes left no doubt as to their race. Their countenances were unmarked by the depredations of age and weather. Their golden hair was cropped short, revealing peaked ears reminiscent of spear points. Except for the black tattoos on their foreheads, the Elves were indistinguishable from each other.

Grael overheard Thomol Mangal's mutterings on the breeze. "Summer never comes, the cheeks of the Pig are stained with blood, and now the Fair Folk walk among us. This is a terrible time, this Year of Bleeding Snow."

A hooded figure detached from the cordon. Donmor brushed back his hood as he splashed through the slush to his father's side. His neat, coppery hair accentuated the tense pallor of his visage. He acknowledged Grael's presence with a nod. "There are four dozen more Elves down by Leaftea Lake," he whispered.

Garscap Torp and Evram Erath forced their way into their company.

"What is happening?" Garscap demanded.

If Widan's glance at Garscap was disdainful, the expression he reserved for the young Erath was withering. "You know as much as we do," he said, turning his back on the interlopers. He climbed atop the slippery earthen mound where the saints sometimes addressed the villagers. From this elevated position, his mountainous bulk loomed above the Fair Folk. "I am Widan Melkath, Politician of Pigsknuckle. What brings you to our village?"

The middle Elf replied, "I am NeverFear for this lifetime, Cor always, and I speak for our group. We are worshipers of the Forelight, pilgrims who have traveled far from our homeland to visit the sacred monastery of Saint Odran."

"It's the custom for visitors to our village to wait at one of the furkas on the edges of our territory," Widan said. "You risk your lives by not observing that tradition."

"We are our own furkas," NeverFear said. "We come here weaponless with arms raised in the sign of the furka."

"And what of your friends by the lake?" Widan asked.

"They await our return with proof of your welcome," NeverFear answered. "We came unarmed to prove our peaceful intent. If it was our purpose to butcher this village, we could have slain most of its population before you realized you were under attack."

Villagers gasped in horror. Spears pressed nearer to the Elves in warning. Widan beckoned Grael. He hurried over, expecting the politician to step down to speak to him, but Widan offered him his hand and heaved Grael onto his earthen podium.

Fearing he might slip on its slick surface, Grael gingerly turned around to look upon the inscrutable countenances of the Elves and the nervous faces of their guards peeping out from under their hoods.

Garscap followed Grael, uninvited, despite Widan's mutterings that there was too little room for three.

"What do you think?" Widan asked.

Grael remembered the circle of dead Jinglemen. "His words are no idle boast."

"Remember Martyrsgrave," Garscap urged.

"You would think of that," Widan muttered.

Garscap ignored the jibe. "What are you going to do?"

"Worry not. Whatever I do, I am certain you will find fault with it."

"What are you going to do?" Garscap repeated.

"Pilgrims are pilgrims, no matter their race." Widan addressed the Elves. "Lower your arms. It has been our custom since the time of Saint Odran to welcome pilgrims to Pigsknuckle. We offer you what hospitality we can, though this wasted year has left us with little to share. Your people can camp tonight at Leaftea Lake. Tomorrow, I will arrange a guide to escort you to the monastery." He added, "Lads, lower your spears. These good people are our guests."

There was a noticeable delay before the Pigsknucklers obeyed.

"We thank the people of Pigsknuckle," NeverFear said. "Their generosity exemplifies the principles of our shared religion. We hope to return their kindness in the future."

"We will hold a feast in my hall tonight to celebrate this unprecedented meeting of our peoples," Widan said. "Circumstances limit our invitation to you and your two companions. Worry not for your comrades at the lake. They shall not find the hospitality of Pigsknuckle wanting."

The Elves conferred in hushed tones. Their faces retained their enigmatic placidity, but the debate was heated. "We will accept your gracious offer," NeverFear announced.

"Very good." Widan sounded pleased. The politician leapt down from the mound with a thud and said softly to

Donmor, "Escort our guests back to Leaftea Lake. Spread the word that nobody is to go near Leaftea without my permission. I don't want some young fool becoming besotted with an Elfin maiden. And tell everyone to keep their children at home."

"You fear the Gilt Spider is among our guests?" Donmor hazarded.

"I fear accusations of his presence, if any youngster is late for supper. According to Grael, the village couldn't hope to win a battle against them."

"Was it wise to invite their leaders to a feast?" Donmor asked, glancing up at Garscap.

"Everyone knows the Fair Folk worship the Golden Light," Widan said. "Yet, these claim to be Stretchers. Their coming is unprecedented and sudden. I would understand the cause better. I have difficulty accepting it is due simply to a spontaneous bout of piety. The one who rescued Grael from the Jinglemen also claimed to worship the Forelight. I conversed with the saints in Pigsback on the matter, and they were perplexed."

"So they told you," Garscap said as he stepped off the mound.

Grael, feeling conspicuous, followed his example.

"What do you mean?" Widan demanded.

Garscap smiled and shrugged. "You know as much as I." He walked away before Widan could interrogate him further.

Donmor and a small escort led the Elves away while the rest of the Pigsknucklers dispersed to their homes.

"Many pilgrims have journeyed to the Pig this year to pray for the sickness in the weather to be healed. Perhaps our guests have come for the same purpose," Grael suggested.

"Perhaps," Widan said. "We will question the Elves tonight, though I suspect their going may prove as mysterious as their coming. Even the name of their leader is a mystery. What did he mean when he said that he was Cor forever but NeverFear for this lifetime?"

Grael shrugged. "My rescuer introduced himself by similar convoluted phrasing."

"You shall sit beside me tonight at the feast for our guests," Widan said. "No need to look so worried. All the senior men will also be invited, including the Changeling. Especially the Changeling. Never give such a man anything he can turn to his advantage, particularly a snub. As the old saying goes, keep your friends close and your enemies closer." Widan's voice softened to a whisper as Grael's dad approached them.

"I would speak with my son alone," Dad said. "If I may."

Widan acquiesced with a gracious nod. Dad threw his arm around Grael and wrenched him from the politician's side. Glancing back to ensure Widan could not overhear him, Dad whispered in Grael's ear, "You must tell Widan tonight you're going to Pigsback and the engagement is over. Any delay may prove fatal."

"I will do what must be done." Grael's assurance was as resolute as it was misleading. By the next morning, he and

Harath would on their way to Cronesglen, and the petty intrigues of Pigsknuckle would be far behind them.

***

Talking of elopement and exile with Harath was inconceivable under Donmor's mistrustful gaze. Grael had to seize a chance to converse with Harath alone while she was about her daily chores. He kept a vigil near the furka, his attention fixed on the great hall in hopes she might emerge.

"Hello there."

Grael ignored Dawan Mangal's salutation and hoped his cousin took the hint, but Dawan was too eager to chat to notice his friend's desire to be alone.

"This is all like something out of a saga," he burbled. "I never thought I would see one Elf, much less such a host of them. Everyone is wondering if any of their womenfolk are with them. I think Widan has their camp under guard more to shield them from our curiosity than to protect us from them."

Dawan's face brimmed with youthful enthusiasm. His cousin had always seemed a little older and wiser, but now Dawan, spared of the sort of adult concerns that plagued his friend, was the more boyish, naive, and excitable. Grael could not share his scheme with him. Dawan wouldn't understand.

"There are furkas hanging over every door in the village and charms, too. The kind Saint Charlin would frown on if he saw them, relics of old, old magic," Dawan continued.

"And there is fearful weeping and loud praying billowing on the breeze. Fair Folk are alarming enough, but Fair Folk who know their catechism—that is something dreadful. How can furkas protect against them?"

While Dawan prattled on, Harath stepped out of the hall, her hood drawn down, a bundle of clothes balanced on her head. It was hard to resist the urge to shove Dawan out of his way and run to her.

"I must go," Grael snapped.

"All right," Dawan said, taken aback.

Grael moved to leave, but his pursuit ended mid-step when one of Harath's male cousins trailed after her, his spear resting against his shoulder.

"See," Dawan said. "Widan welcomes the Fair Folk to the village, but even his daughter cannot wander outside his hall without an armed escort."

Steadying her bundle with her arms, Harath directed a barely perceptible nod of recognition to Grael. He responded in kind. Harath's cousin waved at him, assuming that Grael's salute was meant for him.

"You must be looking forward to the wedding," Dawan murmured saucily to Grael.

Grael shrugged. Tonight's feast was his last chance to speak to Harath. If fate cheated him again, he would lose her forever.

***

Keep your friends close and your enemies closer.

Grael recalled Widan's words when he learned the seating arrangement in the great hall. He was to sit between the Politician of Pigsknuckle and his hated rival. It was not the inconspicuous neutrality that Grael's father craved, but Dad restrained his irritation behind pressed lips. Grael's discomfort was aggravated by Garscap's tardiness, which left Widan on one side of him and nobody on the other.

Donmor led the three Elves into the hall. NeverFear Cor introduced his companions as DayFlambeau Formosus and TrueFriend Peritus. Grael was struck again by how closely the Elves resembled each other. Even they would have found it difficult to distinguish each other without the tattoos on their foreheads.

The Elves were invited to sit on the right side of Widan, while Donmor took his place to their right. The other guests were arranged in a crude ring around the hall. The bearded men of the village constituted most of the front row, while clean-shaven sons sat in their fathers' shadows. The prominent gaps in the circle were uncomfortable. They reminded Grael of Hackit's diseased grin.

"Grael Erol met one of your kinsmen before," Widan said. "The Gilt Spider."

"What is that?" NeverFear asked.

"Nothing more than an old story, it seems," Widan said, taken aback.

"He saved me from slavery in Formicary," Grael said.

NeverFear's smile was wan. "Did this Or have a name?"

"Or?" Grael Erol repeated. The word meant nothing to him.

"The Elf—what was his name?"

"AscendantSun Auctor."

The Fair Folk exchanged glances.

"You know this Elf?" Widan asked.

"He is an old friend," NeverFear said.

"I owe him my life," Grael said.

"Ah, yes," NeverFear said. "AscendantSun told me that tale. He is not with us, though he may join us in Saint Odran's later. Business detains him."

"What business would that be?" Widan asked.

"I wish I knew," NeverFear replied.

The Elves insisted Grael recount his capture by the Jinglemen and his subsequent liberation. They interrogated him in detail, till Widan saved him with a query of his own.

"Why was your friend hunting Jinglemen?"

"I understand he stumbled across them by accident," NeverFear replied. "He recognized their prisoners as fellow Stretchers. Stretchers must help each other. Is that not so?"

"Do many Elves worship the Forelight?" the politician asked.

"Very few," DayFlambeau admitted. "Most still venerate the Golden Light. We call ourselves Orstretcherists."

"And what made you adopt our faith?"

"It was AscendantSun who first converted."

DayFlambeau was about to elaborate when NeverFear interrupted him. "AscendantSun gave us our religious instruction. This pilgrimage will be our first opportunity to converse with saints directly."

"So you have no saint of your own?" the politician asked.

"AscendantSun is almost a saint. He devoted many years to studying the tenets of our faith."

"From Grael's account, he fights well for an almost saint," Widan commented darkly. "And how did he become a Stretcher in the first place?"

"I never thought to ask him," NeverFear replied.

"You aren't a very inquisitive people," Widan muttered.

Grael spotted Harath among the women moving about the hall with beer and trays of food. He could not approach her now. He had to wait for the banquet to descend into a sodden stupor, so that their conversation might go unnoticed.

Jealousy strummed the chords of his heart when her eyes drifted toward the golden strangers. It was hard not to be envious of the Fair Folk. Their beauty was intimidating. He could not compete for Harath's affection against any Elf who chose to reciprocate her glances. At least, she was more discreet than Ashin Carnath. She stood staring at the Elves until one of the older women wrenched her from her daze with a pinch and a few scolding whispers.

"The women of your land are renowned for their beauty," Donmor blurted.

The Elves' amusement was disconcerting. "What do you know of our women?" TrueFriend asked.

"They are hidden from the sight of men and guarded by hundred-limbed monsters, for their beauty drives those who behold it mad with desire." Donmor's voice trembled.

TrueFriend chuckled. "There is some truth in what you say," he admitted, ignoring DayFlambeau's disapproving glance.

"Where did you learn such things?" NeverFear asked.

"From the tale of Alackalas and the Fair Princess," Donmor replied.

"He is our people's greatest hero," Widan explained. "He is my family's ancestor."

"And was this Fair Princess your ancestor also?" TrueFriend asked.

Widan frowned at the Elf's subtle smile. "No. We are descended from Alackalas's first wife, Heldegran."

"Surely your people know of Alackalas?" Donmor demanded.

"Perhaps you can tell us this tale?" NeverFear asked. "We may know your hero by another name."

"We will tell it later," Widan said. "It is a long tale and better told on a full stomach." He threw an irritable glance at the empty place beside Grael, a reminder that a sizable number of the guests had not arrived.

Widan drew Donmor to him with a wag of his finger, and father and son exchanged whispers. Donmor left the hall.

"My great grandfather built this hall," the politician said. "He built it after the old one burned down. His name was Widan also."

"Is the climb to Saint Odran's monastery difficult?" NeverFear asked.

"We have a saying: Don't itch the Pig. It's a treacherous climb, and all the more so in inclement weather. Stick to the track, but don't depend on it too much. Snow can swallow the path, and clouds conceal the furkas scattered along it. Too many pilgrims have lost their way and frozen to death on the mountain. My advice is to start out early tomorrow if the weather isn't too foul and try to reach the monastery as early in the day as possible. Beware of the Crooked Stair. Snow or heavy rain can make that section of the climb especially precarious."

Widan regaled his guests with tragic misadventures of various pilgrims till Donmor returned. He and Widan shared more whispers.

Widan sighed. "Lahan, come sit by your son. Garscap will not be attending. If we delay this feast any longer, the flesh roasting on the spits will drop into the fire."

As Saint Charlin was in Pigsback, it fell to Widan to commence the meal with a prayer to the Forelight. On previous occasions, in consideration of his guests' empty stomachs, the politician had raced through it, but this time, he lingered over every word. Perhaps he did this in deference to his guests, though Widan sounded more plaintive than thankful.

With a nod, Widan signaled to Donmor to begin carving up the spitted pigs. Flat loaves of bread were broken and passed around. Some women doled out small quantities of meat and beer. Others played tunes on flutes and sang.

"I did not realize your people were so musical," NeverFear observed.

"Menfolk may sing a tune now and then, but music is largely the preserve of women and saints," Widan said. "I'm afraid that the fare is meager in comparison to previous banquets. These are hard times, and food is scarce."

"I would not have thought so from this banquet," NeverFear assured the politician as he softened his bread in the beer.

The other Elves agreed. The politician smiled and nodded in thanks as a courtesy, but it was plain that the compliments troubled him.

"The absence of so many guests has plumped the portions for the rest of us," Dad whispered to Grael. "I reckon a third of the village isn't here. It's an ill omen for Widan."

"That leaves two thirds of the village who support him."

"Does it?" Dad snorted. "Evram Erath is filling his belly over there. The Smirk is no supporter of Widan. He probably came to spy on proceedings for his friend Garscap and to gloat at the poor attendance. You can be sure that many others were drawn here by habit or curiosity, or by the lure of a free meal rather than love of the Melkaths.

"This feast was a mistake. Providing a little food and somewhere to rest for the night to pilgrims is one thing. Holding a banquet in their honor is something else entirely. I suppose Widan was a little overawed by our guests. As for the Fair Folk, they're far too exotic for the village to accept them readily as fellow worshipers of the Forelight. I must confess that doubt still lingers in my own heart that they are Stretchers. Squandering the village's precious livestock for their benefit is bound to cause resentment. This feast has damaged Widan's authority more than the Changeling's sniping ever could."

Dad's assessment of the politician and his feast sounded callous, even derisive. Grael's sympathy for Widan mingled with concern for his daughter.

"If you are so politically astute, why do you stay out of politics?" Grael asked.

"It is because I am wise in such matters that I'm content not to dabble in them."

Hot, sodden breath tickled Grael's cheek. Widan murmured something about trust in his ear. How much of Grael's conversation with his father had the politician overheard?

Grael leaned into Widan. "Sorry. Could you repeat that?"

Dad leaned over also, his eyes mirroring Grael's concern.

"I said I don't trust these wretched Elves," Widan said. "They are determined to divulge nothing of their true purpose in coming here. Their conversion to our faith seems miraculous. It is as though they went to bed of one religious persuasion and woke the next morning as another."

"Perhaps it was miraculous," Grael suggested. "Remember the miraculous conversion of Saint Apasapal."

Widan's morose chuckle ended in a belch. "Possibly," he admitted, tipping back his drinking horn. "More drink here, good woman! What you say is possible. Only they know for certain. And the Forelight, of course. From the little they have said, they are exiles. I am certain of it. I don't know, though, whether their professed belief in the Forelight was the cause of their banishment or the product of it. If the latter was the case, these Elves are cynical and dangerous."

"Well, if they are friends of AscendantSun Auctor, I can vouch for their honor," Grael said.

"If they are indeed friends of your rescuer. Remember, you, not they, volunteered his name."

Widan was right, of course. These Elves might have never known AscendantSun. They could even be his enemies.

"Wherever the truth lies, our guests have done me untold harm," Widan whined. "They proved to be the bait in a trap of the Changeling's making, and I have lumbered straight into it. My heart sinks when I think of what slander the Changeling is peddling behind my back this very moment. It is probably far more vicious than the sly barbs he has rehashed again and again at village gatherings since the summer curdled."

He grimaced and shook his head. "The Changeling is clever. He sweetens his sting with honeyed words. He praises my faithfulness to our forbears' customs, while belittling them in the very same breath. *Let the pilgrims starve,* he whispers. *Keep the food for the village.* It's easy for that rogue to scorn the practices of generations. My father and grandfather, and all his sires back to Alackalas, lived and died by these very same traditions, and I'll not discard them."

While the politician demanded another refill of his drinking horn, Grael took the opportunity to rub away the sticky dew of Widan's spittle from around his ear. Dad's frown was a warning to be careful. Grael could hear his father's words ringing in his ear: *Maintain a polite distance from both sides.* That was hard to do while sitting beside Widan.

"It's the custom to ask your politician's leave before you depart for the night," Widan bellowed. The Eraths and several other guests had thrown on their furs and were making for the exit. They were not just sneaking out to relieve themselves. They were leaving for good.

Evram paused, his contemptuous stare directed at the politician. "I know," he said, sneering as he sauntered out of the hall.

Everyone held their breath for the politician's response. Even the Elves fell silent, though they could not understand the significance of what had happened.

Donmor leapt up.

"Sit down," Widan growled. "We promised to tell our guests of our illustrious forbear. Recite for us the tale of Alackalas and the Fair Princess."

Donmor's recitation was shaky and halted often, but Grael was thankful for it. He hoped it staved off further unwelcome confidences from Widan.

"The Changeling's cronies try to goad me into a fight," Widan murmured. "The Changeling wants to start the war, and he wants me to take the blame. Garscap is a subtle one. He would murder me and my family in our sleep if he could escape the saints' wrath. What am I to do, Grael? A vote would solve nothing. Our support is too finely balanced. It would briefly postpone the inevitable."

He sighed. "In my younger days, I would have challenged him to a duel and settled the dispute man to man, but I am past my prime, and the Changeling wouldn't play fair."

The defiance on Widan's face dissolved into pleading. "My death doesn't trouble me, but I fear what that scoundrel may do to Donmor and Harath after I am in my grave. You are my friend and an honest man. What do you think I should do?"

Grael said, "Perhaps you could ask the saints to intervene."

"Perhaps. Old Sebryn has an aversion to village politics, but he may be more amenable given the current circumstances. The saints of Pigsback know the Changeling's mischievous nature. I have always been a friend to the monastery, upholding the rights of the saints, making donations, comforting pilgrims. Saint Sebryn can't ignore an old friend when he is threatened by an old enemy.

"Tomorrow, I will send Donmor to Pigsback. He can accompany the Fair Folk as a guide and appeal to Saint Sebryn on my behalf. A few supportive words from Sebryn will silence the Changeling for good, and our village will be spared a bloody conflict."

"That's an excellent plan." If it succeeded, Grael's betrothal to Harath would be secure. They would not need to slink away from the village in the night like a pair of criminals. But the elopement must happen tonight or not at all. The Forelight damn it! It wasn't even certain that Harath was willing to elope in the first place.

"And will you go?" Widan asked.

"What?" Grael snapped, irritated at the politician's intrusion on his quandary.

"Will you go with Donmor? These Elves make me nervous. I don't trust them. I worry they might spirit Donmor away. Reaching the monastery safely is but half the journey. The thought of him descending the Pig alone frightens me. If you accompanied Donmor, it would be a mighty comfort to me and to Harath."

Grael was at a loss for words. He wanted to help, but it meant remaining in the village, defying his parents, and blatantly siding with Widan.

"Please. I need you. My family needs you," Widan begged. "I'm not asking you to take my side against the Changeling, though I know you would do so willingly, but for Lahan."

Widan raised his hand before Grael could protest. "Don't misunderstand me. I respect Lahan. I admire your gentle submission to his will. A son should honor his father. That is the natural order of things. I wouldn't ask you to do anything that would risk your family's safety. I would rather suffer exile than cause a rift between you and Lahan. But I fear for my son."

Grael glanced over his shoulder. How much of this was his father hearing? Dad stared back suspiciously as his drunken neighbor roared some incomprehensible anecdote into his ear.

Widan tugged on Grael's sleeve to attract his attention. "The Changeling won't consider your escort of the Fair Folk suspicious. Everyone knows about your previous encounter with one of them. Your wish to learn more about his race is reasonable. Donmor will deliver my appeal to Saint Sebryn. All you have to do is ensure he returns safely to Pigsknuckle."

Grael abandoned his dreams of elopement with a reluctant nod. Harath would never consent to forsaking her family at this critical juncture, any more than Grael could desert his.

He sighed. "I'll go."

"Good man!" Widan bellowed, pounding Grael's shoulder.

Dad answered Grael's plaintive glance with a sour expression. Though he could have overheard only incoherent snatches of Grael's conversation, he must have heard enough to know its outcome was not to his liking.

The rest of the evening passed by hazily as Grael prepared for confrontation with his father. It was a surprise when the feast drew to a premature close. Widan's thanks to his guests as he sent them to their homes rang hollow.

The snow-blanketed landscape flushed as the bloody smear of Gules seeped through the overcast night sky. As Grael and his father crunched a path toward their home, Grael spoke of his promise to the politician. Half of what of he had intended to say was forgotten in his fluster. The rest tumbled out in an embarrassing muddle.

"You young fool!" Dad snapped. "Are you so gullible to believe Garscap will not see through this trip to Pigsback? The moment he learns of it, he'll guess its purpose. If he had any doubt about your support for his rival, this escapade will cure him of it."

"I'm a man," Grael said. "I alone am responsible for my actions. What I do and what side I choose should not affect you."

"You live under my roof."

"I'll live elsewhere then. I'm sure Widan would take me in if I asked him."

"He's already taken you in, but not in the sense you mean," Dad muttered. "I'm astonished you can turn your back on your own flesh and blood so lightly."

Grael shook his head in disbelief. Did his father understand him so little? "I don't want you and the rest of the family suffering for my actions. I want you to be safe."

"You're my son, and I won't abandon you. Tomorrow I'll declare my support for Widan."

Grael's gut twisted. This was not what he wanted at all. His father's about-face had to be some kind of cruel joke. But Dad's face was mirthless.

"No. Please, no," Grael begged.

"You've no more influence over my decision than I apparently have over yours. My mind is made up. I must confess no great love for the Changeling. We'd be better off with one of your Elves as our politician than that scoundrel. Don't look so dismayed. There's yet hope the saints will intervene and bloodshed can be avoided." Dad sighed. "My hope of staying out of this mess was probably foolish anyway. Often, in trying to cheat our fate, we cheat ourselves."

"Very true," Grael said. It was hard not to share Dad's sentiment about Grael's now ruined plans.

Chapter 8

Snow and stone that was flesh and bone,
A pig fashioned into a peak,
And on its back, Saint Odran's home –
That is the sacred house I seek.

~From *Alackalas And The Fair Princess.*

Icy wind mauled the Fair Folk and their two shivering guides as they trudged through the narrow entry passage to Saint Odran's monastery.

"They call this the Needle's Eye," Grael said to NeverFear.

"It is not the most spectacular of entrances," the Elf observed. "This monastery is built more like a fortress than a place of worship."

"My brother, Saint Charlin, says the monastery's only enemy is the mountain. At times, it tries to freeze or starve the saints to death."

The outer doors slammed shut, and the inner doors creaked open. Heat and light poured into the dark corridor. An arthritic voice bid them enter. The monastery's familiar musty odor assaulted Grael as he stepped into the reception hall. A great fire dominated it, its light gilding the faded religious tapestries that adorned the walls.

Resting on a walking stick, the hunched abbot, Saint Sebryn, stood with his back to the fire. Saint Charlin stood to his right. Grael, Donmor, and the Elves saluted the saints with the sign of the furka.

"Lower your arms please," Sebryn said, hobbling away from the fire. "Time enough for introductions when you are warm. We have a saying here: All but the cold are welcome. What little we have, we offer to you. Charlin, arrange some hot drinks and food for our guests."

While Grael and his companions peeled off their coats and huddled around the fire, saints laden with trays of cups and bowls, pitchers, and platters of food, streamed into the hall. Bread, cured meat, soup and mulled beer were distributed to the visitors.

A tug on Grael's sleeve distracted him from the feast. "Grael, what are you doing here?" Charlin asked.

"Welcome back, Grael," Sebryn said. He squinted. "And this young man is Widan's son, if I am not mistaken. What is your name again?"

Grael's companion frowned. "Donmor Melkath."

"Do you know who I am?" Sebryn asked.

Donmor nodded. "I remember when you used to visit the village."

"It has been a long time since I was last in Pigsknuckle," Sebryn said. "The journey is too arduous at my age. I will never leave the Pig again, nor do I want to.

When the Forelight calls me, I will be all the nearer to Heaven atop this mountain."

"Saint Sebryn, what about our other guests?" Charlin asked nervously.

It was strange that Saint Sebryn focused his attention on the Pigsknucklers, as if the Fair Folk's visit was in no way extraordinary.

"In good time," Sebryn said. "Saint Charlin, show these two young men to their quarters when they have sated their appetites. I'm sure your brother has news about your family and friends."

"We must talk to you later about a matter of great importance," Donmor said.

"And that is?" Sebryn asked.

"My father begs you to adjudicate between him and his rival Garscap Torp, who seeks to depose him."

Grael could hear Widan in Donmor's words but not in his voice. The son's leaden, over-practiced delivery lacked the father's oratorical finesse. The speech purported to be a plea for the saints to mediate between the rival factions before they tore Pigsknuckle apart, but it was obvious Widan expected any such intervention to be in his favor. Sebryn was invited repeatedly to compare Widan's deference to the saints with Garscap Torp's disdain for the monastery. Widan sought to uphold the traditions of his ancestors while Garscap was intent upon upsetting the natural order for his own benefit. Widan was honest, and Garscap was a rogue. Donmor rambled and repeated himself. Saint Sebryn listened without comment till the youth came to an uncertain halt.

Sebryn nodded solemnly. "Tell your father we will pray for a quick resolution of this matter. However, we cannot intervene." His voice was gentle, sympathetic, but adamant.

"But..." Words failed Donmor. He looked dazed, as though he had been punched in the face.

Grael's desperate glance begged his brother for support. Charlin's fevered visage shone with a desire to challenge Sebryn's ruling, but he remained silent.

"We cannot intervene," Sebryn said firmly.

Donmor looked helplessly to Grael. "We should return to Pigsknuckle."

"Wait till tomorrow. The night approaches. This is not the time to journey on the mountain," Saint Sebryn advised. "Risking your lives will help no one."

Grael admitted the sense in the abbot's advice, though his instincts urged otherwise. After he and Donmor had eaten their fill, Charlin escorted them to their quarters, a pokey, narrow little room crammed with two single beds. Except for a modest wooden furka, the walls were bare stone. The damp cold made Grael shiver.

"You will have to share it," Charlin said. "With so many guests, space will be at a premium." He pointed disdainfully at a lidded, earthenware vessel almost hidden in the narrow space between the beds. "The pot is for any, er, excretions," the saint said, reddening.

"Is there anything you can do to convince the abbot to help us?" Grael asked.

"I will do what I can," Charlin said, but he shook his head. "May the Forelight bless you this night."

With that, Charlin departed.

Donmor stared at the door, then suddenly kicked it in frustration. "Worthless cowards," he hissed. "But for their caution, we could be home this very night. Whatever weather tomorrow brings, I will descend the mountain. The saints may have offered no help to my father against the Changeling, but he will have mine."

***

"You think it wise to ignore this dispute?" Charlin said to Sebryn when he rejoined him in the reception hall.

"Which one?" Sebryn asked, awaking from some private reverie.

"The one in Pigsknuckle."

"Oh, that nonsense," Sebryn said, grimacing. "Not our concern. You may think me too cynical, but a lifetime of dealing with politicians has taught me that no saint is cynical enough for them."

"My family is mixed up in this mess," Charlin said.

"Our duty to the Forelight must come before personal considerations."

Charlin murmured his agreement. So much for the feared power of the saints. What purpose had power, when you lived in terror of its use?

"Let me introduce you to the leader of our guests, until AscendantSun arrives," Sebryn said. "This is NeverFear Cor."

***

The morning smiled. For the first time since the weather soured, the sky cast aside its ashen pallor and shone crystal blue. At last, here was a sign that the worst of the meteorological fever had passed, that the normal procession of seasons was being reasserted.

The saints and their guests packed in the little chapel to thank the Forelight for this miracle. The chapel could not contain such a large number, so some of the Fair Folk were forced to stand in the hall and listen through the doorway. Some saints whispered that the clement weather was in some way connected with their arrival. Even Sebryn joked during his sermon that the Elves had brought the sun with them. The Fair Folk smiled politely, but did not join in the saints' laughter.

Grael tried to hide his stifled yawns behind his hand. His roommate's restlessness had made for tortured sleep. Donmor had tossed and turned and sighed loudly throughout the night.

After prayers ended, as the crowd began drifting to the refectory, Donmor made a final desperate plea to Sebryn for help. The saint's refusal was polite but firm. Donmor persisted, so forcibly decrying the old man's callousness that Sebryn lost his temper.

"Tell the Politician of Pigsknuckle he is beyond the help of an old man," the saint grumbled. "If divine intervention is what he desires, he should direct his appeals to his god. I am sure now that creation is finished, the Forelight has nothing better to do than sort out Widan Melkath's messes."

The saints hovering around Sebryn gasped or tittered, at once amused and aghast at what verged on blasphemy. Sebryn continued: "Warn your father that before he attempts anything as audacious as heartfelt prayer, he must atone for his sins, and that will take a very long time. Good day, goodbye, and may the Forelight bless you."

The abbot stormed away with all the haste his shuffling gait permitted, stabbing the paved floor with his walking stick at every step. The venom of his words left the brazen youth paralyzed behind him.

Grael rested a sympathetic hand on Donmor's shoulder. "I guess it is time for us to leave."

Donmor nodded. "Get our gear, and I'll visit the refectory and get us a few bread rolls. We'll meet at the Needle's Eye. I'm not staying any longer than I must, and I'm certainly not going to sup with the abbot after his discourtesy."

Outside, the mountain glittered in the sunlight. The music of trickling water was everywhere as the snow sweated in the heat. Rocks peeped hopefully through the icy crust. Grael couldn't help but be infected with the bright hopefulness of this abrupt spring, but Donmor was blind to everything except his failure.

His anger swept them both down the still icy mountainside at a dangerous pace. Snorting gusts warned of the mountain's displeasure. By the time Grael and his companion had descended the Crooked Stair, an ominous bank of gray clouds spread across the sky, snuffing out the optimism of the morning.

"We must take care to not itch the Pig," Grael said after Donmor slid on some scree.

"You are right," Donmor admitted. "It's a long way to hop to Pigsknuckle. I will take my time."

"Pigsknuckle is even farther if I am carrying you on my back."

Donmor's hearty laugh echoed around them. "I am happy for my sister that you are marrying her. You are a decent man."

"Like my father," Grael said, remembering Widan's words.

"Don't misunderstand me," Donmor said as they continued down the mountain. "That is a recent conclusion. I always regarded you as an annoying prig till you announced you were going to Formicary. I realized then you were a madman. I can't understand why anyone could leave Pigsknuckle."

Of course, Donmor could not, because Pigsknuckle was destined to be his some day, provided the Changeling did not thwart his father.

"I hope those dreams of distant lands are forgotten now."

"Pigsknuckle is enough adventure for me these days," Grael said.

"Good. Harath wouldn't be pleased if her husband took her from her home."

It was best not to disabuse Donmor of this notion.

"She likes you," Donmor said. "She won't admit it, which is unusual because she is very quick with her opinion on everything. But I can tell she has a soft spot for you. After your last visit, she was a like a different person. I've never seen her so happy."

Grael flushed and bowed his head.

Donmor laughed. "Hey, there is no need to get so embarrassed. Your cheeks won't feel the cold with that color."

Grael was struggling for a suitable rejoinder when something cold tickled his cheek. A single snowflake settled in his open hand and melted.

"Snow," Donmor said with sudden sobriety. Snow was trouble.

More snowflakes danced by. Grael, concerned by the brooding complexion of the sky and the increasing vehemence of the wind, suggested taking shelter in one of the stone huts scattered along their route. But Donmor was insistent that they continue to Pigsknuckle. A few flakes never hurt anyone.

The flurry burgeoned into a storm with alarming speed. Blinded and deafened, they staggered through the falling snow, trying to pick their way through the formless, unending white.

It was hard to hear what Donmor was saying, but in the end, Grael snatched from the tempest's wheezing howl the one word that mattered: "shelter." He agreed enthusiastically. Pigsknuckle could wait. In these conditions, locating a hut was challenging enough.

Worried they might become separated, Grael shouted and signaled Donmor to halt.

Donmor nodded and stopped.

With burning fingers, it took Grael forever to find his rope in his backpack and tie it around his waist. He turned to Donmor to offer him the other end, but he had disappeared. Cursing him, Grael tried to follow his vanishing footprints, but the snow smothered them too quickly. Even Grael could barely hear his own cries in the wind's bitter ululation.

He trudged on, utterly alone, as the storm's icy shroud wrapped ever tighter around him.

***

A child's cry woke him.

The perfume of burning timber filled the darkness. The homey crackling of the fire warmed the silence. Grael's sticky eyelids peeled open. While the faces of Maerbard and Wanyr shone with joy, those of his father and mother were a mixture of concern and relief. He tried to sit, but gentle hands stilled him.

"Sit back and give him some space," Mam told the two children. She took little Miona from Wanyr and gently rocked her on her shoulder till her crying ceased.

"What happened to Donmor?" Dad asked softly.

"I lost him in the blizzard," Grael said. "He slipped away in an instant. He didn't answer my calls, so I continued down the mountain to find shelter, hoping he would do the same."

A swooping screech tore at the darkness, then dwindled to heavy sobs.

Grael continued. "I found a furka. I nearly walked straight into it. I'll never forget the moment its arms reached out to me through the whirling veil of snow. I knew a hut must be nearby, so I fumbled around till I found it, and I waited there for the storm to pass."

"You did the right thing," Dad said. "I doubt anyone could have survived up there without shelter."

"The only help the saints offered us was prayer," Grael said, making no effort to hide his bitterness. Donmor had thrown away his life for nothing.

"I doubt even Alackalas could have moved them," Dad said, patting Grael's shoulder.

"I said it was a fool's errand," Mam muttered, casting a sour glance at the far end of the hut.

There knelt the Politician of Pigsknuckle, his head in his hands, his great bulk shivering with sobs. Harath sat beside him, one arm draped over his shoulders, her face as pale as the murderous snow, her eyes burning with reluctant tears.

Grael avoided her stare. He touched the bandages covering his blistered cheeks, thankful they hid his shame.

Death on the Pig was preferable to living with the knowledge that he had a part in her distress.

"First my wife, now my son," Widan wailed.

"You'll have nothing left, if you don't pull yourself together," Dad growled. "This can't go on. Harassment has driven some of us from our homes. We dare not wander alone through parts of the village for fear of attack. Joraem Scorael was beaten so badly, one of his hands will be permanently crippled. The village faces enough hardship without being torn apart by your rivalry with the Changeling. If the saints will not end this, you must. Either lead or let someone else do so."

Grael shuddered. The situation must be bad if his father felt the need to speak so bluntly.

Widan lifted his face from his hands. "Lahan, you're right. The dead must wait if the living aren't to join them. I'll send word to Garscap Torp to meet us in Horgal's Field tomorrow morning. We'll settle this matter there, for good or ill."

"I'll go," Harath said. She breezed from the hut before anyone had time to argue. She re-entered moments later. "I didn't have to look very far for him," she said. "He is outside and wants to speak to you."

Dad seized his spear. Grael strained to lift himself up on his elbows, but he couldn't. He was useless if this visit turned violent.

"He is making the sign of the furka," Harath said.

"We'll hear what he has to say," Widan said. "Tell him to come in."

As Garscap entered, he nodded to Grael's father. Dad grudgingly put aside his weapon.

"Come to gloat?" the politician asked.

"I understand the Pig has taken Donmor," Garscap said. "I have come to offer my help in recovering his body."

Widan stared hard into Garscap's eyes. The politician relaxed and conveyed his appreciation with a nod. "What of our dispute?" he asked.

"It can wait."

"I suppose it can."

Grael exhaled, but his relief quickly dissipated. The rivals' truce ensured peace for now, but how long would it last?

***

The following days were trying for Grael. Confined to his bed, he learned what was happening beyond the hut second-hand from his mother and Maerbard. His father was away on the search for Donmor's remains. His mother gleaned what she could from the gossips in the village. Maerbard proved to be a better source of information because he hung around the edge of the village and quizzed any searcher returning from the Pig. He complained heartily that he hadn't been allowed to join the hunt for the corpse, but conditions were too severe on the mountain for a mere boy.

Apparently, Garscap's dedication to the search had impressed everyone. Rumors circulated that the politician and his rival were going to come to some sort of compromise. Mam seized upon these and became convinced that conflict would be resolved amicably. Her optimism was infectious. Grael came to share it, and for the first time since the Fair Folk arrived, his heart was light. Even the horrors of the mountain ceased to haunt his dreams.

Then, one evening, Dad returned home, looking tired, dejected, and old.

"Did you find Donmor's body?" Mam asked.

He shook his head wearily. "We gave up looking."

Something was wrong; something his father was reluctant to share.

Mam sensed it, too. "What's the matter?"

"We meet the Changeling's supporters at Horgal's Field tomorrow at noon."

Grael hammered the straw with his fists. His family was in danger, and he could do nothing to protect them.

***

Garscap suppressed a smile as he glanced at the sullen, frightened faces around him. They were all goats pretending to be wolves.

Widan's lackeys lined the opposite side of Horgal's Field, weapons in hand. Widan stood before them, talking to Lahan Erol, scratching the ground with his foot like an annoyed rooster. The crops dividing both factions were stunted shoots peeping through the snow, emaciated by the endless winter, and never would bear anything worth harvesting. The leaders had proclaimed this meeting to be merely a show of strength, a means of measuring their relative popularity, but everyone was tense with the expectation blood would be spilled.

"We have a slight edge in numbers, though it is hardly overwhelming," Evram observed.

"What are you suggesting I should have done?" Garscap asked. "Burn down Lahan Erol's house while Widan was within, grieving for his son? I suspect some of my supporters might think it an uncharitable act."

"Of course not. I am suggesting the Pig is a dangerous place."

The Smirk was so damn eager for his first kill. Would he be as eager after it?

"Too obvious." Also too late.

"So, what do we do?"

There should have been no plural in that question. Sometimes, the Smirk did not know his place, behaving as though he was a partner rather than a toady. The boy was as ambitious as he was temperamental. Was there resentment behind his hero worship? Did he call Garscap the Changeling behind his back?

"I'm going to chat with Widan. Wait here." Garscap strolled midway across the field.

Widan approached him. Lahan Erol accompanied the politician, which was surprising. Widan had never needed anyone's help to talk before.

The Smirk appeared in the corner of Garscap's vision. "I thought it best to keep the numbers even," he explained.

Garscap's annoyance was tinged with admiration for the youth's tenacity.

"So, Widan, what have you to say to me?" Garscap asked.

"You were the one who came forward first," Widan observed.

"That's because I was eager to hear what you had to say."

"I have a question for you," Widan said. "Our village has many family names, but it is really one family. Kinsmen stand on both sides of this field. Would you make brother kill brother?"

"Would you?" Evram retorted.

Garscap waved him silent. Though Widan might have approved, shutting up Evram by punching him in the jaw would have set the wrong tone for the negotiation.

"I'll tell you what I would have," Garscap said. "I'd rather have a whole village than half of one."

For an unbearable eternity, nobody spoke.

"There's been some unpleasantness, but nobody's been hurt so far. Except the Scorael boy who was beaten up by your friend," Widan said, pointing to the Smirk.

"I had nothing to do with that," Garscap said. The Smirk was so naive. It wasn't possible to bludgeon the village into submission single-handed.

"Joraem will have to be compensated," Widan said.

Why was Widan speaking of compensation? What was he up to?

"Our dispute claimed another casualty," Garscap said. "Donmor lies somewhere on the Pig."

"His death was due to his father's foolishness and nobody else's," Widan said flatly. "You did your best to recover his body, and for that I am grateful."

"Joraem will be compensated," Garscap promised. The Smirk would pay it. The incident had more to do with Evram ridding himself of a rival for the lovely Ashin Carnath than Garscap's claim to the thorny crown.

"This is yours," Widan said. "But at a price."

"And what would that be?" Garscap asked.

Widan took a deep breath. "My son is dead. You never had a father."

That wasn't true. Garscap's father was one of the heroes of Martyrsgrave. He'd died defending his village's furka against Elfin invaders.

"Your mother…well, we all know what happened to your mother."

Get to the point, you lump of lard.

"If you permit me to adopt you as my heir, I'll give you the thorny crown this very day."

"Shouldn't that, by right, be your son-in-law?"

Widan cleared his throat as he flicked a glance at Lahan. "That is right. You must marry my daughter, Harath."

Garscap's chuckle expanded into a guffaw. He glanced at the others. Evram was red-faced. Lahan hid his discomfort by staring at the ground. So that was why

Widan had dragged Lahan along—to show there were no hard feelings. Widan's audacity was admirable.

Garscap squeezed a smile from his lips and nodded his assent.

Negotiations followed. The dowry had to be agreed upon, Joraem's compensation settled. Even Grael Erol had to get a little something for his loss. Garscap was generous throughout. It was a small price to pay for his victory.

Slowly, awkwardly, Widan disentangled the thorny crown from his unnaturally red hair. He gently lifted it off his head. Without it, he looked naked, diminished. He held the headdress with both hands, staring at it for the longest time. Garscap resisted the urge to snatch it from him. Widan opened his hands and offered it to Garscap.

Garscap seized it and waved it at both sides of the field. Whether friends or enemies, they must all recognize him as their ruler. This was his moment of triumph. The outcast had subjugated his oppressors.

***

Prayers whispered away the oppressive silence. Mam, beside Grael's straw bed, held his hand—more for her comfort than his, he guessed—while she pressed her infant daughter, Miona, to her bosom. Grael's other sister, Wanyr, knelt by the fire, her arms raised in earnest supplication.

Mam shushed her. "Did you hear something?"

Softened by distance, it sounded like an animal crying. No, it was someone yelling.

Mam passed Miona to Wanyr. "Wait here till I return." She unsheathed her knife as she stepped through the door.

Grael tried to follow, but he could not rise from his bed.

A babble of excited voices outside exploded into laughter. Grael couldn't make out what was being said, but the tone of the conversation was clear. Grael sighed with relief. War had been averted.

One voice silenced the rest. Dad entered the hut. He had an unsettling, somber expression.

"Wanyr, your mother wants you. Take Miona with you." He sat down by Grael, his gaze fixed on the fire. "The good news is you won't have to go to Pigsback. Garscap wears the thorny crown. Widan Melkath gave it to him. Things will settle down now. Hopefully."

"I can't believe Widan surrendered it."

"At a price. It is better you find out now from me rather than from someone else later. Widan has given Harath to Garscap. Your engagement is over."

Grael faced the shadows on the wall to conceal his anguish. As his father tried to soothe him with talk of his own past disappointments that time either healed or proved to be blessings, Grael heaped silent curses on Widan Melkath. The enemy he'd made on Widan's behalf held his beloved in one hand and the future of his family in the other.

Hackit's whip was gentler than Widan's treachery.

PART 2
ASCENDANTSUN

Chapter 9

Matter is part of light, but light transcends matter. The Seven Lights constitute the true fabric of the cosmos, and matter is but the product of their interaction.

~From *On the Matter of Light* by
ShineBright Ferocitas.

The gnomon's golden hand pushed against the ashen sky to no avail. Around it, the priests danced to the rhythm of their prayer, their dizziness growing as they studied the sour, fungal scum stretching from horizon to horizon. No shaft of sunlight pierced this fetid cloud. Not even the tiniest rent existed through which freed souls might fly to their master. The dead, victims of a roof fall in the mine, would remain unburned this day, as they had for weeks. DawnGlow Fulgur glanced at the cold, white disc of the sun struggling against its shroud. Would the pyres ever be set alight?

He tired of watching the priests beg for the sky to open and turned his back on the shrouded sun, continuing on to the ministry of the city of Tincranny. He hurried through the entrance hall, up the stairs, past myriad offices to the private chamber of his friend, the minister-governor of the settlement, AscendantSun Auctor. DawnGlow had come at his friend's request. No explanation for the summons had been given, but AscendantSun's note had stressed that it concerned a matter of utmost importance.

DawnGlow rapped on the door. The silence on the other side was broken by the scrape of a sliding bolt. The door creaked ajar. AscendantSun's smile peeped through the gap.

"Welcome," he said, swinging the door open. With a wave of his hand he indicated to his visitor to take a seat.

DawnGlow planted himself in an armchair and admired the fine upholstery with his fingers. He watched AscendantSun close the door and shuffle to the chair on the other side of the desk. Those mysterious wounds he had suffered in the mountains had left him with a permanent limp. AscendantSun still refused with typical obstinacy to divide, though it would have cured him. The Lineage of Auctor was always so headstrong and peculiar.

DawnGlow glanced about the chamber. Though it was past noon, candles burned to dispel the tyrannical gloom of the Ill-weather. Three golden banners hanging behind AscendantSun's desk dominated the chamber. One was the Golden Light's sigil: a spread, two-thumbed hand. The middle banner, a hammer with faces on both ends of its head, was the symbol of the city of Tincranny. The third bore the emblem of the Lineage of Auctor, the half-face. DawnGlow, like all Ors, was partial to the symmetric, the balanced. Out of friendship, he maintained a tactful silence about his distaste for the Auctors' eccentric symbol, though AscendantSun probably was aware of the strain it placed on others' aesthetic sensibilities.

AscendantSun's personal genealogical chart hung on another wall. Below the first Auctor was a ladder, each rung of which represented a division, one of each set of twins being the progenitor of the succeeding pair. SunGerm and his unfortunate twin MorningHymn were on the top rung, SunGerm's descendants were on the next rung, and so on. Many illustrious names stirred memories of Gleam and its valiant defense against besieging tribes of Mixies. Hatred for Mixies distilled with each succeeding division till it reached its apogee in MixyBane, the last Minister-Governor of Gleam and the founder of Tincranny. After his division, the animosity waned. His progeny sought rapprochement with those who earlier divisions had reviled. They had had successes, too.

AscendantSun and his twin SunTrove had negotiated a decades-old peace treaty with one tribe of Mixies, the Stretchers, which had held even through the Ill-weather. The cost had been great. Several names below MixyBane had disappeared in the wilds, presumably slain by Mixies they sought to befriend. After SunTrove's tragic death in the calamitous flood that submerged the western coast of Sunrest, AscendantSun became the sole survivor of the four divisions since MixyBane.

Which made AscendantSun's inexplicable delay in dividing maddening, even frightening. It was as if he was giving up on his lineage. DawnGlow resolved to try again to persuade his friend of the urgency of adding another rung or two to the chart.

His eyes drifted to a small wooden object on the table beside AscendantSun's ministerial medal. It was a scarred tablet, shriveled and warped by age. He directed his host's attention to it with a nod and asked, "Is that what I think it is?"

"It is. I was given it when I was elected a minister to remind me of the consequences of neglecting my duty."

DawnGlow rubbed his throat. With difficulty, he averted his gaze from the miserable relic of defeat and enslavement.

"Mead?" his host asked.

"Please," DawnGlow replied without hesitation. He hoped his friend would be generous enough not to abuse him with the current year's tasteless produce. No amount of spice could hide its poor quality.

AscendantSun poured two goblets of the honeyed beverage and passed one to his guest. DawnGlow tasted it and smiled. "Last summer's honey."

He gladly accepted AscendantSun's offer of a game of battlefield. The minister laid the gridded board on the desk and poured out pieces from a leather pouch. Both Ors began to sort them.

"You can play the center if you wish," AscendantSun offered.

DawnGlow nodded. "Your pieces are unusual," he said, frowning. They were made of carved bone and veined, yellow marble.

"A holy man of the Stretchers gifted them to me. The marble pieces fascinate me. They are as the Stretchers see us."

DawnGlow picked up a marble piece with two thumbs and examined it. "Judging from these, they find us very ugly," he quipped. Stretchers were just Mixies. The nuances distinguishing one tribe of Mixies from another was immaterial. Only one difference mattered. Two peoples lived in the world of Elysion—those with two thumbs on each hand and those without—Ors and non-Ors.

DawnGlow and AscendantSun quickly set up their pieces on the grid. The gnomon was positioned in the center square and encircled by defending batonaxers. The bone pieces, representing Mixies, were dispersed around the edges of the board, divided as their real-life counterparts. Their greater number was balanced by their inferior ability.

DawnGlow straightened his pieces. AscendantSun made his first move, and battle commenced.

"So, why did you invite me here tonight?" DawnGlow asked as he moved a batonaxer.

"Nostalgia," AscendantSun replied as he advanced a piece. "And a desire to enjoy simple pleasures forever lost with the coming of the dawn."

"What do you mean?" DawnGlow asked as he haphazardly moved another batonaxer. It was a mistake, though hopefully not a fatal one.

"Concentrate on the game," AscendantSun said with a smile. "I do not want to listen to excuses when I win."

They maneuvered their pieces in silence. Dozens of scenarios flitted through DawnGlow's mind, not all of them related to the game. AscendantSun had an ulterior motive for inviting him, but guessing his friend's intentions was like playing battlefield blindfolded and trying to guess his opponent's moves from the sound of his pieces sliding across the board. He had to wait for AscendantSun to make his move.

The slaughter began in earnest. Mixies and Ors were swept from the board in attack and counter-attack. Both sides made errors, missed opportunities. AscendantSun was on the verge of victory when DawnGlow snatched it from him by maneuvering his gnomon into a corner square.

"I am sure you will win our next game," DawnGlow offered in condolence.

AscendantSun sighed. "There might not be a next game." He opened a drawer in his desk and produced an envelope and a parchment. He presented both to his friend and slumped back in his chair.

DawnGlow perused the letter, mentally converting the stilted glyphs into flowing text. As he read, his heart sank.

Speaks Harbinger of the Dawn, Conscience of the Sun, Minister of Ministers, Voice of the Consensus of Lineages, To AscendantSun Auctor, Minister-Governor of Tincranny,

The Consensus of Lineages has learned that a heresy has taken root in Tincranny. A small number of Ors have chosen to repudiate their allegiance to our Bright Lord. These blasphemers, calling themselves Orstretcherists, have adopted as their creed the nonsensical myths and perverse doctrines of the tribe of Mixies called Stretchers. AscendantSun Auctor is accused of leading this movement. The Consensus demands that the minister resign and submit to house arrest till his trial can be arranged. He should appoint NeverFear Cor to act as interim minister-governor. The enclosed envelope should be presented unopened to him.

The seal on the envelope was broken already. DawnGlow's fingers trembled as he removed its contents. The new minister-governor was instructed to arrest an extensive list of other suspected Orstretcherists. They were to be transported to Shiningpeak for trial. Many were DawnGlow's friends.

"I do not know what to say," DawnGlow admitted. "You think they will exile you and the others to Evercloud?"

AscendantSun shook his head. "I doubt the Harbinger intends to extend to us such kindness. Note that we are to be tried in Shiningpeak, where his cult is strongest, where the moderates in the Consensus hold least sway. He plans to have us executed."

"That is preposterous," DawnGlow said. "Nobody has been executed since the Viator War. The Harbinger himself was convicted of treason and heresy and was exiled to Evercloud. Why should he not offer you the same mercy?"

"Different time, my friend. That was before the Ill-weather, this dark age that the Harbinger claims to have foretold. Before its coming, he was ridiculed as a madman, condemned to perpetual exile. Those who once had him imprisoned now proclaim him their savior. They close their eyes, rest their hands on his shoulder, and let him lead wherever he wishes. They willingly submit to his every whim. He wants the Orstretcherists dead. We are the antithesis of all he represents. We want peace. He wants war. We want to prosper with the Stretchers, and other Mixies. He wants them dead."

And of course, the Harbinger claimed to be the Golden Light's prophet, while AscendantSun's followers denied the precedence of Aurelian before the other divine Lights. Indeed, they rejected the divinity of all Lights, preferring to put their faith in the Stretchers' phantom deity.

The grim logic of AscendantSun's argument was irrefutable. The Harbinger was a dangerous and ruthless fanatic. He was certainly capable of putting the Orstretcherists to death.

Many Ors unaffiliated with his cult might agree with him if he did. The Orstretcherists went beyond the Tokenists or the Necrotheists or the Dawn Chorus or the other fringe religious groups. AscendantSun and his followers rejected not merely the orthodoxy of the Consensus but the very nature of the cosmos that Ors had accepted since they left their maturation tubes.

It was very important not to be swayed too much by AscendantSun. He had his own agenda, and he could be very persuasive.

"So, do you intend to obey the orders of the Consensus?" DawnGlow asked.

"No," AscendantSun replied. "The Consensus appears to believe we have no other choice but to do so. It considers us too untrustworthy to be left in peace, but loyal enough to surrender meekly to our executioners. By morning, everyone on that list except me will have departed Tincranny. They will seek sanctuary amongst the Stretchers till they decide a better course of action."

"And you?"

"That is why I asked you here. I am handing over temporary governance of the city to you."

"What about NeverFear?"

AscendantSun laughed. "I think the Consensus would prefer I left you in charge rather than another Orstretcherist. By morning, NeverFear will be beyond the reach of the Consensus." He paused. "I also have a favor to ask. You might not be inclined to grant it."

DawnGlow's chest tightened. "Go on."

"I wish to divide," AscendantSun said.

DawnGlow was too flummoxed to respond.

AscendantSun leaned forward in his seat. "My friend, my heart is pulled in two directions, and I must divide to follow both."

Resting an elbow on his desk, he unfolded the outer thumb from his fist. "On the one thumb, my natural inclination, like all Ors, is to preserve my lineage. I also must aid my exiled coreligionists. Isolated from their kin, they will face great dangers that my conscience demands me to share. I cannot abandon them."

The inner thumb emerged from beneath the fingers. "On the other thumb, the Harbinger must be stopped. He promises the second coming of Aurelian and a golden age for our people, but he will deliver instead suffering and desolation. He wants a holy war, a massacre of every non-Or in Elysion. I'm not concerned just for Stretchers and other Mixies. I fear for our own people. If he was to realize his genocide, our race would be damned by it. Once they understood the gravity of their crime, shame would destroy them. But such an insane scheme is certain to fail. The Mixies are much stronger than our people's pride is willing to acknowledge. We have succeeded against them in the past as much through diplomacy as warfare. The war that the Harbinger craves would be our ruination. I must stop it."

AscendantSun was unrecognizable as he banged the fist on the table. His face was so ugly with violence. It could have belonged to a Mixy.

The list of Orstretcherists was crumpled in DawnGlow's fist. He placed it flat on the table, trying to maintain his calm. "But why turn to me for this?"

AscendantSun leaned back in his chair. The vision of corruption was gone. DawnGlow's friend returned with a smile.

"The method of our propagation must remain a secret from the Stretchers," AscendantSun said. "You know how long division takes and how much food must be consumed. If I attempted it in the mountains, I could not conceal it from my hosts. I want the Stretchers to focus on what our peoples have in common, not become distracted by our biological differences."

"But why turn to me?" DawnGlow asked. "Surely there is some Orstretcherist like NeverFear, unknown to the Harbinger's spies, who could hide you while you divide?"

AscendantSun picked up the list from the table and waved it in the air. "Other than NeverFear, I cannot rely on any Orstretcherist whose name is not on this document, since he might be one of its compilers."

He dropped it on the table. "As for you, aside from our many years of friendship, you can be trusted precisely because you are not an Orstretcherist. You do not share my beliefs, but you harbor the same doubts in our dead god that ultimately drew me to Stretcherism. You have merely drawn different conclusions. I put my faith in the Stretchers' god. You put your faith in none."

"It is hard to have faith in a god who died so ingloriously in battle," DawnGlow admitted, nodding.

"But most of our people still cling to their faith in Aurelian," AscendantSun said. "Their reluctance to accept his death as final makes them vulnerable to the Harbinger and his ilk. I suspect even many Orstretcherists in their hearts long for Aurelian to return, and their adopted faith is an anesthetic to dull the pain of his loss. You are immune to that almost universal longing, so you can appreciate my arguments rationally."

DawnGlow shifted in his seat. "I look on Aurelian and his demise as honestly as I can. Aurelian might have created us, but he brought us little but ruin in his first life. Why should he deliver anything but ruin upon his resurrection? We have prospered without him. The misplaced devotion to him that pervades our society hinders our race from even greater achievements."

He glanced at the murk beyond the windows. "As for this Ill-weather, it is just a meteorological caprice. Aurelian neither caused nor will end the Ill-weather. Coincidence and not providence is the root of the fulfillment of the Harbinger's prophecy."

DawnGlow shook his head. "His famous escape on a pumice raft from Evercloud was likewise just a fortunate accident. Slabs of pumice, great and small, were reported all along the coast. Sailors said they saw islands of the stuff far out to sea. Though the strait dividing Evercloud from the mainland can be crossed by rowboat in a few hours, it took the Harbinger two days to drift ashore. It is not credible that the Golden Light would choose such a haphazard method to liberate his holy prophet from his island prison."

The hollowness of his words mocked DawnGlow as he spoke.

"But," he added, "I condone even less your devotion to a foreign god whose only physical manifestation is the breath of his adherents. In your devotions, you have replaced a god who failed us with one that does not exist." It cheered him to speak with such absolute conviction.

A spasm of irritation flitted across AscendantSun's face. "You have never condemned my beliefs in public or denounced me as a heretic."

"My friend, till now, we have never been frank on the matter. Uncertainty salved my conscience. Besides, I never doubted your loyalty to our people, despite your infatuation with your mountain friends."

"Then do not doubt my loyalty now."

DawnGlow stroked his cheeks as he weighed the decision before him. The division would take between seven to eight months, but AscendantSun would be his guest for much longer, almost a year. DawnGlow would vacillate for every moment of it. He damned his fickle, superstitious heart. He had spent many lifetimes cementing together a perfect mosaic of rational arguments and empirical deductions to seal away forever his true irrational nature. Yet, now, despite all his ingenuity, it burst forth through ignored crevices and blossomed like some impudent weed.

"If I grant you this favor, how do you propose to stop the Harbinger?" he asked.

"Other than betraying our people, any way I can."

"And supposing the Harbinger is truly the prophet of Aurelian?"

AscendantSun stared blankly at him for a moment. He obviously had not expected such a question from a Necrotheist, one who believed their god dead and never to return.

"The Golden Light will stop me," AscendantSun said.

DawnGlow's soft exhale brought no relief. His resolve flickered like a candle between granting and refusing his friend's request.

"I will help you," he said. The decision was shocking, as if he had no part in its making. Friendship had triumphed over good sense. Surprise gave way to regret. How did AscendantSun intend to stop the Harbinger? There could be only one way.

Murder.

Chapter 10

The twingle is the fulcrum of creation on which a single past and two futures balance.

~From *The Medical Primer* by
SunFire Armipotens.

In the dank cellar of the local Hostel of Fulgur, day lasted as long as a candlewick, night endured until another candle was lit. AscendantSun craved sunshine, but DawnGlow dissuaded him from leaving his subterranean lair. The miserable light outside was not worth the risk. The sun, still infected by the Ill-weather, burnt little better than a candle, and the days were sickly and fleeting.

AscendantSun's nursery lay behind a false wall that they had erected at one end of the cellar. Empty mead casks hid its cramped entrance. It was certainly not salubrious, but it was secure from discovery by all except the most suspicious imaginations.

Both the main part of the cellar and the nursery were spotlessly clean. All the grime and cobwebs had been brushed away, in part for AscendantSun's comfort, but also to avoid any telltale disturbances that might betray his presence if the cellar was searched. Nobody would question a basement subject to such obsessive cleaning. Such foibles were not uncommon among Ors.

Hopefully, these precautions were unnecessary. As the only Fulgur in Tincranny, DawnGlow used the hostel as his private residence. Other Fulgurs rarely visited Tincranny. They preferred to frequent more urbane locales. And the home of the interim Minister-Governor was exempt from the frequent random searches inflicted on most buildings in Tincranny since the Orstretcherists' flight.

The Consensus of Lineages was intent on rooting out any remaining Orstretcherists quietly residing in Tincranny. Occasionally, DawnGlow brought news of some old acquaintance of AscendantSun who had been interrogated or incarcerated. Many had never dabbled in Stretcherism. DawnGlow's promises to help them were not particularly convincing.

When AscendantSun finally lost patience, and pushed him on the matter, DawnGlow snapped, "My first priority is our safety. Most of those taken into custody will be freed whenever they repudiate their heresy."

"Even those who were never Orstretcherists in the first place?" AscendantSun asked.

"They will have to get on with it and take the oath," DawnGlow said as he started up the stairs. "I took it, beneath Tincranny's gnomon, under the gaze of most of the city's populace. I did it to put my loyalty to the

Consensus beyond doubt. It's just an empty formula. Nothing more."

"And what about those who aren't released?" AscendantSun demanded. "What about those who disappear?"

DawnGlow paused and looked down at him with a melancholic expression. He sighed. "Only the Harbinger knows." He ran up the stairs and slammed the door of the cellar shut behind him.

Another evening, DawnGlow announced that the Consensus of Lineages had persuaded his lineage to elect him its minister so that his assignment as governor-minister could be made permanent.

The news brought mixed emotions. It increased AscendantSun's security. But, what had DawnGlow done to impress the Consensus so much?

DawnGlow shrugged off AscendantSun's tentative questions. "I would rather keep my private and public lives separate."

In the end, AscendantSun stopped asking. DawnGlow was under enough strain living a double life. His collaboration with the Consensus, whatever its extent, protected AscendantSun. To condemn DawnGlow for it was hypocritical and ungrateful.

Preparation for division began as it always did—with feasting. AscendantSun's lithe frame had to be enveloped in fat to initiate the process of turning one into two, so he consumed as much food as he could stomach. The daily gluttony was a pleasure at first, then a chore. He was permanently bloated and leaden, and sweated through sleepless nights.

His body softened, its brawn smothered beneath spreading fleshy layers. His muscles ached. His skin prickled under the strain. Each day, he surveyed his bloated figure for progress. Every sagging deposit of body fat was stretched, pinched, or patted to gauge its increase. Every day brought dissatisfaction and plaguing doubts that he was losing weight instead of gaining it. The exact mass at which division would begin was random and therefore unknowable. The uncertainty aggravated his disgruntlement. Had he lost the capacity to divide? Was his biology mocking him?

DawnGlow tried to keep up his friend's spirits. "Don't worry," he said whenever AscendantSun spoke of his doubts. "You will be talking out the back of your head in no time."

And then it happened. Desperate feasting became involuntary gorging. The hunger became insatiable. The instinct honed by many divisions assured AscendantSun that the process of one becoming two had begun. As the days and weeks passed, further body changes confirmed this conviction. He shed his golden curls, and his neck thickened. The flexibility of his arms at the shoulders increased, while his spine stiffened. His shoulder blades, pelvis, and ribs ached as the bones began to grow offshoots, stretching and raising the skin on his back to form a large hump. As it grew, sleeping on his back and then on his side became impossible, and he was forced to snatch what rest he could while sitting upright. He was constantly tired, short of breath, and prone to grinding headaches. His facial muscles ticked and twitched, stretched on his elongating skull. Standing up became a chore, as his body became more ungainly. Despite these discomforts, his spirits were high. The protuberance on his back was a second ribcage, a tent of flesh and bone in which a second heart would soon beat.

One morning, a pat on the shoulder woke him.

"Your breakfast is served," DawnGlow announced with a grin as he placed a tray before him. Still half-asleep, AscendantSun scooped up a spoon of thick porridge. Instead of his mouth, it pressed against a foreign, featureless surface. Hot gruel seared his back. He dropped the spoon and cursed. DawnGlow stumbled backward into a corner as he convulsed into laughter.

"What by all the Lights is wrong with me?" AscendantSun exclaimed.

"You blind fool, open your eyes," DawnGlow stuttered through his giggles.

The truth slowly dawned. AscendantSun gently reached for the back of his head. There were the familiar contours of his face, his lips and nose. He opened his old eyes and looked upon the cellar as a dizzying panorama. He had been tracking the development of the eyes in the back of his head for weeks, but dazed by his sudden awakening, he had forgotten their existence. With difficulty, AscendantSun closed his new eyes and twisted around to view his friend with his old ones.

"Good trick, is it not? A nurse played the same prank on me during my last division," DawnGlow said. "I turned you around while you slept, and then I tapped you on the shoulder in such a way that you thought your front was your back."

"It plays nicely on sense confusion," AscendantSun said. "Must try it myself whenever I get the chance." It was great that this crucial landmark in the division had been reached, but his amusement at his friend's joke was tinged with apprehension and sadness. Death or exile would deny AscendantSun the opportunity to perpetrate the same jape.

He practiced blinking and winking his two sets of eyes, till he had mastered them. With his rear eyes, he studied in a mirror the blurry features of the new visage gradually sharpening on the back of his head. He tried to hasten the development of this second face. When not too addled by sense confusion and fatigue, he stretched the new muscles with grimaces and smiles, twitched invisible nostrils, and opened and closed the nascent mouth, still veiled by skin.

When the thinning membrane that sealed his new lips broke, his whole body shuddered with retching spasms, as new lungs struggled to expel viscous phlegm from their airways and gasp their first agonizing breaths. The convulsions disabled him. It was humiliating to be unable to wipe away the creeping rivulets of drool dripping from his new chin, soaking through his cloak and oozing onto the floor.

He was a plant. He had been a warrior, a legate, a minister, a philosopher, and a priest, but now he was reduced to a flesh vegetable. He no longer controlled his body. Its whims controlled him. Why did he decide to divide? Why did the tortures of previous divisions fail to dissuade him? He had let silly, romantic dreams of one becoming two cloud his judgment. He had succumbed to his fear of oblivion. What cost had this vanity? Six months had passed, and all he had done was satisfy his folly. While the Harbinger planned to massacre his friends and bring the destruction of his race ever closer, AscendantSun lay helpless, steeped in his own drool.

When DawnGlow came with AscendantSun's supper, he cleaned up the mess without a word. AscendantSun was too despondent to speak as DawnGlow wiped his face with a dry corner of his sodden garment. DawnGlow stripped him, used the garments to soak up the mucous on the floor, and threw them to one side. He laid a fresh cloak over AscendantSun's naked shoulders. Shivering, AscendantSun squeezed the cloak about him.

"You survived this trial many times before," DawnGlow said. "You know you can get through this."

"I know," AscendantSun said, his old eyes staring at the floor. He wanted to nod but his neck was too stiff.

"And you know there is no way back now. The process cannot be reversed. You must move forward and complete division."

"Yes," AscendantSun said, grimacing.

"I know this is very difficult for you," DawnGlow said. "It is as arduous for me when I divide. You know that. I appreciate how hard it is to be reminded we are prisoners of our biology. But remember, I am with you every step of the way. We are Ors after all, and Ors look after each other."

More indignities followed as AscendantSun's new digestive tract sputtered into life. He detested the worm. He called it that in his lowest moments. It was nothing better than a parasite feeding off of him.

Dizzying sense confusion added to his misery. Reality was slipping away as he sank into the mire of his multiplied senses. His four eyes saw too much in a single glance for him to make sense of it, and he struggled to focus. Sounds echoed in two pairs of ears. Was he hungry or was it the worm? When he scratched his face, which face he was scratching, and was the itch on it?

One morning, as he rubbed his cheeks, powdery flakes of dry skin fell away. With difficulty, he examined his reflection. The first molt had begun. The tattoos on his old face were peeling away with the loose scales of dead skin. The old AscendantSun was dying with them. He had reached the fulcrum of division, the epicenter of creation, the sliver of time between his previous life and future lives.

The divergent drumming of twin hearts heralded that his single consciousness had split in two. They were confused at first. Both controlled the same body, had the same mastery of its limbs, and experienced the same dizzying multiplicity of senses. If they stilled, they could even hear each other's whispery thoughts.

It was futile to worry about which body ultimately would be theirs. The important thing was to expedite division. They agreed on the terms of their joint tenancy of their conjoined bodies, the twingle. If both attempted to use the same limb at the same time, it jammed, and seeing with one pair of eyes would ease their sense confusion. Because each was willing to concede to the other, they drew lots to decide the matter. One took charge of the older body and its left arm, while the other adopted the new body and the right arm. They practiced the same convention regarding the two legs, though this was a formality since they could not stand.

The constant companionship was good. They shared lifetimes of reminiscences. As their sense of confusion waned, they played battlefield against each other on a makeshift board that DawnGlow had carved into the floor. AscendantSun had brought his pieces with him into hiding.

With two of them now feeding the process, the twingle's development accelerated. Buds on the shoulders and pelvis of the new body stretched into new limbs. The new mouth teethed, while a new tooth emerged to replenish the old mouth's lost molar. Further shedding of spent layers of skin smoothed away scars. Spasms toned muscles. It became difficult to tell apart the old and new frames, so perfect was their symmetry. The twins possibly switched bodies by accident sometimes.

Each passing day brought nearer the completion of division, and freedom from their increasingly irksome physical attachment. Division's end was as imprecise as its beginning. As time dragged on, the uncertainty turned eager anticipation into impatience. Every time they closed their eyes to rest, they prayed this sleep would be their last as a twingle.

***

DawnGlow crawled into the nursery. The twins were still asleep. He tickled one of their arms with a feather, and the twingle briefly quivered with movement. They were ready to be woken. He shook them gently till their eyes fluttered open.

"Hungry?" he asked.

"Yes," they chorused.

"You should be. You have been asleep for eleven days," DawnGlow said.

The deep sleep, the last stage of division, was over. They reached back and prodded the bridge of dead skin still binding them together. They began twisting their heads and bodies till the scab broke with a crack and they tumbled free of each other. DawnGlow first checked that they had not peeled from their backs the new skin beneath the dead tissue. Satisfied that all was well, DawnGlow let the twins devour their breakfast, while he rubbed away the loose crusts of dead scales off their backs with a yellow pumice stone.

"So, what are you going to call yourselves?" he asked them.

"I will keep the name AscendantSun," one said.

"I have no name as yet," the other said.

"Then I will call you NoName for now," DawnGlow said. The lightness of his tone masked his disquiet.

As he tattooed the appropriate glyphs on the new AscendantSun's brow, the implications of the new arrangement stampeded through his mind. Did the twins not trust him enough to say what would eventually be on NoName's blank forehead? Perhaps it was destined never to bear a permanent name, just a series of disposable identities to baffle the Harbinger's minions. The other twin's adoption of their progenitor's name reinforced the impression of NoName's ephemeral nature. It was as if he was to be excised from posterity after they parted company. On meeting AscendantSun, the Orstretcherists in the mountains would assume he was the original. They would never know of his twin and the terrible purpose for which he was created.

NoName was more a detached limb than an individual. The revelation was disturbing, but it also made NoName's approaching death a little easier to bear.

Chapter 11

Bright eyes once mine stared back at me,
Fragile mirrors of memory,
A spiritual symmetry
In the ceaseless flow of destiny,
Doomed by writhing currents to change
From the selfsame into the strange.

~From *A Paean to the Other Self* by
SummerDawn Ferocitas.

AscendantSun's Mixies were losing. His opponent's gnomon edged ever closer to victory. Two players of equal ability should play to a draw, but it rarely happened. The Ors had always a slight advantage. AscendantSun was not bothered that the odds were against him. It added to the challenge. Besides, it was his turn to play Ors after this game.

Steps in the cellar stilled NoName's hand in the midst of moving a batonaxer. The twins held their breath. NoName's face was a perfect reflection of AscendantSun's suspense.

DawnGlow announced his presence. He asked AscendantSun to join him outside.

The twins exhaled. NoName finished his move.

AscendantSun crawled into the main part of the cellar.

DawnGlow helped him to his feet and handed him a brace of batonaxes. AscendantSun recognized DawnGlow's most prized possession.

"I want you to have these," DawnGlow said. "NoName can use your old weapons."

With reverent tenderness, AscendantSun took the batonaxes. He had often coveted them. The double-bitted axe heads and spikes shone in the candlelight, the soaring eagles etched across their polished surfaces elevated by the reflected lambency. He stretched them in and out of attack and defense positions. They were light and well balanced, but he was cautious about spinning them till he had more practice.

"I will return them to you in the same excellent condition," AscendantSun promised.

"You misunderstand me," DawnGlow said. "They are a present."

AscendantSun was horrified by his friend's intention to part with such precious heirlooms. He read the golden symbols on the shafts. "The name of one of your ancestors is inscribed on them," he said. "If I am arrested, these weapons can be traced back to you."

"Think of it as an extra incentive not to get caught."

"If I am captured, what will you say when legionaries turn up on your doorstep with these weapons?"

DawnGlow smiled. "I will say, 'Thank you very much for finding my batonaxes. I was wondering where I had left them. AscendantSun must have stolen them.' They will believe me because they think you capable of any crime. And I will find solace in my weapons' return if you are arrested. You are a far greater danger to me than those batonaxes. They, at least, are immune to interrogation."

"I would never betray you," AscendantSun declared.

"Then keep the batonaxes," DawnGlow said. "My weapons will protect you when I cannot."

New bodies had to relearn old skills. Batonaxes were not weapons for unpracticed hands. Wielded with skill, they could defeat any number of attackers, but in a careless instant they could turn on their wielder. As muscles strengthened and reflexes sharpened, AscendantSun and his twin introduced batonaxe drills to their exercise regimen. Each took turns to perform the wielding dances that practiced footwork and the basic thrust, cut, and parry movements while the other tapped out the rhythm with a stick and critiqued the dancer's technique. Time and time again, they danced to the quickening beat till every motion was an impeccable expression of murderous grace.

The twins also practiced casting their batonaxes at targets. When one of AscendantSun's throws went awry and he smashed open a full mead keg, splashing its contents across the floor, DawnGlow thumped down the stairs.

"Are you ever going to duel each other or are you forever going to fight shadows and furniture?" he grumbled.

"Your comment illustrates why the Auctors were always renowned for their skill with batonaxes, while a Fulgur once sliced off half of his hand while playing with one," NoName retorted.

"I am humbled," DawnGlow said, his light manner failing to disguise his chagrin. He helped the twins soak up the spilled mead with rags.

"You seem to be in a rush to get rid of us," AscendantSun said as he squeezed out a rag into a bucket.

"I am eager to be rid of the incessant tapping and the din of batonaxes chewing up my cellar, and not just for the benefit of my mead collection. Your racket travels through the entire hostel. I am afraid it will announce your presence to some unforeseen visitor. Your noise is an unavoidable evil, but I will be glad when it is no more."

After DawnGlow had climbed back up the stairs, NoName asked, "Do you think when he talks of unavoidable evil he is thinking of more than the noise?"

"It is a little late to doubt him," AscendantSun observed. "He has protected us throughout our division."

"He gives you no reason for suspicion. He treats you as the previous AscendantSun. He regards me as a stranger."

"Is this about DawnGlow's batonaxes? He could not split the brace between us."

NoName chuckled. "Do you realize you are as good as accusing yourself of jealousy? Forget the batonaxes. My concern is their former owner. There is deadness in his eyes when he looks upon me, a callousness in his voice when he speaks directly to me. He guesses the true purpose for which I was created. Eight or so months ago, he might have convinced himself otherwise and took succor in the original AscendantSun's vague promises, but now, DawnGlow can no longer salve his conscience with delusion. We should leave the Hostel of Fulgur as soon as possible, lest we test our host too much."

"As soon as you are ready for your mission, we will go. I can always finish my training in the mountains." A great sadness struck AscendantSun. He was not yet ready to say goodbye to his twin. "I wish we had given you a proper name."

"We agreed it was easier if I did not have one. You and DawnGlow cannot betray what you do not know. NoName will suffice for now. I must be able to change my name as circumstances dictate. I will take a permanent name afterward, if I survive.'

"If I could share your burden…"

NoName placed a hand on AscendantSun's shoulder. "Sharing my burden would not lighten it. The knowledge I will live on through you is a consolation."

"Last year, our forbear killed a dozen or so Jinglemen with an untroubled conscience," AscendantSun said. "Is the Harbinger's life more valuable than theirs?"

NoName sighed. "Thank the Forelight that Saint Sebryn freed the old AscendantSun from his vow of pacifism. But for that, I also would have to contend with its breaking. For the first time, I must turn my knife against one of my own kind. Is that not reason enough for guilt? The heart is a balance prone to capricious measure. I know the lives of Mixies and Ors are of equal worth, but my heart tilts otherwise. And the Harbinger's life is as valuable as that of any other Or."

"Think of the lives saved by the Harbinger's death," AscendantSun urged. "Not just the Mixies but the Ors, also."

"It is all that keeps me going," NoName said. "Enough of wielding dances. We're ready for dueling dances."

AscendantSun nodded. "I suppose it is time."

In full armor, they practiced dueling dances of progressive complexity and pace, till they were competent to spar. Even with batonaxes padded to blunt their deadly edges and points, freeform sparring was dangerous. Both duelists suffered bruises and scratches. AscendantSun delivered one blow that knocked NoName to the floor. Begging forgiveness, he knelt beside his moaning opponent and tried to pry open the arms hugging his abdomen. Concern for NoName succumbed to electric fright with the sudden realization that if his twin's injury was grievous, AscendantSun might have to pursue the Harbinger in his stead. NoName's assurance that he was fine brought double relief.

***

DawnGlow's evident dismay at the twins' announcement that they were ready to leave Tincranny puzzled

AscendantSun. Till now, he had been eager for their departure. Perhaps, he had simply become accustomed to their presence.

"Are you sure you are ready?" he asked.

AscendantSun smiled as he tugged at the golden curls on his head. "See? Almost fully grown. We can be seen in public."

"When do you intend to leave?" DawnGlow asked.

"Tomorrow," NoName said firmly.

DawnGlow sighed. "So soon? Very well. I suggest AscendantSun leave in the morning and NoName can set out later in the day. Safer to stagger your departures. This villa is beyond the city walls, but there are frequent patrols of the area. I arranged them."

"And what will we do if we encounter one?" NoName asked tartly.

"Don't worry," DawnGlow assured him. "I will give each of you a letter to present to any city guards who attempt to detain you. It will explain you are acting on my orders, and instruct the guards to let you continue on your business unhindered. Tell them as little as possible. Let their imaginations fill in the gaps. But try your best to evade them. These are suspicious times, and I want to avoid raising any questions, however slight, in the minds of the citizenry of Tincranny regarding my devotion to the Consensus. I will need names for your letters."

He pointed to AscendantSun's forehead. "You'll have to modify your forehead tattoo temporarily to disguise your true name."

"Perhaps we should wait till tonight,' NoName suggested.

DawnGlow smiled. "So you can travel under the cover of darkness? Your confinement here has made you forget how much the Ill-weather has enfeebled the sun and quenched the moon's bloody glow. Day is night and night is a blindness only relieved by torchlight. And carrying a torch would alert every patrol from here to Sunthorn."

After the twins had furnished DawnGlow with their temporary aliases, he bid them goodnight and disappeared upstairs, and the twins set about amending their tattoos. The brush tickled AscendantSun's brow as his twin added the minor strokes to his tattoo to alter its meaning. While it dried, AscendantSun applied the symbols for NoName's new alias to his forehead. He drew the symbols on a piece of parchment and used a needle to puncture along the lines and curves of the pattern.

NoName lay still on the floor, his eyes closed, as AscendantSun positioned the stencil and dabbed paint over it to create a dotted outline. Joining the dots required patience and a very steady hand. The paint dried fast and left little opportunity for correction.

He sighed with relief when he finished. The product of his endeavor was indistinguishable from a genuine tattoo. It would fade over time and have to be retouched. The delicacy required for its application was cause for concern. NoName would struggle to achieve the same perfection by himself if he had to change his name.

AscendantSun woke several times in anticipation of the morning. When DawnGlow finally trundled down the stairs with the breakfast tray in hand, it was both a relief and a disappointment.

While the twins finished their porridge, DawnGlow dashed back upstairs. He returned with a leather backpack and invited AscendantSun to review its contents. The victuals consisted of dry venison sausages, rounds of cheese, and hardtack biscuits, enough by DawnGlow's reckoning for nine days. In the midst of some spare clothes and a blanket, AscendantSun found a sack containing pyrite, flint, and dried fungus for tinder, and another containing ointments and bandages.

"Oh, and you must wear this until you have left the valley," DawnGlow said as he passed AscendantSun a bright yellow hooded cloak.

"A bit flashy, isn't it," AscendantSun said.

"In the gloom outside, it won't be. Civilian garments of any hue other than yellow have been banned for some time and incur a hefty fine. Saffron is restricted for military use. The last thing you want to be doing if you meet a patrol is wearing proscribed colors."

"You should take the battlefield pieces," NoName said glumly to his twin. "I will not need them where I am going."

DawnGlow dashed upstairs and returned with three silver goblets. He filled them from one of his casks and passed one to each of the Auctors.

"When the old AscendantSun ensnared me in this scheme, he plied me with his last decent honey wine. Now I share the last of my favorite vintage with you." He tapped on the cask to illustrate its hollowness. "A toast and a prayer. May the Golden Light illuminate both your paths."

The twins nodded politely and drank from their goblets. AscendantSun said, "My friend, could you leave us again for a few moments. NoName and I need to exchange some final, private words."

"Of course," DawnGlow said. The casualness of his words failed to hide his distress. "But do hurry. Remember the patrols. AscendantSun has to leave as soon as possible," he blurted as he dashed up the stairs.

"Best mead indeed," NoName commented when the door shut. "Tasted as sour as misery to me. I left most of it in the cup."

"I thought it tasted fine," AscendantSun said. "Though I admit it was not particularly good. I guess decent mead is rare these days. Anyway, DawnGlow's prayer reminded me that we have not entreated the Forelight for his protection."

"Not to do so would be a serious oversight. Strange that DawnGlow should invoke a god in whom he holds no faith."

"I suppose he has no better means to express his concern for our safety. Wishing us good luck lacks the gravitas of his true sentiments."

"Possibly."

They were in the midst of the Forelight's Prayer, arms raised in the air, heads pressed against their shoulders, when DawnGlow interrupted them.

"AscendantSun must leave now," he urged. "There is no time to waste."

The twins exchanged final, brief farewells. AscendantSun gathered his gear and hurried upstairs.

DawnGlow shut the cellar door and gave him a slim leather envelope, embossed with a spread two-thumbed hand.

"Inside you will find the pass I promised to give you. Hopefully you will not need it."

As AscendantSun tucked it away, something crashed downstairs.

"I wish your twin would be a little more careful practicing," DawnGlow groaned. "The both of you hacked and slashed so many posts and beams down there, that I feared you were going to collapse the house." He noticed AscendantSun's scowl. "Only joking. Don't get annoyed."

"I know. I'm not," AscendantSun lied, hoping to end the matter. DawnGlow, like all Fulgurs, was so prone to exaggeration at times. Other than the episode with the keg, any damage the twins had caused was minor. Once or twice, a batonaxe might have chipped the wall or scuffed the floor. That was all. AscendantSun was about to set out on a journey that promised at best exile and at worst death, and his friend was needling him about scratches in his furnishings.

DawnGlow led him to the entrance hall and quenched the candles. “A precaution against the light attracting the notice of patrols when we open the door,” he explained.

Both of them slipped outside. AscendantSun looked up at the dark, dreary sky for the first time in over nine months and shivered. Winter’s bite was in the air; its breath whistled about him.

“It is not as dark as you claimed it would be,” he commented as he surveyed the ashen landscape. In the distance, he could discern the wink of lanterns atop of the black walls of Tincranny. A sliver of shadow projected above the battlements—the city’s gnomon—its golden hand unburnished by a reclusive sun. The brittle light from the snowy peaks that girdled the valley of Tincranny barely penetrated the gloom.

“This is a fine day,” explained DawnGlow. “The clench of the Ill-weather is weakening, it is true. The Golden Light breaks the White Light’s grip on the world one finger at a time. The frost’s sting may be fleeting, but it is never far away. The day is stronger, but it still tires quickly. I hear there is hunger and death in the Stretches. The Ill-weather has picked them clean like a famished scavenger. Are you sure you will find a welcome there?”

“The Stretchers are generous hosts and do not forget their friends,” AscendantSun said. “They will provide what they can.”

DawnGlow grimaced. “But they are so”—he searched—“transient.”

"They are transient, but they are not born with the spring and then die with the autumn. They measure their lives in dozens of years. Do not confuse the brevity of their existence with the intensity of their attachment to their loved ones. Though we have been friends since before the beginning of the world, I promise you there are Stretchers who love their friends as much as we love each other, and perhaps even more, since they love in the face of certain death."

AscendantSun was being disingenuous. Some Stretchers could be fickle in their friendships and treacherous in their dealings with others. But if he admitted to such complexities, DawnGlow would seize on them as proof he was right about their natural inferiority.

DawnGlow half-sang an old poem by BrightGleam Risus.

"They are sparks dying in night's arms,
We are of the eternal flame.
They are raindrops flung from the sky
Broken and scattered on the ground,
We are streams rising from the earth
Carving our course with the seasons."

AscendantSun interrupted his friend's rendition. "I had better go," he said.

"Agreed," said DawnGlow. "This is not the time for a philosophical debate." He made the sign of the open hand. "May the sun illuminate your path."

***

NoName lay motionless at the foot of the stairs. The door creaked open. Footfalls descended. He tried to move his head to see who was coming, but it refused to budge. His body was as dead as stone.

"You gave me quite a scare when you made that noise," DawnGlow said as he stepped over him, grabbed his arms, and heaved him across the floor. "For a moment, I feared your twin would want to investigate. I managed to distract him with a bit of banter. You obviously realized you were drugged and tried to get up the stairs. I was lucky to get him out of the cellar before the drug took effect."

DawnGlow looked down on NoName with the detachment of a spider eying its freshly envenomed prey. He rested NoName's arms across his chest, and then evidently changing his mind, placed them by his sides.

As DawnGlow stood over him, batonaxes in hand, NoName groped for an appropriate reaction, but his emotions were as dead as his body.

"Your goblet was laced with an extract of the Purple Bellowtongue," DawnGlow said. "I assume you are unaware of its properties. You never took much of an interest in herbs. Diluted sufficiently, the extract is a pleasurable relaxant. However, at the dosage you ingested, muscles are relaxed to the point of unresponsiveness. The victim is paralyzed, though conscious."

In NoName's deadened state, rage at this betrayal was impossible. DawnGlow, standing above him, looked so far way.

"Before I kill you, I owe you a few words of explanation," DawnGlow said. "You know that many lifetimes ago, I lost my faith in the Golden Light. His defeat in Gules and our subsequent humiliation convinced me he was either dead or had forsaken us. While others found his hand in everything that happened to us here, I saw fickle chance. I grimaced as they praised Aurelian for what we had achieved by our own toil. I loathed them as they engaged in the basest forms of sophism to excuse some capricious punishment he meted us, or his petulant refusal to answer our prayers."

A little feeling was returning to NoName's fingers. He tried to move them. They trembled.

"Yet it was in truth I who clung to specious arguments," DawnGlow said, striking his open hand against his chest. "I ignored the truth to which I myself am a witness—the divinity of Aurelian. Who am I to question the Golden Light? Who am I to judge the ways of my creator or those of his divine kindred? Do I set fire to the sky? Do I breathe life into the earth?"

NoName felt his anger build. The drug was beginning to wear off, but slowly. Too slowly. The only hope was that DawnGlow would be even more long-winded than usual.

DawnGlow shook his head sadly. "I was intoxicated on my own vanity, till the Ill-weather sobered me. All my lives, I treasured reason above all else. I thought it made me an eagle surveying the world in a glance, but I was no more than a buzzing fly, obsessed with trivial details and understanding nothing. My reason is nothing. I am nothing. The Harbinger of the Dawn whom I once condemned as a fool has opened my eyes. Faith foresaw the Ill-weather while reason failed to predict it."

Keep talking, NoName urged as he flexed his fingers a little. *Must be careful. If DawnGlow notices my movement is returning, he won't wait to finish his speech.*

"When the old AscendantSun first involved me in his schemes, I was struggling to admit this to myself. When I finally did, my collaboration with the Harbinger's greatest enemy left me in a quandary. I did not want to betray my friend, but I could not allow him to harm Aurelian's prophet. AscendantSun's division solved this conundrum. The new AscendantSun is the best part of his forbear: the thinker, the dreamer, the idealist. My conscience was easy in aiding his flight to the Stretches. Hopefully, he will realize his folly and repent. On the other thumb, you are the diseased portion of my old friend's character: the fanatic, the assassin. With your death, that rottenness will be destroyed, and I will foil the murder plot against the Harbinger."

NoName tried with all his might to leap up and throw himself at his would-be executioner. His fingers stirred but his limbs remained as dead as stone. He tried to scream, cry for help, curse DawnGlow, anything, but his efforts produced only a dull gurgle in his throat.

DawnGlow turned NoName's head away.

Turn me back around, you coward, NoName raged. *Don't hide from my eyes as you murder me.*

The shadows of raised batonaxes stretched before him. "I am so sorry," DawnGlow whispered.

***

As the banging of AscendantSun's fist on the hostel's front door received no reply, he let himself in. He bristled at this delay, but he had only himself to blame. In his haste, he had forgotten the battlefield pieces. He shouldn't have turned back, but he possessed so few relics of his past, he could not bear to part with them.

A deaf silence greeted his exploratory salutes. DawnGlow had to be with NoName in the cellar. AscendantSun tramped down the hall and swung open the cellar door.

He saw the batonaxes in DawnGlow's hands, the body lying at his feet.

Battle roars shattered the astonished silence. In one motion, AscendantSun swung the batonaxes from his shoulder-rack and flung himself down the stairs.

DawnGlow closed on the base of the steps, his weapons ready to strike.

As the rolling AscendantSun reached the bottom, his legs unfurled. Thrusting through DawnGlow's batonaxes, they delivered a violent blow to the Or's chest, knocking him across the room.

AscendantSun sprang to his feet.

In the far corner, DawnGlow used the wall to begin to crawl from the floor.

"Stay down," AscendantSun pleaded. "I have never killed an Or before. Don't make yourself the first."

But DawnGlow did not stay down. Still winded, he rose unsteadily to his feet.

"Stay down," AscendantSun repeated, though the determination with which DawnGlow picked his batonaxes off the ground made it clear his plea was useless.

His fists clutching his weapons, DawnGlow charged, thrusting the points of the batonaxes at AscendantSun's face.

AscendantSun crouched, and slipping a batonaxe beneath DawnGlow's weapons, yanked them forward, pulling their wielder onto the spike of AscendantSun's other batonaxe.

The spike punctured DawnGlow's chest. His roar choked on the blood surging up his throat. As he collapsed on the ground, batonaxes clattered against the cellar floor.

AscendantSun stood where he was, empty-handed, as DawnGlow spat out his last bloody, gurgling breath.

When he did not rise again, AscendantSun turned to NoName. His gaze shifted helplessly back and forth between his twin's motionless body and DawnGlow's corpse. He had killed before, many times, in many lives, but this was different. This was another Or and a friend—or at least, he had been a friend. AscendantSun was lost in the shock of what he had done, as paralyzed as his twin.

NoName's low groan woke him from his daze. He knelt down, pressed his twin to his chest, and wept for lost innocence.

***

AscendantSun's eyes were drawn to the blood seeping through the cloth over his dead friend. "Everything DawnGlow said since our forbear came here may be false," he said.

"Our comrades in the Stretches may be dead," NoName said. "And the Harbinger's grip over our people is certainly stronger than we were led to believe. If DawnGlow could be corrupted, then nobody is immune to the Harbinger's fanaticism. Nobody can be trusted."

"Both paths before us are precarious," AscendantSun agreed. "I will journey to Sunrest and attempt to stop the Harbinger, while you must seek to learn the fate of our friends in the mountains."

"You will not," NoName declared. "The destiny written on your face is indelible."

"The stains on my forehead are insignificant compared with that on my soul. I have shed the blood of another Or. Despite his treachery, DawnGlow was our friend. You had no part in his slaying. I must bear the guilt of it alone. We both know only another atrocity will stop the Harbinger. Fine words or clever arguments will not dissuade him. He must die."

NoName nodded. "And I am ready to do what must be done."

"You speak as though we are interchangeable. That..." AscendantSun pointed at DawnGlow's corpse. "That differentiates us. The old AscendantSun divided to insulate his lineage from the consequences of the Harbinger's murder. He understood guilt would kill the Harbinger's slayer if he survived the deed. Division provided the means to stop the Harbinger and at the same time preserve our lineage. I am already a murderer. Therefore, I must be the one who deals with the Harbinger."

You can argue as much as you like, AscendantSun thought. *But you are going to the mountains.*

"Do not blame yourself for DawnGlow's demise." NoName waved toward the corpse as if tossing something away. "You acted in my defense. You offered him every opportunity to surrender. We are not long divided. I would have done the same in your place."

AscendantSun shook his head. It all happened so fast. Why hadn't DawnGlow stayed down? Why did he force AscendantSun to kill him? The original AscendantSun should never have dumped this predicament on DawnGlow. It was unnatural, cruel. And it had cost DawnGlow his life.

"What you might have done is irrelevant. The critical point is that you had no hand in DawnGlow's demise," AscendantSun said, wiping a tear away.

"This is foolishness. Shed no tears for DawnGlow Fulgur." NoName's voice escalated with repressed passion. "Had you not intervened, that coward would have merrily butchered me as I lay helpless on the floor. I doubt he would be weeping over my corpse."

"I weep for DawnGlow because he was once our friend. Do you feel no loss?"

"It is hard to be sorry when I still taste his perfidy on my lips."

"I know we had agreed you would head east, that you have prepared yourself for almost certain oblivion. But that fate is mine now. You must live, or our lineage will fail."

Guilt is gnawing at NoName, AscendantSun mused, *the guilt of the survivor. Well, too bad for him. He has a future with which to salve his pangs of conscience. Only death can free me of my guilt.*

But death might be the beginning of his suffering. His adopted religion proclaimed life after death, and the existence of a heaven and a hell. His acceptance of these tenets had been somewhat abstract. The sprawling immortality bestowed by division had permitted his ancestors to ignore the implications of resurrection. Perpetuating their lineage was their principal focus. As long as it survived, their essence would continue on, their memories and thoughts echoing through the divisions. Death, final and absolute, was not a certainty but merely a hazard to be avoided. The luxury of that apathy was gone. The prospect of such a death filled him with dread.

"You assume whoever goes west will avoid having to fight our people," NoName observed. "You may be wrong."

"I do not assume. I hope."

The twins regarded each other in silence.

"I surrender," NoName said, raising his hands. "If you are determined to throw away your life, I will not stop you." He filled two goblets with mead from one of the casks and passed one to AscendantSun. "Let us toast to a successful outcome of your mission."

AscendantSun reciprocated by toasting to his twin's success. NoName made a third toast, a vinous prayer that they might meet again in happier circumstances. Next, he generously proposed a toast in honor of DawnGlow, followed by a meditative quiet. AscendantSun was moved to take a deep gulp of honey wine each time, despite its dissatisfying tartness.

He smacked his lips to relieve their sudden numbness. Vague light-headedness gave way to debilitating giddiness. The room whirled as he fell. NoName's embrace prevented him from slamming against the floor. He could not move. His muscles were insensible to his bidding.

"You made some fine arguments," NoName said as he laid AscendantSun on the floor. "But action is more eloquent than words. I am afraid you are under the influence of the dregs of the same drugged libation that DawnGlow used to incapacitate me. You ingested a diluted dose, so you should recover quicker than I."

His mouth slipped into a wan smile, but his eyes were dull with sorrow. "By the time you can move, I will be well on my way to the land of Sunrest. In time, your angst over the death of our murderous friend will wane, and you will become reconciled to your part in it. Greater tests of fortitude may await you in the Stretches. Your guilt is naive. Your crime, if it is one, is paltry compared with the assassination of the Harbinger. My heart has already committed that sin a thousand times. If our lineage is to survive, then you must be the seed of its continuation. I am unfit for that purpose. I am corrupted beyond redemption already."

NoName was wrong. He was making a terrible mistake. AscendantSun wanted to scream it, but his corpse-like paralysis prevented him. It was hopeless. NoName had said that his digits recovered first from the drug's effects. AscendantSun's fingers shifted a little at his command.

"I had better go," NoName said. "Your fingers are already starting to twitch. If you do not mind, I will take your backpack since it is already packed. I need this as well."

He undid the clasp of AscendantSun's cloak. The soft cloth pulled AscendantSun onto his side as it slipped from under him.

"Do not dally too long after you have recuperated," NoName warned. "DawnGlow's absence from the city is certain to attract curiosity."

He wished his twin a final farewell, before seizing the backpack and dashing up the stairs. AscendantSun raised a hand and groaned, but NoName had already slammed the cellar door behind him.

It was too late to stop NoName now. AscendantSun had no choice but wait for the drug to wear off, and then head for the mountains.

***

AscendantSun climbed the frosty slopes of Broadwall, leaving spring behind him in the valley. He looked down on the valley of Tincranny and the city that dominated it. Even in the sickly morning light, it shone resplendent, like the heart of an enormous flower, its gardens radiating out like petals. The scent of its smelting works wafted on the breeze like an acrid perfume. He had a strange urge to reach out and pick the city like a flower. Despite its bloody birth, he loved the city. He had nursed it through its precarious early existence and shared its disappointments and triumphs for several lifetimes. It was his home since the fall of Gleam.

The familiar heartache stirred that he might never see it again, this time more intense because of its certainty. It was unlikely his twin would share his sense of loss as he, too, beheld Tincranny for the last time. NoName had other concerns.

Was living so hard that the twins should compete for certain death? Their forbear's scheme to protect his lineage was defective. The flaw was analogous to the saints' concept of original sin. The twins and their progenitor were successive stages in a continuum of consciousness reaching back to the moment that the first Auctor's eyes fluttered open in the maturation tube. One twin could not remain free of guilt when the sin began in the parent.

As was his custom on traveling into the mountains, AscendantSun resolved that he would gaze on his city one last time when he summited the ridge, but before he reached it, a mist descended to thwart his plan. He lingered for a while to see if the accursed veil might dissipate, but his wait was forlorn. He recalled the city and seared it into his memory that he might never forget it.

On the col, surrounded by several rocks, stood an anonymous stone stump. AscendantSun rubbed the snow off it and prayed to the Forelight for forgiveness. This was what remained of the furka that the Stretchers of this valley had died defending so long ago. The Ors had broken off the arms after the battle to impress upon Stretchers that the valley was no longer theirs. AscendantSun consoled himself that the sacrilege had been the act of others, but the familiar shame stirred, nonetheless.

The Stretchers hardly remembered the battle. Those whom MixyBane dispossessed were long dead. Time's passage made their descendants forget the wrong done to them. Only AscendantSun remembered. Only AscendantSun cared.

The brevity of the Stretchers' lives was a gift in one respect. The flow of generations cleansed past sin. The remembrance of old wrongs did not haunt them through the ages, as it did Ors.

Then again, few Ors had as much to regret as AscendantSun. He had sinned against two gods: against the Forelight in the past and now against Aurelian. He was damned from all directions as he trudged across the snow-blurred landscape.

His thoughts drifted again to NoName, and shame surged. It did not matter which of them drove the dagger into the Harbinger's heart. The twins were equally culpable for their forbear's premeditation. All that differentiated them was the prospect of redemption. Confession and penance might exonerate AscendantSun in the Forelight's eyes, if not his own. Death without absolution condemned NoName to eternal damnation. Did NoName comprehend that his sacrifice was so profound? AscendantSun declined to dwell on that dark thought. Despair was a luxury that he could not afford as he headed toward an uncertain fate in the Stretches.

Chapter 12

Beware the desolate mountains of the Stretchers,
For that land is as treacherous as its masters,
Prone to trickery and malevolent caprice;
Every rock and stone, every tree and bush,
Every blade of grass, every drop of water,
Desires to betray, a trap for the unwary.

-From *On Hunting* By BrightGleam Risus.

The stone furka's trunk was drenched in the blood of the warriors heaped at its feet, its surfaces chipped by the crossbow bolts that mowed them down. Some of the centurions had bristled at IronWill Defensor's orders, preferring to fight at close quarters, but the legate had been adamant. He had witnessed long ago at the Battle of Tincranny the high price exacted by defenders of a furka in hand-to-hand combat, and he was unwilling to pay it. There would be no songs composed to honor this victory, no trophies made of the red and white halos of the vanquished Stretchers, but his side had not suffered a single casualty either.

He smiled as he remembered how the Stretchers' boisterous chant, dripping with hate and bloodlust, turned to confused silence as the crossbowmen formed neat rows beyond the range of their missiles. As the first round of bolts ripped through the mob, the Stretchers howled their disapproval. The legate laughed at their protests as they decried such underhand tactics. He ordered one volley after another, as indignant demands turned to pleading and then to diminishing groans. In the end, the only remaining sound was the legate's laughter.

IronWill personally snuffed out what residual life clung to the bloody, torn corpses. As, one by one, the dead and dying suffered the spikes of his batonaxes, he relished the defeat on their faces. He had not just taken their lives but also robbed their deaths of meaning.

"The fires in the houses are extinguished," the tribune, SunTalon Risus, said.

"Assign a squad to get rid of this mess before it attracts flies," IronWill said with a dismissive wave at the bodies. "Get them to uproot that forked stone as well. Not even a stump is to remain. As for the dwellings, I want them carefully dismantled. Retain any material that may be reused in constructing our fort. Have the palisade repaired. We will keep it in place till we have built our own wall."

SunTalon nodded. "Pardon, Legate. Perhaps you have noticed there is little enthusiasm for this victory. Many regard the battle as an anticlimax."

IronWill sighed. Must the only battle to satisfy the Ors be one offering them the prospect of heroic death? The Ors were nearly as obsessed with martyrdom as these idiot Stretchers. "When we raise the gnomon, I will remind them this conquest is the first step in the Harbinger's campaign to extirpate the Stretchers. There will be plenty more battles to slake their thirst for glory."

***

In all directions, the Bonefield stretched, a vast, arid plateau flagged with fractured stone. The only hints of life were small plants here and there, bravely eking out an existence in the black crevices, and random sprinkles of small animal droppings, but the blue and gold flesh of the peeled sky promised some sort of summer had come to the mountains. All that AscendantSun had to do was cross this waste to find it. After his incarceration in DawnGlow's dank cellar, the warm sunshine against his skin was a surprise and a sumptuous treat. For a time, the terrible events in the Hostel of Fulgur were forgotten. Then clouds crept across the sky and walled away the sun again, plunging him back into his personal gloom.

He caught the faint sound of flute and drum tossed about by the wind. The tune was familiar—a legionary march—and it was getting louder. The music spurred his progress across the barren plain. When he reached the higher ground on its western edge, curiosity overcame caution, and, concealed amongst the rocks, he waited.

He watched the army slither across the plain like a giant, saffron snake. It was two cohorts or maybe bigger. Batonaxers in the vanguard exhibited their martial prowess by twirling their weapons in the air. The batonaxes would have shone as though afire in the glare of the sun, but in the Ill-weather's gloom the display lost some of its flamboyance. A squad of musicians followed, playing their proud tune, then an endless procession of legionaries interspersed with cattle-drawn carts laden with victuals and other supplies.

The scene was like a memory from Gules brought to life. The war he had hoped to avert was close or perhaps had already begun, but he wanted to know more, so he followed the column. Its blatant trespass was impressive, but the army had little to fear. It was more than a match for Stretchers mustered from a half-dozen villages, and the Stretchers were incapable of such a coalition.

That evening, while the invaders encircled their town of tents with fresh ditches, AscendantSun retreated beyond the range of their patrols and work parties to find less salubrious nocturnal shelter. The blurry sheen of Gules soon reddened the overcast night skies. It was hard not to be jealous of the army's flickering campfires as AscendantSun pulled his cloak about him to squeeze out the chill dampness of his makeshift shelter.

When morning came, he awoke cold and tired. He forced himself to chew on some of his rations as he waited for the army to uproot and continue its journey. Snatches of lighthearted breakfast banter playing on the breeze mocked his isolation.

In the subsequent days, AscendantSun's puzzlement increased at the Stretchers' indifference to the Ors' incursion. The local Stretchers could not defeat two cohorts in pitched battle, but they could have carried out hit-and-run skirmishes or at least harried the column with arrows. Yet the army's brazen parade met no challenge, however cursory. It was as if the Stretches had been emptied of its people, and the Ors marched through virgin lands unclaimed and nameless.

By the fourth day, it was apparent the army's destination was the village of Cliffringden. Perched atop terraced escarpments, the village boasted formidable natural defenses, but it was too small, and its defenders too few to withstand two cohorts for long.

The locals had to be warned. Batonaxes in both hands, AscendantSun slipped ahead of the plodding army and darted through bedraggled forests, across scrubland and lichen-daubed scree. His goal was the Serpentine and the footbridge spanning its blue waters. The bridge was little more than a few logs lashed together. If AscendantSun cut the ropes, it would collapse into the river, slowing the army's advance enough for the Cliffringdeners to make their escape.

Looking down on the narrow valley through which the Serpentine coiled, he discovered the bridge was gone. In its place stood a far grander structure—one broad enough to accommodate the army's rapid crossing. Two squads of legionaries stood guard. The village must have already fallen, its inhabitants having fled or been slain.

Fighting his dejection, AscendantSun descended into the valley. It was important to test his supposition. He had to see Cliffringden's charred remains, to witness the calamity that his own kind had wrought on its innocent populace. He needed a reminder why he had become a traitor to his race.

He descended into the valley and followed the Serpentine upstream till he found a fallen tree spanning the river. Securing his weapons and baggage, he slung himself under the trunk and used his arms and knees to crawl along it. The river's spray moistened the back of his neck. The log groaned and sagged as he reached halfway, encouraging him to redouble his pace. It was a relief to plant his legs on the far bank. Such a foolish risk should not be repeated.

Wary of patrols, he adopted the most circuitous path across the mountains to Cliffringden. From the brink of a plunging cliff, he could see the piled escarpments rising in the center of the valley. Instead of the haphazard collection of burnt-out log cabins and a broken stakewall that AscendantSun had expected, a stern fortress was perched on the summit. The great, golden hand totem rising high above its walls left no doubt as to its occupants.

At the base of the hill a large black smudge indicated a recent conflagration, perhaps a pyre for Cliffringden's slaughtered inhabitants. AscendantSun shuddered. If he had left Tincranny a few days earlier, he might have been in time to save them.

The music of chipped rock and chopped wood echoing through the valley mingled with the marching tune of the approaching army. It crossed the valley and climbed earthen ramps to disappear inside the fortress.

He had seen enough. The stronghold's purpose was obvious. It was a foothold for further conquest.

He set off for Pigsknuckle. Hopefully, it had not yet fallen.

Chapter 13

Beneath the furka, the men stood,
Their spear points and daggers aglow
With the setting sun's fiery blood,
Poised to strike the oncoming foe.

-From *The Martyrdom of Coneyriddle.*

They came as a feeble spring finally pushed aside with great difficulty the long winter's icy pall.

The tattered column of refugees limped through the forest like a wounded animal. Mothers with granite faces hushed weeping children with comforting lies and empty promises. Other women hid tears for lost husbands and sons. The infirm and elderly pleaded to be abandoned, while neighbors and friends patiently carried them. Boys on the cusp of manhood cursed their immaturity, under the delusion their presence might have saved their fathers.

A lucky few carried bundles of possessions on their heads. The rest had not much more than the clothes on their backs and whatever remained in their bellies to sustain them.

Lips whispered entreaties for the Forelight's protection or his forgiveness. Noises real and imagined caused ears to sift the wind for hints of pursuit. Eyes searched for dangerous stirrings in the wood. Everyone who was fit to carry a weapon held one: a spear, a farm tool, a knife, a stone, or a branch.

Crouched like predators behind leaf and shadow, Grael and Dawan watched the ghostly procession trickle through the forest. The refugees wore the red and white halos of Cliffringden. Very soon, their vanguard would stumble on the furka at Leaftea Lake.

"What should we do?" Dawan whispered to Grael. "Should we speak to them?"

"If we emerge suddenly from the forest, the refugees may panic and scatter, or worse, attack us. Our politician should speak for Pigsknuckle," Grael said.

"You can run back to the village and warn Garscap," Dawan said. "I'll continue to shadow these intruders."

Grael resisted the urge to protest. He despised the Changeling, but these lost souls needed an advocate better than Dawan. The arrival of the Orstretcherists had illustrated Garscap's contempt for outsiders. It was unsurprising that they remained in Pigsback and never visited the village.

Grael crept through the undergrowth till he was clear of the Cliffringdeners' searching eyes, then ran to Pigsknuckle. As he reached the great hall, he saw Harath carrying a bundle of clothes, heading in the same direction.

Unable to avoid her, he asked, "How are you?" Now that she was married to Garscap, there was no restriction on speaking to her, but it did not make their encounter any less awkward.

Looking upon her, the anger flooded back, the aching sense of loss opened up again. To think he had let her slip away. He had been a fool to consent to his parents' wishes and delay their marriage till spring. Garscap wed her the day after Widan gave him the thorny crown. While Grael lay in his sickbed, numbing his ache for her with dreams of elopement and a new life together, the Changeling was binding her to him forever.

"I'm fine," she said with ill-concealed discomfort.

He turned to go, not wanting to add to her unease.

"How are you?" she asked.

Her question held him, but he could not answer it honestly. He still loved her. He needed her. His shame at desiring a married woman, his guilt over her brother's death, and the passage of time had failed to blunt his pining. How could he tell her that?

"I haven't seen you much about the village," she said.

"I've been busy," he answered. Busy avoiding her and her husband. He forced himself to look at her. It was a surprise to find his sadness reflected in her eyes. "Harath…" He spied movement from the corner of his eye. Ashin Carnath's eyes were alert with voracious curiosity as she walked toward them. "I need to speak to your husband."

If Harath sensed he had meant to say something else, she showed no sign of it. As Ashin strolled by, they exchanged salutations with her.

"It's an urgent matter," Grael said to Harath. "A crowd of women and children wearing Cliffringden's colors are near Leaftea Lake."

"Forelight protect us!" she exclaimed, her free hand flying to her chest. "What happened to Cliffringden?"

He shrugged. "I don't know. My guess is that the Fair Folk attacked it."

"Garscap was in the great hall when I left him," Harath said. Still clinging to her bundle, she jogged toward the building.

Grael's apprehension built with every step as he trailed after her. He hoped Garscap wouldn't notice he and Harath had arrived together. As Grael entered the hall, he readied for an arched smile from Garscap, perhaps succeeded by some sarcastic remark verging on offensive.

The Politician of Pigsknuckle sat cross-legged by the hearth, mesmerized by its dancing flames, oblivious to the chatter around him. Evram was ensconced to his right. To his left sat Evram's widowed father, Maergan, whose gaunt features were half-submerged in a thicket of wiry hair too black for his age. To Maergan's left was Fapath Carnath, his prominent brow ridges depressed into a permanent frown over dark, suspicious eyes, the black hair on his crown and jaw line streaked with white. Maergan stopped mid-sentence when he noticed Grael. Fapath's scowl deepened. Evram sneered.

Grael struggled to conceal his disgust at finding the politician and his cronies lazing about and drinking beer when there was plenty of work to be done.

"Grael Erol must speak with you," Harath said, breaking the fire's spell over her husband.

"Then be silent and let him speak," Garscap snapped.

Harath flung her bundle away and stormed from the hall.

"I wouldn't countenance my wife behaving in such a fashion," Evram said. "Begging your pardon, Garscap."

"She did what she was told," Garscap said.

"Her problem is pride," Maergan said. "She does not know her place."

"I'm sure she would say much the same about me," Garscap said, eliciting guffaws from his companions. "Grael, come sit down and tell me your troubles."

Grael remained standing while he described what he had seen in the forest. As he finished, despair seized him. What mercy could these wandering women and children expect from men such as these?

"Damn the Fair Folk," Garscap said. "This is their doing."

"The Fair Folk have not attacked a village since Martyrsgrave," Maergan said, his gray eyes stretched with surprise. "The saints promised another such calamity was impossible."

"What do saints know of war?" Garscap asked. "What other devilry could force women and children to abandon their village? Where are their men if they are not dead? The Fair Folk are at the root of this."

He sprang to his feet. "Fapath, send two of your sons as far south as the Witchmilk River in case more than these refugees are heading our way. Maergan, spread the word that the men are to gather by the village furka and then head to Leaftea. Make sure they approach it from the north under the cover of forest so that the Cliffringdeners get no hint of their presence. Grael and I will go ahead and meet the Cliffringdeners at the furka. Evram, you will go to Pigsback and fetch Saint Charlin."

Grael frowned. Garscap had largely ignored his existence since he took the thorny crown from Widan. This sudden desire for his company was puzzling and unwelcome.

"I will stay with you," Evram said as he stood. "Grael is Saint Charlin's brother. He can get him."

"Do as you are told," Garscap said. "And stop annoying me."

"Have you anything else to say before I go?" Evram growled as he stood up.

"Be careful," Garscap said. "On the mountain," he added.

***

Grael walked alongside Garscap toward Leaftea Lake, thankful for the politician's pensive quiet.

"I hope you bear me no ill will over Harath," Garscap said. "My marriage to her was Widan's idea. I had to agree to it if bloodshed was to be avoided."

Grael said nothing. Anything more conciliatory than silence would be a lie.

"You should take comfort in your lucky escape. The woman bludgeons me so often with her opinions that I am forced to question sometimes who is the politician and who is the wife." Garscap's inviting chuckle dissolved amidst Grael's dearth of acknowledgment. "All joking aside, our estrangement saddens me. We were friends once, you and I. I helped you win Widan's permission to journey to Formicary in a roundabout way. The adventure did not turn out too badly for you, despite its trials. As far as I am concerned, any dispute between us was buried in Horgal's Field. I bear only goodwill toward you and your family."

The silence begged Grael to reciprocate. "I will think on what you said."

"Can I at least depend on your support during this crisis, for the sake of Cliffringden's widows and orphans? There are many in the village who will not take kindly to what I intend to do. They will say I am taking food out of their children's mouths to feed strangers. They will accuse me of hypocrisy because I condemned the hospitality lavished on the Orstretcherists."

This was too much. Grael could not believe what he was hearing. Garscap's claims were outrageous. No Pigsknuckler would be so uncharitable.

"You look shocked," the politician said. "Do you think I would abandon women and children to fend for themselves in the wild? Others might claim an inability to feed such a multitude and encourage them to move on, but not I. You must know my history. If Pigsknuckle had not offered a home to my mother after the Fair Folk destroyed her village, I would not be walking beside you now. How could I not extend the same charity to these poor wretches? We can manage. I'm sure we can. We'll prevail upon the saints to increase the mysterious bounty of game that they provide to the village."

They climbed the bumpy hill overlooking Leaftea Lake. Below, knotted clusters of refugees extended from the edge of the forest to the furka near its dark water. A sizable crowd huddled there, their doleful entreaties to Forelight carried across the valley by the breeze. The children sat by their guardians, their natural exuberance spent by fatigue and sorrow.

"I'll do anything I can to help the Cliffringdeners," Grael promised solemnly.

"That will do for now," Garscap said.

They walked on in a more affable quiet, till Garscap's curse tore it apart. "Bitch!" he hissed.

It was a struggle to make sense of his companion's profanity till Garscap thrust an angry finger at the crowd gathered around the furka. In its midst stood Harath, a toddler in her arms, a group of women in intense discourse around her.

Garscap's visage burned with violent fury. By coming here alone, Harath had slighted his authority both as her politician and her husband.

What might Grael have to do to protect Harath from her husband's wrath? Trying to placate him now would only exacerbate his anger. The furka shielded Harath for the moment. By the time she left its sanctuary, Garscap's temper might have cooled enough for soothing words to appease it. It was best not to dwell on what Grael might be forced to do if words failed and action was demanded.

Grael's repeated glances at Garscap searched for some hint that his volcanic rage was waning. In an instant, it was gone. A broad smile spread across his face. The smolder in his glassy blue eyes was the only hint of his former indignation.

"Apologies for my intemperate language," he said. "Concern for my wife was its cause. I was shocked to see her giving succor to the refugees. It's clear her charitable inclination overwhelmed her good sense. There's no telling what danger she might have faced in coming here alone and unarmed."

From what Grael could see, the only threat to her here was her husband. "I am sure her welfare was in your thoughts when you spoke."

Garscap's grin stretched. "My wife is braver than most men. And tougher, too. She would be happier if she was born a man, but then she'd be of no use to me."

Harath stumbled up the scree to meet them. Her face was deathly white, but the look of condescension directed at her husband proclaimed fear of him was not the cause of her pallor.

After a cursory greeting, she confirmed what both men had suspected—Cliffringden had been destroyed. An Elfin army had swept it away. The village had survived five hundred years of hardship, and its founding saint had promised that it would endure till Judgment Day, so a belief was prevalent among the survivors that the end times had come.

Somewhere within the charred ribs of the village, the corpses of their menfolk lay. Piety and honor had made them defend their furka from the teeming hordes of Elfin warriors bent on its destruction. Some of the bereaved took comfort in the hope their loved ones' martyrdom was not in vain and they had exacted a high price from the Fair Folk for their lives.

"I promised you would help them," Harath said.

"And help them I will," Garscap said. "Though it is not your place to speak for me. Our marriage does not give you any special privilege to flout my authority. You would be wise to remember that in future. I promise these poor wretches will receive better help from Pigsknuckle than my pregnant mother did when your grandfather was its politician."

***

Like a wreck of whingeing gulls, the women's thanks pursued Garscap as he returned to the forest. He left Grael and Harath behind to comfort them, claiming he had to head back to Pigsknuckle to meet with the villagers before they set out for Leaftea. But his main purpose was to escape from the desperate, grief-stricken faces. They stirred memories of his mother, emotions too bitter to conceal. He feared the tearful burning in his eyes, the peculiar weakness it betrayed. Harath must not witness him cry. She must never have the satisfaction.

Safe from prying eyes, he could hold back no longer. Hot tears rained down his face, returning him to his miserable childhood.

He chuckled between sobs. This was ridiculous. All the hardships, frustrations, and disappointments of his adult life had not squeezed from him a single tear, and he was suddenly crying rivers for a woman whom he knew only from second-hand remembrances. She had gone mad, he was told. She believed him to be a changeling, and no assurance of the saints could alter that conviction. She threw herself into the Witchmilk, leaving her son playing on its bank alone. The story was worn into his consciousness, but he retained no true memory of it. The face haunting his recollection was the stuff of others' words and wishful thinking, shifting with his mood.

The weight of his grief crushed the attempt to laugh it off. Tears blurred his vision. He had seen something of his mother in those defeated faces by the furka, perhaps not her features, but the shape of her suffering. Granyr's plight after the Battle of Martyrsgrave had been worse. She had become separated from the other survivors. Lost and alone, she had sought sanctuary at the same furka now surrounded by Cliffringdeners. If only he could relive his childhood before madness seized her to have a chance to undo whatever part he had in it, so she might be saved and live to see her son become the politician of the village that had barely tolerated her. Dwelling on such impossible desires was absurd. The past could not be reshaped except in misty dreams that died with the morning.

What laughter failed to budge, pride now pushed aside. It was unseemly for the Politician of Pigsknuckle to bawl like a spoiled toddler. Imagine Widan's ugly sneer on witnessing his rival succumb to such pitiable sentimentality.

As Garscap wiped the tears from his eyes, he promised they would be his last. He shoved his mother from his thoughts and turned his attention to more pressing issues.

He found the Pigsknucklers still mustering in the center of the village. When Maergan and others commented about the redness of his eyes, he blamed an infection, confident they would assume its nature to be physical rather than spiritual.

***

Garscap sat in his old hut, staring into the heart of the fire. He'd left the great hall to the refugees. The Pigsknucklers took some into their homes, bark huts were thrown up to house more, but the great hall was still packed. He had no desire to stay in such cramped conditions, with weeping women and children pressing in from all sides and the dreary thrum of their misery disturbing the night. Here, he was alone with the fire and his thoughts.

The Elfin army had not pursued the refugees beyond the Witchmilk, but that did not mean its invasion of Pigsknuckle's territory was not imminent. It might come tomorrow or the following day, or in a month, or in a year. Garscap didn't know what had reignited their long dormant belligerence, but the Orstretcherists' pilgrimage to Pigsback was probably not coincidental. From the first moment they'd arrived in Pigsknuckle, they had an aura of trouble. If Elves attacked Pigsknuckle, the villagers would be no match for them. Cliffringden didn't even have a chance to summon help from its neighbors before it was annihilated.

A chill draught heralded Evram's entrance. "Saint Charlin will be here presently," he said, blushing. "I apologize for my behavior earlier."

"I sent you to Pigsback because I trust you," Garscap said. "And I needed to sound out Grael. Those disaffected with my rule are likely to rally around him. I had to know if he would exploit the current crisis to attempt to overthrow me. Fortunately, he won't. He's too idealistic. So for the moment, my only concern is Widan."

Evram sneered. "What about him? Widan had his chance. He gave away the thorny crown. Why would anybody give it back? And you are his son-in-law. He should be satisfied that one of his grandchildren will become the politician in time."

"He has no grandchildren yet. Do you think the other Melkaths will suffer to be ruled by my offspring in perpetuity? Widan would rather be seen as their natural leader than let that role slip to another. Perhaps, he may remarry. A male child from such a union would usurp any affection he held for Harath. Her children would be tainted with my blood. If my popularity wanes a little more, Widan may forget his promises in Horgal's Field."

Saint Charlin blessed the hut as he entered. The saint could not hide his discomfort at the politician's extravagant welcome. Garscap's dismissal of Evram was gentle but firm. Evram, still contrite for his earlier transgression, withdrew without complaint.

"Sit down, Worthy Saint," Garscap said, indicating a place by the fire.

"I can't stay," Charlin said, waving his hand. "Pressing matters elsewhere in the village demand my attention."

"Sit down and rest yourself a few moments," Garscap said. "You visited the Cliffringdeners. You must give me an account of what you found."

"I should be with them now," the saint said as he sat down. "They mourn for dead fathers and sons, husbands and brothers, even well-regarded neighbors. Their bereavement is so immense they can scarcely comprehend it. For the present, the absence of tangible proof of their loss tempers their sorrow a little, but in the coming days, that lack will turn grief into anger. You will face heated demands for an expedition to Cliffringden to reclaim the bodies of beloved dead. For now, the survivors most keenly feel the loss of their village. Everything they have ever known is gone, and with it, in some instances, their faith. Those cases demand intense religious counsel."

"And their physical needs?" Garscap asked.

"My primary concern is their spiritual welfare," Saint Charlin said, blushing. "The flesh passes, but the soul is everlasting. However, from what I have seen, Pigsknuckle has provided amply for their material wants."

It was annoying the saint gave him so little credit. But for Garscap, the refugees might be still starving at Leaftea Lake. With no advantage to be gained by antagonizing his guest, he chose not to draw the saint's attention to this fact. He broadened his smile. "Thank you."

"Of course, your leadership deserves great praise in this matter," the saint said hoarsely as if choking on his words.

Garscap sniffed opportunity in Charlin's awkward commendation. The scent was intoxicating. "I am gratified you think so, Saint. I fear others who covet my position might not be so charitable to these widows and orphans. Some of my rivals whisper against my magnanimity. They claim it overburdens Pigsknuckle's resources and puts the well-being of its people at risk. They say I should have offered the refugees a meal and then sent the majority of them on their way, permitting only the few who might be of long-term benefit to the village to remain. The old and the infirm can find shelter elsewhere."

"No true Stretcher would condone such sinful cruelty," Charlin said.

"My detractors cast their arguments less bluntly than I put them to you," Garscap said. "These are hard times. First, the Year of Bleeding Snow brought famine to the mountains. Now, as the world recovers, the Fair Folk destroy Cliffringden. People are frightened, and the fearful are susceptible to hate and cruelty. Actions dismissed as barbarous in happier times garner a creeping reasonableness in more desperate circumstances. I am afraid very soon I will be deposed and my good deeds will be undone."

Charlin scowled. "Saints do not dabble in politics." It might have been Sebryn speaking.

"Of course," Garscap said, feigning innocent shock.

Thankfully, the saint's intervention had prevented him from overreaching. Patience and delicacy were required. "The thought never occurred to me that you might meddle in affairs properly my remit. You've always acted with such fastidious impartiality and propriety. I'd never be so bold to ask you to favor me over my rivals. However, the future welfare of the refugees is our common concern. If you spoke to the village on the merits of charity and the damning sinfulness of forsaking fellow Stretchers at their time of greatest need, I'm sure your sermon would put the kindness shown to the Cliffringdeners beyond debate."

Charlin's eyes narrowed. "It would also undermine your enemies."

"You may be right," Garscap admitted. "But that is a political matter and therefore not your concern. If it eases your conscience, I am sure my foes will find fault with me on other issues. The most important and most lasting legacy of your discourse would be the protection of the refugees."

"I will contemplate on what you have said," Charlin promised too smoothly to mean it. He started to rise.

"There is something else that you must consider," Garscap said.

Charlin sighed as he sat back down. "What is it?"

"The men of Cliffringden died to defend their furkas. Before them, the men of Martyrsgrave did the same. What are you going to do to prevent the same happening in Pigsknuckle?"

Charlin blushed. "If the village is attacked, I will deconsecrate the furkas."

"I'm sure the saint in Cliffringden might have deconsecrated its furkas if he had been there instead of away at his monastery," Garscap said as he stoked the fire. "You, too, are not always in Pigsknuckle."

Charlin shrugged and opened his hands. "Well, that can change immediately. We can maintain a saint here at all times, if not me, then someone else from St. Odran's."

"There are seven furkas scattered around Pigsknuckle," Garscap said. "Can you really deconsecrate them all in time for us to escape?"

Charlin frowned. "If I get enough notice."

I'll tell the Elves to give us fair warning of their attack then, Garscap thought.

"I understand that you have lookouts posted now..." Charlin offered.

Garscap nodded. “Everyone gets their turn to guard the village. But that’s no guarantee that you would get sufficient time to deconsecrate seven furkas. It’s no guarantee that you would get any warning at all. The Elves could kill the guards like that.” He snapped his fingers. “So quick that they would be dead before they realized that they under attack. Remember these Elves are the Gilt Spider’s kin.

“And I’ll tell you something else,” Garscap said, pointing a finger at Charlin. “Now that Cliffringden’s fallen, there’s no other village between us and the Elves. An attack is not a matter of *if* but of *when*.”

Charlin’s mouth hung open for a moment. “So what are you suggesting?”

“I’m *suggesting* that all of Pigsknuckle’s furkas should be deconsecrated and knocked down. Now.”

Charlin nodded. He continued to nod as he stood. “I will meditate on your advice.” His voice shivered with unease.

“That’s all I can ask,” Garscap said. *For now.*

Chapter 14

For countless years a village thrived,
In a day, it became a grave,
But the tragic tale has survived
Of its heroes, pious and brave.

~From *The Martyrdom of Coneyriddle.*

The footbridge across the Witchmilk was gone. No trace of legionaries was present in the area, either. Hopefully, the Pigsknucklers had demolished the bridge as a precaution against sudden invasion.

AscendantSun detoured upstream to another crossing point. A series of broad boulders peeping through the brink of a squat waterfall served as a natural bridge for one who was nimble enough to bound over the white water sluicing through the gaps. He crossed it without incident and made his way to Leaftea Lake.

The furka that had stood near its reposing water was shattered. The fractured trunk lay on the ground, surrounded by fragments of the arms. He searched the rubble for clues about its destruction. The sharpness of the breaks, the lack of peeling of the painted surfaces, and the absence of lichen and moss suggested that its demolition was recent. Only Ors could have committed such a sacrilege.

He was too late. He kicked at the grass with frustration. Again, he had failed.

The Pigsknucklers would have never brooked such violent sacrilege, but the area gave no indication of battle. No telltale fragments of bone or weapon lay strewn in the vicinity of the broken stone. The Ors must have passed here before the Pigsknucklers became aware of their approach. Perhaps the invaders had even entered the village before the alarm was raised.

The prospect of what might await him in the ruined village was sickening. The gruesomeness of massacre and its various phases of decomposition were already too familiar. His acquaintance with Pigsknuckle and its inhabitants, even if it largely came second-hand from the saints of St. Odran's or from his own distant observation, added an aching poignancy to his horror.

And what was the monastery's fate? Was it also destroyed? What about his friends who had sought refuge there? Were they dead, too?

A pebble clattered down the scree to his left. He was being observed, and the watcher wanted him to know. It must be a Stretcher. Legionaries would not be so circumspect.

AscendantSun eased his batonaxes from their rack and laid them on the ground. He discarded his knife in the same fashion. He stretched his arms in the air and pressed his head against his shoulder.

From behind the rocks, two awkward figures emerged with taut bows. They wore the white and blue halos of Pigsknuckle. It took a few moments to adjust to their large noses, woolly eyebrows, strange eyes, lopsided faces, and odd proportions. The taller one had a tanned complexion and dark wiry hair. He was young and quite handsome by the standards of his race. Sparse white frizz hugged only the sides of his companion's head, forcing him to secure his halo by means of a chinstrap. His face had the quality of weathered stone. His jaw was fringed with gray hair. Both men had the same gray eyes. Perhaps they were father and son.

"Peace, friends," AscendantSun said. "I honor the Forelight, like you. I am on a pilgrimage to St. Odran's monastery."

The Stretchers glanced at each other uneasily. The furka that might have guaranteed AscendantSun's safety lay broken at his feet. Perhaps the other Orstretcherists were dead. Perhaps, they came here and were murdered.

"If you're telling the truth, you have nothing to fear from us," the younger Stretcher assured him.

"If you can prove it," the older Stretcher added.

"The saints of Pigsback will vouch for me," AscendantSun promised.

"If you fail to do exactly what we say, they won't get the chance," the older Stretcher said as he gathered AscendantSun's weapons. "Put your hands behind your back. Grael, tie them together. Do not even twitch, Elf. Make sure the knot is tight. Our lives may depend on it."

Grael. That name was familiar. The younger Stretcher was possibly the same boy whom AscendantSun had rescued from the Jinglemen, though a year had elapsed since their last meeting, and it was easy to mistake one Stretcher for another. It was tempting to ask, but neither Stretcher would welcome the revelation that the Gilt Spider now stood before them.

"I thought the people of Pigsknuckle were cordial hosts," AscendantSun said as the rope burned into his wrists.

"So were the people of Cliffringden," the old Stretcher said.

AscendantSun made other attempts to converse with his captors, but his tentative queries were either ignored or elicited the curtest of replies. He tired of his guards' terseness and decided to take a risk.

"We have not exchanged introductions," he said.

"We know," the old Stretcher said.

"I am Auctor always, AscendantSun for this lifetime."

The youth's eyes widened with recognition. "This is the Elf who rescued me. The Orstretcherists have been expecting him."

The old Stretcher halted the Or with his spear. He stared hard into AscendantSun's eyes. "What do you think we should do, Grael?"

"He saved my life and nearly paid for it with his own," the young man said.

The old Stretcher introduced himself as Lahan Erol, Grael's father. As he interrogated AscendantSun on the details of his son's rescue, Grael confirmed that the Or's answers were correct.

"If you promise to honor our trust, we will free your hands," Lahan said, sternly wagging his finger. "But you must swear it by two gods: the Forelight, on the assumption that you've told us the truth, and the Golden Light, in case you are a liar."

AscendantSun complied, and Lahan cut his bonds.

"Are there any of my people in the village?" AscendantSun asked, rubbing his wrists.

"Your friends stay in Pigsback," Lahan said. "Many refugees from Cliffringden are sheltering in Pigsknuckle. There's not much welcome for your kind here."

"But we are Stretchers like you," AscendantSun protested.

"You may be Stretchers but you are not like us," Lahan said. "Understand, my family bears you no grudge. We are beholden to you because of your kindness to my son. I am telling you like it is. You'll find no trouble in Pigsknuckle unless you make it. We'll make sure of it. But a lot of people will be none too happy to see an Elf wandering about."

So much for the hospitality of Stretchers! The hostility was understandable given what had happened to Cliffringden, but now was the time for Stretcher and Orstretcherist to come together against their common enemy.

The entire village stared at him as he entered. Chiding mothers dragged their children from his apparently hypnotic presence. Men and women forgot their chores and regarded him in stony silence. On some faces was wonder, on others fear, but on most, loathing. Hands drifted toward weapons as he passed. Without his batonaxes, his two escorts were his only protection. Their warning glances to the other villagers were all that prevented their simmering hatred from boiling over into violence. AscendantSun's apprehension increased when Lahan disappeared inside a small hut, leaving him alone with Grael.

A child with curly brown hair and brown eyes wandered by. It was hard to tell if it was male or female. It stood no taller than AscendantSun's knee. He could not help returning its surprised stare. Mixy children were so peculiarly incomplete.

"Go home to your mother," Grael commanded. "Be a good girl and leave us alone before you get us into trouble."

Urgent arms snatched the child up. Her mother put a good distance between her and AscendantSun before pausing to check her daughter. Then, with a final menacing glance at him, she swept up her child again and continued her flight.

"Keep away from children," Grael cautioned. "People believe Fair Folk steal them."

A chill raced down AscendantSun's spine. "Why would we want them?" he asked.

Grael shrugged. “People believe it. From when I was no older than that child, I was warned not to wander the forest in case the Gilt Spider caught me.”

“I would never hurt a child.” It would be like injuring a twingle. Absolutely heinous.

“I have no doubt of it, but plenty in the village are inclined to believe otherwise. That woman will take her child to Saint Charlin to prove she’s not a changeling.”

“A what?”

“One of your own disguised as a child.”

“You cannot be serious.” The concept was preposterous in so many ways.

“The politician of this village is a changeling according to some, though it would take a man braver than I to say it to his face.”

Lahan peeped out of the hut and beckoned them inside. Grael waved AscendantSun to enter ahead of him.

The man sitting by the blazing fire carved a menacing silhouette against the hut’s shining walls. He lifted his gaze from the hearth and scrutinized AscendantSun, who forced himself to meet the politician’s gaze. His blue eyes possessed a coldness that no flame could touch.

“AscendantSun, this is our politician, Garscap Torp,” Lahan said.

“His hands aren’t bound,” the politician observed. “If he was an assassin, our corpses might now litter this hut.”

“We’re not dead, so he’s not one,” Lahan retorted.

Garscap’s eyes narrowed. “That’s not the point.”

Lahan interrupted the politician before he could elaborate. “He’s the one who saved my son.”

Garscap’s demeanor brightened. “So, you are the Gilt Spider, or at least that was what you claimed to be.”

Could Garscap trust the Gilt Spider? Could the inhabitants of Pigsknuckle learn not to fear him? Impossible.

“What else would one of my kind call himself if he traveled through this land and discovered he must fight a dozen Jinglemen? My adoption of that guise was a ruse to daunt Grael’s captors.”

Garscap’s smile slipped. “So does the Gilt Spider not exist?”

AscendantSun couldn’t be sure what NeverFear and the others had already said on the matter. “I believe another of my race may claim the name.”

Lahan withdrew behind him.

“NeverFear Cor often praises you,” Garscap said. “I have met him a couple of times on my visits to Pigsback. I understand NeverFear intends to relinquish leadership of the Orstretcherists to you on your arrival. Being so esteemed, you must have much influence amongst your comrades.”

“I have what influence they are willing to lend to me.”

“May I speak candidly?”

AscendantSun nodded. He glanced over his shoulder. Grael and Lahan quietly stood behind him. Evidently, they were content to let their leader speak for them.

Garscap threw a log on the fire, creating a splash of sparks. "The Fair Folk's invasion brings a war unfamiliar to most of my people. Our saints ensure conflicts amongst Stretchers are tame affairs. The annihilation of entire villages and the massacre of women and children are horrors with which my people are little acquainted. I used to be a mercenary for the Shadow Folk in Formicary. I fought in conflicts like this. I understand their pitiless nature. But my people do not. They think we have done the Fair Folk some dishonor to bring this calamity to the mountains. It is beyond their comprehension that the Elves want to destroy us utterly. Is that not their intent?"

AscendantSun nodded. "It is."

"You saw the toppled furka by Leaftea Lake? As a Stretcher, you understand its religious significance. It had stood there unharmed for all the generations since Alackalas. Every man in this village would have died to protect it. That is why I had it deconsecrated and destroyed. It was a decision over which I agonized. I knew many would condemn me, but I had no choice. If your friends in the Elfin army blundered across that furka, my people would be compelled to defend it though it meant their death. It happened in Cliffringden, and in Martyrsgrave before that."

Horror shuddered through AscendantSun. The man was correct. Stretchers would sacrifice everything for their sacred objects.

"I hope my words have not offended you," the politician said, inviting AscendantSun to join him by the fire with a wave of his hand. “You must not think I blame you and the other Orstretcherists for these atrocities.”

“Of course not,” AscendantSun said, kneeling down beside him. Fortunately, the politician could not divine the reason for his consternation. Garscap could not guess the Or who stood before him was responsible for the massacre at Martyrsgrave.

“The furka in the village still stands,” Garscap said. “The saints are as reluctant as the villagers to part with it. However, they have agreed to maintain a saint in the village at all times to undo the stone’s deadly blessing at the first hint of invasion.”

Garscap tossed another log on the fire. “That’s not my people’s sole sacrifice. Their village has been overrun by strangers, victims of Cliffringden’s fall. My people go hungry so that their guests have enough food to survive. Pigsknucklers must endure the unedifying spectacle of their politician wandering like a beggar from village to village, flattering and cajoling old enemies like Ogresquern to donate unwanted crumbs to feed our guests.”

He voice was soft, but his eyes burned with anger.

“The people of Pigsknuckle bear all of this without complaint, but on the very rare occasion they do grumble, they direct their ire at Pigsback. They ask me what sacrifices the inhabitants of the monastery make. I tell them the Orstretcherists and the saints pray for us, but the villagers are unimpressed. They can pray for themselves, they say. I say the Elves seek fresh meat for us in the mountains, but the malcontents are unimpressed. My people want to know that, when the war comes to Pigsknuckle, the Orstretcherists will do more than pray and hunt game. I promise them your people will fight by their side, but in truth, I speak in hope rather than certainty."

"Have you discussed this with NeverFear?" AscendantSun asked.

"I've tried," Garscap said, his voice growing louder. "But he is only interested in philosophical vagaries of the type that so enthuse his hosts. He seems unable to understand his moral quibbles won't protect my people in this current crisis. His theological dialog with the saints of Pigsback may have tied him in knots or he can't bring himself to take up arms against his own people. Either way, he needs to cease his dithering and choose a side. We need more warriors, not more saints, if the Fair Folk's invasion is to be halted." His finger thrust at AscendantSun to the rhythm of his rage.

"NeverFear was drawn to Stretcherism because of its compassion for life," AscendantSun explained. "He went into exile to leave war behind him. He wants to live in peace. You are asking him to put aside that dream."

"But that is exactly what it is—a dream. Not reality. You must realize this?"

Too well. NoName must be well on his way to Sunthorn now, drawing ever closer to his victim. "I will talk to NeverFear and the others on your behalf. I can promise nothing, but I will do my best to convince them."

Garscap nodded. “Very good. I can ask for no more than that. Grael, you and Dawan can escort AscendantSun to Pigsback.”

“I will go in Grael’s place,” Lahan said. “We can set out in the morning. It is too late in the day.”

“Nonsense,” Garscap said. “You could easily reach the monastery before nightfall. If you will not accompany AscendantSun there now, he must go alone. In these impassioned times, I can’t guarantee his safety if he remains in the village overnight.”

“I’ll go with him,” Grael said, pointing to AscendantSun. “I would let no Stretcher, whether he is man or Elf, ascend that mountain alone.”

“There is no need,” Lahan said. “I can go in your stead. You haven’t been up there since your…accident.”

“I will go,” Grael insisted. “I’m fit enough for the climb, and I’ll not let the Pig sneer down on me evermore. Dawan can come with me. If you go, too, it’ll double Mam’s worry.”

“You’re a man and know your own mind,” Lahan said.

Mother, father, son, daughter, brother, sister, male, female—such strange concepts. Mixy propagation was so much more convoluted than division. Man and woman joined together, though they never properly knew each other, to create a stranger, an empty mind blind to the past. And yet Mixies loved their kin as much as any Or loved his lineage.

“Then it’s settled,” Garscap said. “Grael, you can return our guest’s weapons after you are clear of the village and its more excitable inhabitants. No need to invite trouble. It has been a pleasure to meet you at last, AscendantSun. I am sure we will meet again very soon."

Prompted by the politician's rising, AscendantSun stood up. AscendantSun took Garscap's offer of his hand.

In midst of their handshake, Garscap frowned and, lifting AscendantSun's hand, stared at it intently. His eyes rounded. "You have an extra thumb on your hand." His eyes shifted to AscendantSun's free hand. "On both hands."

AscendantSun smiled. "No. You are missing thumbs on your hands."

"So all from your race have these appendages? I never noticed before," Garscap said.

"You need to shake their hands more often," AscendantSun quipped.

Grael and Lahan chuckled quietly. It was hard to tell if the expression on Garscap's face was a smile or a grimace.

He tightened his grip on AscendantSun's hand. "Hopefully, I will get the chance."

After their handshake ended, AscendantSun followed Lahan and Grael out of the hut. They led him to a rock outside the village. There, he and Grael waited while Lahan fetched Dawan. After what seemed ages, a scowling youth appeared. He had dirty blond hair and a freckled face. In one hand, he held a spear. In the other, he carried two small sacks.

"Your father asked me to give you this," he said, dropping one of the sacks at Grael's feet.

"Dawan, where's your usual cheer?" Grael asked.

"I won't need it on this trip," Dawan replied, eyeing AscendantSun with deep suspicion.

AscendantSun and his companions followed the trail up the Pig. Grael walked alongside him. Dawan kept a good distance ahead of them, checking over his shoulder at intervals, probably to confirm AscendantSun had not done some terrible mischief to his cousin. AscendantSun regarded this constant reminder of the villagers' mistrust of Elves with a mixture of annoyance and amusement.

"Of the villagers I have met, you seem most comfortable with my presence," he said to Grael, at some length.

"You saved my life," Grael said.

"Your father was eager to accompany us," AscendantSun observed.

"He's concerned for my safety, but he best serves it by staying at home. He is not as spry as he used to be. The Year of Bleeding Snow has taken its toll on him. His presence would only add to my worries. Besides, I refuse to be carried up and down the mountain on another's back like an invalid."

The youth greedily eyed the fragments of hardtack that AscendantSun was sucking on to distract him from his empty belly. He offered Grael a morsel. "This is a kind of bread that sustains us on long journeys."

Grael grimaced as he tried to chew the biscuit. "It is as hard as stone but not nearly as tasty. Until I managed to gnaw off a few crumbs, I thought you had played a trick on me and switched the piece you had offered with a pebble."

AscendantSun's chuckle opened into a belly laugh. It was the first moment of unrestrained merriment he had experienced since he left Tincranny. "It sustains the body though it offends the mouth. It is a staple for our legions. Soaked in mead, it is more palatable. I promise you would find the rest of the cuisine I brought on this trip far more pleasing if I had any left to offer."

Grael produced something that looked like a sheet of gnarled bark. He cut off a sliver and offered it to AscendantSun. "It is an acquired taste, like your bread."

"It is nothing like hardtack if it has a taste," AscendantSun said as he bit off a chunk. He masticated it till it softened. The flavor was not offensive. He ate a second piece, and then a third.

"How fares the Jinglemen's other prisoner?" he asked.

Grael's mood turned somber. "Harath is married to our politician."

"I am sorry," AscendantSun said. Obviously, this was a painful subject for his new friend.

Grael gave a wistful smile. "No need to apologize. You couldn't know."

As they continued the climb, he explained about his engagement and the circumstances of its ending. After a reticent start, he warmed to the subject, evidently glad to confide in a sympathetic ear from outside the village. Fascinated, AscendantSun listened, though he could not delve too much in case he exposed his naivety about such matters. He had received rudimentary explanations of courtship and marriage from the saints, but their practical knowledge was limited. Grael spoke of alien emotions and concerns. AscendantSun grasped that Grael's sentimental attachment to Harath persisted long after it was practical, and because of this, despite his protestations to the contrary, Grael despised her husband, the politician.

This was unfortunate because Pigsknuckle was lucky to have Garscap Torp as their leader. The politician was perceptive in his reading of the Ors' invasion and practical in his response to it. He was someone with whom AscendantSun could do business. Indeed, they had no choice but work together if Pigsknuckle was to survive. Hopefully, the Orstretcherists in Pigsback would prove as clear-sighted.

Dawan stopped by a furka, sat down, and waited for them.

"Do you promise to tell nobody what I said?" Grael's murmur had a plaintive tone.

"Who would I tell?" AscendantSun replied. He liked Grael. His hostility to Garscap might wane in time and the two might become friends. After all, they were both Stretchers.

"Beyond this point, you won't be able to see Pigsknuckle," Grael said as they reached the furka.

AscendantSun looked back at the village, a random collection of huts dispersed like some wild weed across the valley. It lacked the purposeful regularity and aesthetic virtue of his people's settlements. He had beheld it from this location before, but never until this day had he visited it. Though he had encountered great suspicion and even paranoia there, the villagers' reactions were understandable, given what had happened in Cliffringden. If Grael and his father were typical of its denizens, then it had much to be admired. Pigsknuckle must survive if NoName's sacrifice and indeed DawnGlow's death were to have any meaning.

A holler attracted his attention to a black-clad figure scurrying up the mountain toward them.

"It's my brother, Saint Charlin," Grael said. "I wonder what he wants."

The saint was puffing and red-faced when he reached them. "Grael, may I speak to your charge in private for a moment?"

He didn't wait for his brother's answer. He grabbed AscendantSun's batonaxe rack and pulled him beyond the inquisitive ears of his companions.

"We meet again," Charlin said. "I wish to ask a favor of you." The blush of exertion deepened to an embarrassed scarlet. "Please make no mention of the deconsecration of Pigsknuckle's furkas in Saint Sebryn's presence. The lives of the villagers may depend on it. Saint Sebryn might demand the furkas' reinstatement. If the village was attacked, I could never deconsecrate all of them in time for the villagers to escape."

AscendantSun frowned. "Are you asking me to lie to the abbot?"

Charlin's eyes rounded. His arms shot above his head. "Oh, no no no. That would be a sin. I would never ask you to do that. No." He pressed his hands against his mouth and slowly drew them down to his chin. "If the abbot asks you a question, you must answer him honestly. All I ask is that you make no comment on this matter without Saint Sebryn's prompting."

AscendantSun was dubious. It still sounded a lot like lying. But the Pigsknucklers' lives were at stake. "I'll do it. I will swear it on the Forelight, if you wish."

Charlin's eyes bulged. "In this circumstance, that would be sacrilege," the saint said, almost choking on his words. "I trust your word."

Clearly relieved to have finished his odious business, the saint made his farewells and headed back down to the village. AscendantSun watched him shrink into the distance. What other secrets might await him in Pigsback?

Chapter 15

An individual is more than a limb of his lineage. His lineage has no right to destroy him if it considers him diseased. He is an independent entity. He is more than the sum of his predecessors. He is himself and all the divisions that follow him.

-From *The Book of Judgments.*

Night's icy fingers closed in on the screaming mountain as Grael and his companions reached Pigsback. There was an unnerving lag before their hammering on the great doors roused a response. The door creaked open, and a muffled figure beckoned them inside. They left their weapons outside to honor the sanctity of the monastery. They passed through the Needle's Eye into the reception hall.

The saint who had let them in discarded his fur cap and cloak. He was unfamiliar, little older than Grael or Dawan, obviously a recent recruit. Blinking excessively, he introduced himself in a whispery voice as Saint Finshin, recently arrived from the village of Wyrmery. He invited Grael and Dawan to warm by the fire while he conducted AscendantSun to Saint Sebryn.

Dawan smiled as he presented his open palms to the flames. “At least that’s done. I must admit I’m not very comfortable around *them*. I don’t know how you do it. You seem so at ease in their presence.”

“I trust AscendantSun more than some Pigsknucklers I could mention,” Grael said.

Dawan glanced around. “Like our politician and his cronies?”

Grael nodded.

“I don’t think the stories about Garscap are true,” Dawan said. “He can’t be a changeling. Even the Elves don’t like him.”

Not all the Elves. AscendantSun was surprisingly naive about Garscap. He seemed blind to the politician’s deceitful nature.

“My father wants to speak to you as soon as we get back to Pigsknuckle,” Dawan said.

“What does Lormak want with me?” Grael asked.

Dawan shrugged. “Something too important to tell me, apparently.” He cupped his yawn with one hand. “Where is that saint gone? I’m starving. Forelight!”

Three Elves flitted by them and out through the Needle’s Eye. The open doors slapped against walls with thunderous bangs, as the howling wind swept into the reception hall, ruffling the fire and tearing at the tapestries.

The Elves re-entered, slamming the doors shut behind them. They carried batonaxes.

A fourth Elf entered the hall, waving his arms. Grael recognized the symbol on his forehead. It was NeverFear Cor. "Don't do this," he begged. "If it's AscendantSun—"

"And if it's not? What then?" the leader of the armed Elves said. "Ask him nicely to surrender?" It was TrueFriend Peritus.

"He is AscendantSun," Grael said.

The two Elves stared at him.

The corners of TrueFriend's mouth hinted at a smile. "You don't understand…Elfin magic."

He and the other Elves dashed down one of the corridors leading from the reception hall. Grael made to follow, but NeverFear waved him back. "Leave this to us. We'll take care of it."

***

Saint Finshin led AscendantSun through narrow, dank corridors to the chapel. Saint Sebryn stood before the great furka on the altar, his back hunched by the weight of his age, his shriveled hands clinging to the supports that helped him to maintain a prayerful pose for extended periods.

AscendantSun and his guide waited patiently for the abbot to finish his prayers. After some time, Saint Finshin coughed. As if jolted from a beautiful dream, Sebryn dropped his arms and turned a vexed countenance toward the source of the unwelcome intrusion. His ire melted when his gaze rested on AscendantSun. The old man pottered over to him and shook both of his hands.

AscendantSun found it hard sometimes to accept this wizened little man as the vigorous youth whom he had met a lifetime ago. It was as if Saint Sebryn and Sebryn Costan were separate people, one forever young in AscendantSun's memory and the other growing more frail with each meeting.

Sebryn dismissed Saint Finshin and invited AscendantSun to sit with him in one of the pews.

"You have been missed," the abbot said. "What have you been doing?"

Before AscendantSun could answer, three curly-haired Ors burst into the chapel, batonaxes at the ready: TrueFriend Peritus, PureFaith Nitor, and StrongArm Servitor. Unarmed, NeverFear Cor followed behind them, his face taut with apprehension.

AscendantSun stood and stretched as batonaxes encircled him.

"My friends, please," Sebryn exclaimed, rising stiffly to his feet. "There's no need for hostility."

"Forgive us, but this stranger might not be whom he claims," TrueFriend said.

PureFaith studied AscendantSun's forehead. "What are those faint smudges on his name tattoo?" he asked nervously.

AscendantSun had forgotten about the temporary alterations made to his tattoo in Tincranny. It was surprising that traces of the paint were still visible.

"The password we agreed was *Broadwall*," he said.

NeverFear exhaled and confirmed with a nod that the password was correct.

"You could have said that in the first place," TrueFriend quipped as he lowered his weapons.

Laughter dispelled the tension as NeverFear and his companions greeted AscendantSun.

"We were beginning to think you would never come," NeverFear said. "Whatever have you been doing?"

"I will explain later," AscendantSun promised, hoping to stave off detailed interrogation for the moment. It was great to be surrounded by his friends again, to be in the company of Ors.

Sebryn did not succumb to the general camaraderie. "Where did these weapons come from?"

"I am sorry, my friend, but we must be careful," NeverFear said. "The Consensus might have sent an impostor to infiltrate us, or worse."

The old man's face reddened. "You have not answered me. You bear weapons in this sacred place. This is sacrilege."

"The Harbinger's servants would not respect the monastery's sanctity," TrueFriend observed. "Which is the greater sacrilege? That the faithful carry batonaxes or that innocent blood is spilled?"

"And did you agree to this?" Sebryn asked NeverFear.

"I carry no weapon."

"You let others bear them for you."

"You are being hard on NeverFear," TrueFriend said. "He tried to dissuade us."

"Their impulses were generous," NeverFear said. "They acted out of concern for your safety."

"Their impulses may have been generous, but they were wrong. Not since Saint Odran laid the foundation stone of this monastery have weapons violated its sanctity. If you must vet new arrivals, do it outside. There's a whole world for war beyond these walls, but this is a holy place. To disturb it with even the threat of hostility is an affront to the Forelight. Get out of my sight. I wish to converse with AscendantSun in private."

AscendantSun stifled a laugh as beings who remembered the birth of the cosmos were hustled from the chapel by a frail sexagenarian over a millennium their junior.

NeverFear tried to resist, but in the end Sebryn drove him out with the others.

"Interesting crowd you sent me," Sebryn commented as he plopped down on a pew. "They're different from what I imagined."

AscendantSun sat beside him. "Why? What did you expect?"

"More like you. They are a bit of a mishmash. Even the best of them, like NeverFear, lack your refined sensibilities. They worship the Forelight with a whole heart but not with a whole head, or vice versa. Others, like TrueFriend, are chronically confused about the tenets of the faith they espouse. I am at a loss why some came here. Their motivations are opaque, even to themselves."

"My friend, none of them chose exile on a whim. They are all committed believers in the Forelight. Remember what I was like when we first met. Those refined sensibilities that you admire took many years to mature. And it is not as though you and I have all the answers."

"Indeed. So much about your people remains perplexing," Sebryn admitted. "Over the years, we have had many debates about their place in creation. They have been entertaining, sometimes infuriating, occasionally revealing, but never conclusive. The answer to each riddle is another riddle. I fear one day we will come full circle and find ourselves back where we began, none the wiser."

"I doubt that. As I seem to remember, you were hanging upside down at our first meeting."

"Sometimes, I feel that I am still inverted, metaphorically. I'm beginning to wonder if we hold enough shards of the truth to piece it together. My peoples' tales sometimes speak of your kind, but most of what they tell is either untrue or too shallow to enlighten. The fragments of our holy book, the blessed Godward handed down by Saint Odran and his predecessors, do not mention your kind at all. They speak of angels and devils, but your resemblance to either immortal species is superficial. Our third source, your memory, is the best, and at the same time, the worst."

"For my race, history and memory are indivisible."

"But even your recall of the distant past may be imperfect. I'm but a fraction of your age, and my memory sometimes deludes me."

Unlike poor Sebryn, Ors were immune to the depredation of age, and the passage of time did not tarnish their recollection. AscendantSun declined to share these self-evident truths with his friend so as not to remind the saint of his increasing decrepitude.

"Then there is your Golden Light," Sebryn continued. "He informed your perception of your primordial experience, and he is an unreliable authority. Much of what he told you must be fabrication or at least a distortion of the truth." He paused. "You are uncomfortable."

"You speak as if Aurelian was a voice whispering lies in my ear," AscendantSun said. "He was a physical presence, flesh and flame. When I close my eyes and think of him, his image still blazes in the darkness as if singed onto my eyelids. My skin burns as if I once more stood before him. An audience with Aurelian in his martial aspect was akin to stepping into a furnace. We referred to it as the Divine Calefaction. Common wisdom held that his flame would incinerate anyone who dared to touch it. In that endless day, that eternal noon, when I served the Golden Light, my heart burned, too, with love for him. Even now, when the memories stir, it sometimes smolders."

AscendantSun looked to Sebryn for reassurance. In all their diverse theological discussions, he had never before admitted this to the saint.

Sebryn sighed. "If you still feel so strongly for your former god, why then do you choose to disdain him?"

"Because he is dead. He failed us. He promised victory but brought defeat and slavery. He professed love for us while butchering us for sport." Anger built in AscendantSun as he spoke. The old bitterness was always there, ready to reignite.

He smiled to reassure Sebryn. "Do not mistake nostalgia for remorse. I do not regret my conversion to your religion. I have never seen the Forelight, but I know his worshipers. I first encountered your people on Gules. They served the Blue and White Lights as I served Aurelian, but the Stretchers never loved their masters. Because of this, my people condemned them, like all other Mixies, as faithless and duplicitous. We did not understand that Stretchers served a greater power than the squabbling tyrants we considered gods. The Stretchers' faith endured all the marvels and horrors whirling around them during the Light War. It survived slavery and exile on Elysion."

He glanced at the golden furka, encrusted with precious gems, sparkling in the candlelight. "Of course, my people could make similar claims, but in one sense, the Stretchers' achievement is the more admirable. Ors' recollection of Aurelian remains vivid, whereas your people's faith must transcend the churning of the generations and the death of memory. Even Saint Odran never beheld the deity whom he spent a lifetime serving."

Saint Sebryn smiled. "You always did say our faith's endurance played a significant part in your conversion."

"It was an important reason, though not the sole one," AscendantSun continued. "I cannot imagine Aurelian encouraging his myrmidons to love others as they love themselves or offering salvation to all races. That the saints entertained my conversion was, in itself, inspiring."

"You gave me a bit of a scare there," Sebryn admitted. "Your conversion is very important to me. It is the reason I became a saint. I thought that if an Elf could become a Stretcher, even I might be worthy of sainthood. I wouldn't want to think your faith was waning. It is a little late for me to start over at my age."

AscendantSun concealed bitter thoughts behind his smile. He tried not to dwell on what the saint's reaction might be if he learned the true reason for his tardy arrival at Pigsback. NoName's dismal fate made every word spoken to Sebryn hollow. While AscendantSun was trading philosophical niceties, NoName was closing on his quarry.

"You look exhausted," Sebryn observed. "Even I can see it."

AscendantSun's tiredness was not merely physical. It was mental, spiritual. "I feel fine."

Sebryn was unconvinced. "I will have you escorted to the Elves' dormitory. We can talk more tomorrow, when you are rested. We haven't scratched the surface of your adventures." He hobbled over to the door, and holding it a little ajar, bellowed hoarsely for Saint Finshin to return, but it was NeverFear who popped his head inside.

"Come in, come in," Sebryn said wearily. "Have you been waiting out there all this time?"

NeverFear nodded. "I suggested to Saint Finshin that there was no point in two of us waiting in the hall, so he went to tend AscendantSun's guides."

"That was very good of you," Sebryn said. "I'm sorry about my earlier behavior. I was a bit harsh. Anger got the better of me."

"I should have stopped TrueFriend and the others."

"You tried."

"I should have done more than try. The Orstretcherists chose me as their acting leader. I should have taken charge. That is what leaders are supposed to do." He glanced at AscendantSun. "At least I am relieved of that burden now that our true leader has been restored to us."

AscendantSun protested. He cajoled. He begged. In the end, he acquiesced. If NeverFear was so determined to give the leadership of the Orstretcherists to him, why deny himself that honor? He accepted with the proviso that the other Orstretcherists endorsed the change.

"Of course they will agree," NeverFear assured him. "We have missed you. Since we departed Tincranny, your fate has been a persistent topic of discussion. Now, at last, that mystery can be solved."

"I was chatting with the Politician of Pigsknuckle," AscendantSun said, hoping to change the subject. "He asks for our aid against the Harbinger's invasion of the mountains."

NeverFear frowned. "He is a tricky character, not to be trusted. Is that not true, Saint Sebryn?"

"He has a reputation for underhandedness," Saint Sebryn said. "Not undeserved."

"So we are not going to help our friends in Pigsknuckle?" AscendantSun asked.

NeverFear's brows lowered. "Our efforts to help are unceasing. The Pigsknucklers would have starved this winter but for the meat we put in their pots. We are willing to help in any peaceful way we can. But we did not come here to kill, to murder. We may be pariahs estranged from the rest of our kind, but the Ors in those legions are still our lineagemen and friends. For all I know, my own twin could be serving as a legionary. Do you think I could turn my batonaxes against him?"

"He would turn his batonaxes on you," AscendantSun said. "Make no mistake about it."

"There are better ways to help," NeverFear insisted.

Was NeverFear already ruing his hasty promise to relinquish the Orstretcherists' leadership? The direction that AscendantSun favored was obviously not to his liking. It wouldn't be surprising if NeverFear found some pretext to rescind his offer. "What do you think, Saint Sebryn?"

"Saints do not dabble in politics," the saint said. Concern was carved into his face. He was about to add something else, but for whatever reason, would not bring himself to say it.

AscendantSun smoothed away the sharpness in his voice. "I am only the messenger."

NeverFear's mood lightened. "I know. I know. We can discuss this further tomorrow."

"You have taken no vow of pacifism?" AscendantSun asked.

"I considered it," NeverFear said. "But no. None of us have. This matter is not for you or me to decide, here and now. The entire group should make the decision after a proper debate tomorrow. We should be off to our dormitory. We have disturbed the abbot's prayers enough, and the others will be sore with me for not bringing you to them sooner."

"Could I have another few moments of privacy with our friend?" Sebryn asked NeverFear.

NeverFear nodded. He closed the door as he stepped outside.

"Politics is not the concern of saints," Sebryn said. "But there is something you should know about Garscap Torp. He is an orphan of Martyrsgrave, or as you know it, Tincranny. He is the same child whom you rescued from wolves. His mother believed him to be a changeling. She went mad and killed herself. Pigsknuckle, infected by her fear, refused to take him in, and the monastery was forced to receive him. He has no reason to love you or your kind."

"Then I have wronged him twice," AscendantSun said. "My blind hate took his father from him, and then my botched act of generosity robbed him of a mother."

"I meant this to be a warning," Sebryn said. "It was not my intention to inspire a deeper sympathy for a man who has every reason to be your enemy. As for your sins, the Forelight has already forgiven them through baptism."

Not all of them. Not DawnGlow's death. Not the sins of his twin that he abetted. Not the hypocrisy of his every word since he'd arrived in Pigsback. He was about to ask for absolution, when Sebryn drew their conversation to a close by inviting NeverFear to return. It was just as well. AscendantSun was not finished with sin yet.

He and NeverFear bid Sebryn farewell and headed toward the Ors' dormitory.

"What was that about?" NeverFear asked him.

"The sins of the past," AscendantSun said.

"You are not hobbling anymore," NeverFear observed.

AscendantSun heaped mute curses on his stupidity. He had forgotten about his antecedent's limp. "My leg healed. The limp comes back sometimes when I am tired."

NeverFear's eyes glimmered with suspicion, but he said nothing.

The Orstretcherists swarmed around AscendantSun as he entered the dormitory. In place of cropped or straightened hair, every head bore riotous curls, a subtle acknowledgment, perhaps, of the group's outcast status. Their tunics were civilian colors—mostly yellows and greens. He struggled to read the names tattooed on the joyous faces whirling around him; to disentangle the clamor of well-wishes and questions crashing against his ears and shake the anonymous hands competing to seize his.

It was difficult not to feel like a fraud in the midst of the frenzied welcoming. They were greeting their friend, not a stranger with the same name. Such melancholic notions were dangerous. He was every bit his forbear. They were the same person. He would be foolish to think otherwise.

As salutations waned, the interrogation began.

He claimed he had traveled to Sunthorn to seek allies against the Harbinger, but the effort proved fruitless. He found much sympathy but little willingness to act. He was trapped in Sunrest until recently, when his accomplices there judged it safe to smuggle him out. Promises to protect their anonymity forbade him to reveal more detail. His audience was oblivious to his deceit, but with every lie, the gulf separating AscendantSun from his comrades yawned a little wider.

He shared what hearsay he had gleaned from DawnGlow without divulging its source.

"So, what news of DawnGlow Fulgur?" TrueFriend asked. "You have not mentioned him."

"DawnGlow is now Minister-Governor of Tincranny," AscendantSun said. "As far as I know."

He shifted the conversation to other matters and asked the others about their life in Pigsback. Since their arrival, they had left the monastery only to hunt game. Some, like TrueFriend, expressed boredom with their spartan existence, while others had become inured to it. A few even welcomed it as penance for past misdeeds.

A subtle remoteness tinged the Orstretcherists' easy banter. Was it a symptom of lingering doubts about his story? No, it was most likely a product of his long absence. He had disappeared inexplicably from their company in the midst of a great crisis. While he was a captive of division in Tincranny, exile had molded them into a close-knit community. He returned as an outsider. Their generous welcome for their former leader was surprising, given the circumstances of his departure.

That was what he was—their former leader. NeverFear was their leader now. The deference once reserved for AscendantSun had transferred to his successor. That was the real price of his dereliction. NeverFear's talk of passing the leadership back to AscendantSun was naive to the point of farce. AscendantSun should have not abandoned his friends. He should not have divided. Nothing good had come of it.

"You look ill," StrongArm observed.

"I am tired," AscendantSun said. "It has been a long trip."

"Of course, of course, you should rest," NeverFear said. "You can use my bed. I will make up a new one for myself."

"AscendantSun can take mine," TrueFriend said.

"Doing penance for your sins?" DayFlambeau Formosus scoffed.

"Something like that," TrueFriend admitted.

AscendantSun made his good-nights, climbed into his bunk, and turned to the wall. The others' whispered conversations kept him awake, but he pretended to sleep to put off the inquisitive and the concerned. As the Orstretcherists drifted to their beds and the low hum diminished to silence, sleep remained elusive. The events of the day swirled too fast in his mind.

The notion he was a sham continued to nag. Sebryn had once said sin was a prison. It was more like a tomb, every untruth another brick sealing AscendantSun inside. The only way to escape this sepulcher of lies was to confess all and unburden his conscience. Absolution would be worth the censure of his friends.

But was it worth the devastation of Pigsknuckle? NeverFear's precious detachment to its fate was appalling. The Pigsknucklers could not defend themselves with principles, theory, and wishful thinking. They needed practical aid from the Orstretcherists if they were to survive the Harbinger's genocidal campaign.

If AscendantSun admitted his sins to the Orstretcherists, they might forgive in time, but they would never forget. Whatever slim chance he had to influence them would disappear forever. NeverFear would keep them in splendid isolation in the monastery till an ocean of blood drowned it. Convincing the Orstretcherists of the wrongness of such fatalistic pacifism was more important than easing AscendantSun's personal torments.

If he failed to move his comrades to action, he would return to Pigsknuckle alone and do whatever he could to help the villagers. It was likely to prove a futile gesture against such overwhelming odds, but at least he might die with some honor. His division had been an act of cowardice. He could no longer live in its shadow. Endurance of his lineage meant nothing, if spinelessness was its means. Contentment overcame him, the racing of his thoughts slowed to a saunter, and a soporific serenity wrapped around him, nursing him to sleep.

***

The next morning, the bustle of yawning Ors rising from their beds woke him. After AscendantSun washed in a basin of ice-cold water and dressed, he sought out NeverFear and reminded him of his promise to debate Garscap's plea for help.

"After breakfast," NeverFear promised. His voice hinted irritation. "It is best to deal with such matters on a full stomach." He paused. "We should discuss the leadership question at the same time. That also needs to be settled by the group. It's not mine to give away."

"It's not mine to take," AscendantSun said. "I said as much yesterday, if you remember."

NeverFear took a deep breath. An orange tint brightened his cheeks. His eyes shied from AscendantSun's gaze. "I will be asking the group to endorse me as their leader. We all owe you a great deal, but we have reached a fork in the road. You beckon us in one direction. Someone must champion the other."

AscendantSun smiled at his prescience. "That is your right. Of course, neither of us might be chosen. A third candidate may emerge."

"Of course. TrueFriend might put himself forward, or DayFlambeau, or even NoonBlest Libamen."

The bell for morning prayers tinkled through the corridors, cutting short their conversation.

The Orstretcherists gathered together, NeverFear at the center. AscendantSun expected them to join the saints in the chapel, but NeverFear explained that, as the chapel was too small to accommodate the entire population of the monastery, the Orstretcherists usually conducted their communal orisons in the dormitory.

"As AscendantSun is our guest, perhaps he would like to lead the prayers," NeverFear suggested.

AscendantSun smiled to conceal his irritation over being described as an outsider. Anger made him dash through the prayers. Nobody appeared to be perturbed by his curt delivery. Only a few stifled yawns disturbed the others' prayerful mood.

"Time for breakfast," PureFaith chimed after AscendantSun finished.

AscendantSun hardly tasted the porridge that he shoveled into his mouth. He was focused on preparing his speech to the Orstretcherists. When NeverFear demanded the Orstretcherists' attention, it was like waking from a dream.

"Our friend AscendantSun Auctor has something he wants to discuss with us. Perhaps, AscendantSun, you wish to elaborate."

By accident or design, NeverFear had out-maneuvered him by making him speak first. Any attempt to quibble would be viewed as churlish by the others.

As the Orstretcherists sat on beds around him, AscendantSun cleared his throat and began. "My friends, the Politician of Pigsknuckle has begged for our aid against the invaders who threaten to swat his little community out of existence. How can we refuse him? NeverFear already gave me a reason. He says we came here to live peaceably, and he is right. We did not come here to kill our own lineagemen or friends. Yet those same lineagemen and friends now threaten to massacre both Pigsknuckle and this monastery. Don't imagine that they would spare any of us, either, if they caught us."

"They would never kill us," NoonBlest insisted, shaking his head. "Unless we gave them cause."

"If they posed no threat to us, why did we flee Tincranny?" AscendantSun countered. "More than a desire for peaceful living brought us here. We feared for our lives. The Consensus wanted to arrest us for heresy."

"Arrest is one thing. Killing is another," NoonBlest muttered.

AscendantSun fumed at the Or's willful ignorance. "It's easy to say that while perched atop this lofty mountain, for the moment safely beyond the reach of the Harbinger's murderous onslaught. The legionaries' actions in Cliffringden were murder, pure and simple. Does anyone dispute that?"

He paused, letting the silence answer. The truth could not be denied.

He continued, his confidence growing. "I cannot accept NeverFear's argument that cowardice is a requisite of our adopted religion; that all we can do is pray and dither while legions butcher our coreligionists. If Mixies raided a nursery, all of us would bear arms to defend it without hesitation. How can we refuse to do the same for the children of Pigsknuckle? Are their lives less valuable than ours? Are they inferior because of their fleeting nature?"

Every Or attempted to speak at once. Their words were incomprehensible, but their yelling amply communicated their contempt for AscendantSun's insinuation. It took some time for NeverFear to diminish them to simmering indignation. AscendantSun's own words were turning them against him.

"Perhaps you should apologize for your remark," NeverFear said. His tone made clear that it was more than a suggestion.

AscendantSun raised his open hands in a gesture of apology. "I beg your forgiveness if my words cause offense. Passion goads me to speak so hotly. I'm frightened that my talent for oratory is too poor to dissuade you from the course on which you seem intent. If I question your empathy for our fellow Stretchers, I do so because I am painfully aware of the shortcomings in my own compassion for them."

Lowering his arms, he pressed one hand to his chest. "Intellectually, I consider Mixies to be our equals, but my unfettered instincts would cry otherwise. However hard I try, I cannot escape these wayward impulses, the product of prejudices accumulated over many life times."

As he spoke, his gaze roamed the room, demanding all eyes it met to accept his sincerity.

"Remember, I was once MixyBane," he said. "Back then, my hatred of Mixies rivaled the Harbinger's. My lineage sacrificed many lives to defend Gleam from them.

When some ill-tempered Light tore down its defenses, I was one of the last to accept its abandonment."

"I remember," TrueFriend said. "I was one of those who dragged you from its ruins."

AscendantSun nodded. "Much more than any love for Gleam, I was motivated by my hatred of Mixies. Their victory appalled me. I ordered that the city be torched so only embers remained for them to scavenge. It took a long time for that hatred to cool."

Some of his audience nodded. Others looked pensive, sad. The floorboards creaked as, behind AscendantSun, NeverFear shifted his position slightly. NoonBlest crossed his arms and deepened his scowl.

"After the massacre at Tincranny, I tentatively reached out to my enemies in hope of negotiating a peaceful co-existence," AscendantSun said. "I sought it on my terms. I made little effort to understand Stretchers till I realized my efforts were doomed unless I did. Had I known I might repudiate the Golden Light and embrace the Forelight as my deity, I would have been horrified. Initially, I pretended to honor the Forelight to ingratiate myself with his followers. Later, as I became drawn to Stretcherism, I feigned my pretense. It took me a long while to admit my conversion was genuine, even to myself. I became the first Orstretcherist."

"We've all heard this before," NoonBlest said. "We've all lived some version of it. I fail to see the point you are trying to make."

AscendantSun ignored the interruption. "You perhaps imagine my dedication to the Forelight is implacable, that my relationship with our Mixy friends is entirely comfortable; that my only challenges are the theological conundrums Saint Sebryn and I have struggled to solve. My devotion to the Forelight is a somewhat brief period in a much longer existence. I retain residual biases. I struggle with them every day, tearing them from my heart like rude weeds."

TrueFriend admitted to similar misgivings. Reticent at first, then with increasing frankness, the others took the opportunity to share their doubts and fears.

"Saint Sebryn is aware of our method of propagation, and he heartily approves of it," PureFaith said. "He says it makes us immune to the sins of the flesh. But supposing he is wrong. When we fatten up for division, are we not indulging in a form of gluttony? If that is so, how can we divide without sin?"

"I have lived a long time," StrongArm said, bowing his head. "I have committed many sins in the name of Aurelian and later Gleam and Tincranny. Can the Forelight forgive so much? Saint Sebryn says so. But I can't even forgive myself."

Even NoonBlest chose to voice his doubts. "I find some of the Stretchers' beliefs difficult to accept. For example, they claim this mountain was a giant pig petrified by Saint Odran. I was on the first expedition through this region, before the Stretchers settled here. The mountain was already here."

"The saints suspect the story is apocryphal," NeverFear said.

"But they permit the villagers to believe it. By their silence, they give it credence. What else are the saints allowing us to believe that they themselves have no faith in? What do they believe that they choose not to share with us?"

Blushing orange, DayFlambeau said, "I sometimes wonder…not often, just sometimes…I wonder what we would do if Aurelian returned."

TrueFriend broke the stunned silence: "Beg for forgiveness."

Nervous laughter filled the room as if everyone had been tickled at once. DayFlambeau had touched on everyone's greatest fear.

AscendantSun waited for the others to sober before continuing. "The wrong done by our inaction to Pigsknuckle is plain. The harm to our own people is perhaps less obvious but just as grave. Very soon, they will forsake their unrequited attachment to a dead god. We must all believe that this will come to pass. Otherwise, why would we be here? When it does, when their delusions shatter and fall away, they will find blood on their hands that no number of divisions can wash clean. Past crimes torment us all. Imagine if our whole race suffered that crushing guilt. It would be the end of our race."

"Why should it?" DayFlambeau asked. "The pangs of conscience of which you speak have killed none of us."

"But the Forelight blesses us with the strength to bear our shame," AscendantSun said. "He gives us hope."

DayFlambeau bowed his head.

"When Aurelian died, we were plunged into darkness," AscendantSun said. "But the Harbinger's rise to power has inflicted on our people a more terrible blindness. Dazzled by his promises of Aurelian's second coming, they cannot see the terrible abyss that he has opened before them. By the time he is exposed as a charlatan, our people will have plummeted down it. What will sustain them when they have no faith in either their god's return or their own innate goodness?"

As he spoke, his gaze drifted across his audience, challenging and seeking understanding in equal measure. "We can save our people from this calamity. Our example can be a beacon to guide them from that despairful darkness. We can inspire a new hope in our race when all other has been snuffed out. All that is needed is for our actions to match our words. By joining the war on the Stretchers' side, our bravery can save two peoples. Let the world bear witness that we did not abandon our coreligionists at their time of greatest need, that we resisted the murderous excess of the Harbinger with more than platitudes."

He lowered his head and his voice. "Whatever we decide here and now, the unfolding catastrophe will eventually force us to act, though, by that stage, our intervention will be too late. Only if we act now, can we make a real difference."

He looked up and pressed one hand to his chest. He had saved his most powerful argument, the most emotional one, for last. "My life is precious to me. I am all that remains of four divisions." It could be true. His twin might be already dead. "I am the single thread by which the continuation of my personal lineage now hangs. All that it was and all it could become lives or dies with me. I stand here before you and advocate a course that puts my life and my lineage in jeopardy, because I know that, whatever the personal risk, it is the right course. Ultimately, it is the only one we have."

His final sentence lingered in the mesmerized silence.

He turned to NeverFear. "I assume you intend to make a rebuttal argument."

NeverFear admitted defeat with a silent shake of his head.

NoonBlest leapt to his feet. "Well, I'm not convinced. AscendantSun's persuasiveness is what forced us into exile in the first place. Are we yet again to yield to it unchallenged?"

"The Harbinger was responsible for *our* exile. Not me," AscendantSun retorted.

NoonBlest sneered. "Ah yes, the Harbinger and AscendantSun—two sides of the same coin."

"You reject Stretcherism?" AscendantSun asked.

NoonBlest shook his head. "It is typical of you to consider yourself and Stretcherism the same. If our religion has any merit, it must be bigger than any one of us. Even you. You are no more a prophet than the Harbinger."

A few of the Orstretcherists gasped.

What was NoonBlest doing here anyway? Since the first Auctor met the first Lumen in the deserts of Gules, the two lineages had never got along. Did NoonBlest regard Orstretcherism as merely another opportunity to pursue their ancient rivalry?

AscendantSun's eyes narrowed. It was best to stay calm. "I never said I was a prophet. Have you a better argument than insults?"

"The saints oppose us entering this war, but of course, AscendantSun Auctor knows better."

"Their concern is with the next world. My concern is this one." AscendantSun retorted.

"The saints don't trust Garscap Torp," NoonBlest said. "Why should we?"

A few supportive murmurs rippled through the gathering.

"So we should let a village be massacred on account of one man?" AscendantSun challenged.

NoonBlest growled as he sat down.

"Let's vote," NeverFear suggested. "First, those in favor of AscendantSun's proposal."

AscendantSun exulted as NoonBlest and a small number of other objectors became lost in a forest of raised hands supporting his motion.

The same hands stretched into the air to endorse NeverFear's nomination of AscendantSun as the group's leader. AscendantSun took careful note of the dissenters—NoonBlest, DayFlambeau, and their smattering of sympathizers. It was a warning to not try his comrades' loyalty and patience so much in the future. During NeverFear's tenure, his democratic inclinations had infected the group. Once, AscendantSun's word had been enough for his followers. Now, it needed the legitimacy of a vote. If NeverFear had not been swayed by his arguments, the vote would have been much closer. AscendantSun might even have lost. Any future threat to his leadership would likely coalesce around NeverFear.

"I want to thank you for your support," AscendantSun said. "I also must commend NeverFear Cor for his hard work and dedication over the past year. Leadership is never easy, particularly in trying times such as these. As my first act as leader, I am appointing NeverFear as my deputy."

He brought the meeting to a close, and then slipped out of the dormitory to inform Sebryn of its outcome. The abbot was praying alone in the chapel. When he learned the Orstretcherists intended to leave for Pigsknuckle the next day, knotting wrinkles and deepening lines carved his aged face into an icon of indignation.

"You have no faith," he snapped.

AscendantSun's surprise at his friend's ire turned to anger.

"I forsook my homeland for the Forelight. To serve him, I cast aside many lifetimes of devotion to Aurelian. I sacrificed everything I had, and you accuse me of faithlessness. Perhaps you are the faithless one. You released me from my vow of pacifism in the first place."

Saint Sebryn swallowed his reply. He blessed AscendantSun and curtly bid him farewell.

***

Grael smiled. It was a relief to be safely off the Pig and nearly home.

He accompanied Dawan to his home. As usual, the cabin was so crammed with young Mangals that they spilled out the front door. Their grandfather, old Thomol, sat by the fire, mumbling about the cramped conditions, while Dawan's heavily pregnant mother waded across a sea of children as she went about her chores. Even taking into account that the cousins and friends would eventually go back their own homes, it was hard to imagine all the inhabitants of the house would fit in it, once they lay down to sleep.

"I don't know how your mother manages," Grael confided.

"The big ones mind the little ones. Most of the time," Dawan said.

Lormak emerged from the middle of a pile of children, and picked his path carefully through the throng beneath him. He warmly shook hands with the new arrivals. His resemblance to an older Dawan with a beard was uncanny. "Welcome back, Grael. We might go for a walk. It's impossible to hear anything in this bedlam. Dawan, run to Grael's home and let his parents know he is home safe."

Grael and Lormak strolled through the forest, discussing the journey to Pigsback, AscendantSun's arrival, and the slow improvement in the weather. Lormak's head swiveled about dramatically. He rubbed the back of his neck. "Have you any idea why I invited you here?"

Grael shook his head.

Lormak bit his lip. "We need a new politician. One who puts the village before himself for a change."

Grael's eyes narrowed. "If this is about the Cliffringdeners, I want no part in it."

"There may be some folks unhappy about taking in the refugees. You have to take your allies where you find them. But most just want rid of the Changeling and his cronies, Maergan and Evram Erath, Fapath Carnath, and their ilk. What sort of future have my children with a man like Garscap Torp as their politician? What future has any of us?" Lormak was trembling.

"And who is going to replace him?"

Lormak pointed a finger at Grael. "You are. We want you to have the thorny crown, if you are willing to wear it."

Grael's heart skipped a beat. "My father does not know about this?"

Lormak nodded. "We haven't talked to him, but you can be certain of his support."

"You want me to risk my family's welfare in this…conspiracy."

Lormak's face burned with indignation. "I'm risking my own."

"Why choose me?"

"You had a fortune, and you gave almost all of it away to feed the village. That sort of selflessness is what we need in a leader. And it should be rewarded."

Lormak had used *we* a lot, but he hadn't divulged the names of the other conspirators. "Who else is part of this?" Grael asked.

Lormak's blush deepened. He shook his head. "It wouldn't be fair to the others to give you their names yet. Not until you decide you want in. But our number is significant."

"What about Widan?" The answer might give a clue as to the fate awaiting Harath.

Lormak snorted. "He gave the thorny crown to the Changeling in the first place. His daughter is married to Garscap. Even the Melkaths don't want him back."

If Grael was politician, he might be able to protect Harath, prevent her from being exiled with her husband. He might be able to keep things peaceful. But it was a huge gamble, and not just for him, but for his whole family. If Garscap somehow won…

Grael wet his lips and asked, "Are you sure you have sufficient support to overthrow the Changeling?"

Lormak's eyebrows arched. "Of course! The whole village wants rid of him!"

Grael shied from Lormak's look of feverish anticipation. He just couldn't decide here and now. "Let me think about it overnight. I'll give you my answer in the morning."

"Very well. I can understand that you need time to mull it over." Lormak sounded disappointed. "It's a big decision."

Grael spent the rest of the day wandering the forests, absorbed in his dilemma. As night fell, he found a secluded spot on the edge of the village. Using a hollow log as a seat, he waited for his family to go asleep. He was in no mood for questions. As he sat alone in the dark, the Erols' home was probably filled with games and stories and laughter. He didn't need a reminder that his family's happiness might rest on his decision. It was very late when he tiptoed back to the silent cabin. The dull light of the dying fire revealed his sleeping parents and siblings. They looked so peaceful and contented. He lay down on his straw bed and prayed to the Forelight for guidance. He closed his eyes but his predicament kept him awake through the night.

It was long walk back to the Mangals' house the next morning. Lormak answered Grael's knock on the lintel. He had that expectant look again.

Grael took a deep breath. "I'll do it." Every word felt momentous.

Lormak patted him on the back. "Good man. Good man." His eyebrows furrowed a little. "What made you decide to accept?"

Grael shrugged. "Something my father once said to me." *Often, in trying to cheat our fate we cheat ourselves.* Whatever Grael decided, his family would ultimately be forced to choose a side in the coming conflict. Knowing his father, it wouldn't be the Changeling's.

Grael ignored Lormak's puzzlement. "So, what is to be done?" Grael asked.

"Nothing as yet. Still gathering our strength. But soon, very soon, we'll rip the thorny crown from the Changeling's head."

PART 3
GARSCAP

Chapter 16

Nimbly his fearsome axes danced,
Flaming steel that consumed all foes,
No shield could withstand their advance,
No spear could pierce their maze of blows.

~From *Alackalas and the Fair Princess.*

The men of Pigsknuckle gathered at Leaftea not long after daybreak. AscendantSun spun his batonaxes as he addressed them. Many were uninterested. Some were hostile.

"These are the most fearsome weapons you will ever face. Imagine fighting four men, each with a double-bitted axe in one hand and a dagger in the other. Imagine these four warriors fighting in perfect coordination. That is what you must withstand when you face a single batonaxer. Batonaxes are dangerous. In inexperienced hands, these weapons can kill their wielder as easily as his opponents. On the other thumb, inexperienced hands amongst our race are long gone. All are well versed with using these weapons."

He nodded to Grael and Evram Erath to attack. They approached him cautiously, spears at the ready. Evram circled to the left so that AscendantSun was forced to stand in profile and glance back and forth between his assailants.

"Observe, they wield spears, not axes. Batonaxes are short-range weapons unless thrown. The spears give the advantage of distance," he lectured.

Evram lunged. AscendantSun hooked the spear with one batonaxe, and pulling the surprised youth forward, delivered a kick to his torso. As Evram tumbled to the ground clutching his belly, the spear flew from his hands and barely missed Grael. Grael charged, but AscendantSun parried his spear thrust and swirled into him. Before Grael could react, a spike pressed against his neck.

"Sorry," AscendantSun said as Grael wiped a drop of blood from his throat. "I did not mean to knick you."

"What about kicking me in the stomach?" Evram asked.

"I was fighting two. It was your misfortune to be the first." He offered Evram a hand to help him up, but the youth refused it.

AscendantSun thanked Grael and Evram, and then continued. "Be under no illusion. For you, tackling a batonaxer alone is suicide. To have any chance of winning, you must work in pairs, at the least, and coordinate your attack. You must maintain distance from your opponent, read his moves, force him into over-committing, and kill him with your first strike."

NeverFear and NoonBlest watched, heeding every word.

The drilling continued through the morning. The tactics of batonaxers were dissected, and counter-measures explained. Many were theoretical, concocted by the Orstretcherists from their intimate knowledge of wielding batonaxes rather than their scant experience in countering them with other weapons, and AscendantSun had to modify and refine these techniques as he taught. The effectiveness of most of them would be temporary. The legionaries would adapt quickly. However, the Stretchers would have surprise on their side in early encounters, and that edge might be enough for them to triumph.

Disgruntled mutterings emerged among his pupils as the noon approached, but he ignored them. Only when the concentration of his best pupils flagged did he end the lesson and let the hungry, exhausted Stretchers disperse to their homes.

"That went well," AscendantSun commented to NoonBlest as he and NeverFear approached. "Our students' apathy waned as the lesson progressed."

"You were teaching them how to kill us. Of course they would be interested," NoonBlest observed. "As for your techniques, well, two against one is hardly fair."

"We discussed this and agreed as a group this was the best way to help the Stretchers defend their families," NeverFear reminded him.

"I did not agree," NoonBlest pointed out.

"We voted," AscendantSun said.

"A vote does not make it right."

Clearly shocked by NoonBlest's arrogance, NeverFear's eyes bulged. He believed group decisions were sacrosanct.

His shock quickly turned to a frown. "Would you rather batonaxers mow the Pigsknucklers down in battle?"

"You too agreed this was distasteful," NoonBlest replied.

"Sometimes the distasteful is necessary." NeverFear said. "We promised to aid the Stretchers. Our number is small, and our most effective means of helping is to train the Stretchers to defend themselves against legionaries."

"I came to the mountains to live in peace, not to start a war," NoonBlest muttered.

"So did I," NeverFear said.

"And I," added AscendantSun.

"That is why you dragged us into this war within a day of arriving at the monastery," NoonBlest muttered before he stormed off.

"He will calm down," AscendantSun said, more in hope than certainty.

"I hope you are right," NeverFear said. "Only men participated."

AscendantSun shrugged. "I suggested the women should attend the sessions, but Garscap and Saint Charlin were against it."

"A shame," NeverFear said. "If the women were permitted to fight, it would more than double Pigsknuckle's defenders. I suppose they know their womenfolk better than us."

"This feminine pacifism is not universal among Mixies," AscendantSun said. "In some tribes, women fight alongside their men. Garscap hinted that if I could assuage Charlin's objections, he might look on my proposal more sympathetically. I tried, but the saint is adamant that a battlefield is no place for women, even if it engulfs their own homes."

"What about the other villages?" NeverFear asked. "Are we going to train their warriors also?"

"Garscap commended the idea, but I suspect he is not as enthusiastic about it as he claims. He said he would prefer the warriors come here to be trained rather than *scatter across the mountains*, as he put it. He promised to make the necessary arrangements with the other politicians."

"I suppose it makes sense," NeverFear said. "I…" His eyes fixed on something behind AscendantSun. "Here comes your friend."

AscendantSun twisted around to take a look. Grael was strolling toward them, his spear resting against one shoulder.

"I need to talk to you, AscendantSun." Grael glanced at NeverFear. "Alone."

***

The Elf's tent was a novelty to Grael. Its scent was reminiscent of honey. The light seeping through the fabric painted everything either black or a pale yellow. Everything was neat, in its place, just so. The only dirt was a footprint stamped onto the mat across the floor. His boot must have made it. He blushed and pretended not to notice.

AscendantSun folded his legs as he sat across from him. How long would his smile remain after Grael explained the reason for his visit?

Grael's deep breath failed to quell the fluttering in the pit of his stomach. "This conversation must remain a secret between us."

"Of course," AscendantSun replied. Did he look nervous? It was hard to tell. "I assume this is connected to our discussions on the way to Pigsback."

"In part. I need you to answer a question. If Garscap Torp was no longer politician, would your alliance with Pigsknuckle still stand?" Grael braced for the answer.

AscendantSun's eyes widened a fraction. "It would depend on whether the new politician would wish to retain it."

"If I was the politician?"

"I trust you, Grael. If you were the politician, our alliance would stand. But…"

"But?"

"I am going to ask this because I consider you a friend. Are you sure replacing Garscap would be to Pigsknuckle's advantage? He is the only person in your village who has fought in real wars. He is the only one who grasps what is required to survive one. And this is a real war, not some skirmish over a couple of stray goats."

"You've fought in wars," Grael said. "You can advise me."

A spasm of emotion flitted across AscendantSun's face. Annoyance perhaps. "I've won a few, but I've lost the ones most important to win."

"I doubt Garscap has won many wars. Otherwise, he would be somewhere else."

AscendantSun poured a brownish yellow liquid into two small cups, and passed one to Grael.

"I hope that this is better than your bread," Grael said with a smile. He took a sip. A spicy sweetness pervaded the alcohol. "Very nice."

"This matter must remain our secret," AscendantSun said. "My people would be disturbed to discover that there is dissension among our allies. If Garscap is to be replaced, it is better that they learn after the event."

"Believe me," Grael said with a chuckle, "I don't want this matter becoming common knowledge either."

"And how soon will this… change of leadership take place?" AscendantSun asked.

Grael ignored the cautious urges of his instincts. He trusted AscendantSun. "By the end of the week."

***

Garscap and Evram sat on the fractured trunk of Leaftea's deconsecrated furka, watching the Orstretcherists' camp.

Evram chuckled. "My friend, you're a lucky man. You're the most powerful man in Pigsknuckle, and you have an army of Fair Folk at your command."

Garscap's yawn curled into a smile, not of triumph but of patience. "Keep that type of talk to yourself," he chided gently. "As many mercenary captains learned to their great cost in Formicary, it's not advisable to overestimate one's position. As for the Orstretcherists, they fight for their own reasons. I do not pretend to understand them."

He picked up three stones and began playing with them, throwing and catching them with such rapidity that they seemed to fly of their own accord.

"I'm forced to be a juggler," Garscap said, grinning. "I've to juggle the villagers, the saints, and the Orstretcherists. It appears as though I am in control, but if I make one mistake..."

He let the stones drop to the ground.

"My dear father-in-law came to me this morning with an interesting story. Apparently, he was approached some time ago by certain parties in the village about replacing me as the politician. Turned them down, or so he claims."

Evram's face stretched with surprise. He leapt to his feet, his hands curled into fists. "Did he name any of these plotters?"

Garscap waved him to sit back down. When he reluctantly complied, Garscap continued. "He gave me one name. I can guess the others."

"What are you going to do about them?"

Garscap winked. "Leave it to me. I have a plan. If they are scrounging around for a leader, I have a little time. Matters like this are always about timing. Speaking of which...quick, stand up before Saint Charlin sees us."

"The stone is deconsecrated."

"In reality but not in the heart. Get up. Get up!"

"It is in mine," Evram grumbled as he rose to his feet.

"Over here, Worthy Saint," Garscap cried, waving his hand above his head.

Saint Charlin's acknowledgment was reluctant. "You wish to speak with me?"

"I need your advice, Worthy Saint."

As the saint approached, Garscap whispered to Evram, "Leave me. I must speak with Saint Charlin alone."

Evram scowled but obeyed without protest.

"What do you want?" the saint demanded.

"I must talk to you about the Orstretcherists."

"You are very amiable toward them, given your history."

Garscap could hear his sobriquet in the saint's tone. "I like them well enough, when they train my men how to fight the Fair Folk's soldiers."

"War is not the business of saints. I cannot advise you on such matters."

"Of course. I understand that. I wish to offer other villages the same instruction."

Saint Charlin looked askance at the politician. "You want the Orstretcherists to train Pigsknuckle's rivals? It's very generous of you."

"Old rivalries must be set aside if we're to defeat the invaders. Risks have to be taken if we're to survive. I need your help to reach out to Ogresquern, Cronesglen, and the others."

Saint Charlin shrugged. "It should be no problem. You do not need my help to visit them. Unlike Pigsknuckle, their furkas still stand. I'm sure if you explain your proposition to their politicians, they would see the benefit of it."

"It's not so simple," Garscap said. "Why should they trust me? Why should they trust the Orstretcherists who are kinsmen of their enemies? My rival politicians would be a lot easier to convince with your help—"

"Saints do not dabble in politics," Saint Charlin insisted.

"—and a lot less likely to take liberties with my generosity."

Saint Charlin frowned. "What do you mean?"

"Well, they could use the offer as an opportunity to attack the Orstretcherists or Pigsknuckle."

A disbelieving smile spread across Saint Charlin's face. "They would not dare."

"They might. Without your direction, they might." His foot struck a stray fragment of the furka, but, fortunately, Saint Charlin was too lost in thought to have noticed.

"I will contemplate on what you have said," Charlin said finally.

"There's something else you should consider. If my own people learn what I am proposing, they'll drive me from the village. Only your advocacy can protect me."

Charlin looked uncertain. "You raised a similar concern when the refugees from Cliffringden arrived in the village. I will seek the abbot's advice on the matter."

"Whatever you feel is appropriate," Garscap said, meeting the saint's glance.

Charlin's gaze drifted to the broken stones at Garscap's feet. "I don't have to answer to the likes of you for my actions," he growled.

"Of course you don't," Garscap said. He was careful to maintain a reverential demeanor. "I'm surprised you feel the need to climb the Pig to ascertain Saint Sebryn's attitude to my proposal. Do you believe there is even the slightest chance he would be favorable? He distrusts all politicians. He hates me. Yes, he despises me. Don't pretend otherwise. You already know he'd be against my plan if he knew of it. You must decide for yourself if you'll help me. Just as you made up your own mind about this furka. Saint Sebryn would have forbidden its destruction had he known. You knew that, but you went ahead anyway because you understood it was the right thing to do. I recall at the time you said you preferred Saint Sebryn's disapproval on your conscience to the wailing of widows and orphans."

"Clever words," Saint Charlin chided. "Clever words."

Garscap let the breeze whisper his response. A clever silence followed the clever words.

"I will consider what you said," Charlin said.

"That is all I ask," Garscap replied.

***

Gules washed the night in bloody light, as the conspirators gathered in Horgal's field. Most of them were hooded, their faces lost in shadow. Grael counted somewhere between three and four dozen. It was a disappointing turnout. Lormak had promised more.

"The rest will do their bit when Garscap is gone," Lormak assured him. "How many men are needed to deal with just one man?"

"And what about the Eraths, Carnaths, and other families who support him?"

"By the morning, he'll be gone, and there'll be nothing they can do. They'll see sense. Most of them just wanted to be rid of Widan. They have no particular love of the Changeling. They can't go against the will of the entire village."

"I doubt that's true of Evram."

"Evram can go chasing after Garscap for all anyone cares."

A few of the others chuckled grimly.

Lormak demanded everyone's attention. "This is the plan. Garscap will be in his hut on the outskirts of the village. About a dozen of us will rush inside, while the rest of you stand guard outside. We tie his hands behind his back, gag him, and take his thorny crown. Then we take him to Saint Charlin's house. We tell Saint Charlin that Garscap isn't wanted in the village anymore. Either he takes Garscap away, or we'll have to kill him."

"I'm killing nobody!" someone in the crowd cried.

"We're not going to kill him," Lormak insisted. "It's just a threat. The saint will accept our word on the matter and just take him away."

"But isn't that a lie?" an uncertain voice asked.

"No no no," Lormak said. "It's not lying. It's the custom in circumstances like this."

"What about Harath?" Grael asked. He had to make sure of her safety, whatever else happened.

"What about her?" Lormak replied. "She probably won't be there. She sleeps in the great hall with the Cliffringdeners most nights, so I hear."

"Grael makes a point, though," a hoarse voice said. "If we drive the husband out of the village, is it right to leave the wife?"

A few hoods nodded.

"Can't get between a man and his wife," someone said, raising a few chuckles.

"The father-in-law should go with them," someone else chirped, eliciting louder guffaws.

"Harath is not going anywhere," Grael insisted. "Our quarrel is with Garscap."

Lormak gave Grael a nervous glance. "Grael is right. We're not here to threaten women, are we? We'll get rid of her husband first. If she wants to go after him, that's her business. Anyway, back to the plan. After Charlin has taken Garscap away"—Lormak rested a hand on Grael's shoulder—"and this man here is wearing the thorny crown, we'll pay neighborly visits to the Eraths, Carnaths, and so on to let them know we have a new politician. Any questions? No? Let's go."

Lormak, Grael, and Dawan led the way. The rest trailed behind, a long, slithering shadow.

"At long last, we'll be rid of the Changeling," someone murmured. "And his Elfin friends will follow him. We'll drive them out, too."

Lormak's whisper tickled Grael's ear. "Don't mind loose talk like that. When you wear the thorny crown, you'll make the decisions."

Would he? It was hard to believe it. How long would it be before some of these men were plotting against him?

The only sound they made as they approached Garscap's house was the swish of their feet through the grass. The crowd coiled around the hut. Lormak thrust a rope into Grael's hands.

"Are you all ready?" Lormak whispered. He pulled back the flap over the door and dashed inside. Grael followed. He caught a glimpse of a shocked Garscap sitting up in his bed before one of the other conspirators jostled him out of the way. The rope was snatched from his hands. From behind a wall of backs came sounds of a struggle.

"Get off me, you..." Something choked off Garscap's voice.

Grael shoved his way through the crowd. Garscap squirmed on the floor, prostrate, trussed up and gagged. Four men pressed down on his legs. He raised his head to direct a malevolent stare at his captors.

A wide-eyed Lormak picked up the thorny crown from its resting place by Garscap's bed. As he passed it to Grael, he almost dropped it. Lormak cleared his throat. "If you give us no trouble, Garscap, then you have no need to fear us. We'll escort you to Saint Charlin. He'll remove you from this village, and you can go somewhere that wants you."

Garscap shivered. The sound that he made was like a sob. Surely, he was not about to cry.

The gag could not prevent Gascarp's snicker from filling the hut, chilling Grael to the bone. A boot kicked Garscap in the side to shut him up, but it only served to redouble his laughter. It continued all the way to the saint's home.

Lormak knocked on the door of the stone building. It swung open.

Charlin stood in the doorway, frowning. "Who dares disturb a saint's rest with such raucous merriment in the middle of the night?" Anger turned to shock when he saw the gag in Garscap's mouth. And then to understanding and horror.

"You have to release him," he said. His voice was soft, even apologetic.

"You don't understand—" Lormak began.

"*You* don't understand. His thorny crown is protected by saintly blessing. No man in the village may raise a hand against him. You must set him free."

Laughter shook Garscap to his knees. A few plotters turned and ran. Then the rest followed their example, stampeding into the night, leaving only Lormak, Grael, and Dawan staring at one another, aghast.

Lormak drew his knife. He walked behind Garscap. He looked at the saint with pleading eyes.

Charlin averted his gaze. "You have to free him."

Anger trembled through Grael. "I have never before heard the like of this blessing. Who gave Garscap this blessing?" he demanded.

Charlin bowed his head and massaged his forehead with one hand. "I did."

Grael managed to wring out a few words through his choking outrage. "Why? Forelight, why?"

The saint sighed. "He convinced me that it was necessary for the common good."

Lormak's knife was right behind Garscap's back. One quick thrust, and the Changeling would cease to be a threat. But the wielder of the blade would earn eternal damnation.

Snip.

With his freed hands, Garscap pulled the gag from his mouth. His grin brimming with malevolence, he stood up, strode over to Grael, and snatched the thorny crown from his hands.

"Thanks for minding it," he said. "Now, what am I to do with you three?"

"I was the instigator of this plot," Lormak said, his voice trembling. "The blame for it should be mine alone."

Still smiling, Garscap glanced slyly at Charlin. "But Grael was the one who would wear the thorny crown. This is a strange twist of fate. When Saint Charlin gave me his blessing, only this evening, he could not have realized his own brother would lead the plot against me this very night."

"Whatever you are going to do, do it," Lormak snapped.

"Dawan, go home to your mother," Garscap said.

Dawan did not move, just stared at his father.

"Go!" Garscap cried. "Get out of my sight before I change my mind."

Dawan ran.

"Wise man, wiser than the father," Garscap said. "Keep running. By rights, I could put you both to death and cast your families out of the village. Is that not so, saint?"

"It is." Charlin's words were barely a murmur.

"As a personal favor to Saint Charlin, I am going to put down Grael's involvement to youthful folly. Grael, the rest of your fortune"—Garscap smirked—"is mine now. Think of it as a fine. Now, go home to your parents before I change my mind."

"Thank you," Charlin whispered

"What about Lormak?" Grael asked.

"You won't be seeing him again. What did he say to me again? *He can find somewhere else that wants him.* Now, get out of here, before I regret my generosity."

As Grael fled into the night, he glanced back at Charlin's house. Lormak was kneeling on the ground, and Garscap was tying his hands behind his back with the same rope that had once bound the politician.

"Grael, here," someone whispered. "Over here."

Grael followed the voice to Dawan, who was lurking behind a clump of bushes. The tears streaming down his cheeks briefly shone red in the moonlight, before he buried his face in his hands and sobbed. Grael threw his arms around him.

"At least, his fate is exile," Grael said. "He's not dead."

"I can't go home to Mother and tell her," Dawan said. "She knew nothing about this. How can I tell her that he's gone forever? How can I tell my brothers and sisters?" He growled as he pushed free of Grael's hug and punched the air. "Damn the Changeling and damn the saint who saved him! I'm sorry, Grael. I didn't mean what I said about your brother. It was grief speaking."

It was hard to watch his friend so distraught. But for Charlin, Grael might have also been cast out of the village, and his family might have suffered this same agony.

Dawan wiped his eyes. "Will you come back to my home? I don't want to go back there alone."

"I will, but I'll not stay long," Grael said. "I must tell my father what has happened."

They walked back to the cabin in silence.

"I'll wait here," Grael said as they reached the door. He could go no farther.

"You're family," Dawan said. "Come in."

"No," Grael said firmly. "I can't."

Dawan nodded. "Wait here then." He opened the door and stepped inside the cabin. The door slammed shut. Grael sat on the little wooden doorstep, and cradling his head in his hands, he prayed. "Forelight, forgive me. I beg you, return Lormak to his family and spare them this grief."

A woman's raised voice came from inside the cabin, and then a pained wail. Other voices rose up and joined its keening. Morning stirred in the east before this lamentation halted. The door opened, and Dawan peered out.

"Grael, sorry. I forgot you were out here," he said. "You must be freezing, sitting there. Come inside"

"If you insist," Grael said with some reluctance. The cold had been preferable to being in the midst of their grief. He stiffly rose and entered the cabin.

Smiles greeted him, but they were forced, even desperate. Eyes, hollow with sorrow and exhaustion, watched him.

Dawan's mother fussed over him as an honored guest, embarrassing him with offers of food and drink. He was an impostor here. He had to get away, but he did not want to offend them by spurning their hospitality.

"I must go," Dawan said. "I must find out what exactly they are going to do to him."

"I must go, too," Grael said, seizing his opportunity. "I must tell my father what has happened."

Relief at escaping the Mangals' cabin quickly dissipated. Grael's apprehension grew with every step that brought him nearer his home. His father's reaction, on learning of the plot and Grael's part in it, was not going to be pleasant.

When he reached his father's house, the door was shut. Grael shied from entering. He knocked respectfully.

The door opened, and Grael's father filled the entrance. He regarded Grael with flinty eyes and crossed his arms.

His face burned with indignation. Anger sweated from every pore.

"You have to leave," he said. "Right now." The callousness of his visage denied any possibility for appeal.

"So you know," Grael said, swallowing.

The redness of his father's face deepened. "The Changeling already called around to gloat."

"I was a fool," Grael pleaded.

"You were warned," his father said. "But you wouldn't listen. You put your family's lives at risk for some stupid bit of cloth."

Grael had not done it for the thorny crown. He did it to protect Harath, but it was pointless to explain. His father would never understand.

"I cannot risk keeping you under this roof any longer," Lahan said, his voice thickening with emotion. "You are going to have to make your own way in the world." He wiped his hand across his eyes before he slammed the door shut.

***

Garscap let Evram push the bound Lormak ahead of them with a spear. They were a good distance outside Pigsknuckle. The Witchmilk roared beside them. The river's foaming waters, splashing against its rocky banks, sprayed them with gentle mists.

"Here's where the journey ends." Garscap drew his knife.

Lormak stared into the frothing waters before him. "I knew you had no intention of letting me go."

Garscap laughed. "But you kept quiet for the sake of your family. How noble."

Evram's smirk faltered. He licked his lips. "Did you not promise Saint Charlin to free him?"

"I promised to escort him from the village. I never promised to release him." He began to strip off his clothes. "I can't have him wandering from village to village gossiping about me, telling everyone what a monster I am."

"What in the Forelight's name are you doing?" Evram asked.

"He doesn't want to get my blood on his clothes," Lormak muttered.

Garscap sat up on a rock. "Let this be your last lesson in this life, Lormak. It's something I learned long ago. If you knock a man down, make damn sure he never gets up. Lormak, turn around. Evram, if you please." He waved toward Lormak.

"What?" Evram cried.

Garscap shrugged. "You are the one with the spear. Kill him."

"Don't do it, son!" Lormak cried. He was still facing Evram. "For the love of the Forelight, don't listen to him."

Evram glanced back and forth between Lormak and Garscap. His spear shook. He looked more scared than Lormak.

Garscap sighed. "All this talk of killing this one and killing that one. I knew it was no more than talk."

Evram grunted as he lunged. Lormak roared and crumpled as the spear tore through his belly. Garscap hopped off his perch as Evram pushed Lormak toward the water.

"Wait!" Garscap cried. He raced over and grabbed Lormak's head by the hair. He stared into Lormak's eyes. "I want you to know your sacrifice is a waste of time. When I get the chance, I am going to kill your son, and Grael Erol, and the rest of those stupid bastards who followed you."

Bloody spittle spattered upon his face. Garscap twisted Lormak's head to expose his neck. The knife jerked as it sawed through sinew and bone.

The bloody deed finished, Garscap sliced the corpse's bindings. If the body was ever found, it would be better not to give the impression that it was anything other than a fair fight.

"Push him over the edge into the river," Garscap panted.

Instead, Evram wept.

Thought he was a big man, found out he was a child. Garscap grumbled under his breath, "Oh, in the names of the seven divine Lights." He wrenched the spear from Evram's hands and poked the corpse into the Witchmilk.

He threw the spear at Evram's feet. "Clean it well. There can't be a hint of blood on it, or you. I'm going to have a wash to clean off this filth." He fanned his fingers toward his blood-spattered torso. "You did well, Evram," he lied. At least Evram was blooded now. Hopefully, he would find it easier to kill in the future.

"Were you serious about what you said about Grael Erol and the others?" Evram asked. His face was as pale as the Witchmilk's waters.

"Of course," Garscap said. "They'll all pay for their treachery."

"And when will that be?"

Garscap blessed Evram with an indulgent smile. "I told you before. It's all about timing."

Chapter 17

From across the mountains they came,
A council to answer his need,
Heroes of honor and acclaim,
The wise of word and great of deed.

~From *Alackalas And The Fair Princess.*

Early in the morning, beneath the long shadow of the furka, Garscap waited. Saint Charlin emerged from the woods. A white-haired man followed, his arms raised high, his head jammed against his shoulder. On his head was a thorny crown of twisted black and white. Garscap stood and made the sign of the furka.

"This is the Politician of Cronesglen, Radal Faral," Charlin said. "Radal, this is Garscap Torp. I'm sure the other politicians will arrive shortly. I'll leave you. Saints should not intrude in politics."

Garscap smiled. Did saints ever stop meddling?

Radal stretched to acknowledge the saint's departure. Garscap imitated him.

"Welcome to Cronesglen," Radal said. "Or at least its periphery."

This was an unfortunate byproduct of the demolition of Pigsknuckle's furkas. As the gathering of politicians could not take place in the middle of his village, Garscap was forced to cede the honor of hosting it to the Politician of Cronesglen.

"I hear strange things about Pigsknuckle. I hear its furkas have been destroyed," Radal said.

"Not all of them. One still stands. The saints deconsecrated the rest."

"Aren't you afraid?"

"Afraid?"

Radal pressed his hand against the trunk of the furka. "We couldn't stay in Cronesglen without our furkas. It's a haunted place. The ghosts of the old witches who gave the valley its name still linger."

"You mean the waterfalls?" Garscap asked. The seven cataracts in Cronesglen were said to be the endless tresses of the witches, turned to water.

"Their malevolent spirits are soaked into the valley. They're in the water, the earth, and the air. Sometimes, their murderous wails shiver through the night. I have heard them myself. No beast could make those cries. They want their valley back, their forest bearded again, and their altar restored and glistening with blood. The furkas protect us from their evil. You smile?"

Garscap struggled not to laugh at the old man's superstitious nonsense. "I find your faith inspiring."

Radal's arms reached into the air. Garscap turned to see a young man approaching. His gaunt, hungry face reminded Garscap of the thieving urchins in Formicary. A thorny crown of green and black rested on the stranger's greasy brown hair. The light redness of his beard accentuated its scarcity. He responded to Radal Faral's salute with a half-hearted flap of his arms. He introduced himself as Mogod Kulum of Stonegarden.

"You came without a saint," Radal observed.

"One accompanied me to the edge of the forest, but he would go no farther. He was afraid if he came any closer, he might be corrupted, I suppose."

Radal appeared to wrestle with Mogod's comment for a few moments. "What do you mean?" he asked.

"Never mind," Mogod Kulum said. His smile was too worldly for Garscap's liking.

"You look familiar. Have you ever been to Formicary?" Garscap asked.

"I've never left the mountains," Mogod replied in a tone implying those who did were failures.

The drip of politicians became a trickle and then a stream. The faces of many were young and lean, perhaps indicating the Year of Bleeding Snow had given them their thorny crowns. Some hailed from Pigsknuckle's neighbors, like Highstep and Wyrmery. Others represented villages on the fringes of the Stretchers' territory, places of which Garscap knew little other than their names, such as Kneadlea and Wolfden. A few. like Beardwood and Skullridge, were unfamiliar. The distinctively colored halo on every head flavored the throng milling around the furka with an exoticism that Garscap had not experienced since his days in Formicary. The crowd's size impressed upon him how numerous his race was. If each of these politicians led a community as large as Pigsknuckle, then they could muster an enormous army.

Lohor Teevan weaved through the crowd to salute Garscap. He was a short, stocky man. The yellow and blue of Littleknuckle rested on a balding pate, while his gray beard extended with threatening length from his jaw. His bulging brown eyes and grotesquely broad smile made him look like a hairy frog. Lohor's community was Pigsknuckle's nearest neighbor. He greeted Garscap with all the exaggerated bonhomie that had once been reserved for Widan. Garscap welcomed him in the same fashion, all the while remembering that, despite Lohor's affability, he had failed to help the orphans and widows of Cliffringden. For such a holy people, Stretchers could be not very charitable.

Radal was calling the meeting to order as the last politician arrived. Wearing the yellow and red thorny crown of Ogresquern, he introduced himself to the assembly as Avel Kuny. Black hair circled his face. His complexion, tanned and speckled by the sun, emphasized the ghostly pallor of his large blue eyes.

"I believe one of you might be a distant kinsman of mine. Which of you is the Politician of Pigsknuckle?" he said as he joined the group.

"I am. I'm Garscap Torp."

"You're not a Melkath?"

"The Melkaths no longer rule Pigsknuckle. I'm its politician now." Garscap declined to mention his marriage to Widan's daughter.

"You deserve congratulations. You achieved something my ancestors couldn't. Of course, I feel some sympathy for the Melkaths. I'm grateful to them. Had they not driven my family from Pigsknuckle, I might have ended up ruling that heap of excrement instead of Ogresquern."

Garscap shrugged and smiled.

Radal hushed the titters rippling through the crowd. "You shouldn't speak like that beside a furka. Perhaps we should begin with a prayer to the Forelight for guidance."

A few nodded enthusiastically. The countenances of others expressed groans they did not dare utter. The majority accepted Radal's proposal with stony silence. The Politician of Cronesglen began the Forelight's Prayer, and the others joined in.

"So, why were we summoned here?" Mogod asked when they had finished.

"We represent every village in the Stretches," Garscap said. It was hard to believe this motley gathering comprised the noblest leaders that his race could find. "Each of us is responsible for the protection and welfare of his community. I'm sure I don't have to remind you of that burden. This is an unprecedented gathering, but if it had taken place not so long ago, another politician would have attended. I'm referring to the Politician of Cliffringden. That village is no more. The Fair Folk destroyed it. They have built a mighty fortress on its corpse, from which they intend to strike deeper into our lands. If we don't join together, they'll destroy us one by one. Any of us could be their next victim."

"Stonegarden is beyond their reach," Mogod Kulum said.

"True, for the moment," Garscap admitted. "But when the Fair Folk have wiped out all the villages between what was Cliffringden and your village, what chance has Stonegarden alone to withstand their onslaught? If we are to survive, we must put aside old enmities and join together to defeat our common enemy."

"So you propose some form of alliance?" Avel Kuny asked. "Fine words, but what does it mean in practice?"

"Well, for example, I have a group of Elves at my disposal," Garscap said.

A few jaws dropped, but most of the politicians didn't show any surprise. Evidently, they had already heard the rumor.

"They're Stretchers like us. They're training my people to fight the Fair Folk's legions. I'm offering the same instruction to your warriors."

"And what do you want in exchange for this generosity?" Mogod asked.

"Nothing."

"Nothing?" Mogod repeated.

"*Nothing*," Garscap emphasized, relishing the gasps and bewildered countenances. "Of course, guarantees will have to be given before saints that my hospitality will not be abused."

"I'm not interested," Mogod said. "Stonegarden doesn't need Pigsknuckle's aid to look after its own. What you propose is akin to inviting the Gilt Spider for supper or seeking advice from witches."

Other politicians voiced concern that their communities would disapprove of fraternization with Fair Folk, whatever their religion.

"I'm leaving," one politician declared. "I can't see where the trick in this lies, but I can smell it."

As he stood to go, Avel called him to a halt. "You're foolish to leave without a saint's protection. Warriors from rival villages may be lurking in the forest. Wait for your saint."

"If warriors are out there, I assure you they're not from Cronesglen," Radal said.

"This alliance will need a leader," Garscap said. "One of us must be senior to the others to prevent our league from being wrecked by disputes and petty rivalries. I'm ideally qualified for the role. Given my experience as a mercenary captain in Formicary, I'm uniquely equipped for the sort of war we face."

The other politicians laughed. Even the pious Radal Faral could not suppress a chuckle.

"What could you offer to make us agree to such absurdity?" Mogod asked.

"How long have you been Politician of Stonegarden?"

"Half a year."

"And you?" Garscap pointed to another youngish politician.

"A season or so," he admitted nervously.

"Times are hard," Garscap said. "In hard times, people have little patience for their politicians. That impatience bestowed to some of us our thorny crowns, but it could take back those crowns just as easily. Mine is absolutely safe. None in Pigsknuckle would dare to challenge my authority because it is guaranteed by a saint's blessing."

"That's preposterous!" Mogod cried. "No saint would dabble in politics so flagrantly."

Garscap placed one hand on the furka. "I'm telling the truth. And I promise if you accept me as your leader, the saint will extend the same blessing to you."

"Nonsense!" Mogod protested.

"Impossible!" someone else cried.

"If the saints are so amenable to his rule, then I must accept their wisdom," Radal said.

"And what do you say?" Garscap said to Avel.

"I'm interested." Avel responded to the gasps from the crowd with a shrug. "I bear his people no love. The enmity between our villages is renowned but paltry in comparison to my family's detestation of Pigsknuckle. However, his offer still interests me, if he can deliver on it. I would sleep a lot easier at night knowing my crown was secure. Be honest. Can any of you say anything different?"

"My village will never pay tribute to Pigsknuckle!" someone in the crowd roared.

Garscap shook his head. "None is sought. Your sole obligation is to place your warriors at my disposal to fight the Fair Folk."

"If I go back to my people and tell them I agreed to that, they would fling me off the nearest cliff," Mogod said.

"The saints back Garscap's proposal," Radal said, drawing a disgusted grunt from Mogod and grumbling from other politicians.

"You are missing the point," Garscap said. "The saint's blessing will shield you from the indignation of your village. Saintly decree will make your rule perpetual."

That was enough for several politicians, including Mogod. Victory was within Garscap's grasp. He was about to request a vote when Lohor demanded to speak.

"Your offer is an attractive one," Lohor said to Garscap. "I'd like to know if every monastery is party to this blessed edict."

"It only needs one saint to be convinced of its merit," Garscap said. "What one saint binds, no other saint will unbind. And I have such a saint."

"I have never heard the like before," Radal said. "It has the smell of intrigue. I don't like it."

"Relying on subterfuge to secure our reigns may serve to hasten our ruin," Lohor said. "The monasteries might not take kindly to such trickery, when it is discovered."

"I won over this saint not by some tawdry ploy but by logical argument," Garscap said. "I told him any politician who sent his men to be trained by my Orstretcherists placed his thorny crown in jeopardy. Some of you have made the same observation. My pious collaborator agreed that, in this time of crisis, any politician brave enough to submit his men to the Orstretcherists' tutelage deserved saintly imprimatur for his authority. If this proves to be wrong, the blame shall fall on him and me alone. Any of you who earn the blessing will be no worse off than you are now in the unlikely event that it is ever rescinded. While it stands, nobody will dare challenge you."

"The repercussions of losing that blessing for those who lean on it too much might not be as slight as you claim," Radal said.

"The Politician of Cronesglen talks of consequences that might happen in some distant future," Avel said. "My worries exist in the present. Unlike Radal, who has ruled his village since before I was born, I haven't such a tight hold on my thorny crown that I can ignore Garscap's offer. I advise others in my position to do the same."

"I find it hard to believe you are so willing to swear allegiance to your most bitter enemy," Lohor said.

"The breadth of that fealty is narrow," Avel said. "And its reward is so great."

"Perhaps you are right," Lohor admitted, rubbing his jaw as he cogitated. "This saintly blessing would be a boon. However, the permanence of my thorny crown is of no matter if Littleknuckle becomes another Martyrsgrave. I won't make a promise that places my people in jeopardy. The safety of my village takes precedence over any pledge of support I might decide to offer Garscap. I reserve the right to disregard his orders if they put Littleknuckle in danger."

Garscap's heart sank as several heads in the crowd nodded in agreement. "I would never ask you to do that. You can trust me."

Lohor grinned and shook his head. "It's not about trust. It's about the principle."

Garscap nodded and tried his best to sound sympathetic as he nervously eyed the crowd's growing restlessness. "Of course. I've no quarrel with what you are saying." The validity of Lohor's condition was so obvious that any argument Garscap might make against it would only serve to alienate his audience. He had no choice but to concede it.

Avel smiled. "I've heard enough." He strolled over to the furka and placed a hand on the stone. "I recognize Garscap Torp as the leader of our fight against the Fair Folk's invasion. I pledge my fealty to him in that capacity, provided it doesn't endanger Ogresquern."

One by one, other politicians followed his example, including Lohor and Mogod. Some of the more long-reigning politicians demurred, claiming they needed more time to consider the matter, but their opposition faltered when Radal placed his hands on the furka and solemnly promised his fidelity.

A long train of shadows stretched behind the furka when the saints began to dribble back to take away their charges. As the evening sank into night, only Garscap and Avel remained.

"That went well," the Politician of Ogresquern said. "I didn't mention we had met before this gathering. Of course, it wasn't my intention to deceive the other politicians." He shrugged and smiled. "I simply feared it might complicate the debate."

Garscap smiled. "I can vouch you uttered no untruth." Though Avel had been extremely misleading.

"Apologies for my unflattering comment about Pigsknuckle," Avel said. "Of course, I meant it in jest."

"I realized that," Garscap said. "It was good to remind the other politicians of our villages' former enmity."

"I thought so," Avel said.

Garscap and Avel had a lot in common. Both were outsiders in the villages they ruled. Both hated the Melkaths. Both desired power. And Garscap offered something his rival could not resist.

"So, when will you take my sister Talida as your wife?" Avel asked.

"Very soon. I have a few matters to resolve first," Garscap replied. Like getting rid of his current wife. Avel would doubtless be amused on learning the truth. It would add some extra spice to the prospect of his nephew wearing the thorny crown of Pigsknuckle. But now was not the time to mention it. Not until it had been resolved. Hopefully, Talida was not ugly.

"I suppose we should be thankful to our pious friend from Cronesglen," Garscap said. "Even if he's a bit slow-witted, without his support, we might have struggled to convince the dissidents."

Avel chuckled. "You underestimate Radal Faral at your peril. He has worn the thorny crown of Cronesglen longer than either of us has lived. He is wilier than we and all the other politicians combined. Remember the boy and girl from your village that were kidnapped by the Jinglemen? Their captors' carts were recovered, and Radal insisted on giving the vehicles and their contents to the boy. Some say he was afraid such a trove would spark disputes among his own people. Some say he knew it was cursed. You can scoff, but the Jinglemen died at the Gilt Spider's hands, and the politician who accepted it is politician no more."

The implication was unflattering. Garscap's rise in power was not due a curse. It was preposterous nonsense. Still, he would be more wary of the Politician of Cronesglen in the future.

He would also remember Lohor Teevan's contribution to the debate.

"You're looking very serious," Avel said. "What's bothering you?"

"The oath's not as strong as I would like."

Avel chuckled. "Come on. Do you really think any politician worth his thorny crown would pledge unconditional loyalty to another?"

Avel had come up with the oath's wording too easily. He must have composed it before Lohor voiced his objection. Why wouldn't Avel want to limit Garscap's authority? Of course, he had been content to let another propose the restriction and become the target of Garscap's ire. Perhaps, Avel had even prompted Lohor's idea. Avel was another tricky character.

Having to deal with all these deceitful politicians made Garscap nostalgic for when Widan was his only rival.

Avel slapped Garscap's shoulder. "You should rejoice. No matter the oath's strength, it has made you the most important leader of our people since kingship was abolished."

Garscap broke into a smile. It was true. And this was but the beginning. The other politicians were slier than he had imagined, but his cunning exceeded theirs. Eventually, they would bend to his will, as Charlin had.

Garscap spied the saint at the edge of the clearing. "Ah, here is my escort. I must bid farewell till our next gathering."

Garscap quickly shook Avel's hand, and then jogged over to the approaching Saint Charlin.

"It is good to see such friendliness between old enemies," Charlin observed.

"Blessed are the peacemakers," Garscap said, smiling.

He chatted with the saint about inconsequential matters till he was certain they could not be overheard by Avel. "The meeting was a great success," he said. "We agreed to form an alliance against the Fair Folk. And the other politicians chose me to be its leader." He was giddy, like an excited child.

The saint's wan smile spurred Garscap's generosity. "This wouldn't be possible without your help. Future generations will recall your wisdom in the same breath as Saint Odran or Saint Valclar or Saint Apasapal."

"Please stop," Charlin pleaded. "I'm unworthy of your praise."

Garscap nodded. "I meant no offense."

"None taken," Charlin assured him. "Thank you."

Garscap silently thanked Grael Erol for all his help, too. Out of gratitude for sparing Grael or fear for his future safety, Charlin had shed a little of his circumspection and become more amenable to Garscap and his schemes.

Charlin stopped walking. "You understand your role is to lead the politicians, not to rule them," he said. He wagged a finger, but he was friendly, even apologetic. "The days of kings and their sinful ways have long past."

"Of course," Garscap said, pretending dismay that anyone might suspect him of such grand ambitions. The golden thorny crown, the one Alackalas, Braer, and the other kings of old had worn, lay in some dusty corner of the monastery of Skyaltar, but some day it would be his. While he protested his innocent intentions to Charlin, he looked forward to the time when some saint placed that crown on his head.

Chapter 18

She was a year's beauty distilled -
Fierce as winter, gentle as spring,
Gold lips ripe as autumn's harvest,
Eyes dancing with summer's flowering.

~From *Alackalas and the Fair Princess.*

The weeks following the Orstretcherists' return to Leaftea Lake were a happy time for TrueFriend Peritus. The feeble spring gradually strengthened into a healthy summer, and the hardships of a seemingly endless winter were forgotten. Though he disclaimed the Pigsknucklers' assertions that the Orstretcherists had brought the good weather with them, he nonetheless took pleasure in such superstitious gossip. More importantly, the cramped, sedentary existence of Pigsback, relieved only by the occasional hunting trip, was over. Frenetic activity packed his day. Much of it related to preparing the Pigsknucklers and other visiting Stretchers for combat, but there were many other chores to be done. Food to gather and cook. Fires to feed. Damaged equipment to repair or replace, and dirty clothes to clean.

TrueFriend enjoyed all these tasks. Except the laundry. He hated the laundry.

Unfortunately, that job, due to its general unpopularity, was on a strict rotation, and TrueFriend's turn had come. DayFlambeau and PureFaith took pity on him and helped carry the piles of dirty garments from their encampment to a nearby stream.

TrueFriend sighed as he observed the daunting mountains piled in a semi-circle around him. "I am outflanked by washing. Reinforcements would save the day. You two would not like to give me a hand?"

"You're right," PureFaith said. "I would *not* like to give you a hand."

"On the other thumb, I would, but unfortunately both of my hands are still raw from doing it the last time," DayFlambeau said, as he passed a wooden paddle to TrueFriend. "Enjoy."

"At least keep me company a while," TrueFriend begged.

"We have to get back to the camp," PureFaith said, yawning. "Duty calls."

"I heard another bunch of novices arrives today," DayFlambeau said glumly.

"They are from Wyrmery," TrueFriend said.

"I do not care where they are from," DayFlambeau muttered.

"I know what you mean," PureFaith said. "New names and faces replace the old before I am familiar with them. First, it was Littleknuckle, then Highstep, then Bittenglen, and now Wyrmery. Their sojourns are so brief. They leave in the same hurry as they arrived. They hardly have a chance to master even the most rudimentary combat skills."

"That is not what I meant," DayFlambeau said, his voice sullen and low. He turned for camp.

"I have to go," PureFaith said, hurrying after him.

TrueFriend sighed as he surveyed the mounds of disheveled garments. It was a pity that AscendantSun had not brought some decent soap from Tincranny. The Orstretcherists had been bereft of this vital commodity for some time. He had no choice but beat the dirt out of the clothes.

He immersed so many garments in the stream that they threatened to soak it up completely. Then he picked an item from the soup of apparel and began to pound it on a stone, rubbing the stained fabric together till the marks were gone. He wrung it out, threw it to one side, and then snatched another garment from the stream and put it through the same pummeling. Then another garment. Then another.

"You wash your own clothes. Have you no woman to do it for you?" It was an unfamiliar voice. A Stretcher's voice. A female voice.

TrueFriend continued with his laundry, careful not to glance at the speaker. The pliant gentleness of her voice was alarming. The Orstretcherists were aware of the lust they inspired in some of the village women. The saints had taught them about the sins of the flesh and how women were especially prone to them. It was not clear why casual copulation was so terrible, but the saints must know what they were talking about.

"Have you no woman to do it?" the girl repeated.

"I have none," TrueFriend admitted. "Here," he added. The Orstretcherists had agreed to maintain the subterfuge that they had women in their homeland. They had settled on this plan by themselves, being unsure of the wisdom of saintly advice on such matters.

"I thought you were without desire like the saints," the girl said. "You must get lonely without your woman."

"I miss her terribly," TrueFriend declared, redoubling his frenzied washing. Was she attempting to proposition him? If so, his professed devotion to another would stop her.

"My name is Ashin Carnath." A long pause followed. "If you ever want company," the girl said, her voice trembling.

"Thank you," he blurted. Maybe he shouldn't have said that. He lay the breeches in his hands down on a stone, straightened his back, and looked around, but she was gone.

***

"So, what's this about?" Grael asked.

"I will let TrueFriend explain. I cannot," AscendantSun said as he lifted the flap of his yellow tent and waved Grael inside.

He stooped and entered. NeverFear and TrueFriend sat cross-legged on a blanket. Elfin countenances were as a rule inscrutable, but TrueFriend's face radiated distress as it looked up at Grael.

After AscendantSun and Grael sat down, TrueFriend related his encounter with the girl at the stream. Horror crept up Grael's spine as he listened. Everything about the story was disconcerting, including TrueFriend's obvious naivety about affairs of the heart.

TrueFriend sighed and rubbed his hands down his face. "In the end, I thanked her. I have no idea why. I suppose I panicked."

Grael rolled his eyes.

"She may not have even heard that. She was gone when I looked round." TrueFriend pressed his hands against his cheeks and formed a triangle with his outer thumbs under his lower lip. "I don't understand. My professed devotion to another woman should have ended the matter."

Obviously, it hadn't. Otherwise, Grael wouldn't be here. "You didn't get a glimpse of her?" he asked.

"I was afraid to look upon the face of my would-be seductress in case my glance aggravated her passion," TrueFriend admitted. He lowered his hands and took a deep breath. "However, lately, I have been followed around the camp by a plump-cheeked girl with dark hair and light brown eyes."

"It sounds like Ashin Carnath," Grael said. "It must be her." It explained why she was hanging about the Orstretcherists' camp so much. If the details of this infatuation became common knowledge, she would be ruined.

TrueFriend rested his head in one hand. "I've tried to find the humor in the situation, but the girl's misplaced passion disturbs me. I am incapable of reciprocating it."

"Grael, please understand, TrueFriend means no offense," NeverFear said. "After you have beheld an Elfin maiden, you become blind to all other feminine charms."

"Everywhere I go, she follows," TrueFriend said. "Even when I cannot see her, I can feel her gaze on me. I despise those imploring eyes. Even in sleep, I cannot escape them. They invade my dreams."

He shook his head. "Her ability to pick me out from the midst of my comrades is unnerving. I wonder why I alone must endure her obsession? We all look alike to Mixies. I have overheard Stretchers comment to that effect. What have I done to inflame her fascination?"

"I can recognize you all by the tattoos on your foreheads," Grael said. "She can probably do the same."

"Recognition is one thing. Attraction is something else. Your suggestion is reasonable but it fails to explain why her passion fixed on me before all others," TrueFriend said.

Grael thought of Harath. "The heart's impulses are sometimes wayward, and the root of its caprice is obscure even to its owner."

"We learned of this matter only this morning," NeverFear said.

"I have been hinting about it for some time," TrueFriend said, directing a sharp glance at NeverFear.

"You must admit, your clues were pretty cryptic," NeverFear observed.

"Embarrassment does not lend itself well to eloquence," TrueFriend replied. "And what was my friends' reaction to my plight? They made light of it."

"Our mirth was not spiteful or mocking," AscendantSun said. "We acted out of kindness. We hoped humor might ease your distress. Having never experienced such unwelcome attention, we had little appreciation of its gravity. Your stricken countenance quickly dispelled our levity."

He turned to address Grael. "I invited you here because we need the advice of someone whose discretion can be trusted. We realize the delicacy of this matter, and we want it resolved with minimum fuss. If we tell Saint Charlin, he is liable to demand the girl's public censure. Saints despise sins of the flesh above all other wickedness. As for Garscap, he might consider the affair to be the concern of saints rather than politicians and hand it over to your brother. What do you advise that we should do?"

"Women have no business hanging around your camp," Grael said. "Widan would have never tolerated their presence. Ask Garscap to impose a general ban on their visits. That will prevent Ashin from harassing TrueFriend without singling her out."

AscendantSun smiled and nodded. "NeverFear and I had considered what you propose already, but we needed to hear it from you to be sure of its wisdom. Of course, it will not prevent her from approaching TrueFriend outside the camp."

"I will not leave it," TrueFriend said. "At least, not until her ardor has cooled."

"That might take a very long time," Grael admitted. "These feverish vexations can take months and even years to wane." He was a hypocrite to speak of love as someone else's disease.

"You could talk to her," TrueFriend suggested. "You might be able to dissuade her of this foolishness."

Grael's cheeks warmed. "It would not be appropriate for me to make such an overture. It should come from another woman." There was only one candidate for the task, though he was eager to avoid her. "Garscap's wife, Harath, is the ideal choice."

"Are you sure?" AscendantSun asked.

"Yes," Grael said. His face and ears burned. "There's an independent streak in her character which would make her more sympathetic to Ashin's situation than, for example, my mother. I might as well tell my brother as ask for my mother's help. Charlin might be more forgiving."

"I understand there may be some difficulties in speaking frankly to Harath," AscendantSun said.

"It'll not be easy," Grael conceded. "It may take some time before I get an opportunity."

"In the meantime, we will ask Garscap to banish women from the camp," AscendantSun said. "Perhaps, that by itself will be enough."

***

AscendantSun lay awake in his tent, watching the dull yellow light passing through its fabric slowly brighten. With the ban in place, TrueFriend hopefully had slept more soundly.

A swooping screech lifted him from his mattress. Wearing just his tunic, he grabbed his batonaxes and dashed outside. More screams drew him southward. The camp rattled awake. Dazed faces peered out of their shelters. Tents shuddered with frantic movement as their occupants dressed and armed.

On the fringe of the encampment, AscendantSun discovered the origin of the distressful cries. Ashin's face, so raw with murderous fury, was hardly recognizable. Tearful streams coursed from her bloodshot eyes. Her body shivered as if in the grip of fever. Her screams were reminiscent of those that a wounded animal might direct at its injurer, brimful with pain and warning. Though NoonBlest, PureFaith, and NeverFear barred her way, they were intimidated by her ferocity. Their glances pleaded for AscendantSun's intervention.

"You are not welcome here," he said. It was a relief to see two approaching Stretchers, undoubtedly posted by Garscap to maintain a discreet vigil over the Ors' camp.

"You can't keep me from him!" Ashin roared. "TrueFriend and I are meant to be together. He avoids me only because you make him." She punched NeverFear in the face.

The two Stretchers grabbed the girl's arms from behind and began to drag her away.

One of them chided, "Daughter of Carnath, you should be ashamed of yourself. Pull back your claws and end your fussing. You bring shame on your family's name by striking a guest of Pigsknuckle and carrying on like a cheated strumpet from Formicary."

Nodding at NeverFear, who was trying to staunch the blood pouring from his nose, the other Stretcher quipped, "She doesn't need much combat training."

"Let us hope this settles the matter," NeverFear said, tilting back his head as he pressed a handkerchief to his nose. "Older Pigsknucklers will have more experience of this sort of wayward attraction than us, or your friend Grael. They will know how to cure her affliction."

AscendantSun agreed, despite his doubts.

Days passed, and the girl did not reappear. None of the Stretchers mentioned her. When pressed by AscendantSun, Grael politely refused to speak of her. The incident gradually slipped from conversation. With so much to be done to prepare the Stretchers for war, and so little time to do it, nobody had much opportunity to reflect on distractions like Ashin Carnath. Even TrueFriend forgot his misguided tormentor.

Then, one evening, Grael raced into the camp. Sensing something was terribly wrong, AscendantSun put aside his dinner, and ran over to him.

"What's happened?" AscendantSun asked, unnerved by Grael's wide-eyed stare.

Through labored breaths, Grael said, "Ashin has disappeared."

***

Fapath Carnath pointed out the distant figure scrambling over the boulders by the Witchmilk's raging waters. "There she is. We've found her." He waved to his sons, who were farther down the river, and signaled them to head upstream.

"It's a great relief she's alive," Evram said. He wanted to maintain a grave mien suited to the circumstances, but he was unable to restrain a smile.

"You respect my daughter still, despite her bewitchment," Fapath observed.

"She is an innocent victim of the Orstretcherist's magic. She is to be pitied rather than hated."

"Would you marry her?"

"She wouldn't want me," Evram said. She had been cold toward him since the incident with Joraem. Still, that cheeky flirt had to be taught a lesson after trying to muscle in on Evram's girl.

"Her wants have little to do with it," Fapath said, patting Evram's shoulder. "In all honesty, I doubt she'd find a better husband."

"My father might not approve," Evram admitted. Maergan was a potential rival for Ashin's hand. Since his mourning for his wife had drawn to a close, Maergan had made no secret of his desire for another wife.

"I'll give a dowry more than adequate to silence his objections. All you've to do is stand firm against his remonstration. You're a man now, not a child that your father can bully."

"Will we go down to her?"

Fapath's chronic scowl deepened a little. "I think it may be best if you approached her first. We don't want to startle her into doing something even more stupid."

With the care of a predator closing on his prey, Evram crept down to the river, using the rocks and foliage to hide his approach. Ashin halted atop a large flat boulder and stared into the churning water. He was only a couple of feet away when she turned.

"Go away!" she screamed. She looked a frightful mess. Even her halo tilted to one side. Her left eye was swollen and bruised. Did the tears streaming from it hurt?

"Your father sent me," Evram said, trying to sound gentle. "He's worried about you."

"More like worried about his good name," she hissed. "The coward hasn't even the guts to come himself." She moved a little nearer the river.

"Please, Ashin," Evram said. "I love you."

"Is that why you crippled Joraem Scorael?" Her smile was scornful. "Poor Joraem. All he did wrong was to show me a little kindness. Despite his injuries, he's twice the man you or TrueFriend will ever be. My beauty has brought me only misery."

"I love you," Evram pleaded.

"Stay away from me!" She backed a step too far and tottered over the edge.

Evram lunged toward her, but he could not reach her before she hit the water. He followed her in, thoughtless for his own fate. Icy terror tore at him as he smashed into the Witchmilk. He struggled to keep his head above the frothing water as it coiled about him and pulled him downstream. He could not hear his own screams above its thunderous roar. As he slammed against rocks, he tried to cling to them, but they were too slippery, and he was too weak to fight the urgent force of the river.

A spear reached out from the bank and dangled above his head, keeping pace with the current. He seized it with all of his will, and Fapath's sons dragged him from the river's murderous clutch.

"Where is Ashin?" he asked through struggling breaths, as he hugged the dry stone.

"She's gone to wherever the Witchmilk takes her," Ilyam Carnath said. "She was face down when I last saw her. May the Forelight have mercy on her tortured soul."

Ashin had not meant what she said. She had been in the grip of a delirium of the Orstretcherist's making. TrueFriend had taken her from Evram, and he would have his revenge.

***

The training session with visitors from Rockstack was nearing its end when someone grabbed AscendantSun's arm.

"I need to talk you now," Garscap whispered. "It can't wait."

AscendantSun turned to his pupils. "I must go."

"So, are we finished for the day?" one of the Rockstackers asked.

AscendantSun glanced at the sun. "No. NeverFear will take over for me."

The Rockstackers emitted a collective, exhausted groan.

NeverFear winked at AscendantSun as he shouted, "Enough of that! Your foes can fight from sunup to sundown, and you must learn to do the same. Let's do some sparring."

Clanging of metal and cries of exertion drifted from the training area as AscendantSun followed Garscap in silence to the remains of Leaftea's furka. Why was Garscap being so secretive? Was this about Ashin Carnath or some other matter? Perhaps he had somehow learned of Grael's visit to AscendantSun before the attempt to overthrow him.

They halted over the broken stone. Garscap cleared his throat. "Ashin Carnath is dead."

The news numbed AscendantSun. He took in only fragments of Garscap's account of her death. Apparently, she had leapt into the Witchmilk and drowned. His shock was nothing compared with what TrueFriend would suffer when he found out.

"I'm telling you in case you experience increased hostility from some of the villagers," Garscap said. "Many have no love for your kind as it is, and this incident is certain to deepen their hatred. To tell the plain truth, her father demanded I put to death the Orstretcherist who was the focus of her attention. Fapath claimed TrueFriend had cast a spell on her."

AscendantSun shook his head. The Pigsknucklers had an infuriating propensity for superstitious nonsense.

"Of course, I told him I had no interest in punishing the innocent, and he should keep his slander to himself," Garscap said. "For all we know, she ran away from home for reasons unconnected to her passion for your friend. Perhaps, old Fapath was responsible. Perhaps, he was a bit too generous with his fist after she made a show of herself."

"You seem certain of TrueFriend's innocence," AscendantSun observed. "You are not swayed by my people's reputation for seduction?"

Garscap kicked the shattered trunk of the furka. "If he had ravished her, then my view might be different. He had no interest in her. I guess his taste is spoiled by the women of his own kind."

"Something like that."

Garscap shook his head as he kicked the stone again. "What possible motive could he have to seduce her and then reject her? What would he gain by driving her mad? He had no reason to ruin her. Nobody does anything without a reason."

AscendantSun thought of the Harbinger. "Perhaps he is evil."

Garscap chuckled. "Are you trying to sow doubts in my mind?"

"No. I am astonished by your faith in us."

"I trust my friends. You are my friends, are you not?"

AscendantSun nodded. "Of course." He smiled at the questions about Garscap that NeverFear and Saint Sebryn had attempted to sow in his mind. Garscap had proved them wrong. He was someone who could be trusted.

AscendantSun excused himself and set about locating TrueFriend. It would take only a stray word from a Stretcher for news of Ashin's death to spread rapidly through the Orstretcherists' camp. TrueFriend had to be prepared for the revelation before it became common knowledge.

He arrived at TrueFriend's tent to find a sheepish NeverFear standing at the entrance. From inside came the jangle of metal, the soft plop of fabric being stuffed into a leather backpack, and the scrape of leather cords being tautened and knotted.

"I already heard," AscendantSun assured NeverFear before he could launch into an explanation.

"He will not listen to reason," NeverFear said. "He is determined to leave."

A backpack and a shoulder-rack were tossed out of the tent. TrueFriend followed, clad in full armor, a batonaxe in each hand. Rising from his stoop, he laid the weapons to one side and began strapping on the equipment.

"I am going back to Pigsback," he said. "One innocent death on my conscience is plenty. I want no more."

"Don't go," AscendantSun begged. "None of this is your fault. Nobody, not even Garscap, blames you. You're needed here. Here, you can make a real difference."

Deaf to AscendantSun's pleas, TrueFriend prepared for his departure. After he had secured his batonaxes on his shoulder-rack, something gurgled briefly in his throat but got no further. His eyes glistening with emotion, he nodded farewell and headed out of the camp towards the white peak as his defeated friends watched in hopeless silence.

***

Streaks of venom rolled down Evram's cheeks. Rage had wrung all sorrow out of him, and as he leaned over Garscap, he burned with hate like the vengeful hero of some forgotten saga. Garscap would have found the spectacle more impressive if it wasn't because of a silly crush on a stupid, dead girl.

"I want Ashin's seducer dead," Evram demanded.

"On what grounds can I arrest him?"

"Who said anything about arresting him? I said I want him dead," Evram rasped. "He'll die, even if I have to raze Pigsback."

The politician leapt from his seat and connected his fist with Evram's jaw, knocking him to the ground. Garscap had forgotten how good it felt to punch someone in the face. Evram's astonishment was quite comical. Lying on the floor, he looked as small as his concerns.

"You hit me," Evram whined as he gingerly rubbed his jaw.

"Only to knock some sense into you. For your own good. Never speak such nonsense again. Understand?"

"I understand," Evram muttered, his voice filthy with accusation.

Garscap sighed. It had been a mistake to take this petulant child into his confidence. He had sought to mold Evram's naive adulation into the admiring audience so long denied him, but the material was poor. Evram was too impetuous, too temperamental. He was not clever enough. He lacked subtlety. He didn't understand finesse. Though his loyalty was undeniable. And loyalty was worth a lot. Loyalty was better than intelligence, if a choice had to be made. Besides, Evram was learning. Garscap had to be patient.

Still rubbing his jaw, Evram wobbled to his feet. "Ashin's murderer is to remain unpunished because his friends are too precious to your schemes to risk upsetting them."

Garscap smiled. Here was evidence of Evram's learning. He made no spurious assertion that Garscap was motivated by fondness for the Orstretcherists. Evram understood political considerations were Garscap's paramount concern.

He nodded at his student. "They are like the scorpion who wanted to cross the river."

"What?" Evram grunted.

Garscap shrugged. "It is a tale I picked up somewhere. Maybe I heard it in Formicary." He sat down by the fire and invited Evram to join him with a tilt of his head. Evram plopped down on the far side of the little hearth.

Garscap smiled. "The story begins when a scorpion finds a river fat with rainwater. Searching for a crossing point along the bank, he spies a frog trapped beneath a fallen branch.

"The scorpion says to the frog, 'I wish to cross the river, but I can't swim. Promise to ferry me across on your back, and I'll release you from your prison.'

"The frog is suspicious. 'I can't trust you. You're my bitter enemy.'

"The scorpion says, 'You have no choice. If you refuse my help, you will die slowly of starvation.'

"'But you'll sting me with your tail while we are crossing,' the frog whimpers.

"The scorpion says, 'If I do, we'll both drown, so it's not in my interest to poison you. To make it worth your while, I promise from this day forth I'll never strike any frog again.'

"The frog agrees to the bargain. The scorpion uses his tail and claws to free the frog. The frog lets the scorpion crawl onto his back and wades into the stream. All is fine till they're about halfway across. The frog suddenly disappears beneath the swirling water. When he emerges at the far bank, the drowning scorpion calls to him plaintively, 'Why did you abandon me? I promised to not sting you.'

"The frog calls back as the river swallows the wriggling scorpion, 'You said it made no sense for you to poison me while we traversed the stream, but what would stop you from stinging me when we reached the bank? True, you might have kept your promise, but by letting you drown,

I'll ensure your murderous tail will never bother me again.'"

Evram's eyebrows squished together into an expression of puzzlement. "I don't understand."

Garscap sighed. "The Orstretcherists are our scorpion. They may be a temporary boon, but they're a constant threat. Their consciences could carry them in any direction. They renounced the god of their ancestors. They betrayed their own flesh and blood. They claim they did so as martyrs for our religion, but their actions speak of their fickleness. Their consciences could lead them to betray us as they betrayed their own kind."

Evram's eyes narrowed. "So, we are the frog to the Orstretcherists' scorpion?"

Garscap nodded. "Exactly. Fear not. When the Elves have served their purpose, I'll gladly help you to exact your vengeance. You must be patient till then. We must do nothing to make the Elves suspicious of us. When the moment is right, we will strike, and by the time the Orstretcherists realize what is happening, they, like the scorpion, will be already dead."

Chapter 19

She was the most resplendent gem
That graced the night's starry booty -
Atop a tower that scraped the sky,
Shone bright this jewel of beauty.

~From *Alackalas and the Fair Princess.*

Garscap stood beneath Pigsknuckle's last furka. Harath stood to his right, her head bowed. The breeze riffled through the heap of her belongings to his left. Before him stood her father, bewildered and suspicious.

"Widan, I'm returning Harath to you," Garscap said.

"What?" Widan blurted, his face boiling with indignation, his eyes darting from his sullen daughter to Garscap and back again.

"I've no further need of her as a wife," Garscap explained.

"What? The saints will never sanction this!"

"But the marriage was never consummated."

"What?"

"Your daughter remains chaste. We never…" Garscap cleared his throat. "We never engaged in the purpose for which the Forelight created marriage."

"You never? What? That cannot be true."

"He never touched me," Harath confirmed. "He never even hinted he might, and I had no desire to encourage him."

"Don't you realize what you have done?" Widan wailed. "You've ruined us. You've made us outcasts in the village ruled by our family for generations, because you were too stubborn to perform your wifely duties."

"If you loved the Changeling so much," Harath snapped, "you should have married him."

"Even if she had begged me, I wouldn't have slept with her," Garscap said. "I don't find her attractive."

Widan seized Harath's hand before it could connect with Garscap's face. "You cannot strike him here, however much he might deserve it. So, Garscap, this is how you reward me for giving you the thorny crown and staying loyal to you even when others begged me to depose you?"

Garscap snorted. "Come now, we both know that's untrue. You only warned me of that plot because the conspirators had no intention of giving you the thorny crown. To think you once called me a has-been. Who's the has-been now?"

Harath screamed as, with outstretched arms, she placed herself in front of Widan to prevent him from attacking Garscap. She clung to Widan as he tried to push by her.

Widan shoved her away and stared at Garscap with murderous eyes.

Drawn by the commotion, several women peered out from their doorways. The men were training with the Orstretcherists at Leaftea. It was a pity that they were not also here to witness the Melkaths' humiliation.

Garscap bowed. "Now, I must take my leave of you both. Saint Charlin will be arriving soon with my new wife."

As Garscap walked away, Widan violently castigated his daughter. "To think I raised a fool like you! You are unfit to bear the Melkath name!"

His talk of disowning her made Garscap smile. Their pretenses of nobility lay scattered in the dust, tossed and turned by the breeze, like her possessions.

He awaited his bride in his hut. The saint entered first. Talida Kuny followed with the hesitant trepidation of a kid taking its first steps, round-eyed and skittish. As Charlin introduced them, her wan smile pleaded for reassurance, before it wilted under Garscap's critical gaze. She was scrawny, underfed. He would have to fatten her up a bit. He must purchase some powders from Forge to conceal her acne scars. Otherwise, she was pretty enough.

Sanctimonious layers of clothing, no doubt imposed by her protector, concealed her figure. Garscap would have the pleasure of discovering her true shape soon enough. He had to be patient. He would buy her expensive dresses, jewelry, and perfume. His intimacy with the whores of Formicary had taught him such feminine ornamentation could transform the plain and ugly into an arousing beauty. She must be regarded as the most beautiful woman in the village. Every man in Pigsknuckle must desire her and envy him. He must deny his enemies the satisfaction of claiming that the Politician of Ogresquern had bested him in the match.

Most of all, his wife should be a constant reminder to Harath of what her own dowdiness and lack of feminine charm had cost her.

"When do you wish to hold the wedding?" the saint asked.

"Today," Garscap said. "Right now."

"This is not the custom."

Garscap smirked. He declined to point out that changing wives was not customary either. "Do you think the village will welcome a daughter of Ogresquern marrying their politician? Every moment we wait is an opportunity for dissent and mischief. It's better to marry us now and give the villagers no choice but to accept our union."

Charlin admitted defeat with a nod. Talida's brittle smile could not hide her despondency. She probably had expected her wedding to be a more salubrious affair with a great feast and all the other usual trappings. But for Garscap, to suffer through such nonsense once was enough. Besides, it was important for her to learn her place. She had no friends in this village, and her fate depended upon him.

As Charlin droned through the wedding liturgy, Garscap's attention drifted to his bride. He could feel his excitement growing. How ironic that a man who had known the joys of the most beautiful women who could be bought now trembled at the prospect of feasting on this tatty morsel. He had played the part of a celibate far, far too long. He had much to teach her. She would become the pet of his desires.

The saint's insistent prompts to recite his vows interrupted his reverie. As he repeated Charlin's words, the tears rolling down Talida's cheeks excited him even more. He rubbed his hand over his wolfish grin, assuming it was the cause of her anxiety. His voice thickened and hoarsened as desire choked him. He struggled to retain his composure as the ceremony drew to a close. As soon as Charlin pronounced them man and wife, Garscap wanted him gone. He could hardly breathe till he had swept away this suffocating impediment to his gratification.

Then, at last, he was alone with his sobbing bride. Deprived of the saint's reassuring presence, Talida shriveled into an even more pathetic, helpless creature. Imagining himself as a bird of prey, Garscap swooped on her, clutched her in his talons, and carried her, still crying, to his bed.

***

Grael found Harath weeping over the broken furka. He approached her cautiously, afraid that she might not appreciate his intrusion on her grief. As soon as she became aware of his presence, she stopped crying.

"What do you want?" she demanded as she wiped the back of her wrist across her eyes.

He took a deep breath. "I heard what happened. I came to see if I could help."

"My husband has cast me aside. My father has disowned me. Every door in the village is closed to me. How do you think you can help?"

"My door is not closed."

She snorted. "What door have you? You've no home, other than the Mangals' floor."

"That's right," he muttered. "You're not the only outcast in the village."

She stared down at the broken stone. "At least you have hope," she said as she drew her hands down her face and behind her neck. "In time, you may earn your parents' forgiveness. I, alas, cannot."

The shiver of despair in her voice brought a twinge of panic. It was too reminiscent of Ashin Carnath and her dark fate. Last year, Grael would have happily offered to take Harath away from the village and build a new life together elsewhere. But with the Fair Folk threatening Pigsknuckle, he could not leave. He had to stay here to protect his family. Anyway, she was unlikely to accept such an offer from him.

"You can't give up."

Her laugh was mirthless and bitter. "I'm going to Pigsback."

The suggestion that a woman might visit Saint Odran's monastery would have been preposterous to some, but this age of miracles and woes had inured Grael to such novelties. He had no hesitation. "I will go with you."

Her hand touched the hilt of her dagger. "I will go alone."

"You've never climbed the Pig. I can guide you."

"As you guided my brother?" Her retort was another punch in the gut. "Sorry," she said. "That was unfair. I know you nearly died up there, too. It's been a hard day."

"The climb up the Pig is dangerous for even those familiar with the route," Grael said, staying calm. "Are you sure you won't let me accompany you? Let me find Saint Charlin. I am sure he would be glad to be your guide."

"I would prefer your company to his," Harath said. "He brought the harlot from Ogresquern that the Changeling intends to marry. The saint's presence would remind me of her."

"My brother is decent and honorable," Grael said.

Harath turned her gaze toward the Pig. "When will we start out?"

"In the morning. It's too late in the day to reach Pigsback by nightfall."

"Where will I go till then? Wander the forest?"

"I know a hunter's lodge where you can stay."

They barely talked as he led her through the maze of twisted paths crisscrossing the forest. Grael attempted to strike up a conversation a few times, but his questions drew terse responses, and his comments were answered with silence. In the end, he stopped trying. Sometimes, he heard her sobbing just behind him, but he thought it best to feign ignorance. Harath's pride would brook no consolation.

The hut was farther than Grael remembered, and he struggled to find it. Preoccupied by her own troubles, Harath was oblivious to his difficulty. The sight of the bark shack was a relief. He peered into the darkness within. Its black bark skin was speckled with stars of daylight. The shack was empty, except for some cold ash in the little hearth.

"You should be safe here," he said, stepping out of her way so that she could have a look. "Hopefully, I'll be back before nightfall."

She peered inside, her face full of apprehension. "Hopefully? You're going to leave me alone in this wilderness with nothing more than a knife to defend myself?"

"I must get some provisions for the journey. I'll leave you my spear."

She folded her arms. "Be gone then. I hope you don't regret your decision."

"I'll be back as soon as I can," Grael promised. He propped the spear by the entrance. As he walked away the urge to repeatedly peek over his shoulder at her was irresistible.

She appeared oblivious to his glances as she stooped to pick up fuel for a fire. His last glimpse of Harath before the forest blocked his view was of her standing outside the lodge, cradling a pile of sticks, watching him go.

After borrowing some spare clothes and food from the Mangals, he hurried back to the shack, spurred by the fear he might lose Harath as he had lost her brother.

Her smile as she greeted him was surprising.

"You seem brighter," he observed.

"No point on dwelling on the past," she said, her mood turning somber again.

This emotional turmoil continued throughout the evening. She was smiling one moment and dour the next. He tried to keep her talking for his sake as well as hers. It was difficult to keep the conversation from steering back to the cause of her despondency. Innocuous topics led invariably back to her family. Sobbing and laughing, she recounted her brother's childhood adventures or some story about her mother as if she was impelled to pick at her pain.

"Donmor and my mother are dead," Harath said. "And as far as my father is concerned, I may as well be. We are dead to each other."

Each time she lapsed into tearful melancholy, Grael patiently waited for her to reclaim her composure. He was at a loss about what else he could do. They talked late into the night. She clung to the conversation, as if afraid to be alone with her thoughts.

Eventually, weariness overcame Grael, and he bid her goodnight. He lay down on one side of the fire and she on the other. He closed his eyes but was too tired to sleep. She sobbed for a while, then fell silent. Her snore was a surprise and a relief, the gentle purr a welcome intrusion of domesticity in a day heavy with drama.

***

Panic that Harath was gone jolted Grael awake. It was still night. The fire had died down. She lay on the far side of the hearth, her sheathed dagger held to her bosom. Her eyes were open. She was watching him. He lay down again and waited for the dawn to release him from this sleepless night.

Grael wasn't fooled by the blithe sunshine that greeted them as they set out for Pigsback early the next morning. Though the snows had retreated somewhat in the preceding weeks, the weather on the Pig was as changeable as Harath's mood. He was unsurprised when the day turned somber and a fog closed in around them.

"We'll be all right as long as we stick to the path and follow the furkas," Grael said, pointing to the shallow scar winding up the slope. Of course, it was not so simple. The trail branched in a multiplicity of useless directions. Some sections blended so well into the landscape that they could be easily missed. Explaining this to Harath was pointless. It would only worry her needlessly.

She resisted his attempts to hold her hand, but the memory of her brother made him persevere till she acquiesced. He let go when they reached the furka near where he and Donmor had become separated. He joined

Harath in a prayer for her brother's soul, and then gripped her hand anew, tighter than before.

"I do not blame you for my brother's death," Harath said, squeezing his hand. "The mountain took him, and you can't fight a mountain. If the fault lies with anyone, it's my father. He sent you both on that ill-fated journey. Thank you for showing me this place. It's probably the only grave Donmor shall ever know."

They wandered through the mountain's frosty breath for what seemed an eternity till a forbidding curtain of rock blocked their way. Grael assured a daunted Harath they did not have to scale the impossible obstacle. He gave no indication they had gone astray in the mist as he led her along the barrier to the Crooked Stair. Grael scrambled up the higher steps first, and then, after advising Harath where to place her feet, hoisted her up the cracked faces by the hand. It was good that the Crooked Stair was clear of snow. Precipices loomed over the passage on the right, while on the left side, a murderous plunge awaited the unwary.

Beyond the Crooked Stair was a series of steepish inclines punctuated by sections of more gentle terrain. The sporadic tatters of snow littering the stony mountainside increased in size and frequency, till they merged to form a featureless white mantle.

This, combined with the fog, plunged the travelers into a blankness as blinding as the darkest night. Grael encouraged Harath to join him in prayer. His spear led the way, probing the snowy mantle for hidden dangers.

Satisfied, he waded forward and gently pulled Harath along behind him. Progress was slow. Their only firm reference point was each other. Even their tracks seemed to bleach into the white monotony.

Luckily, Harath did not fully appreciate the precariousness of their circumstance. Their lives depended on Grael's sense of direction—a fragile talent. His only consolation was that Pigsback was not far.

When they emerged without warning from their blurry shroud, Grael greeted the brilliant sunshine with a triumphant cheer. A furka emerged from the mist as if conjured by their prayers. He pointed out the monastery of Saint Odran perched some distance ahead, a squat, granite bastion across a sweep of glittering white.

"I thought it was on the summit," Harath said.

Grael chuckled at her disappointment. "Be glad it is not."

"Grael Erol, you are a good and kind man," Harath said, twisting her hand free of his grasp. "Forgive me."

"There's nothing to forgive," he said.

She hurried toward the monastery. He followed in puzzlement.

The outer door of the Needle's Eye was shut. Harath and Grael battered it with their fists till it creaked open and a saint's head peeped out. His eyes bulged at sight of Harath, and he withdrew, slamming the door shut again. Harath redoubled her pounding.

"I never experienced such blatant inhospitality at the monastery before," Grael said.

"You never brought a woman with you."

The door opened to reveal several saints crammed into the Needle's Eye. Saint Sebryn wormed his way through them. Never before had Grael seen the frail old man so angry.

"You should be ashamed, bringing this woman to this hallowed place," the saint said. "Go back to Pigsknuckle and no longer desecrate this mountain with her presence."

"But it is too late to return this evening," Grael said. "We'd die, descending in the dark."

"You should have thought of that before you committed this sacrilege."

"The fault is not his," Harath said. "It's mine. I took advantage of his generous nature."

"I'm sure you did," Sebryn said.

"I'm Widan Melkath's daughter. And Garscap Torp's wife till Saint Charlin annulled my marriage."

"I'm sure he had good reason to do so," the abbot said.

"I suppose he had good reason to have all the furkas around Pigsknuckle destroyed."

Sebryn's gape was at once comical and disconcerting.

Harath ignored Grael's whispered pleas to say no more. "He also blessed the Changeling as the Politician of Pigsknuckle, making his reign unchallengeable."

"This cannot be," Sebryn said.

"But it is. He has done the same to the politicians of other villages, and he has aided the Changeling to become their leader. Garscap's influence extends across the Stretches. Saint Charlin nullified my marriage so the

Changeling could strengthen his alliance with the Politician of Ogresquern by marrying his sister."

"These allegations are preposterous," Saint Sebryn declared. "Grael Erol, is there any truth to them?"

Grael wanted to deny it, but he could not lie to a saint. He nodded. "It's all true."

Sebryn's head dropped, accentuating his hunch, diminishing his stature, as if the old man had crumbled. "Is this why you came here? To spread malicious gossip?" His accusation was without fire.

"I came here because I've nowhere else to go," Harath said.

"I'll not say you are welcome. You aren't. But charity must be shown to the least of the faithful. You can stay, for the moment."

They shuffled through the Needle's Eye and entered the reception hall, where a saint conversed with an Elf.

"TrueFriend Peritus, perhaps you might attend to our female guest, as Saint Sebryn says you are immune to lustful desire."

"Keep her away from me," TrueFriend said, averting his face from her sight.

Saint Sebryn rested his hand on Grael's shoulder and murmured. "Tomorrow, when you return to Pigsknuckle, find your brother and tell him I want to see him."

***

IronWill Defensor hunched over his desk and studied the map of the Stretches. With every passing day, his cartographer filled in the blank void at its heart with mountains, and valleys, and lakes, and rivers, and villages. Soon, the entire range would be mapped, and the purging of the Stretches could begin in earnest.

Yet, he might not get the chance to lead it. The arrival of the Harbinger's envoy had put him on edge. Several of the more hawkish officers had petitioned the Consensus to have him removed on account of what they perceived as his excessive caution in combat. In less strained times, these pleas would be ignored, but with the Harbinger in charge, anything might happen. Perhaps this new arrival was to be his replacement.

Someone knocked on the door. He rolled up the map, revealing the neat piles of parchments beneath it. He grabbed the topmost document from a pile of reports and spread it on the desk. "Come in," he said.

IronWill saw the armor first. The stranger wore a golden cuirass embossed with a spread two-thumbed hand. On his golden helmet, auric fingers and thumbs radiated through the orange hair on his transverse crest in the manner of a senior officer. His arm-shields were shaped like golden wings. His greaves bore the same motif. Finely meshed, golden mail covered his forearms and thighs. It was the panoply of a member of the Harbinger's new order of sentinels. Its wearer was a Pugnus. The helmet bore only the number five. His name was missing. Wearing that armor, he had little need for one.

IronWill saluted the sentinel. "Welcome to Fort Lumen. I hope you find the hospitality of the Third Reconstituted to your liking."

"Yes. Thank you, Legate," Sentinel Five said. "The Harbinger of the Dawn asked me to convey his congratulations for your victory and his thanks for all your hard work in building this fort."

IronWill braced for bad news. The sentinel's tone was too amicable, too full of false politeness.

"The Harbinger has charged me with a special mission," Sentinel Five said. "He has come into possession of information regarding the location of AscendantSun Auctor and the other Orstretcherists. I am to take charge of two of your centuries and eradicate this menace at last."

IronWill's surge of relief dissipated. "Are two centuries sufficient? I can spare another if you wish."

"The Harbinger believes so," Sentinel Five said. "The Orstretcherists number about four dozen. Two centuries will outnumber them six to one."

You know all about killing Ors, IronWill thought. *You slew enough of them already to get that precious armor.* "But the Orstretcherists must have allies. What about them?"

"We are to exterminate them as well if they get in our way. You have already illustrated that the denizens of these mountains are no match for legionaries," the Pugnus said.

"No doubt two centuries are enough to secure victory, but casualties on our side would be minimized if you took three."

"The concern for your legionaries is admirable, but we have our orders. Our duty is to obey them."

Duty demanded that IronWill agree, though his heart urged otherwise. "Very well. I will make the necessary arrangements. I will instruct my tribune, SunTalon Risus, to accompany you. Have you no qualms about hunting AscendantSun Auctor? Your lineage and his share a history."

The sentinel snorted. "We are over a millennium old. All Ors share a history. In any case, the cutting away of a diseased limb is an act of healing. The Lineage of Auctor will be all the better for his passing."

Sentinel Five gave the legate a farewell salute. As he exited, he paused at the door. "Remember this, Legate. We are the myrmidons of the Golden Light. We all must be as prepared to die as kill in his name. Death is but a joyful return to his sacred flame."

"And to become a sentinel, you have already sent eleven Ors back to him," IronWill retorted. "Or two short of two dozen, if you include those whom the first Pugnus dispatched to earn his armor." His regret of his outburst was immediate.

The sentinel indulged IronWill's pique with a smile. "Very soon I will add four dozen to that tally. When the Golden Light receives their corrupted essence, I wonder what he will do with it?"

Chapter 20

He ached to glimpse beyond the glass
At her, not her reflection,
Though his love forbade such trespass
Lest that glance bring ruination.

-From *Alackalas and the Fair Princess.*

A hand shook AscendantSun awake. He rubbed his eyes and yawned. "What time is it?"

"Just after dawn," NeverFear said. "DayFlambeau is here. He wants to talk to us."

"What about?" AscendantSun asked. Surely, whatever it was, it could wait till later.

NeverFear shrugged. "He wouldn't say." His eyes shifted to the entrance of the tent. DayFlambeau's head was sticking through it.

"Come in, DayFlambeau," AscendantSun said wearily as he sat up. "Tell us your trouble."

"Thank you," DayFlambeau said as he entered. "I apologize for your early waking, but this is a matter of some importance."

The tension in his voice filled AscendantSun with dread. Had DayFlambeau become another victim of girlish fixation?

NeverFear sat beside AscendantSun. They folded their legs to permit their stooped guest to sit down.

The silence stretched as DayFlambeau struggled to find his voice. "I am leaving you," he said, steadying his quivering breath. "I am going home."

Stunned silence turned to anger. "You cannot just return to your old life in Tincranny," AscendantSun growled. "The Harbinger will not be content with an apology and a shrug of the shoulders from a heretic. They will imprison and torture you."

DayFlambeau shied from his glare. "It may not come to that. My lineage might help me if I throw myself on its mercy. It has the means to reinvent me as another and conceal my return from the authorities."

It was nonsense. Either DayFlambeau considered AscendantSun and NeverFear to be gullible fools or he was delusional.

AscendantSun took a deep breath and swallowed his anger. Losing his temper would only serve to deafen DayFlambeau to what he was trying to say. "If your lineage proves less charitable than you hope, what then?"

"If your conscience demands that you leave us, take sanctuary in Pigsback," NeverFear urged.

"I would never betray you," DayFlambeau assured them. He made hesitant eye contact with AscendantSun.

"If I am arrested, I will tell the Consensus the Stretchers killed you and I am the sole survivor."

AscendantSun thrust a finger toward him. "And when the legions face us in battle, what you will tell the Consensus then? You made a mistake? The Consensus will repay your lies with death."

"That is a risk I must take," DayFlambeau said. "I have come to the realization I do not believe in the Forelight."

NeverFear sighed. "But, you were so convinced."

DayFlambeau shook his head. "My conviction was a fraud, and I was both the perpetrator and the victim. I wanted to believe, and I convinced myself I did, but I was living a lie. My faith in the Forelight was merely an affectation."

"So you cast aside the god to whom you swore unceasing devotion and slink back to your former master!" AscendantSun snapped. He could no longer dam his anger.

DayFlambeau frowned. "Your conscience prompted you to cast aside many divisions of devotion to the Golden Light. Why is my change of heart any different?"

"When I changed my religion, it was not some whim," AscendantSun muttered. "I changed only once."

"Thus speaks the great servant of the Forelight, would-be prophet of an invisible deity," DayFlambeau mocked. "So devoted to your god that you are willing to break his most solemn commandments. You shall not kill. Remember? You speak of piety as you prepare to sin."

The words stabbed AscendantSun's heart. He could not help thinking of his twin. Would that wound ever heal?

“Calm down,” NeverFear pleaded, his hands flapping.

“I suppose you will kill me now that I pose a threat,” DayFlambeau said with a sneer.

“Calm down,” NeverFear repeated. “Nobody is killing anybody. DayFlambeau, have we your solemn word that you will not betray us to the Consensus under any circumstances?”

“A promise is not enough,” AscendantSun said, pounding his foreleg with his fist. “He must swear it by the Golden Light.”

DayFlambeau snorted. “That is not going to happen.”

“He intends to betray us,” AscendantSun said. “Why else would he decline?”

“I will not betray you,” DayFlambeau said. “I simply do not see the point in swearing on the Golden Light or the Forelight. I believe in neither.”

“Perhaps,” AscendantSun muttered. DawnGlow, too, had claimed to have no god. Visions of red blots spreading across his makeshift pall flashed in AscendantSun’s mind. “Perhaps not. In truth, you do not know what you believe. You think you are a Necrotheist, as you once thought you believed in the Forelight. Some minor portent will seize your heart, and it will beat for the Golden Light again, and your rediscovered devotion will be all the more fervent because of your past heresy.”

“And do you know what you believe?” DayFlambeau asked him.

NeverFear interjected before AscendantSun could answer. "This repartee is getting us nowhere. There must be some way this can be sorted to everyone's satisfaction."

DayFlambeau said with a shrug, "Either you let me go or hold me prisoner for the duration of the war. I bear you no ill will, but I cannot pretend to serve your false god."

"If the Consensus captures you and demands you swear fealty to the Golden Light, what will you do?" AscendantSun asked.

"How lucky you and the others here are!" DayFlambeau moaned. "How fortunate is the entire race of Ors but me! I am without a god, alone and hopeless in the world. Yes, AscendantSun, I must concede your point is valid. I had not considered the Consensus might force me to pledge my devotion to the Golden Light, much as you wish me to prove my good faith by his name. Let me withdraw for a short spell to the broken furka by the lake and reflect further on this matter."

AscendantSun responded to NeverFear's uncertain glance in kind. He acceded to DayFlambeau's request with feigned nonchalance. He and NeverFear followed DayFlambeau out of the tent and escorted him to the edge of the encampment. There, they waited, their eyes never leaving him as he walked to the ruined stone and commenced his deliberation. His every movement was evaluated as a possible prelude to flight. DayFlambeau appeared oblivious to their intense scrutiny, his eyes fixed on the smashed stone, his face animated by mute debate, his hands dancing to the tune of his conflicted emotions, but his relative indifference might have been a ploy to put them off guard. It was a great relief when DayFlambeau sauntered back to them.

"I will take your oath," DayFlambeau said. "I will take it by Aurelian and the other Lights, and the Forelight, and any other deity that you wish. For me, such ostentation adds nothing to my solemn word, but I will take it to put your minds at ease."

"An oath by the Golden Light will suffice," AscendantSun said. Aurelian was the only Light that mattered.

DayFlambeau waited while AscendantSun and NeverFear agreed on the exact wording, and then flew through the oath with disdain.

"I will leave in two days' time," he said. "Much of tomorrow will be spent making private farewells."

As the black fingers of the Stretches snuffed out the sun, the Orstretcherists gathered around the main campfire for their evening repast. After DayFlambeau had quietly filled his bowl with stew and slipped away to his tent, AscendantSun asked for his comrades' attention. Bewilderment, dismay, even panic, swept through his audience at the news of DayFlambeau's departure. It took a lot of effort on the part of AscendantSun and NeverFear to placate them. The vow that DayFlambeau had sworn was parsed and analyzed. The discussion entered a purposeless spiral as the participants rehashed variations of the same arguments over and over till conversation petered out due to general exhaustion.

As the Orstretcherists scattered to their tents, NeverFear asked AscendantSun, "What, if anything, do we tell the Politician of Pigsknuckle?"

"I have wrestled with that question all day," AscendantSun said. "In the aftermath of Ashin Carnath's unfortunate end, Garscap has proved to be a good friend to us, risking his popularity to protect TrueFriend, but he would be alarmed to learn of DayFlambeau's intention to leave. On the other thumb, if we do not tell him, and he learns of it by chance, we would forfeit his trust and wreck our alliance before it has had a chance to bear fruit. I think it best to inform him and try to convince him that DayFlambeau's departure poses no serious threat to his village."

"It will not be easy," NeverFear said. "Given your doubts."

"The challenge is greater than you realize," AscendantSun said. "I dare not divulge to Garscap the change of mind that spurs DayFlambeau's leaving. Born into his faith, the politician could not appreciate the doubts and dilemmas pestering converts like us. He would be unsympathetic to DayFlambeau's plight. I consider DayFlambeau's plan naive, but I am as certain of his integrity now as I was when I invited him to convert to Stretcherism. Garscap would be blind to such nuance. If he understood the reason for DayFlambeau's departure, Garscap would condemn DayFlambeau as a traitor and us as fools."

"But we cannot lie to Garscap either," NeverFear said. "Lying is a sin."

"Agreed," AscendantSun said. "I'll tell him DayFlambeau's motivations are not his concern, and hope Garscap does not press the matter too much."

"And if he does, what will you do then?"

"I do not know," AscendantSun admitted. "We find ourselves bereft of choice. DayFlambeau cannot be dissuaded. Placing him in captivity solves one problem, only to create another. Our comrades might gripe about what they perceive as DayFlambeau's betrayal, but most of them would not condone his imprisonment. Others who secretly share DayFlambeau's doubts might become more inclined to forsake us and join the ranks of our enemies. We have only one course open to us. Unfortunately, it is not a good one."

***

Stares—some suspicious, others hateful—followed AscendantSun as he walked through the silent village to Garscap's hut. He missed having NeverFear by his side, but he had promised Garscap he alone would enter Pigsknuckle when circumstances demanded, and now was not a time for broken promises.

He hurried by the great hall. Its seething residents poured outside to shower him with salivary invective. A few stones struck his armor, flung by childish hands in the midst of the spitting women. They did not care that he was Pigsknuckle's ally. His kinship to the murderers of their relatives and neighbors was sufficient reason to hate him. Deference to their host—and fear of his wrath—was probably all that prevented them from worse violence. AscendantSun wiped the spittle dripping from his face with a handkerchief. Thankfully, they did not pursue him.

Garscap's new wife answered AscendantSun's rap on the politician's hut. No halo rested on her disheveled hair. Her eyes were sunken and listless. Her general paleness exacerbated the rash of pimples about her chin. She regarded him coolly.

"The Orstretcherists' leader wishes to see you," she said to the smoky darkness behind her.

"Then get out of his way," Garscap growled from somewhere inside.

A shiver of fear passed through her. She jerked aside as if pushed, dropping the leather flap across the door. AscendantSun lifted it and entered the hut. Garscap was braiding his thorny crown into his hair. The stubble along his jawline was a new development. On seeing AscendantSun, the politician's sour mood dissipated. His welcome was as cordial as always.

"AscendantSun, please sit down. Talida, stop standing there," he said. "Get our guest some refreshment."

"Thank you, but there is no need," AscendantSun said. "I just finished my breakfast. There is a private matter I must bring to your attention." He cast a meaningful glance at Garscap's wife.

"Talida, go for a walk," Garscap said.

"I am in no fit state to go anywhere," Talida pleaded.

"Bring your halo here."

She offered him a circlet of yellow and red cloth. He threw it in the fire. She reached for it, but he held her back while the flames consumed it. Her distressed cries made AscendantSun uncomfortable.

"Forget Ogresquern," Garscap said. "You wear the white and blue of Pigsknuckle now."

"That cloth was blessed by a saint," Talida said. "To treat it such is sacrilege."

While she knelt sobbing by the fire, the politician did a hasty rendition of the Forelight's Prayer.

"That's better," he said. He rummaged through bags of possessions till he seized a white and blue halo. "Thus is the cost of love," he muttered as he pulled his weeping wife to her feet and lashed the halo to her head with fistfuls of her hair.

"Now get out and bother me no more till I look for you," he said when he was done.

"What am I to do?" Talida begged. "Wander through the village like a vagrant?"

"You have a strange attitude to your village. This is your village now. Your husband is its ruler. It's time you knew more about it than this hut."

After the door flap closed behind her, Garscap muttered, "Women."

AscendantSun, at a loss as to what the statement meant, nodded politely.

"So, what brings you here this beautiful morning?" Garscap asked as he sat down on the far side of the fire.

AscendantSun tried to make DayFlambeau's return to Tincranny sound like a trivial matter, but the politician looked troubled.

"You have not explained the reason for his departure," Garscap observed.

This was the question that AscendantSun dreaded. He had spent a lot of time concocting possible responses the night before, but now, beneath the politician's probing stare, his nerve wilted.

"I would rather not say. It is an internal matter," he answered, silently cursing himself as the words tumbled leadenly from his tongue. His reply would not satisfy Garscap's curiosity. If anything, it would heighten it. "All I can say is that his return to our people poses no risk to your village."

A reassuring smile spread across Garscap's face. "Of course, it's your own business. I was merely curious. I thank you for your courtesy in informing me. When does DayFlambeau intend to depart?"

"Tomorrow morning," AscendantSun answered, doing his best to hide his surprise. "Thank you for your trust in this matter."

"If you and I cannot trust each other, our alliance is worthless."

The conversation drifted to other matters. The warriors from Stonegarden had requested to stay for an extra week of training while the arrival of the delegation from Beardwood was delayed another week due to the sudden death of its politician. AscendantSun expected that, at any moment, Garscap would steer the conversation back to DayFlambeau's departure, but the politician appeared to have forgotten the matter. AscendantSun departed Garscap's hut, relieved and bewildered. He could not believe his luck.

***

"You are getting better," AscendantSun said as he offered a hand to the prostrate Mogod Kulum.

"Not good enough," the Politician of Stonegarden muttered.

A few of the Pigsknucklers chuckled, but none of the Stonegardeners dared a smile. Their politician was a proud man and not one to forgive a slight, however innocent.

Mogod's pride was the main reason for the Stonegardeners extending their sojourn at Leaftea. The politician was determined to best an Orstretcherist before he departed. His persistence was admirable, as was the rate of his improvement, but it would take a miracle for a Mixy to defeat a fully equipped legionary in single combat.

"Again," the politician said as he retrieved his spear. "Perhaps my obsession with beating you is pigheaded, but we are the guests of a village where calling someone pigheaded is considered complimentary."

The Stonegardeners' laughter was hearty and unrestrained. The Orstretcherists expressed their amusement with chuckles and smiles. The Pigsknucklers' reaction was mixed, some taking it as innocent fun, others expressing their displeasure at being the butt of Mogod's joke with icy silence.

From the edge of the crowd, NeverFear waved at AscendantSun.

"There will be time for a rematch later," AscendantSun said. "In the meantime, I want you all to break out into your pairings and take turns sparring with my comrades. I have to go."

He jogged over to NeverFear as the crowd dispersed. AscendantSun's eyes widened as NeverFear whispered in his ear, "We must make haste. Garscap has cornered DayFlambeau in his tent."

AscendantSun cursed his naivety. He was foolish to presume Garscap would drop the matter.

By the time they reached the tent, DayFlambeau stood outside, arms folded, waiting for them. He winced as he spoke. "I had a visit from your friend, the politician. He insisted on knowing why I am leaving. I tried to stall him till you arrived, but I had to tell him in the end that it was none of his business. He was not very happy when he left."

"Should we tell him the truth?" NeverFear asked AscendantSun.

"Garscap may be suspicious, but he can be little more than that. Tell him the truth, and we confirm his worst fears. Tell him nothing, and he has little more than conjecture."

"So we say nothing?" NeverFear asked.

"No," AscendantSun said. "We confront him about his interrogation of DayFlambeau. Garscap needs our help.

We are his best hope against the invading legions, and he knows it. Without our training, his warriors would be wiped out by a couple of squads of legionaries. Garscap will not want to alienate us. He will act contrite and keep his suspicions to himself. After DayFlambeau has left, the matter will be forgotten."

AscendantSun and NeverFear caught up with Garscap when he was halfway back to the village.

Garscap smiled. "Good day, my friends. To what do I owe this pleasure?"

AscendantSun covered his mouth with his hand and cleared his throat with a cough. "I understand you visited DayFlambeau." His tone was polite and casual, even nonchalant.

Garscap scratched the back of his head. His cheeks reddened, though his smile remained fixed. "I'm sorry about that. I am in the wrong. I admit it." He raised his hands and shrugged. "Curiosity got the better of me. I intended no offense."

AscendantSun smiled at NeverFear's eyes darting nervously back and forth between him and the politician, as the silence dragged. What would NeverFear have said in AscendantSun's place?

"No offense taken," AscendantSun said. He stared hard at Garscap. "*If it doesn't happen again.*"

Garscap's smile wavered for the briefest of moments before it widened. His head dipped slightly. "It won't. I promise."

"Then let us speak no more of this matter," AscendantSun said.

NeverFear gave a cautious nod.

Garscap's head bobbed enthusiastically. "Thank you," he said. "I must go. I have pressing business in the village."

The Ors watched the politician walk away. When he was some distance from them, NeverFear asked, "Do you think he got the message?"

"Hopefully," AscendantSun said. "For all of our sakes."

***

The next morning, pouring rain did not delay DayFlambeau's departure. He kept his final farewells to his comrades light and quick. More heartfelt goodbyes might cause awkwardness, given the circumstances of his leaving. The other Ors were cordial, but DayFlambeau sensed a chasm opening between him and them. How quickly fast friends had become strangers. He departed the camp with only the rain for company.

It was almost noon when the precipitation eased to a drizzle. A tingle creeping up his spine made him freeze. Was someone stalking him? The forest whispered innocently. The curtain of leaf and shadow draped about him on all sides offered nothing to confirm his suspicion. He walked on.

A branch snapped.

DayFlambeau looked behind him, but the source of the noise was lost behind impenetrable foliage. Briers snagged his cloak. He tugged it free and pretended to examine the stitching, listening to the wind playing on the trees. It carried a murmur, too faint to be coherent.

Again, his eyes scanned the wood with more subtlety than before. A face stared at him from the bushes. The Mixy wore no halo, but DayFlambeau had seen his impressive brow before in Pigsknuckle. The man looked straight at him, his expression as fixed as stone. DayFlambeau continued to look about the forest, partly to convince the Mixy he remained undetected, partly to determine the presence of any accomplices. If they were there, they were better hidden.

Why was this Mixy spying on him? Curiosity? Perhaps it was that innocent.

An arrow breezed by DayFlambeau's head. The archer was somewhere behind him, but DayFlambeau, ripping his batonaxes from their rack, charged at the Mixy in front of him. The Mixy rose to his feet, pulled back his bow, and loosed an arrow. DayFlambeau leapt toward him, his whole body curled behind the embrace of his arm-shields. The arrow scraped against the shields as it sped past.

DayFlambeau rolled out of the leap and swung his batonaxes wide, tearing through his foe's body. Pain distracted him from the bloody mess slumping at his feet. An arrow had struck his left shoulder. His left batonaxe slipped from his fingers. He hooked it with the other, and as two other Mixies broke cover, he flung it at the nearest. It smashed into his face, toppling him to the ground. His companion loosed his bow. DayFlambeau roared as the arrow struck his foreleg. He stumbled backward and slammed against a tree trunk, banging his head against its knotty surface.

The Mixy's eyes flicked from DayFlambeau to his fallen comrade. "Ilyam, get up!" he hissed, kicking the corpse to no avail. "I guess it's just you and me," he said, breaking into a smile, as he slowly reached for his quiver. "I wonder how many arrows it will take to kill you."

Evram Erath's lopsided grin was unmistakable.

DayFlambeau was dizzy with pain. He could hardly stand, much less close the distance between him and the politician's toady. Somehow, he had to draw Evram nearer.

DayFlambeau laughed as Evram began to pull an arrow from its container. "Coward!" DayFlambeau shouted, waving his remaining batonaxe. "Put away that child's toy and fight me like a man!"

Evram's smile faltered. He scowled as he let the arrow slip back into the quiver. He slung the bow over his shoulder, drew an axe from his belt, and walked so very slowly toward DayFlambeau.

His hand tightened around the shaft of his batonaxe as he waited for the fight of his life.

***

A warm tap on his forehead briefly disturbed AscendantSun's slumber. A second warm drip trickled down his face. He wiped its tickle from his cheek. A hand ripped him from his sleep. It was greased with warm blood. In the dimness of the early dawn, a vision of agony and horror stared into his uncomprehending eyes.

"We are betrayed," DayFlambeau growled hoarsely, thrusting a bloody halo into AscendantSun's hands. It could be white and blue, but it was hard to be sure in the dull light.

"Help me," DayFlambeau groaned. He rolled onto his back, revealing the broken arrow shaft jutting from his shoulder.

"NeverFear, wake up!" AscendantSun cried. "DayFlambeau is injured."

They needed to carry him to the campfire to get a better look at his wounds. With NeverFear's help, AscendantSun slid DayFlambeau onto a blanket. They picked it up by the corners, turning it into a makeshift stretcher.

Outside, DayFlambeau's crawl had left a long black slick on the grass. AscendantSun raged. Why had the Orstretcherists on guard duty not spotted DayFlambeau before he reached AscendantSun's tent? They would regret their laxity.

"Everyone get up!" AscendantSun roared as he and NeverFear weaved DayFlambeau through the maze of tents to the main campfire. DayFlambeau groaned as he rolled about on the blanket.

PureFaith Nitor and GoldTear Furcifer were sitting on a log beside it. They stood, their faces stupid with surprise.

"Wake up the camp!" AscendantSun snapped.

GoldTear scurried away.

PureFaith helped AscendantSun and NeverFear to lay DayFlambeau down by the fire.

While NeverFear set about treating DayFlambeau's wounds, AscendantSun examined the halo. It was white and blue—Pigsknuckle's colors. Disgusted, he flung it into the fire.

"He shouldn't have had to drag himself to my tent," AscendantSun said to PureFaith. "You should have found him."

PureFaith crossed his arms. "He should have called us."

"And what if he had been a spy or assassin?" *Or a legion.*

PureFaith pursed his lips as he gazed at the fire. "Sorry. I don't how we missed him. Everyone is alert and at their posts. The perimeter checks took place at the usual intervals." PureFaith was not the sort to shy from the truth.

"If that's true, we need more perimeter checks, and sentries," AscendantSun said. He knelt down beside DayFlambeau and asked, "What happened?"

DayFlambeau recounted how he had been ambushed. "I killed two. The third escaped, though I gave him a nasty slash across his abdomen. He was the politician's favorite flatterer, the one called Evram Erath. They weren't wearing their halos, but one of the men I killed had his headdress stuffed into a pouch on his belt.

"I hobbled most of the way here on a makeshift crutch and splint. When the crutch broke under my weight, I crawled to the camp."

"I don't how you got here with these wounds," NeverFear said.

DayFlambeau winced as NeverFear explored his shoulder wound. "Sheer stubbornness," he said with a wan smile. "And fear for your safety."

"Bite on this," NeverFear said, lifting a stick to DayFlambeau's mouth.

DayFlambeau regarded it with disdain. "Will the analgesic you gave me not suffice to protect me from the pain?"

NeverFear shook his head and shoved the stick into DayFlambeau's mouth. He glanced at AscendantSun and PureFaith. "You two might hold him down…as a precaution."

News of DayFlambeau's return was rippling through the camp. A crowd of onlookers began to gather in an arc around them.

DayFlambeau roared and writhed against AscendantSun's grip as NeverFear withdrew the broken arrow from his shoulder. It seemed to take forever. As NeverFear cauterized the wound, DayFlambeau suddenly went limp. NeverFear touched his neck and lifted his eyelids.

"I think he has passed out," he said. "Keep a tight hold of him just in case he comes round while I am working on the arrow in his leg."

AscendantSun exhaled a long-held breath when NeverFear had finished. The arrow wounds were not DayFlambeau's only injuries. The gash in his side needed several stitches. Three fingers on his left hand had been sliced off by an axe blow.

"Do you think that he will live?" PureFaith asked.

NeverFear smiled and pressed his hand to his chest. "I may not be an Armipotens, but I don't usually kill my patients either. DayFlambeau has lost a lot of blood, but he should survive." He added in a whisper, "Though he requires a division to make a full recovery. Till he does, he'll be a cripple."

AscendantSun rose to his feet and addressed the assembled Orstretcherists. "We must strike camp immediately. PureFaith, can you arrange a litter for DayFlambeau?"

PureFaith nodded and stood, but he didn't leave. He just stared at DayFlambeau, mesmerized.

"Where are we going?" NeverFear asked.

"Pigsback," AscendantSun replied. "And we must be well on our way before our allies wake."

"Are we not going to ask the politician about this?" PureFaith asked, looking very shaken.

"We will," AscendantSun said. "But not until we are safe in the monastery. If it is his intention to do us harm, he will not attack us there."

"I thought he could be trusted," NeverFear said.

DayFlambeau's eyes opened. He tried to raise his head but quickly gave up.

"For all we know, he is no longer the politician, and the villagers' new leader views us as a menace rather than as an ally," AscendantSun said.

NeverFear propped DayFlambeau's head on his knees.

"Are you sure we can believe him?" PureFaith asked, pointing to DayFlambeau.

The latter's face twisted with derision.

"Do you think he did this to himself?" AscendantSun asked.

"I suppose," PureFaith conceded.

"Get the litter," AscendantSun commanded, finally rousing PureFaith into action. "The rest of you get packed. We're leaving."

Chapter 21

My princess, freed from her glass cage,
Is captive of her reflection,
And I too am slave to her image,
Taunted by its imperfection,
So I came to this saintly place,
To seek a cure for our affliction,
That I might look upon her true face
Without fear of retribution.

-From *Alackalas and the Fair Princess.*

A persistent rapping pummeled Grael's head, but he clung to his straw mattress and the illusion of sleep till Dawan's determined nudges forced him to abandon his pretense.

"Someone's outside. Go and see who it is," Dawan growled.

With sullen weariness, Grael slipped from under the blanket and shuffled to the door. As he opened it, the morning light flooded inside, stinging his eyes with waspish malevolence. The Politician of Pigsknuckle was only recognizable by his thorny crown. The Garscap standing before him was a stricken creature bled of his usual poise.

"Any news of your brother?" Garscap asked. He was trembling.

"I've heard nothing of Saint Charlin since he last ascended the Pig," Grael said. It was better not to mention Harath's outburst or Sebryn's summons, though they almost certainly were responsible for Charlin's delayed return.

"The Orstretcherists have abandoned us," the politician said. "They were spotted on the trail to Pigsback. The Stonegardeners are readying to depart. Mogod Kulum maintains there's no point staying with no instructors. Evram Erath, Fapath Carnath, and his son, Ilyam, are missing. I've a bad feeling these disappearances are connected in some way to the Orstretcherists' flight. I had hoped to ask your brother for his advice on this matter, but he's gone, too. I'm at a loss as to what to do. While there's no saint in the village, we're at the mercy of its furka. If Fair Folk attack us, we'll have to defend it, and we'll be massacred like the men of Cliffringden and Martyrsgrave."

"Perhaps you should go to Pigsback."

"If I do, will you come with me?"

Grael wanted to refuse. He burned with embarrassment at the thought of another encounter with Harath. She had made a fool of him. While he was fumbling to help her, she was planning her vengeance on his brother. As for Garscap, he was a worse schemer than his former wife. If she was the agent of Charlin's humiliation in Pigsback, he was the ultimate cause. He had abused the saint's trust to turn him into an innocent accomplice in his intrigues, and brought Harath's wrath toppling down on Charlin by implicating him in her ruin. It was a pity Grael and his brother had not heeded their father's sage counsel to keep clear of village politics.

"What's going on?" Dawan asked as he sauntered over. He started when he saw Garscap.

"I'm going to Pigsback," Grael said. He would rather climb the Pig alone than travel to Saint Odran's alongside the man standing before him, but the village's safety was paramount. He started to gather what he needed for the climb, while Garscap told Dawan about the Orstretcherists' disappearance.

"I hope you find them," Dawan said, his voice taut with suppressed anger. "I ask the Stretchers who come here to train with them if they have met my father."

"Have you heard anything?" Garscap asked.

Dawan snorted. "As if you care. You banished him. Grael, please hurry up, and take this…man from my door."

***

Grael's low opinion of Garscap had not improved by the time that they reached Pigsback. The politician had drawn his habitual veil of smarm across his earlier jitters and was unrecognizable from the tremulous man who had stood at the Mangals' door begging for his help.

They pounded the frost off the door of the Needle's Eye till it creaked open. Charlin's eyes rounded when he saw Garscap.

"Worthy Saint, it is a joy to see you," Garscap exclaimed.

"Come in," the saint said with resignation.

A group of Orstretcherists were gathered in the reception hall, AscendantSun among them. Their chatter died as they recognized Garscap. The Politician of Pigsknuckle was unfazed by their stares.

"Murderer," one of them muttered.

Garscap's puzzlement appeared genuine. "I'm afraid I don't know what you mean. I've always been a friend to Orstretcherists."

"Saint Charlin, must your brother always bring trouble to our door?" Sebryn asked as he shuffled through the crowd.

"Trouble? Your once-beloved ward, Lilak, is home once more," Garscap said, smiling. "I have such fond memories of this place."

"I wish this place had fond memories of you," Saint Sebryn said. "Only you ever called yourself Lilak. Nobody here ever called you by any name other than your true one, Garscap."

"My mother called me Lilak," Garscap said wistfully. He smiled. "I must admit that I was a difficult child."

"I suppose you have come here to find them," the saint said, waving his hand at the Orstretcherists.

"I came here to seek an explanation for their disappearance and to make amends if I was in any way the cause."

This brought a scornful chorus from the Orstretcherists.

"Perhaps we might continue this conversation in private," AscendantSun suggested.

"AscendantSun and Garscap, please follow me," Saint Sebryn said. "Saint Charlin, you can stay here and entertain your brother."

"NeverFear, you should come, too," AscendantSun said.

"You must be hungry," Charlin said to Grael, his eyes darting about the crowded room. "Let me take you to the refectory."

The famished look on Garscap's face made Grael smile. "Sure," he said. "I am starving."

***

The warmth of the mutton dumpling soup poured down Grael's throat and massaged his chest. His fingers cupped the bowl and basked in its heat. "I was worried about you," he said to Charlin, who sat across from him on the bench.

"You shouldn't have. What could happen to me here?"

"Are you in trouble?"

Charlin glanced around the empty room. "Not any more. I was in trouble. It was of my own making. But for Saint Sebryn's intervention, there's no telling what damage my folly might have caused. I'll not be returning to Pigsknuckle for some time."

"What do I tell our parents?"

Charlin's eyebrows lifted. "Tell them my duties confine me to the monastery for the foreseeable future."

"Damn the Changeling. This is his fault."

Charlin winced. "Refrain from swearing in this sacred place, please."

He folded his hands on the table, his thumbs tapping together as he spoke. "This is more my fault than Garscap's. He cannot rise above his nature, but I am a saint and must. He used me to further his own selfish ends, but he succeeded because of my vanity. My actions were unsaintly, as were my impulses."

His hands parted into two imploring gestures. "I presumed to know better than Saint Sebryn and his predecessors. I was contemptuous of their disdain of secular politics. I thought it precious, even hypocritical, in this time of crisis. For the best of intentions, I took upon myself the right to exercise the authority that they feared to use."

Both hands dropped to the table. He shook his head sadly. "Vanity, vanity, all was vanity. I lied to myself by specious argument, to Saint Sebryn by omission, and to the saints of other monasteries by both."

It did not matter how much Charlin blamed himself. Garscap was the real culprit. He had exploited Charlin's generous nature to lead him astray.

Charlin glanced from behind the hand rubbing his forehead. “I feel particular guilt about annulling Garscap’s marriage to Harath Melkath. I observed the word of our laws but not their spirit. I dealt with the matter in indecent haste. The marriage had not been consummated due to willful abstinence on the part of not just Harath but her husband, as well. I should have encouraged them to complete their union, or at least, denied Garscap permission to marry the Kuny girl.”

Charlin took away his hand and leaned toward Grael. “What do you think of Harath? She thinks very highly of you.”

“She is as devious as her husband,” Grael muttered.

Charlin frowned. “If she is, necessity has made her so. Can you condemn her for saving your brother? But for her, my folly would have been my ruin.”

Grael shook his head. She had abused his trust. He would never make that mistake again.

“Harath speaks to me of you often,” Charlin said. “She praises you as her savior and considers you to be the noblest soul in Pigsknuckle. Her misuse of your benevolence is her greatest anguish. The thought of your disfavor weighs heavier on her heart than her estrangement from her father or the opprobrium of Pigsknuckle or the quandary of her future.”

Grael’s heart soared. What was this power Harath had over him that a hint of her favor was enough to make him forget the wrong that she had done to him? He had sworn off her only moments ago. A grin slipped out despite his best effort to suppress it.

Memories of how fate had stolen her from him before dampened his elation. "What will become of her?"

The saint shrugged. "She can't stay here forever. A home will be provided for her in Pigsknuckle or some other village. There's no reason other than inclination that prevents her from taking a new husband. Her honor is intact. If she chose to marry again, the monastery would provide a dowry."

"Tell her I have no quarrel with her," Grael said.

Charlin rose from his seat. "It would be better if you told her. Wait here. I'll get her."

***

AscendantSun sat on one side of the table, between NeverFear and Sebryn. Garscap sat on the opposite side with his back to the fire.

"Why did they try to murder DayFlambeau?" AscendantSun demanded, staring hard at the politician.

"I swear I knew nothing of this," Garscap insisted. "The culprits will be punished. I promise it."

"Evram Erath was one of them," NeverFear said.

"What? Are you sure?"

"His victim recognized him," AscendantSun said.

Garscap sighed. He placed an elbow on the table, rested his cheek against his hand, his eyes turning heavenward. "This is in part my fault." He shook his head. His lips pressed into a narrow line. "I may have mentioned to Evram that DayFlambeau was leaving."

He straightened, his eyes round with sudden desperation, his hands spreading into a beseeching gesture. "I never imagined that Evram would do anything like this. He was very upset about Ashin's death. He was a bit besotted by her, to tell the truth. There was some loose talk of avenging her. I dismissed it as youthful bluster, but I admonished him nonetheless. My scolding cooled his temper, and he forswore all thoughts of revenge. I presumed the matter settled and forgotten. I never imagined he'd dare to break his promise and follow through on his threat."

Sebryn's eyes narrowed. "Well, he did, and two others helped him."

Garscap sighed. "I've my suspicions as to who they might be. The Carnaths reported Fapath and Ilyam missing. They are the obvious candidates."

"Whoever they are, they are dead," AscendantSun said. "DayFlambeau slew them. Evram escaped, despite being wounded."

Garscap rubbed his mouth. "That's a terrible tragedy. Of course, Fapath is probably to blame for this calamity. Evram might have told Fapath of DayFlambeau's intention to leave, but I am sure that attacking the Elf was the older man's plan. As far as I am concerned, DayFlambeau did nothing wrong. He had no choice but to defend himself."

"Of course DayFlambeau is innocent," AscendantSun muttered. "That is self-evident."

"Evram must be found and brought here for trial," Sebryn insisted, stabbing the table with his finger.

Garscap nodded. "Of course. Do not mistake my sympathy for Evram as endorsement of his wrongdoing. Hate the sin but love the sinner, as you saints like to say. Justice must be done. If the case against him is proved, and it seems certain that it will be, our former friendship will not prevent me from having him stoned for his crime."

Sebryn shook his head. "He must be tried, but not by you."

"I am his politician," Garscap said, tapping his chest with a finger. "His trial is my responsibility."

"But you are not the Orstretcherists' leader," Sebryn said. "They are a village unto themselves, and AscendantSun Auctor is their politician. This monastery claims jurisdiction over any crime one of your people commits against them. Or perhaps you imagine that because the politicians of other villages consider you to be their leader, you have some special authority over this matter."

"The word of a saint is law," Garscap said with a defiant smile.

"That's right," Sebryn said. "A saint's word is law."

The politician and the saint locked stares in a goading silence.

Garscap trembled beneath the abbot's glare, but his voice resounded with defiance. "If you have something more to say on the matter, now would be an opportune moment."

Sebryn's gaze dropped to the table.

"What of the Orstretcherists?" Garscap asked, turning to AscendantSun. "Will you return to Pigsknuckle now that you know the truth?"

"It must be put to a vote," AscendantSun said, glancing at NeverFear. "We will tell the other Orstretcherists what you said."

"If there's anything further I can do to reassure them…"

"You must be famished," Sebryn said. "You should get something to eat in the refectory. We can continue this discussion later."

Garscap's brows knitted. "I have no appetite. I prefer to continue."

"I prefer to pause," the saint said.

Garscap stared at AscendantSun with pleading eyes, but AscendantSun fixed his gaze on the table. Garscap's chair squealed against the stone floor as he rose to his feet. "No need to call a guide. I can find my own way there," he said.

Nobody spoke as he strode out of the room.

AscendantSun was about to speak, but Sebryn silenced him with a wave of his finger and pointed to the door. The politician had left it slightly ajar. The saint shambled over to it, and scanned up and down the corridor outside. He shut the door.

"I would not have put it past him," he muttered.

"Can we trust him?" AscendantSun asked as he watched the saint's painful progress back to Garscap's vacated seat.

"That is a big question," the saint said as he angled Garscap's vacated chair to view the fire and sat down. "There is a smaller but more urgent question. On this occasion, is Garscap telling the truth?"

"Sometimes, we find it hard to read your demeanors," NeverFear said. "They are more intense than ours. Expressions you might consider subtle strike us as violent. You may think this an advantage, but we find it hard to hear the music from the noise."

AscendantSun did not bother to contradict NeverFear's assertion, though it did not apply to him. Having been immersed longer in the company of Mixies, he was used to their exaggerated miens.

"And what is your perhaps oversensitive reading of the politician's demeanor?" Sebryn asked.

"His shock at the attempted murder of DayFlambeau seemed sincere," NeverFear said. "His bewilderment at Evram's complicity also appeared genuine. The whole incident is a deep embarrassment to him. He is eager for us to return to Pigsknuckle."

"And he fears you, Worthy Saint," AscendantSun added.

"He would be wise to do so," Sebryn said with a devious chuckle as he turned to one side on his seat and stoked the fire.

***

Grael searched for the admiration his brother had spoken of in Harath's scowl.

"I will leave you two alone," Charlin said as he disappeared out the door.

"What do you want?" Harath demanded.

Her bluntness tangled Grael's thoughts. "I…Saint Charlin said…I forgive you. I mean, I bear you no grudge. I hold you in high esteem."

"I bear you no ill will either, though I cannot say the same of your brother," Harath said, glancing at the exit.

"Saint Charlin respects you," Grael protested. "He told me so himself."

She shook her head. "You misunderstand me. One of us is bait in a trap of your brother's making. He knows I like you. It's the custom when a marriage is dissolved in the manner mine was that no unwed man can refuse the spurned woman's proposal of marriage."

Grael's brows furrowed with disbelief. Such things occurred in old epics, but they didn't happen now, in this more prosaic age. Of course, the saints were desperate and clever enough to seize upon such an ancient precedent to rid them of Harath.

She raised an open hand. "Fear not. I've no intention to abuse your kindness a second time. I suffered one loveless marriage and have no desire for a second."

Though his heart sank at her pronouncement, he mimicked her outrage. "The deceitful monster! No wonder Saint Sebryn chose to confine Charlin to Pigsback."

"I am sure Saint Sebryn approved this scheme. The saints are desperate to free their monastery of my presence.

Don't think too badly of your brother. I'm certain he acted with the best of intentions."

"I hope I'm not interrupting anything." It was as if Garscap had appeared from nowhere. The sneer fixed to his lips reminded Grael of a wart. "I came to get something to eat."

"Get your food and be gone!" Harath snapped.

Garscap slipped by them into the kitchen. They were silent as he rummaged inside. "Of course, you could leave and let me eat in peace," he yelled. "This is, after all, a refectory, not a place for idle gossip…or courting."

Harath seized Grael by the shoulder before he could bolt into the kitchen. "Ignore him," she murmured. "He's trying to provoke us."

Surprise at the calmness of her voice tempered his anger. Harath's heroic composure was admirable. Here she was, in friendless exile, despised by her own kin, barely tolerated by the saints, her fate bent and twisted by others' political expediency, and yet she maintained an ethereal tranquility against the taunts of her cruelest tormentor.

Garscap emerged from the kitchen. The wooden tray in his hands held a bowl of soup, a mug of beer, and a loaf of bread. He sat down at one of the tables, drew his dagger, and began cutting chunks off the loaf, dipping them in the soup before he ate them.

"I'm starving," he said as he stuffed bread into his mouth. He slurped the beer and swallowed, his eyes fixed on the couple. "I hope you'll be happy together."

"That's none of your business!" Charlin bawled as he strode into the refectory from the hallway.

"Saint, do you ever stop meddling?" Garscap asked, grimacing into an unpersuasive smile. His hands curled into fists.

"Get out!" The ferocity in the saint's voice made Grael shiver.

"I'm not finished eating," the politician said with low menace.

"Yes, you are," Saint Charlin said. "Get out."

Garscap rose to his feet very slowly. He picked up his knife from the table.

"Apologies to you all," he said as he slipped it into its scabbard. "I'm not myself today." He bowed extravagantly to Harath and Grael, and gave Charlin a nod as he passed him.

"I have never witnessed Garscap in such brutal temper," Harath said when he was gone. "He was determined to pick a fight, with no care for the consequences. He's normally so poised, even at his most villainous."

"He's learning that even he's no match for even the humblest of saints," Charlin said as he strolled over to their table. "Which is me."

"Brother," Grael said, "Harath informs me the humblest of saints has been plotting my marriage."

Charlin raised an eyebrow. "Brother indeed. You never refer to me so casually outside family. I am a humble saint and know nothing of romance, but it is plain even to me that Harath loves you."

Feverish with embarrassment, Harath seized his sleeve. “Cease your nonsense. I can speak for myself. Grael, don’t listen to your brother. He’s plainly not in his right mind.”

Smiling, Charlin gently pulled free of her grasp. “And I know you love her. Lahan told me that the night you learned she was betrothed to Garscap. You…well…you were very upset. You two could find no better match than each other.”

“You risk bringing the Changeling’s wrath down on your brother with this nonsense,” Harath warned.

“The damage is already done, if there is any,” Charlin said. “I suspect Garscap is too preoccupied with other matters to take any interest in either of you. Now I must leave you two alone. Saints have no business meddling in affairs of the heart.”

He strode toward the exit, leaving Harath and Grael crimson and dumbstruck. He paused in the doorway. “Don’t descend the mountain alone with Garscap. Just in case.”

***

Charlin’s high spirits did not survive the abbot’s somber mood. The old man sat by the fire, collapsed inward like a derelict ruin. His every breath rattled like his last. Never before had Charlin seen him so haggard and weary. The younger saint tried to lighten the gloom by recounting his altercation with Garscap.

“Do you think your brother will relieve us of our stray?” the old man asked.

"I believe so," Charlin said, sitting down on the seat at the opposite side of the fireplace.

Sebryn rubbed his lower lip as he studied the fire. "It would be something, at least, to be rid of her. She makes the monastery itch with the threat of licentiousness. Even the Orstretcherists fear her, though they are immune to the temptations of the flesh."

"The girl is innocent. It was her chastity that brought her here."

Sebryn glared at Charlin. "Did I say otherwise? Saint Odran and his followers built this place to hide away from the corruptions of the world, but their hearts carried their vices here. They couldn't escape their nature, and nor can we. We are weak-willed men, easily led astray."

Charlin's face warmed as he remembered his recent indiscretions. He smiled. "Come. Enough of this despondency. What ails you? Have you slipped into your dotage and imagine yourself a beau for our misfortunate damsel?"

Sebryn's hearty laugh was a tonic. "You cheeky rapscallion, my dusty old heart is well past such giddy passions. My funk stems from another source. I couldn't pick apart the edifice you built. The politician retains his precious immunity to challenge."

"What devious ploy did he use to secure it?"

Sebryn shook his head. "None. I chose not to remove it. He sat across from me, fragile and trembling as a newborn kid, and I let the moment slip." He stabbed the fire with a metal rod, and threw three chunks of wood on it. “When a saint delivers an edict, he speaks for the Forelight, not for himself. For one saint to undo the word of another is to invite doubt into all the hearts it touches. If I stripped Garscap and the other politicians of your blessing, my pronouncement would shake the mountains. There is no telling the consequences, the number of faithful hearts it might poison with doubt.”

Charlin winced. His hubris had created this mess.

“To deprive Garscap of your blessing is to sentence him to death,” Sebryn said softly. “Malcontents would have torn the thorny crown from his head already, but for your protection. I suspect Garscap, believing his position unassailable, has exploited that luxury to the full to shed not just his marriage to Harath but other inconvenient alliances, also. The number and vehemence of his enemies in Pigsknuckle is far greater now than when he first became politician. He is as likely to be murdered as overthrown. I don’t want his death weighing on my conscience.”

“You hate him,” Charlin said. He was not in the mood for euphemism.

Sebryn rubbed his forehead. “That makes sentencing him to death all the harder. Besides, obnoxious he may be, and a ruthless schemer, but he has not murdered anyone.”

“Are you sure?” Charlin wasn’t.

“I believe he spoke the truth when he claimed he knew nothing of the plot to murder DayFlambeau. Even he is not so brazen as to come here and tell a lie.”

“Are you sure?” Charlin repeated.

"His shock at learning of DayFlambeau's ambush was genuine. I'm certain of it."

Charlin fingered his halo and sighed. "So, yet again, despite all our vaunted power, we fear to act."

"Impatience brought us to this impasse in the first place," Saint Sebryn chided. "In your urgency to tease apart the knot, you risk snapping the yarn."

Charlin made no rejoinder. The truth was undeniable.

"Your chance will come to undo the harm you caused," Saint Sebryn said. "You have to be patient."

"And what of his request for a saint to replace me in Pigsknuckle?" Charlin asked.

"Tomorrow is Saint Odran's feast day." Sebryn said, leaning back in his chair. "Garscap can wait till the day after tomorrow for his saint. The politician's heart will learn to love us more by our absence."

Charlin smiled and nodded, though the petulance at the root of the abbot's decision troubled him. Once again, the all-powerful saints reduced themselves to children. Instead of striking at the wolf at their door, they played games with it. Nothing good would come of it.

***

They left Pigsback the next morning. Garscap kept his back to his companions as they descended the mountain. If only he could forget them. Harath walked beside Grael. AscendantSun kept a few steps ahead of them. The saints were certainly behind his offer to accompany the Pigsknucklers back to their village. His presence was an implied insult. Garscap would never resort to arranging an accident on the Pig for the lovers. He was more subtle than that. And more patient.

In a sense, it was gratifying that the saints continued to underestimate his cunning. Enamored with their own lofty intellect, they failed to appreciate his more worldly genius. Their blindness was to his benefit. As long as they regarded him as a fool, albeit a dangerous one, they remained susceptible to delicate manipulation.

He smiled at the certain horror and outrage of Grael's parents when they learned that their son was engaged to Garscap's former wife. Any slim chance of reconciliation between Grael and his parents would be gone. Insinuations of barrenness and unconventional living—most of them spread by Garscap—wafted about the annulment of her marriage like a bad smell. Disowned by her father, her dowry was whatever charitable donation the monastery chose to bestow. Grael's parents would regard a vagrant as a better wife for their son than Widan's wayward daughter. And the mother, Myryr, would never forgive her saintly son for arranging the match. She would no longer speak of Charlin with such conceited reverence. His name would be a curse on her lips.

Garscap looked back to share his triumphant grin with the couple, but when his eyes met AscendantSun's, the smile died. Instead of wasting time as an unnecessary escort, AscendantSun should have stayed in Pigsback to press the other Orstretcherists to return to Pigsknuckle.

Garscap had said as much to his companion several times, but he could not resist reiterating his point.

"As I explained before, we set aside this day for private contemplation on the matter," AscendantSun said. "The final debate will wait till I return to the monastery tomorrow."

Garscap asked the question foremost on his mind, though he feared its answer. "And do you think you will win?"

AscendantSun shrugged. "The events that sent us back to Pigsback have divided us. Our united purpose has fractured along our private inclinations. We are like a mirror smashed on the floor. Before, there was a single reflection. Now the image differs slightly on each shard."

"Better to make your mirror out of polished metal than glass. It isn't so fragile," Garscap said.

"Better to not drop it in the first place."

"I had nothing to do with the attack on DayFlambeau," Garscap growled. "The fault lies with Evram and the Carnaths. Two are dead, and when the third is found, he will be delivered to Pigsback. What more can I do?"

"Be patient," AscendantSun said gently.

"Be patient," Garscap scoffed. "Tell our enemies to be patient."

"Whatever my comrades decide, I will fight by your side."

"Forgive me. Your prowess in combat is indisputable, but what difference can one make against an army?"

"What difference can four dozen make against a legion? Victory lies in the hands of your own race."

"Then we are doomed," Garscap said, too softly for Harath or Grael to overhear. "Our mirror was shattered long ago. The saints scattered its fragments across the mountains. Without the help of your friends in Pigsback, I cannot bind the pieces together. Saint and Orstretcherist must rally to our cause or it is hopeless."

They were about to pass the last furka on the trail down the mountain, when Harath said, "Let's pause here a while. I could do with a rest."

Garscap was inclined to continue if only to annoy her, but it was important not to appear petulant in front of AscendantSun. He shrugged and smiled. "We aren't in a rush. Take as long as you like."

Harath and Grael shared a boulder as a seat, while Garscap and AscendantSun strolled a little further on to take in the view. From this vantage point, they could see the village, the valley beyond, and the mountains that enclosed it.

"Look!" AscendantSun cried.

Garscap followed the Elf's pointing finger. At first, his straining eyes detected nothing extraordinary in the shadows drifting across the distant mountainside. Then something gleamed in the midst of the shifting cloud. The sun's glare revealed a saffron thread extending downward from the rugged horizon like a misplaced hair.

"Our enemies are patient no longer," Garscap said. "War is upon us."

Chapter 22

Nacreous steel and sun-forged gold,
Like lightning, arms and armor flashed,
Like thunder, their bearers' roars rolled,
As the saffron storm onward thrashed.

-From *The Martyrdom of Coneyriddle.*

Pigsknuckle was wide-eyed with terror. As Garscap looked down on the swarming villagers, he was reminded of a kicked ants' nest. People scurrying in all directions, the desperate cries and barked orders—all lent to a general aura of panic and confusion. Women prepared their families for flight while their menfolk readied their weapons. Pairs of girls struggled to prop up aged grandmothers on their slim shoulders as they crawled out of the village in the hope of getting a head start on the impending exodus. Young men helped their grandfathers to the furka before getting their own weapons. It was fitting that Widan stood near these ancients as he tried to shape the chaos. The Cliffringdeners were quieter and sadder as they organized their departure. They had witnessed all this before, and they knew how it would end.

"Harath, are you tired?" Garscap asked, glancing back at his two remaining companions. The suspicious scowls on their faces were comical.

"What do you want?" she asked.

"Someone must seek Littleknuckle's aid," Garscap said. "I can spare no man."

"Send someone else," Grael said. "She's too tired. Send a boy who knows the way there."

"The Politician of Littleknuckle may ignore the pleas of a child. This mission requires someone more headstrong, and I can think of no woman more suited to the task than your betrothed." She was tougher than most of the men in the village.

Harath hushed Grael before he could speak. "I thought the politicians made you their leader. Surely, he must obey your command."

Garscap snorted. "He must, as long as it poses no risk to Littleknuckle. In this circumstance, he may be tempted to invoke that exception." Garscap would, if the situation was reversed. "Someone must remind him of his duties as a Stretcher."

"I'll go," Harath said, glancing at Grael. "Nobody will have rest this day."

"Do you even know where it is?" Grael asked.

"We passed near it on our journey from Cronesglen," she said. "Have no fear. I will find it."

"You mustn't dally at one of Littleknuckle's outer furkas," Garscap said. "You mightn't be discovered there in time. You must strike for the one in the center of the village."

Grael threw up his arms. "Are you mad? Do you realize the risk that you are asking her to take? Harath, don't listen to him."

Ignoring him, Garscap stared into Harath's eyes, demanding her attention. "Tell Lohor Teevan Pigsknuckle is under attack, and he must honor the sacred pledge he made on Cronesglen's furka and come to our aid. It's his duty as a Stretcher. Now go, and may the Forelight protect you."

She planted a kiss on Grael's cheek and ran.

Garscap waited till she was a good distance away. He waved his arms and cried, "Wait!"

She halted and looked back, her head tilting quizzically.

"I forgot to say something to her," Garscap explained to Grael as he dashed toward her. "You stay where you are. I'll be back in a minute."

She scowled suspiciously as he neared. "What do you want?"

Garscap halted beside her and took a moment to recover his breath. A glance back at Grael confirmed that he was too far away to hear what Garscap was about to say. The last thing that Garscap needed today was Grael holding him to his word. "If Lohor is less than willing to help, tell him that I am dispatching other messengers to every monastery and village in the mountains. If he doesn't come to our village, Littleknuckle will be known evermore as a village of cowards and liars."

Harath gave him a dubious look. He had already protested that he could not spare a single man, and now he was talking about scattering men across the Stretches.

Garscap smiled. "Those are my words. If they prove false, the sin is mine alone. Now go!" Of course, he might forget to send the messengers, or circumstances might deny him the opportunity. But Lohor wouldn't know that.

She nodded reluctantly, and raced away.

"What was that about?" Grael demanded as Garscap reached him.

The politician smiled innocently and shrugged. "Just a little more detail on how to deal with Lohor Teevan."

Harath had already disappeared into the forest.

Grael frowned. "If anything happens to her, you'll be sorry."

The politician chuckled grimly. "Your concern is admirable but misplaced. In Littleknuckle, she may be safer than the rest of us."

"Unless it, too, is under attack," Grael muttered.

They ran down the slope and hurried to the village. Faces vivid with terror and anticipation crowded around Garscap. He pushed through them, sprinkling morsels of hope behind him, inviting them to follow. Thus, it was at the head of a procession that he reached the furka and his old rival.

"I'm glad you have returned," Widan said. "It would be a shame to die without you."

Garscap stared into Widan's defeated eyes and filled Pigsknuckle with defiant laughter. "It was a lucky day for this village when you handed me its thorny crown." He leapt atop the earthen podium and shouted to the departing Cliffringdeners. "Where are you going?"

"Away from here!" one of the women cried.

"You took our hospitality, and now, in the midst of this crisis, you abandon us. You shame the memory of your village and those who died in its defense."

A few of the women booed. Others protested against his slander.

One shouted, "What do you expect? We aren't warriors."

"You can't fight but you can carry," Garscap retorted. "You can help to carry our infirm and aged. You can help shoulder the provisions for our flight."

"And where will we all go?" another asked. "What village will bear such a host?"

Garscap pointed to the Pig's icy summit. "To Pigsback. The saints' miraculous hospitality will sustain us till we can return here or find a better home elsewhere. There's no need for despair while hope lives. AscendantSun is racing up the mountain to rally his friends to our aid. A messenger is on the way to Littleknuckle to summon its warriors. We can survive this calamity, but only if we stand together."

"The men of Pigsknuckle have no choice but to stand together under this furka, like the Cliffringdeners," Widan muttered. "It remains blessed and must be protected from sacrilege."

"Pigsback will send a saint to deconsecrate it as soon as AscendantSun reaches the monastery," Grael said. "Saint Charlin promised as much."

"He'll be too late even to bury us," Widan muttered.

Garscap sneered. "Someone get me a hammer. The biggest one you can find."

A furka would not murder him like his father.

***

Tossing his batonaxes aside, AscendantSun threw himself against the door of the monastery and pounded his fists against it till the sound of movement in the Needle's Eye made him step back. The door creaked open, and Saint Charlin peered out.

"What are you doing back here so soon?" he asked, opening the door.

"Make haste to Pigsknuckle," AscendantSun said as he pushed by him. "The Fair Folk's army closes in on it as we speak."

"I'll inform Saint Sebryn. He is in the chapel with the other saints celebrating Saint Odran's feast day," Charlin said weakly, stunned by AscendantSun's revelation.

AscendantSun's soaring voice filled the reception room as he ran through it. "No time. Go now!"

The labyrinthine corridors through which he raced were awash with the overspill of devout chanting from the chapel. He burst into the Orstretcherists' dormitory, slamming the door against the wall. They were all gathered there, eating lunch. DayFlambeau lay in bed, propped up on pillows, sipping from a spoon that NeverFear pressed to his lips. Heads swiveled in almost perfect unison to regard the unexpected arrival.

"To arms!" AscendantSun yelled. "Pigsknuckle is under attack!"

"We agreed decisions on our involvement in this conflict should be made by the group," NoonBlest said. "Is that not so, NeverFear?"

NeverFear nodded slowly.

"There is no time for debate," AscendantSun insisted. "Every moment we delay brings our allies' ruin closer."

"These same allies crippled DayFlambeau," NoonBlest said.

"Garscap gave his word he had nothing to do with that," AscendantSun said. "He promised that Evram Erath would be punished for his crime. Is that not so, NeverFear?"

NeverFear nodded.

"Lost your tongue?" AscendantSun sneered.

"The politician meant what he said, but that does not mean his followers can be trusted," NeverFear said.

AscendantSun shook his head. "So you think we should let them all die."

"I'm not saying that," NeverFear said. "I think the group must decide the matter. Not you or I. The group."

NoonBlest and his sympathizers nodded. They were exploiting NeverFear's democratic inclinations to thwart AscendantSun. His foresight of this possibility was little consolation. With time, he might have unraveled their machinations, but time was one thing that he did not possess. The Pigsknucklers would be dead long before the debate was concluded.

"Enough talk. I am going to Pigsknuckle," TrueFriend declared as he walked to AscendantSun's side. "Anybody of the same mind should come with us. The rest can stay here and pray for our souls to salve their consciences."

"But the group…" NeverFear protested.

"The *group*?" TrueFriend cried. "What about the group? Different reasons brought us here and different reasons made us stay. I am responsible for one innocent's death, and I will not stand by and be party to the murder of others."

"You risk facing your own twin in combat," DayFlambeau croaked.

TrueFriend shrugged. "If I do, I will leave the moral dilemmas to him."

"My twin is a cobbler, so unless legionaries need emergency repairs to their boots in the middle of a battle, I am unlikely to meet him," PureFaith Nitor said as he, too, joined AscendantSun.

StrongArm Servitor followed him.

AscendantSun addressed the others. "We are leaving now. If you want to come with us, do not delay or we will be gone."

NoonBlest's voice, brimming with triumph and mockery, followed them down the corridor. "I guess AscendantSun has as much respect for the opinion of the majority as he has for the precepts of his religion."

As they passed through the Needle's Eye, TrueFriend said, "Our weapons are beneath a cairn by the graveyard around the back. I thought it was kind of appropriate."

AscendantSun quickly retrieved his batonaxes and followed the others around the back of the monastery. Snow furred the mound. It formed a ridge along the spine like hackles. TrueFriend brushed away part of the icy cover, and they began to pick away the stones from the mound. As they pulled free leather parcels containing weapons and armor, AscendantSun thanked his companions for their support.

"You know me. TrueFriend by name, true friend by nature. To be honest, Ashin is the reason I am here. In my legionary days, the slaughter of Mixies never bothered me. Yet, the death of this one girl, though it was not by my hands, haunts me as much as our defeat at Gules. She taught me what words could not. I need no more lessons in the value of a Mixy's life."

"I am sick of listening to the others' whining," PureFaith said as he slipped into his mail shirt. "Your disappearance for a year does not make you any less our leader as far as I am concerned. I am sure you had good reason for it. Some of us suffer from too much ambition to serve. Whereas once their object of veneration might have been the Golden Light or the Consensus, now it is the group, but as TrueFriend rightly pointed out, there is no group, just a collection of individuals."

"I must go because of them," StrongArm said, grinning and pointing to his friends. "I probably would go anyway. It beats talking."

With numb fingers, AscendantSun helped the others strap on their armor. They walked past the Needle's Eye for a second time as they headed down the mountain. In their hasty exit, they had left its doors wide open. The hot breath of the monastery pouring through it turned into a cloud. AscendantSun kept glancing back at the entrance for some hopeful glimmer of activity, but it cradled only darkness, silent and hollow.

***

Grael paused before the open door of his parents' home, apprehensive about the welcome he might receive there. He peered inside. Mam was stuffing clothes, edibles, and a few treasured possessions into leather bags, while Wanyr tried to keep a struggling Miona, now a robust toddler, from climbing out of her arms. Dad, red-faced and sweating profusely, watched them in silence, his obvious desperation for their departure undoubtedly tempered by the knowledge that their lives might depend on whatever was in those sacks. A fearful Maerbard, spear in hand, stood quietly in his shadow.

Dad glanced in the direction of Grael's cough. He nodded to Grael, and Grael nodded back. They smiled.

"Trust you to come for a visit on a day like today," Dad said.

Grael stepped into the cabin. "Where is the hammer I gave you?" he asked his father.

Dad waved vaguely towards one corner. "Are you ready?" he asked the others.

Grael found the hammer, still in its original leather wrapping.

"Should we put out the fire?" Myryr asked.

"Does it matter?" Lahan asked. "I will take care of it. You should go now."

"Garscap told everyone to head for Pigsback," Grael said.

"I'm staying with you," Maerbard said to his father.

"None of that nonsense. You are going with your mother and sisters," Lahan said.

"I'm near manhood."

"Be thankful you're not yet a man," Dad muttered, glancing at Grael.

"But people will think I'm a coward," Maerbard whined.

Grael rolled his eyes. Poor Maerbard did not realize that by the end of the day, there might not be anyone alive to judge him.

"This is Grael's fault," Mam hissed. "Maerbard got these notions from him."

"Myryr, no harsh words, please," Dad said calmly. "Maerbard, I don't think you are a coward. Do you, Grael?"

Grael shook his head.

His father smiled at Maerbard. “See, Grael doesn’t think you are a coward either. It would be a relief for me to know that your mother and sister and baby brother are safe with you.”

“I would feel safer with you to protect us,” Mam added.

Maerbard’s agreement was grudging, but his relief evident. The family trooped outside, and Grael made his final farewells.

As he hugged his mother and kissed her cheek, she whispered in his ear, “Look after your father.”

His hug with Maerbard was little more than patting each other’s backs. He picked up little Miona and hugged her, and then it was Wanyr’s turn. She clung tightly to him and started to cry, and their mother had to gently pull her away.

He went to hug his father, but Dad waved him away, grinning. “I’m coming with you, remember. Besides, we’ll all be together soon enough. Don’t worry.”

***

Foreboding gripped Garscap as Grael placed a heavy hammer in his hands. It had been part of the Jinglemen’s cursed trove. Too ornate for a common tool, its embellishment made it strangely apt for Garscap’s purpose.

“Hear me,” he said to the assembled warriors. “Saint Charlin gave me absolute authority over this village. Does anyone here challenge the word of a saint?”

Silence answered.

"Then I will honor the word of Saint Charlin. I will deconsecrate this furka with this hammer."

"It's easy for you to talk of tearing down this furka," the ancient Thomol Mangal said. "You're not from here. It has protected the village since its foundation. Saint Odran planted it here with his own hands. To damage that stone is sacrilege and makes you as much our enemy as the Elves. I, for one, will not let you destroy it."

Some part of Garscap longed to turn his back on the Pigsknucklers and leave them to their fate. But another, stronger part of him wanted to accept the old fool's challenge and show him what his threats were worth.

"Perhaps you are so old, Thomol, that you wouldn't notice death. The rest of us want to live to defend our families. Is this stone worth more to you than Dawan and your other grandchildren? A saint raised this furka, and a saint ordered its destruction in the event that it proved a bane instead of a blessing. Who are you to question the word of a saint?"

"I hear no saint," Thomol growled. "The only word I have is yours."

"If I am lying, then the sin of the furka's destruction will be mine alone," Garscap said. "We've no more time for debate. If any man knows for certain that I speak falsely, let him strike me down now. Otherwise, get out of my way."

The men cleared a path before him to the furka. As he walked toward it, he looked upon faces filled with fear and awe and hope, and smiled. He basked in the silent adulation of the men whose village had once spurned him. Only he could save them. Only he could do what must be done. Not Widan nor his dead son, nor Grael, despite his inclination for unorthodoxy. No one had the imagination to conceive this deed, much less the audacity to carry it out. Perhaps, this was the reason the Gilt Spider had singled him out as a child. Perhaps, he was what he had always dreamed of becoming—the new Alackalas.

This day, he was the hero.

As the furka loomed before him, he paused. The crowd held its breath. He could feel them silently urging him to strike. The hammer's shaft twisted in his hands. He raised it over his head and brought it down on the center of the furka. The force of the blow shuddered through his hands and arms. One arm of the stone broke off with a thunderous crack and dropped to the ground, followed by a few quickly stifled cheers. He stared at his handiwork for a moment. The one-armed furka reminded him of a wounded bird for some reason. He swung again and again, pounding the stone till only a stump remained.

When he finished, he returned the hammer to Grael. Garscap looked at Thomol. "Anyone who wants to stay here can do so." He pointed to the Pig. "The rest of us are going up there."

***

Harath steadied her gasps as she waited behind the hut. Eventually, the traffic of Littleknucklers through the center of the village would ease, and the moment would come to run to the furka. The village's buildings and their layout were similar to Pigsknuckle in many ways, but it lacked its neighbor's impressive setting, its view of the Pig being obscured by lesser mountains. The central furka was within sight, but she was so tired and her legs so leaden, she feared that she didn't have the strength to reach it.

She brushed away the loose hair that tickled her cheeks. The smell of stale sweat and exhaustion was overpowering. She must look a sight.

Someone screamed behind her. An old woman, her face contorted with terror, pointed to her. Harath bolted by a young man who came to investigate the shriek, and dashed for the furka. A second man stood in her way, his hand drawing a dagger from its sheath. She managed to swerve beyond his arms, but his foot tripped her, and she tumbled to the ground. She crawled for the sacred stone. Hands grabbed her foot, but she managed to kick off the sandal and reach the furka.

Clinging to its base, she cried, "Get your politician now!" She propped her back against the stone trunk and laughed at the irony of her earlier concern for her appearance. She had only one sandal, and mud and grass stains streaked the front of her dress.

Littleknucklers crowded around her, though none dared to touch her. Someone tossed her missing sandal at her feet.

Lohor Teevan emerged from the village's great hall, demanding to know the reason for the commotion. He stopped mid-sentence when he saw Harath, his angry demeanor turning to puzzlement.

"The Politician of Pigsknuckle sent me here to remind you that it is the duty of every Stretcher to help his fellows," Harath said. "Our village is under attack by the Fair Folk. Garscap Torp demands that you honor your sacred promise to him, and come to the aid of your neighbors."

Lohor shook his head sadly. "My first duty is to protect the furkas of Littleknuckle. Garscap must look elsewhere for help."

Harath could not repress a sneer. "Garscap has sent other messengers to villages and monasteries across the mountains seeking aid. Know that the names of this village and its politician are also on their lips. Good or ill, your actions on this day will not be forgotten."

Harath glared back at Lohor's angry stare. He pursed his lips, and turned to the crowd. He pointed a finger at a youth. "Gather half a dozen men of your age. I have an errand for you. If Littleknuckle must go to war, it won't do so alone."

***

Saint Charlin blessed the fleeing women and children as he ran by them in the opposite direction. They were a mixture of Pigsknucklers and Cliffringdeners. Most of them were laden with leather sacks or wicker panniers brimming with foodstuffs and spare clothing. He wasted no time in acknowledging salutes, though he noted those who made no effort to make them.

He had already flown past his mother before he recognized her gaunt face. He glanced over his shoulder at the children in her company. Little Miona was in her arms. Wanyr and Maerbard were by her side. Charlin thanked the Forelight for this merciful vision, but there was no time to stop. The lives of Grael and Lahan depended on him reaching Pigsknuckle in time.

Imagine Saint Sebryn's consternation when this stream of refugees reached the monastery. One woman demanding entry to Saint Odran's spurred the old man to unheard-of indignation. Such a vast influx of femininity pouring through the Needle's Eye had the potential to drive the abbot to fatal apoplexy. Perhaps Sebryn would be more tolerant toward them than Charlin supposed, given the circumstances of their flight. It was hard to know where the saints were going to put them all, much less feed them.

Charlin thanked the Forelight for the clement weather and pleaded for it to continue. The mountain's climate was so capricious. If the Pig decided to scratch this unprecedented itch, the impact on the refugees would be catastrophic.

The thread of climbers followed the meandering path up the mountain. A good distance behind the tattered rear of the column was a second, more compact group, predominantly devoted to the transport of the old and invalid. They were either carried on younger shoulders or dragged on crude litters. It was good that their helpers were not confined to family and neighbors. Irrespective of the colors of their halos, Cliffringdeners and Pigsknucklers shared the burden of their advancement. They progressed at what was little more than a crawl. Yet, despite the urgency of their flight, they had a laudable determination that nobody was to be left behind. The Pig watched, ready to bring death to stragglers.

Talida was with this group. She walked by herself, overloaded with sacks doubtless containing her husband's possessions, staggering beneath their weight, ignored by the rest. The saint avoided her harsh stare as he rushed past.

Beyond this group, there was only the lonely mountain. Charlin fought the leaden ache in his legs and the stitch in his side as he skittered and stumbled down the shifting scree. Down the Crooked Stair and through the maze of false tracks he raced. As he passed by each furka, he whispered breathless prayers for his family, his village, and his people.

Before he reached the final furka on the descent, he found some old men from Pigsknuckle squabbling with a group of Cliffringdeners. Five ancients, sitting on the side of the track, resisted the women's attempts to lift them. Thomol Mangal was the most vociferous, his arms folded in grim defiance of the attempts to seize them. "Unhand me! I won't be carried up the Pig like a child or an old woman. But for my respect for your gender, I'd answer your harassment with the point of a spear."

"But your politician ordered us to take you to Pigsback," one of the women said. "And he ordered you to let us."

"If I was twenty years younger, I would teach that young buck some manners."

"If you were twenty years younger, we wouldn't be having this conversation," another woman said as she made another unsuccessful grab for his arm.

"Please, Worthy Saint, save us from these witches," Thomol pleaded, emphasizing his desperation with outstretched arms.

Charlin struggled to contain his temper. "Do not insult pious women with that name. If you want to be treated as men, then behave like men and treat these ladies with respect. Do as your politician commands. He is the authority in temporal affairs. My sole concern is with spiritual matters."

As Thomol's countenance crumbled into abject defeat and despair, the saint regretted his harshness. He was about to offer a few consolatory words when Thomol's eyes flashed with brazen malevolence.

"So, is the destruction of a consecrated furka a temporal or a spiritual matter? For instance, our politician has destroyed the furka that Saint Odran built in Pigsknuckle with a hammer. He says he acted with your leave. Is this true?"

"Thomol Mangal, no more nonsense!" Charlin roared as he wagged a finger at the cantankerous ancient. "Let these women help you, or you will have more to contend with than their generosity. You should know better than to invite the wrath of a saint."

As Thomol mumbled earnest apologies, Charlin stamped away. If the old man had spoken the truth, Garscap would pay for his sacrilege. He would learn the price of usurping a saint's power and abusing Charlin's name.

A short distance farther, he found most the menfolk of Pigsknuckle gathered together. "Where's the Garscap Torp?" he barked as they divided to let him pass.

"He's standing by the ruins of the furka over the brow," someone murmured.

Not content with destroying one furka, the Changeling had smashed a second. Charlin's head filled with the terrible punishments that were meted out to sinners before the saints became afraid of their own power. Most were too gentle for the Changeling.

The politician was in permanent genuflection near the site of his latest crime. The broken trunk of the furka stood, pointing upward like an impertinent finger. Leaning casually against it was the hammer, the tool of its demolition. A dozen other Pigsknucklers, including Grael, Lahan, Widan, and Maergan Erath, were huddled in various low postures around him. Their attention was focused on the valley below.

Garscap glanced over his shoulder, and smiled at Charlin. "Worthy saint, you're too late, or at least you would have been if we had awaited you in Pigsknuckle. Come and watch. The Fair Folk are about to attack."

Shock skewered the saint's anger. Stunned, he walked to where Garscap and his companions gathered. As he stood over them, hands tugged at his sleeves.

"Worthy saint, please kneel down, lest our foes spot you," Garscap said.

In a daze, the saint complied. He was mesmerized by the activity in the valley. Two saffron curves approached the village on opposite sides like hands slowly closing around a fly. Their progress had a ghostly quality as they passed through copses and outlying huts with no apparent loss of cohesion. The legionaries charged. Charlin imagined a thunderous clap as they rushed into Pigsknuckle. The heart of the village burned with the color of their uniforms.

"Thus falls Pigsknuckle," Garscap said with surprising nonchalance. "Hopefully, they'll be content with its capture like they were at Cliffringden, and harass us no more this day."

***

While the legionaries secured the village, their tribune, SunTalon Risus, and Sentinel Five stood beside the broken furka and contemplated its meaning.

"This is a new development," SunTalon commented, managing to smile despite his disappointment. "I guess the Stretchers have learned to escape this trap of their own making. The legate must be apprised of this as soon as we return to Fort Lumen."

"Tell me," the sentinel said, "were you a Gleamer?"

"I fought for Gleam till the walls came tumbling down," SunTalon replied. "I was a member of the Harbinger's Dawn Chorus before it became fashionable."

"As one Gleamer to another, tell me what you think of your legate, IronWill."

SunTalon was slow to respond. "He was a good Gleamer. Like all of his lineage, he is resourceful and clever. He is personally very brave. But when it comes to his troops, he is a coward. He loves them too much. He is a legate more suited to peace than war." His voice had trailed off to a whisper. Sharing such a bold confidence with one of the Harbinger's elite guards held a giddy intoxication.

Sentinel Five nodded. "I have heard similar comments from others."

"Take this current situation as an example. Presented with the surprising abandonment of this village, IronWill's natural instinct would be to err on the side of caution. He might even retreat." SunTalon was about to expand on his point, but the approach of the centurion superior, WarSage Galea, silenced him.

WarSage saluted SunTalon, but his eyes drifted to the sentinel. "We have searched the village and found none of the inhabitants. The livestock have been let loose, probably because the villagers were in too much of a rush to take their animals. Warm ash in some of the hearths suggests their flight was recent."

"So we have a chance to catch them," SunTalon said.

"Their extermination is not the primary objective of this mission," Sentinel Five said. "The Orstretcherists are our main quarry."

Irked by the sentinel's rebuke, SunTalon hastily dismissed WarSage.

"Your help since I arrived at Fort Lumen has not gone unnoticed," the sentinel said. "I have not the authority to offer promotions, but I promise my report to the Harbinger concerning your part in this expedition will be highly complimentary."

"I am gratified to hear it."

"You know many of these Orstretcherists were Gleamers."

SunTalon nodded. "All the more reason that they must be extirpated. Their very existence insults all who lived and died to defend Gleam."

Sentinel Five expressed his approval with a nod. "If the Orstretcherists are not here, then they must be hiding in the temple somewhere up there." He pointed to the mountain. "Perhaps, your missing villagers are with them. Much of the day has passed, and we have little yet to show for our exertions. Let us delay here no longer and scale the mountain."

***

Harath hugged the base of the furka, afraid to forsake its reassuring protection. Why was Lohor Teevan taking so long to gather his men? She could see nothing beyond the women encircling her. They were all lean, no doubt due to the hardship of the Year of Bleeding Snow. She thanked the Forelight that Pigsknuckle avoided famine due to the generosity of Pigsback and the treasure of her former captors. Perhaps, her relative plumpness was the reason they glared at her with such malevolence. She faced their accusatory stares with mute defiance till her patience ran out and she challenged them to explain their animosity.

"You came to take our men away," one of them said.

"I came here for help. If the Fair Folk are not stopped now, your village might be next."

"They are attacking Pigsknuckle because your people meddled in their affairs. You consorted with the Orstretcherists, their enemies. You invited bad luck into your homes and bad luck accepted your invitation."

"Tell that to the widows of Cliffringden."

The cordon retorted with silence. Harath's comment had shamed a few, mostly younger women, but the faces of the rest radiated absolute certitude in their convictions—some unknown moral failing of the Cliffringdeners must have brought their ruin. The Forelight would not let decent people suffer such a terrible calamity.

Harath bristled at their self-righteousness. She was about to disabuse them of their delusions when a child pushed through the crowd. She clung to her mother's hem with painfully thin arms as she stared at Harath, her brown eyes far too big for her bony little face. It was ironic that these women blamed others' misfortune on their sinfulness, given the signs of famine in their village. Fear motivated their condemnation. These women were frightened for their families. Pigsknuckle had let them starve through the Year of Bleeding Snow, and now their neighbor demanded that their husbands and sons sacrifice their lives to save it. If these women's illusions eased their distress, Harath should not dispel them.

"What is delaying Lohor Teevan?" she asked, trying to sound conciliatory.

"Did you not know?" a woman said with genuine surprise. "The men have already set off for Pigsknuckle."

She was about to strike the furka with her fist, but good sense prevented her from committing such a sacrilege, and she redirected her blow into the ground. Of course, Lohor would never think to bring her along. In his eyes, she was a woman and unsuited to war, even if she must endure its consequences. The furka was as much a trap as a sanctuary. Her part in Pigsknuckle's defense was over. Resting one hand against the sculpted stone, she turned to the furka, closed her eyes, and prayed to the Forelight to protect Grael and the others.

***

The disgusted moans of Garscap's companions choired with his own as saffron began to spill out of the village. The column of legionaries pointed like an arrow toward the Pig. Garscap stood. Hiding any longer was pointless. As he ran over to the broken furka, the others followed. He seized the hammer and thrust it into the saint's fumbling hands.

"Every furka between here and Pigsback must be smashed," Garscap said. "Deconsecrate them if you must, but be quick with your prayers."

Saint Charlin stared at him, and then at the hammer.

"What are you waiting for? Go!" Garscap roared, sending the saint running through the massed Pigsknucklers.

The politician addressed the crowd. "As you probably gathered from our groans, the Fair Folk are on their way up the mountain. We have no choice but to fight them. Calm down. Take heart. My former profession as a mercenary taught me a few tricks that will not be to our enemies' liking." His laugh promised more than he dared to commit in words. Even if the Orstretcherists arrived in time, even if the Littleknucklers came, their interventions would hardly be sufficient to defeat the invaders. His only consolation was that his people would not die like sheep. Their lives would exact a heavy price from their takers.

Chapter 23

The heroes of Coneyriddle,
Undaunted, made their final stand,
Their arms breaking but not their will,
Spear turning to knife, knife to hand.

~From *The Martyrdom of Coneyriddle.*

SunTalon Risus climbed the mountain alongside the sentinel. Legionaries in bronze and saffron stretched before and after them. Was this climb a fool's errand? Scouts had discovered another broken furka and indications of recent activity on the trail, but there had been no sighting of Orstretcherists or Stretchers. It was possible that the monastery was deserted, and SunTalon was risking his legionaries' lives for nothing. This mountain was a dangerous place to bivouac. His preference was to return to the village, camp there overnight, and then restart the ascent in the morning. That would give them a full day to make the round trip to the monastery.

The problem was that Sentinel Five was set on reaching it today. He feared any delay might give the Orstretcherists and their allies time to escape. There was no point in incurring the sentinel's wrath unnecessarily. Memories of what the sentinel had said about IronWill Defensor were still fresh, and SunTalon was eager to avoid the impression he lacked courage like his legate. It would be a dereliction of duty, if he failed to express his concerns at some point, but it was not an absolute necessity yet, so he postponed the unpleasant conversation for later. Hopefully, the sentinel might see sense on his own.

The legionaries reached the top of the ridge and filed past the ruined furka. SunTalon took it as a good omen and put aside his qualms. Ors would never destroy a gnomon in this fashion. They would defend its golden hand to their last breath, though their sacrifice would not be as heedless and ineffectual as that made by the Stretchers in the past. The destruction of these objects of veneration was a symptom of despair.

SunTalon glanced upon the noon sun, a whitish blaze in the sky. Surely, the fineness of the day was another omen. Aurelian was smiling down on the expedition.

Two scouts in camouflaged attire raced down the column. One, nudging a legionary aside, reported with a fluttering voice to the tribune. "We spotted Stretchers farther up the trail. There are a dozen of them gathered on a series of low escarpments."

SunTalon repressed the urge to whoop for joy. Some of the legionaries around him were less restrained, forcing him to shut them up. The sentinel's grin stretched from ear to ear, and his eyes sparkled with wild delight. At last, they had found some enemy to kill.

"A dozen Stretchers are no great challenge," the tribune said to sober himself as much as to his troops.

"One rat is never alone," the sentinel observed. "There may be an army beyond this dozen. The Orstretcherists may be with them."

"I hope you are right." SunTalon had no doubt that whatever force awaited them on the mountain, the two centuries under his command were more than a match for it.

***

Grael stood at the back of the crowd gathered around Garscap at the top of the Crooked Stair.

"This is where we'll meet them," the politician said. "I'm going to send a detachment of young men to wait for the Elves at the bottom of the Crooked Stair. They'll draw the Elves up it, breaking their cohesion. The rest of us will meet them here, using the height of the top terrace and the relative narrowness of the plateaus below it against them."

"What if they scale the cliffs?" someone asked.

"Hopefully, they'll be too focused on the Crooked Stair to think of it. If they try to scale the cliffs, our lookout will spot them." Garscap pointed to Joraem Scoral zigzagging up the mountainside.

"And what happens if we cannot hold them here?" Dawan asked.

Garscap winked. "I have a trick up my sleeve for that eventuality. Grael Erol will lead the decoy group. The others will be Dawan Mangal—"

"I'll go in my son's place," Lahan declared.

"No," Grael and Garscap said in unison.

"Lahan, you're too old," Garscap said. "The decoy group must be young men spry enough to stay ahead of pursuing legionaries."

Grael pushed his way through the crowd to his father's side. "Better I risk my life than you end yours. Garscap, I'll go."

***

Grael wished his palms would stop sweating as he wiped their excess moisture on the front of his tunic.

"Did Garscap give any indication as to when we should retreat?" Dawan asked, his voice heavy with tension.

"He said I must decide." Grael glanced around at his comrades. They were all young men like him and Dawan, though the value of that advantage during their inevitable retreat was yet to be determined. Two whittled pieces of wood. Another inspected his spearhead lashings and the edge of his knife with grim intensity. Two more propped themselves against boulders, their eyes closed in a vain search for forgetful sleep. Several made sporadic traversals of the terrace whenever their nerves got the better of them. The rest stared with hypnotic intensity down the mountainside, their eyes sifting the barren landscape for the tiniest movement, for the first telltale flicker of saffron.

If the Smirk was here, Garscap might have put him in charge and spared Grael the burden of command. Evram's absence deepened Grael's contempt for the politician's pet.

The coward should be here defending his people during this crisis, and, if he survived it, face justice like a Stretcher, instead of hiding in the wilderness like a frightened animal. Evram had done so much damage, denying Pigsknuckle its allies at this critical moment. Worst of all, his crime might prove his salvation as much as his people's doom.

"We're being watched," Dawan murmured. "Look at the humped rock with the bitten side yonder."

It took some time to identify the boulder from Dawan's description. Grael began to suspect his cousin was the victim of an overeager imagination, when a flash of movement came from behind the rock.

Grael's orders drifted on whispers through the group. "Make no sudden movements. Be ready for an attack."

With growing impatience, Grael watched four Elves creep nearer. They were dressed in ragged greens and browns rather than the brighter plumage of regular legionaries, though the camouflage was not very effective against the gray terrain. Their swift advances from the rock to rock were punctuated by long pauses while they decided their next move. Part of Grael wanted to yell at them to hurry up, but he had to be patient with them, like any quarry.

Without warning, the Elves broke cover and dashed toward the Stretchers. The only sound they made was the flutter of their cloaks in the breeze and the patter of their naked feet on the stone. As the nearest closed on Grael, he ignored the distracting twirls of his opponent's weapons and picked his moment to thrust his spear at the scout's face. The point smashed through the scout's mouth and out the back of his neck. The Elf slumped to the ground, his batonaxes clanging against the bare stone. His gored neck and head clung to Grael's spear, pulling it downward. Grael was about to use his foot to push the corpse off his weapon when whooshing batonaxes forced him to fall backward. He rolled away, expecting death at any moment. Safely beyond the dancing legs of his companions, he swung around to see his men form an arc around his attacker and skewer him with their spears.

The other two scouts were dead. One lay in a crumpled heap on the terrace. The other lay face down, his legs draped over the ledge. Splashes of blood mapped the course of the battle across the stone slabs that paved the little plateau.

The hand with which Dawan helped Grael to his feet was oily with blood. They hugged each other as their companions cheered, stabbed the air with their spears, and clapped each other's backs and shoulders.

Grael made sure to shake each man's hand. The whoops of their comrades farther up the mountain, thinned by distance and wind, were just audible. His joyful delirium brought tears to his eyes. He had lived an eternity in that instant of combat, and life was sweeter and brighter in its aftermath.

"I can't believe you did that," Dawan said. "You killed one by yourself."

"The accomplishment nearly cost me my life," Grael said in hope of fending off his cousin's worship.

The Stretchers were unhurt. The only damage that they had suffered was to their weapons. A few obsidian spear points had broken, their shards left buried in their victims. The iron beak of another spear had bent, and its owner was forced to straighten it with his foot. A couple of axes had broken against Elfin armor. The owners of the damaged weapons rummaged through the spares for replacements. Their loss was a minor quibble compared to their victory. They had felled four Elves without suffering a single casualty.

Grael glanced down at the batonaxes at his feet. The heads had been blackened with some tarry substance to prevent them from reflecting the sun's glare. He kicked the weapons off the terrace.

"This was a feat worthy of Alackalas himself," Dawan commented.

Grael chuckled. "If he had been twelve men, maybe. We were three times their number. Don't think that because we dispatched these four we can take on a legion by ourselves."

One of the others pointed out a bright speck in the distance. The Stretchers' precious respite from despair and fear shriveled as saffron fringed the mountainside. The sun sparking against burnished metal created the impression of a spreading blaze as the legionaries marched toward the defenders.

The others' stares fell upon Grael.

"Prepare yourselves," he said.

***

SunTalon had little sympathy for the four slain scouts when he learned of their misfortune. Their attack had been unsanctioned. It had been an act of hubris on their part, fueled by ambition to serve and an excessive confidence in their superiority in combat. It was surprising, given their long military experience and their lineages. Their rashness had served to get them killed, embolden their enemies, and undermine the morale of their fellow legionaries. Their foolishness was all the more infuriating because the Consensus would reward it with a posthumous commendation.

IronWill's reaction would not be pleasant—his words of consolation, the righteous twinkle in his eyes, the false sorrow depressing his smile. Four Ors were dead, no sign of the Orstretcherists, and not one Stretcher slain. So far, the expedition's only success, if it could be described as such, was the capture of an empty village of no strategic importance whatsoever.

To add to the tribune's woes, a messenger from the village had arrived. SunTalon had left a small detachment, two squads, to hold it, and now he received a report that a large force of Stretchers was closing in. His instinct was to turn back and deal with this threat. This handful of Stretchers was probably a decoy to distract the main force of legionaries while their comrades attacked the little garrison in the village. But the sentinel would not brook retreat, not when he had the scent of his elusive quarry, and it would be unwise of SunTalon to split his force. He sent the messenger back to the village with orders for the garrison to abandon it. Hopefully, the messenger would reach them in time.

The tribune called his troops to a halt while he summoned WarSage and the two centurions.

"What is the meaning of this delay?" Sentinel Five demanded.

"I am going to lead the attack," SunTalon answered. "In the event of my death, I want to make sure everyone knows what must be done."

"Is it wise for the most senior officer to join the front line?"

"I need the exercise. One officer is as good as another. WarSage Galea is more than capable of replacing me if I am incapacitated. You lectured the legate on the virtues of courage and sacrifice, and now, when their time is at hand, you counsel caution."

"I will lead the attack," Sentinel Five said.

"As the senior officer here, that is my privilege to decide, not yours."

"I am one of our Bright Lord's bodyguards. I outrank you."

What is the point of a bodyguard when there is no body to guard? SunTalon resisted the temptation to say it. The sentinel would regard the question as blasphemous, a slur on not him but his god, and he was liable to answer it with his batonaxes.

"Sentinel, your original argument was that the senior officer should not lead the attack. As you hold that position, you have precluded yourself from the front line."

SunTalon took a moment to savor the sentinel's sulky admission of defeat before turning his attention to his subordinate officers.

***

Garscap watched the work party pick their way down the scree-littered slope toward the rest of the Pigsknucklers at the top of the Crooked Stair. In the distance, the amorphous Elfin army formed neat, saffron blocks. The regularity of its structure showed confidence and discipline, but it also suggested a mental rigidity a canny foe could exploit.

If the Pigsknucklers failed to hold the top of the Crooked Stair, they would retreat up the sharp incline to their left, while a party above them set off an avalanche of rocks and boulders to scourge their pursuers and, perhaps, kill a substantial number of them.

He turned to the five ancients and their hard-pressed bearers.

"Thomol, you must decide when the chocks holding back the rubble should be knocked away. The life of every Pigsknuckler may depend on that decision."

Thomol puffed up with irksome glee.

"Of course, if you had your way back in Pigsknuckle, you wouldn't have lived to enjoy this opportunity," Garscap observed. That plucked Thomol's crowing.

He started downhill to join rest of the Pigsknucklers. Halfway down, he stopped and beckoned two of the old men's minders to him. Beyond the reach of Thomol's hearing, Garscap instructed the women to take the initiative if Thomol dithered.

Garscap was not happy with the size of the mound that the work party had built, but time was against them, and its progress down the slope would hopefully dislodge more material, expanding the avalanche. The slender, flexing trunks that held the pile in place were a bigger worry. If they gave way at the wrong moment, the Pigsknucklers might be victims rather than beneficiaries of the resultant onslaught of debris.

Everyone at the top of the Crooked Stair greeted Garscap's return with respectful nods. Even Widan saluted him with genuine deference. A few arms jolted with the impulse to stretch upward. Garscap's past no longer mattered. Old enmities were forgotten. He had already saved their lives once this day by an act both blasphemous and miraculous. Every face held the hope, the prayer, that he was capable of more wonders.

Lahan and a few others whose sons were bait in Garscap's trap didn't subscribe to this general reverence. Lahan's eyes were focused downward as if he was trying to stare through the curve of the mountain to view his son. Only Joraem Scoral, whom Garscap had positioned on the mountainside, had a proper view of what was happening below.

“Our landslide is prepared,” Garscap said. “Hopefully, it’ll not be needed.”

An almighty crack reverberated above them. There were gasps of horror as rocks and debris poured through the broken struts down the side of the mountain. As a herd, the Pigsknucklers ran up the mountain out of the path of the oncoming landslide. As fast as the slip had started, it ceased. The bulk of the falling rubble slowed and settled back into the mountainside. Only a harmless trickle of pebbles and sand traveled far enough to shower the Crooked Stair.

Some relieved Pigsknucklers proclaimed their escape a miracle, while others assured Garscap that he would make good this setback. It was a blessing in disguise, they said, that the faultiness of his backup weapon had been discovered before they relied upon it.

Garscap smiled and nodded and agreed with their optimistic sentiments. He spoke of holding the Fair Folk at the Crooked Stair as though it was a small feat. Without the distraction of the landslide, retreat was impossible. They must hold their position or die.

Repressing his dismay, Garscap raged in silence at Thomol for no other reason than he had been a persistent nuisance all day. If the old fool had tumbled down the cliff with the debris, it might have proved more effective. He was in love with death. His carcass should have been left in Pigsknuckle for the Elves to pick clean.

The old men’s retinue descended the slope.

"Where do you think you are going?" Garscap demanded.

"Our charges are safe where they are," one of the women answered. "We thought we might be of more use down here."

Before Garscap could reply, a signal from Joraem demanded his attention. The Fair Folk were on the march.

***

SunTalon's force was divided into four rectangular formations, two at the front and two at the rear. Three had a full complement of six squads—seventy-two legionaries. The right half-century at the rear was missing the two squads posted to guard the village. The sentinel walked behind it. SunTalon, flanked by the remaining scouts, marched between the leading formations.

At the tribune's signal, the legionaries drew their batonaxes from their racks. Patches of bright light danced in the shadows where the Stretchers lurked as the metal heads of the Ors' weapons flung the sun's glare at them. SunTalon thrust one batonaxe forward and began to sprint toward them. As the half-century to his left followed, the steady beat pounded out by their synchronized step quickened to rolling footfalls.

The Stretchers stood still as if mesmerized by the spectacle. As the legionaries closed on them, the Stretchers' inertia was peculiar. Suddenly, they sprang to life. The Stretchers cast a halfhearted volley of spears and stones, then turned and ran.

SunTalon smiled as he watched them scramble from terrace to terrace. They had left their flight too late. The legionaries were closing on them fast. The Stretchers took too long negotiating cliffs that their pursuers glided over. The hindmost straggler was soon within reach of his batonaxes. SunTalon's stride wobbled as he spiked the Stretcher in the back, sending him crashing downward. As SunTalon bounded over the prone man, he didn't bother to glance down as his handiwork. It had been a killing blow. SunTalon was already focused on his next victim.

He hooked the foot of the second Stretcher, and tripped him. SunTalon left him for others to finish off. Ahead of him, two more Stretchers were chopped down by legionaries. A fifth stumbled as he was climbing a cliff and fell prostrate on the ground as legionaries poured over him. Two more made a stand in a futile attempt to gain their comrades a little time, but a flurry of batonaxes tore them apart.

The sport of the pursuit was making SunTalon merry. It was a trifle annoying that a bolt felled the leading Stretcher, but the important thing was that none escaped. He counted down as the remaining Stretchers were felled.

Four. Three. Two. One remained. He was climbing onto the top terrace, nothing above him but sky. SunTalon flung a batonaxe at him but it missed and struck the cliff-face. As he followed his quarry over the ledge, he was dazzled by the sun glinting on metal just before a spear struck him in the face.

***

Garscap and Lahan heaved the survivor over the cliff.

"Dawan, where is my son?" Lahan demanded.

"He fell, I think. He may have been hit. I was afraid to look back," Dawan gasped.

Along the edge of the terrace, lines of Pigsknucklers thrust spears at the oncoming foes, while others rained arrows and stones down on the attackers. Intoxicated with bloodlust, the Elves appeared oblivious to their losses. They were packed too close to use their batonaxes properly. When they threw their weapons at the Pigsknucklers, the batonaxes became ensnared on the defenders' spears. If the Stretchers held this line, victory was theirs.

"I promise you the sacrifice of Grael and the others won't be in vain," Garscap said.

"You knew you were sending him to his death," Lahan roared. "It was a trap for him as much as the Fair Folk."

It was grief talking. Everyone was too busy fighting to notice what Lahan said. "Direct your anger at your real enemy. You have a wife and three children who'll need their father tomorrow."

"Grael once said something similar to me when he first proposed going to Formicary. He tried to persuade me by saying we had so many children, we would hardly miss his going. He couldn't understand why I got so angry. He was too young to understand. Myryr and I lost our second baby to the Blood Stipple. Neither of us slept for three days while we tried to nurse her through her fever, but it made no difference in the end. No number of children lessens the sadness of one who is lost."

Lahan's meandering speech was getting irksome. Garscap had no time for it. "I'm sorry. I don't understand the relevance of this story to our current circumstances."

"You wouldn't," Lahan said with a smirk. His eye had a dangerous glimmer. "I was trying to explain to you why I must do this." Spear in hand, he pushed his way to the front line. "Some of our sons and brothers may be alive down there. Let us get them!" he roared as he jumped down from the terrace. Garscap's heart dropped with the spearmen as they followed Lahan. The victory within his grasp began to slip away.

He joined them as they pushed the enemy from one terrace and then the next. He found Lahan lying amongst the corpses. His shoulder and thigh were bloody messes. Friend and foe had trodden upon him. One cheek was a massive purple bruise, and the impression of a dirty boot sole was imprinted across his forehead. Bones jutted through his left arm. His right leg was crushed so badly it looked more like a snake than a limb. Despite all these wounds, somehow he clung onto life.

"I hope you're happy," Garscap muttered.

Lahan answered him with a crooked smile and laughing eyes.

***

Screams rippled down the column as AscendantSun and his comrades flashed by. Mothers hugged children in a final farewell. A few women closed their eyes and surrendered to despair. Treasured possessions spilled on the broken ground as refugees dropped them and grabbed for weapons. As they drew knives or raised axes, some cursed Garscap Torp for forbidding their training in the arts of combat, denying them the chance of extracting an even heavier price from their attackers. A few shook tightly-gripped spears in warning, while others seized stones from the trail and flung them at the oncoming warriors.

The Elves flitted by them, dodging missiles and ignoring curses. They had no time to explain to the panicked refugees that they were on the same side, and that they were hurtling down the mountain to defend their village.

It was a relief when they had passed the two straggling columns and faced only empty mountainside.

In the distance, Saint Charlin stood with arms raised before a furka. As AscendantSun approached, the saint ended his prayerful pose, picked up a hammer, and struck the furka. He shuddered, as if the blow passed through him and not the stone. Holding the hammer too far over his head, he dropped it when he saw the Orstretcherists coming. His arms rose again, this time in salutation.

AscendantSun raised his hand and signaled his three companions to halt. It was a relief to learn the Pigsknucklers had escaped from their village, though Charlin was coy about the details of this miracle. The saint could not tell him much, either, about Garscap's plans other than he intended to make a stand against the Elfin army climbing up the mountain. From Charlin's description, the force that the politician faced was perhaps two centuries.

AscendantSun bid the saint a quick farewell, but before he could leave, Charlin asked, "Are the other Orstretcherists far behind you?"

The question held AscendantSun, though he had little desire to answer it. He shook his head mournfully. One of the others could explain.

"They are on their way!" TrueFriend pointed excitedly up the mountain. A slender cascade of flashing bronze spilled down the scree toward them. "I guess the debate is over."

Vital moments dripped by as AscendantSun waited for the descending Orstretcherists to reach them. The boon was worth the delay. Hopefully, he and his comrades were not misreading the intent of the approaching force.

NeverFear led the procession, his cheeks tinted orange with embarrassment, his eyebrows pressed into a scowl. He halted before the damaged furka. As somber faces gathered behind him, he saluted the saint with a shy nod, though his eyes remained fixed on AscendantSun.

"Is the debate over?" AscendantSun asked, yawning with feigned nonchalance.

NeverFear grinned. "It is for us. NoonBlest and his supporters are still in Pigsback, preaching to the walls about the rightness of their convictions."

"I suppose we all answer to our consciences," AscendantSun said, referring as much to himself as NoonBlest or NeverFear. "So, what is our plan?"

"You tell us," NeverFear said. "You are the leader."

"If you are sure." His departure from Pigsback might have been interpreted as a renunciation of his authority.

"The debate was about our role in this war. It was never about the leadership, whatever NoonBlest might think. Unless you want another vote…though I doubt we have the time for it."

A chorus of voices joined AscendantSun in agreeing another ballot was unneeded.

"My immediate plan is to join forces with the Pigsknucklers farther down the mountain," AscendantSun said. "Circumstances will dictate the rest. The task before us will not be easy. Perhaps two centuries oppose us."

Some of his audience gasped at the odds. Apprehension was etched on the faces of the rest. It was unlikely that the Pigsknucklers and forty or so Orstretcherists could beat such a force.

"Take heart," AscendantSun urged. "Put your faith in the Forelight and in each other. This is already a day of wonders. We will triumph!" Hopefully, the Orstretcherists were moved by the sentiment of his words without realizing their implication. The Forelight needed to perform another miracle.

***

Grael lay face down, afraid to move, the stone slab beneath him as cold as a corpse. It sucked the warmth from his body, leaving only an aching lethargy. The batonaxe that punched him to the ground had torn a gash in his side. Flowing blood tickled through the burning pain, but blinded by his position, he feared the least twitch of his finger might betray him. An Elf might be standing right beside him this very moment, waiting to deliver the killing blow.

He heard distant shouts of triumph, shrill cries of despair and death, the clash of weapons, and the crash of falling armor. But closer by, something dripped above him. From below came the thunder of myriad stampeding feet, sometimes breaking stride to scale a cliff or some other obstruction. As it grew louder, Grael's back muscles tensed in readiness for a pummeling by Elfin boots. The ground trembled as they closed in. Shadows flickered as legionaries raced by him. From the corner of his eye, he could see the boots moving up and down as they passed.

The sound of them splashing through shallow pools was strange. He didn't remember water puddles on the terraces. The gory scent, presumably originating from his wound, grew more intense. A steady drip became a ragged trickle. Rivulets of blood meandered across the stone in front of his face, tickling his nose and cheek. Who did this blood belong to—his people or the invaders?

Two sets of unhurried steps approached. They stopped beside him. A third set of feet came careering down the Crooked Stair to meet the others.

"Centurion Superior, Sentinel," said a panting voice. "The Stretchers are pushing us back down the terraces. We cannot use our batonaxes up there. I have never witnessed Mixies fighting with such discipline."

Centurion superior was a familiar term thanks to AscendantSun's instruction on legionary ranks, but what was a sentinel?

"The Orstretcherists must have a hand in it," declared a second, gruffer voice. "We must break these Stretchers. We should send the second century up there."

"Sentinel, I will obey your commands," said a third voice, whom Grael guessed was the centurion superior. That meant that the second voice was the sentinel. "However, it is my duty to point out we have another option, one that is certain to win this battle for us. We pull back."

"Retreat?" The sentinel said it like a curse.

"A tactical withdrawal. Give them the scent of victory. Draw them down from these cliffs into open ground where the terrain favors our tactics. We have almost a full century below. We can cut them down with crossbows with ease."

Something prodded Grael's back. Was the tap of the batonaxe spike an idle action of a preoccupied mind or was its intention more sinister?

"What you suggest might work, but it is not in keeping with the Harbinger's philosophies," the sentinel said.

"We have lost at least half of a century so far," the centurion superior snapped. "Our casualties increase with every passing moment. The Harbinger may demand sacrifice, but I doubt he considers stupidity a virtue. I suspect you were not so highly principled in the Faith Melee. You did not win that gold armor without a few cunning ploys."

Grael jerked as the spike bit into his leg. He waited for the Elves to react, but they were too preoccupied by their conference to notice.

"Insulting this armor is an affront to the Harbinger of the Dawn. It is an outrage against our Bright Lord," the sentinel said as he banged his fist against his chest plate.

"I intend no insult to your armor. I mean to save it from becoming a Mixy's trophy."

The spike began to prod Grael once more. Its tap became so insistent that he had to bite his lip to keep from screaming.

"We will follow your plan," the sentinel said at last. "I may have become a little heated there. I promise your contribution to this mission will be reported favorably to the Harbinger."

"I am pleased to hear it," the centurion superior said. "But my main concern this day is avenging our dead. I want the sun to set on their murderers' corpses."

Grael's right hand now rested on the hilt of his dagger. It had crept there, spurred by some unconscious desire. A bold plan formed in his mind. His fingers tightened around the hilt. If he could leap up, he might be able to deliver a single, killing blow to either the sentinel or centurion superior before he was slain. If he was really lucky, he might even slaughter both Elves and throw their troops into confusion. Whether he succeeded or failed, he was certain to die in the attempt, but it promised to be a nobler demise than lying in the sewage of battle, waiting for life to ebb away.

He jerked upward. Violent dizziness and the pain in his side pushed him down again. He waited for a batonaxe to deliver oblivion but the Elves had not noticed his movement. Perhaps what he perceived as a massive leap was little better than a twitch. He lay face down, as he had before, waiting for his life to bleed away.

Chapter 24

The furka that they fought to save
From barbarous sacrilege
Now serves to mark these martyrs' grave
Atop a lonely mountain ridge.

~From *The Martyrdom of Coneyriddle.*

Despite Garscap's efforts to hold back his warriors, their progress down the terraces had a slow inevitability. The ranks of Elves were thinning as a growing trickle of deserters forsook their comrades. The Pigsknucklers smelled victory in the ineffectiveness of the Elves' batonaxes, in their cries of frustration, in the quickening pace of their retreat. The Pigsknucklers could not resist its intoxicating scent. Every time a gap opened between the two lines, they stepped forward to fill it.

There had to be purposeful calculation in their enemies' disarray. The Elves' retreat was too orderly to be the product of despair or panic. Any moment, the legionaries were going to break into a full retreat, and the Pigsknucklers would spill after them in wild confusion and be slaughtered in the resulting melee by their regrouped foes.

The clamor of shouts on both sides drowned out Garscap's warnings. The men whom he peeled from the back of the crowd were too stupid with triumph to comprehend what he was saying. He was trying to pull an impossible weight uphill, but instead, it was dragging him inexorably downward to destruction.

He managed to get the attention of Dawan and another youth. With spears raised high, the three of them began pushing their way through to the front of the mob. The youths labored at its extremities, while Garscap burrowed through the middle, negotiating his advancement with his crown and sometimes a well-placed knee or fist. The throng squeezed ever tighter around him, till, about two rows from the front, it held him fast. He could progress no farther, nor could he retreat. He was trapped by the implacable momentum of the crowd, impelled to flow forward with the rest.

A panorama of heads denied him a vision of the battle's course. The fetor of staling sweat stung his nostrils. A dew of spittle and perspiration drenched his face. A relentless inundation of roars pulverized his cries, as the crowd pressed from all sides, constricting about him with such bone-cracking force that it left him breathless and dizzy.

The front rows fell away. Another terrace was being descended. Garscap threw himself forward, jostling his way into the unsettled front line. Gripping the midpoint of his spear, he turned it not toward the enemy but perpendicular, along the front of his own men. Dawan and the other youth had managed the same feat.

A batonaxe flew at Garscap, but the spears on both sides of him blocked it, and it dropped to the ground like a stoned bird. The few Elves who remained on the terraces were less interested in attacking than in goading the Pigsknucklers onward. The ploy was so obvious that it was hard to believe that everyone around Garscap was blind to it.

Fear shivered through him. He was puny against the colossal, seething mass thrusting him forward. He questioned the premise of his plan. Could three spears halt its crushing advance?

This was not a time for doubt. Garscap leaned back against the surging Pigsknucklers, his spear holding them back as he begged them to go no farther.

"Turn back! It's a trap! Turn back!" he cried, but the Pigsknucklers' triumphant cheers swallowed up his warnings. His shoulders and arms burned as they strained to withstand the monstrous force pressing on the spear. Warriors pushed past Dawan's spear and spilled onto the next terrace.

Two terraces down, Garscap spotted an arm rise, and a human hand opened like a bloody flower. His spear snapped, and the Pigsknucklers poured forward.

***

Cries of human exultation drew Grael's hand into the air. A rattling thunder made him roll against the rocky curtain to his right. Garscap must have deployed his landslide against the Fair Folk. At any moment, a torrent of earth and stone was going to slam into Grael and end his suffering. Hopefully, it would sweep away the Elves as well.

The amorphous, shuddering rumble resolved into racing footsteps. Grael looked over his shoulder at the Pigsknucklers flitting by. He tried to warn them they were running toward an ambush, but none of them noticed his low moan.

A voice called on the stampede to stop. More voices joined its cry, as if the Pig itself was squealing. The running feet stuttered to a halt.

"Get that man up the mountain." It sounded like Garscap.

Water dribbled into Grael's mouth. Hands grappled with his body. Something softly prodded the wound in his side. As arms lifted him off the ground, he smiled at the knowledge that he would not die alone.

"Hang on in there, Grael. You'll be fine," a familiar voice assured him. It was Maergan.

Grael's gentle glide up the Crooked Stair was punctuated by awkward lifting and painful manhandling as his bearers negotiated the cliffs. It was a relief when he finally reached the top.

"Place him beside his father," Maergan said. "How is he?"

"Not good."

Grael's heart leapt. Was that Harath's voice? No, that was impossible. The hope that she was somewhere safe compensated in part for her absence. It was funny how fate kept teasing them with happiness, only to tear them apart.

A blonde woman, wearing Cliffringden's halo, knelt beside him. Her lined face was spattered with blood. "Grael," she said as she wiped his face with a wet rag. "You'll live. The fabric of your tunic staunched the wound in your side. Your father…" She paused. "Your father is dying. He should be dead already, but stubbornness makes him cling to life."

"Lahan led the charge down the Crooked Stair," another man murmured. "He did it to find you."

Grael's bearers sat him against the rock beside his prostrate father. He fought his dizziness to look down upon Dad's awkward smile. "You should have not risked your life to save me. I might have been dead," he said.

"Sounds like something I might say," his father answered. "All that matters is that you are alive. You must look after your mother and the children."

"You'll be fine."

A sour face briefly interrupted Dad's smile. "It's right that a parent dies for his children. They are all that remains of him in this world when he has gone to the next."

"Don't talk nonsense," Grael said, holding back his tears. His father would brook no weeping.

"Parents die a little for their children every day. Sometimes slowly, sometimes fast." And with that, Dad fell silent.

Grael hugged the corpse and wept.

***

"Listen, lads," Garscap said as he led his men back up the Crooked Stair. "I want no more foolery. The only voice I want to hear from our side is mine, and when I give an order, obey it as if your life depends on it. Because it does."

"We shout to show we are unafraid," Maergan Erath protested gently.

"They don't care if you fear them. And your shouts don't frighten them, either. The only thing that scares them is the dead bodies of their friends strewn down the Crooked Stair."

He glanced back down the terraces. Legionaries were giving chase. A few had paused to prime crossbows. The Elves realized too late that their foes had avoided their trap. The Pigsknucklers were already pouring onto the top terrace.

Garscap ordered his men back from the ledge to deny the Elfin archers easy targets. He crawled to the edge of the terrace and surveyed the activity below. A new Elfin force was making its way up the Crooked Stair. The foremost legionaries skidded as they tried to pick their way over stone made slick by gore.

He was gleeful as he readied his men. It didn't matter how many legionaries tramped up the Crooked Stair—they would descend again as corpses. As long as the Pigsknucklers held their nerve, this day was theirs.

As the first legionaries began scrambling over the ledge, the Pigsknucklers pushed forward, their spears skewering some and shoving others back on top of the Elves massed behind them. Behind the spearmen, archers loosed arrows in a high arc to rain random death on their enemies. This time, the Pigsknucklers, disciplined by confidence in themselves and their leader, stood their ground as Garscap commanded. There were grunts of exertion but none of the boisterous shouting on their side. The air was filled instead with the music of the pain and exasperation of their enemies. And an annoying buzzing sound.

It was too soft for a bee, too loud for a blowfly. It was coming from above. Garscap looked up the slope. Thomol was standing, waving one arm, his voice thinned by distance to an incomprehensible whine. What did the old fool want now?

Something swooped across the mountainside. Perhaps it was an eagle. No, it glinted in the sun. The batonaxe struck the ancient, felling him. Garscap followed its course back to its point of origin. At the head of two-dozen legionaries was a warrior clad in the dazzle of the sun. Garscap had never imagined they might scale the cliffs beside the Crooked Stair, but he had not counted on their inhuman agility and their thirst for victory. They must have taken poor Joraem unawares.

As their march quickened to a run, Garscap fought the urge to raise his arms in prayer. He directed his archers at the oncoming warriors. The volley of arrows hit their targets but failed to strike down a single warrior, bouncing off their helmets or breastplates or the locked arm-shields covering their faces.

A second front was needed to face this onrushing menace. “Grab your spears!” he yelled to the archers. Men stared stupidly at him as he peeled them from the back lines at the Crooked Stair and shoved them toward the new battle line. As the legionaries closed, the line that faced them was a paltry, fragile thing.

The Elves leapt into the air, spreading their arms and batonaxes like massive wings. Glinting sunlight fringed their dark outlines as they flew over the awed defenders.

Thunder filled the sky as competing silhouettes crashed into the attackers. Garscap roared and punched the air in triumph, as legionaries and Orstretcherists rained from the sky.

***

AscendantSun fought his screaming instinct to flail his weapons about him as he sprung to his feet. His batonaxes were as likely to strike friend as foe. He scanned the sprawled warriors struggling to their feet. Most of the legionaries were too stunned by the Orstretcherists’ intervention to put up much of a fight. AscendantSun dashed toward the nearest one, batonaxes at the ready.

“This one is mine,” a warrior in golden armor cried, leaping over the rising legionary. “The Harbinger will consider our lives a small price for the heresiarch’s death.”

This sentinel was a crude caricature borne of the Harbinger’s conceit. This was not Gules, and Aurelian was dead. The golden armor was an encumbrance rather than an advantage. Its weight sapped the wearer’s stamina.

At the same time, the Or was an apparition from a more heroic age, a gleaming panoply bought with eleven lives. Its bearer, a Pugnus, was the scion of the surviving member of Aurelian's bodyguard. Perhaps, this was the product not of a madman's caprice, but proof of a bright power rising once more.

"Greetings from your nameless twin," the sentinel said.

As AscendantSun wrestled to make sense of the sentinel's words, his opponent linked his batonaxes and whipped the chain at his face. AscendantSun jerked his head clear of the blow, but he failed to hook the sentinel's weapon with one of his own. Before he had recovered his balance, the sentinel was upon him.

It took AscendantSun's full concentration to fend off the frenzy of blades and spikes pushing him to ground. He tried to roll free, but the sentinel closed too fast, and AscendantSun was pinned again by the dance of his foe's batonaxes.

He kicked at the sentinel's legs. Batonaxes writhed against each other as the sentinel sprawled across him. The sentinel's perspiration dripped on AscendantSun's face as his opponent pressed a batonaxe down on his chest. His own weapons forgotten, AscendantSun held the same batonaxe with both hands as he tried to halt its grinding creep up his chest toward his neck.

***

The thunderous clash above Grael wrenched him from his grief.

Elves and weapons rained from the sky and smashed against the ground. In front of him, a prostrate legionary snatched a random pair of batonaxes and leapt toward him.

A batonaxe thrust at Grael, but it struck his dead father. Instinct made him seize the head of the weapon. He cringed as he waited for the legionary's second weapon to smite him, but an Orstretcherist blocked it with one batonaxe and beheaded Grael's attacker with his second.

Grael crawled as fast as he could to escape the battle raging above him. He was sick and dizzy, every movement hurt, but at any moment, a batonaxe could swoop down on him and finish him.

Ahead of him, on the edge of the melee, a legionary in gold armor had an Orstretcherist pinned to the ground. Grael recognized the symbols on the forehead—AscendantSun. Grael drew his knife. He crawled toward the golden legionary. He was too weak to stand, but he was close enough to strike a blow with his weapon.

The legionary's greaves didn't protect the back of his legs. With all his strength, Grael stabbed the nearest exposed calf. The leg shifted as the blade struck, preventing it from boring deep into the flesh, but for an instant, the legionary forgot AscendantSun. He roared and swiped his batonaxe above his head at an imaginary enemy.

AscendantSun threw off his attacker and seized the batonaxes beside him. Two Pigsknucklers attacked the legionary, but with a fluid sweep of his batonaxe, he felled them both. He lunged at AscendantSun, but he had already rolled clear of the legionary's reach. As the legionary stood, his eyes fixed on Grael lying nearby, the bloody knife in his hand.

Grael, on his back, tried to crawl away on his elbows and heels.

If the legionary had thoughts of revenge, he had no time to act on them. AscendantSun was upon him. The rage on the legionary's face turned to fear as he retreated before AscendantSun's onslaught, his single batonaxe struggling to parry two.

AscendantSun drove a spike into the legionary's shoulder. The armor resisted the blow, snapping off the spike, but its distraction allowed AscendantSun to hack off one head of his opponent's batonaxe. The legionary swung the remainder of his weapon like an axe, but AscendantSun's batonaxes yanked it from his hands and forced him to the ground. Blood sprayed AscendantSun's legs and chest as his blade hacked through the legionary's throat.

AscendantSun racked his batonaxes, seized Grael's arms, and pulled him clear of the melee. It was already nearly over. Most of the legionaries lay dead. The remainder were outnumbered, their defeat certain. A few even chose to leap down the cliff rather than die at the hands of Stretchers.

AscendantSun propped Grael against a rock and crouched beside him. "You saved my life. Thank you."

"I owed you mine," Grael said.

"I think you've repaid that debt in full today."

"That debt will never be settled," Grael said firmly.

AscendantSun patted Grael's shoulder. "Likewise."

***

Garscap reviewed the progress of the battle with satisfaction. The surprise attack had been defeated, and the Pigsknucklers' lines along the terrace were holding. He climbed atop a boulder and peered down at the terraces awash with blood and littered with corpses. At the bottom, another force of warriors had gathered. They were Stretchers.

"Forward!" he cried to the Pigsknucklers.

The legionaries' ferocity redoubled as they understood what was happening, but they couldn't resist the relentless push of the Pigsknucklers down the terraces.

Stretchers swarmed up the Crooked Stairs to attack the Elves from the other side. The halos of the new arrivals indicated that they were from the villages of Littleknuckle, Highstep, and Wyrmery. Harath must have delivered her message. They fought with far less discipline than the Pigsknucklers but their number was much greater. Facing enemies on both sides, the legionaries chose to make their last stand against the new arrivals. Their bravery was as desperate as their plight, but in the end, valor and skill couldn't save them. A roar of murderous triumph shook the mountain as the last of them fell.

Lohor Teevan scrambled up the treacherous rocky steps to where Garscap waited. The startled expression on Lohor's face amused him.

"How did you do this?" Lohor asked. "How did you defeat such a number? I see so few bodies of your people. I lost many men dealing with your scraps."

Garscap smirked. "Some hunt wolves. Some hunt gilt spiders." He noticed AscendantSun was looking up at him with a pained expression. The politician leapt down and shook the Orstretcherist's hand.

"I didn't mean you," Garscap assured AscendantSun. "We owe you our lives." Lohor was listening to every word. Being overgenerous in his praise might be misinterpreted as weakness, a symptom of dependency. "Let the mountains echo with news of the victory of Pigsknuckle and its allies. For the first time since Alackalas, Stretchers have faced an army of the Fair Folk and triumphed."

NeverFear murmured something to AscendantSun.

"We request that the wounded legionaries be placed into our custody," AscendantSun said.

"Are there any? They all must be dead," Garscap replied.

"There is at least one over there," NeverFear said as he pointed to where a group of women huddled. When he comprehended what they were doing, he raced at them, shouting and waving his batonaxes, scattering them like flapping vultures from a wounded beast. He examined the legionary.

"They murdered him," he cried. "They must have been doing this throughout the day, tending their own wounded while murdering their helpless enemies. Is this the behavior of true Stretchers?"

"Their enemies are your enemies also," Garscap observed.

One of the Cliffringdeners shouted back: "This is the behavior of women when the murderers of their husbands and sons lie at their feet."

AscendantSun tugged Garscap's arm to get his attention. "Unless you want our alliance to end here and now, you must promise that the murder of wounded prisoners will be not be tolerated now or in the future."

Garscap's nod was grudging. He glanced at Lohor. The Politician of Littleknuckle appeared oblivious to his embarrassment.

"NeverFear, gather a party together and search for survivors," AscendantSun commanded.

"AscendantSun, please, no," NeverFear begged. "I might see my face among the dead."

Garscap pondered what the Orstretcherist meant as AscendantSun cajoled TrueFriend into taking NeverFear's place.

***

AscendantSun watched tears wash the bloody spatter from NeverFear's cheeks.

"I am sorry. I could not do it," NeverFear said.

"Forget it," AscendantSun said. "It has been a trying day for all of us."

"Well, if any doubt remained about which side we are on, we buried it today." NeverFear cupped his face in his hands and sobbed. "I killed an Or. A Galea, I think. I admire your strength. You slew that sham sentinel, but you maintain your composure in spite of your sorrow."

AscendantSun stopped himself from saying that his first kill had already drained his tears. The sentinel's words echoed again in his thoughts. *Greetings from your nameless twin.*

Chapter 25

Of those brave heroes of old,
Alackalas, Witchhammer and Braer,
Many wondrous tales are retold,
But this lay tells of their true heir.

-From *The Fair War.*

Around the blazing campfire, the Orstretcherists gathered for their evening meal. AscendantSun ladled some stew into his bowl and sat down. PureFaith was recounting some humorous misadventure that had befallen him when he lived in the town of Summerly, but AscendantSun was too distracted to follow it. How could he feel so alone in the midst of his friends? He forced a smile as they laughed around him. He scooped up a spoonful of stew, stared at it in the hope of inspiring his appetite, then poured it back into the bowl.

NeverFear sat down beside him. "Are you not hungry?" Since the Battle of the Crooked Stair, he often enquired how AscendantSun was feeling. AscendantSun sometimes caught NeverFear watching him. Obviously, he was aware that AscendantSun's temperament had turned more withdrawn and melancholic. No doubt, he ascribed it to the battle.

Greetings from your nameless twin. Did that riddle have an answer, or was it merely a ruse to distract him at a vital moment in his duel with the sentinel?

"How was your meeting with Garscap?" NeverFear asked.

"Fine," AscendantSun said, stirring the contents of his bowl. He wasn't in the mood for small talk.

"Any word of Evram Erath?"

AscendantSun shook his head. "They're still looking."

"Will we be getting any more pupils?"

AscendantSun put down his bowl by his feet. "In the next couple of weeks, we are going to be inundated with them. We may have to train two or three villages at a time. Every politician is pleading for his village to be given priority."

"Great," NeverFear said. His raised eyebrows made AscendantSun smile.

"Oh, one other thing," AscendantSun said. "I asked Garscap to appoint Grael as his proxy on all matters related to our alliance." AscendantSun had done more than ask. He had insisted.

NeverFear's frown impelled him to ask, "Must every decision, no matter how inconsequential, be put to a vote?"

"No," NeverFear said, shaking his head. "I'm merely surprised you saw the need for one."

AscendantSun shrugged. "Garscap is a busy man these days. I don't see the point of bothering him with daily minutiae." It was a less than subtle warning to Garscap. If any harm came to Grael, the politician would answer for it to AscendantSun.

Demands for silence relieved AscendantSun of the necessity to speak further. TrueFriend put his flute to his lips and started to play. The sickly sweet tune was familiar, though AscendantSun couldn't remember its name.

If the sentinel knew of NoName, then his mission had ended in failure. NoName must be dead. How close did he get to Harbinger? NoName might have been captured and interrogated. It would explain why the legionaries climbed the Pig after they found the village empty. They knew the monastery was there. No. NoName would never permit himself to be taken alive. AscendantSun was being paranoid.

NoName was dead and AscendantSun was alone.

***

Grael awaited Harath by her new hut on the outskirts of the village. She returned from the fields, her skin glistening from exertion. She blushed when she saw him.

"You shouldn't be here," she said, looking about. "Not alone."

Grael's cheeks burned at his thoughtless indiscretion. "I could get Dawan."

"No." Her voice dropped to a whisper. "Wait for me at the old bark hut in the forest where we stayed the night before we climbed the Pig."

"Are you sure you know the way?"

She answered his question with an arched eyebrow and an indulgent smile.

"Of course, you know. You suggested it," he said, decoding her expression.

The sun rested on the Pig's shoulder when she arrived at their rendezvous. Tempted by the evening's fineness, he had a fire blazing outside the hut. The signs of her day's toil had disappeared. Gone were the stray hairs and the smudges on her face and dress. As she drew near, he caught a flowery scent. There had to be a bouquet of wild flowers secreted on her person.

"You didn't come to my father's wake," he said.

"I attended the funeral."

"I saw you hiding at the back."

"I didn't want to upset your mother."

"Of course." Mam was upset enough already about their engagement. She had even dared to curse Charlin to his face for his betrayal.

"Let's sit by the fire."

"How are your wounds?" Harath asked.

"Not too bad. An itch I must not scratch."

She studied him, then, comprehending his puzzlement at her gaze, returned it to the fire. "I hear they are building new furkas on the Pig," she said.

"They are to be made of wood, not stone. And they won't be consecrated. Easier to tear down in an emergency."

They chatted about their kidnapping, their first engagement, and the events that followed. When Grael asked her about her father, her silence encouraged him to move on to another topic.

"How do you like your neighbors?" he asked her.

"The Cliffringdeners are fine. I should call them Pigsknucklers since they wear our colors. I'm surprised the Changeling was in such a rush to rehouse them. It's a miracle we didn't have to rebuild the entire village."

"One of many," Grael said. "Garscap wanted his hall back, now that every politician is coming to pay homage to him. And have their men trained by the Orstretcherists. It's starting to rain. Perhaps we should go inside."

As the shadows of evening spread over the land, a cloudy gloom crept across the firmament and gently wept on them.

"It is little more than a mist," Harath said "And the fire's too inviting. Let's stay."

He panicked a little as her head lay on his lap and she stared at the fire. He ignored the urge to move. The events of the last few months had weakened his respect for some of his people's more fussy customs. The firelight set the beads of moisture on her hair alight like precious gems. Harath was more advanced in her contempt for the meddlesome edicts of saints. She was always a little ahead of him.

"Oh, I didn't tell you the big news," he said. "Garscap has made me his official intermediary with the Orstretcherists."

Harath lifted her head and regarded him awkwardly. The puzzlement on her face made him smile.

He shrugged. "Apparently, AscendantSun insisted."

She frowned. "When can we get married?"

It was his turn to be silent. Mustering his courage, he said, "My mother insists on a full year of mourning."

"In a year, we might all be dead," Harath grumbled,

"That's what she says. I've tried to convince her otherwise. Please don't get upset. Don't let her ruin this evening. We may have so few together."

She rested her head again on his lap and returned her gaze to the fire. They basked in each other's company as much as the fire's comforting warmth, as night blinded them to everything beyond the reach of its light.

"We should go back to the village," Harath said. "Myryr will be wondering where you are."

It was tempting to argue for an extension to their sojourn, but she was right. He put out the fire and escorted her home through the darkness.

***

Garscap crept inside the cave. Something stirred in the blackness beyond the candle's timid light.

"Evram, are you there?"

A sigh of relief answered. "I wasn't sure if it was you." A black shape staggered toward him. Evram's head emerged from the darkness. His halo was lopsided, his hair disheveled. Tears merged with the beads of sweat trickling down his feverish face to carve lines in the smudges on his cheeks. His face burned with fever, but the familiar skewed grin was still there.

"This dank air cannot be good for you," Garscap said. "Let us go outside and get you cleaned up."

They emerged, blinking, into the sunlight.

"Be careful you don't go too far," Evram said as he shielded his eyes. "It's a long way down."

"I'll be careful," Garscap said, peering over the edge of the precipice. Far below, the Witchmilk was a ribbon of white.

"You've not come in a long time," Evram said.

"I've been busy. I brought some food." Garscap passed the bag to Evram.

Evram weighed it with his hand. "Not a lot here."

"I have to avoid suspicion."

Evram's grin spread. "That's nice, but it won't fill my belly."

"How is the wound?"

"I am putting herbs on it. I don't know if they are healing it or just hiding the smell. When can I go home?"

"Very soon. Remember the frog and the scorpion."

"That's fine for you. You're not stuck out here, living in a cave." A fit of coughing doubled Evram over.

Garscap seized his chance. He shoved Evram toward the cliff. Evram tried to cling to him but Garscap tore free of his grip. Evram toppled over the edge of the precipice, his screaming ceasing abruptly as he struck the cliff face. He glanced off it again before he disappeared into the Witchmilk's white water. Poor Evram could not have survived the drop. If his body washed up anywhere, people would assume he threw himself in. Garscap could feel safe again.

***

"What is wrong?" Talida asked.

Her genuine concern surprised Garscap. Of course, she was dependent on his fortunes. "Nothing," he said as he rose from their bed. "I need some air."

"You were screaming in your sleep," she said.

"Did I say anything?" he asked.

"No. You just screamed."

Suspicious, he studied her a moment. Was she telling the truth? It seemed so.

"I'll be back in a while," he muttered. He slipped through the curtains around their private sleeping area, tiptoed across the drunken casualties of the evening's revelry, and plunged angrily into the cold, hard air of night.

Evram, leave me alone. Haunt my dreams no more.

What did the young fool expect? Garscap had to defend himself. He had to. If it became common knowledge that he had ordered DayFlambeau Formosus slain, everything achieved so far would be lost.

If Evram had done the job properly in the first place, he would still be alive. His panicked reaction to the gash across his abdomen was understandable, but he should have never let the injured Elf escape. Or he should have let the Carnaths deal with DayFlambeau by themselves. At least that way, his involvement would have been secret, and both he and Garscap would have been safe, and there would have been no need for any unpleasantness.

Evram had always been too hotheaded, too eager. Garscap was probably better off without him. Still, he would be missed. He was Garscap's only confidant. A friend who could be trusted was a rarity in these precarious times. Who would Garscap brag to now?

If Evram had put up a real fight, if it had been more of an effort, Garscap might have been less melancholy. To the end, Evram had clung to the conviction that Garscap could solve his mess with a wave of his hand. A pity it was not so easy. If only Garscap could reverse what he had done. If only he could find another way to protect himself. But it was too late for that now. Too late.

Damn the Orstretcherists! It was their fault. DayFlambeau had been up to no good. The Elves' emotions were hard to read, but the discomfort of the others around DayFlambeau was so evident, and none of them would divulge the real reason for his departure. They answered Garscap's questions with obfuscations and lies. And Elves were poor liars.

He had not trusted the Fair Folk from the start. They were like a mercenary force, loyal to a point but ultimately looking out for themselves. The difference was that they weren't motivated by something tangible like wealth. Their coming to the mountains was some sort of spiritual quest that Garscap did not understand. Perhaps, they didn't understand it either.

The palaver about the prisoners was a perfect example. It was lucky that they found none alive. And AscendantSun had forced Garscap to make Grael his liaison to the Orstretcherists, in effect to elevate a man who had tried to steal his thorny crown. Yes, such random perversity made Orstretcherists dangerous.

Then again, Garscap, too, could be dangerous. The Battle of the Crooked Stair had proved his specialness to the world. He was indeed destined for greatness. Even his mother, before her madness, had recognized it. Her pet name for him was Lilak—his childish effort to pronounce Little Alackalas.

His jaw shivered as he yawned. It was cold. He headed back to the warmth of his bed.

Coming Soon

The Concluding Part Of
The Golden Rule Duology

The Unconquered Sun

For More Information On This Book
And Other Future Projects, Check Out
http://photocosm.org/

About Noel Coughlan

I live with my wife and daughter in Ireland.

From a young age, I was always writing a book. Generally, the first page over and over. Sometimes, I even reached the second page before I had shredded the entire copy book.

In my teenage years, I wrote some poetry, some of which would make a Vogon blush.

When I was fourteen, I had a dream. It was of a world where the inhabitants believed that each hue of light was a separate god, and that matter was simply another form of light. Thus, the world of Elysion was born.

I tinkered with the idea for a couple of decades, putting together mythologies, histories, maps, etc., but world-building isn't worth much without a gripping story. Finally, I discovered a tale so compelling I just had to write it. The story was originally to be one book called *The Golden Rule*, but it expanded so much in the telling that I had to split it into two volumes, *A Bright Power Rising* and *The Unconquered Sun*.

Printed in Great Britain
by Amazon